Kavita Kané is a former journalist and the bestselling author of five books. She is considered a revolutionary force in Indian writing because she has brought in feminism where it is most needed—mythology. Her five novels are all based on women in Indian mythology: *Karna's Wife* (2013); *Sita's Sister* (2014), on Ramayana's most neglected character, Urmila; *Menaka's Choice* (2015), on the apsara, Menaka; *Lanka's Princess* (2016), on the female antagonist in the Ramayana, Surpanakha; and *The Fisher Queen's Dynasty* (2017) on Satyavati, the grand matriarch in the Mahabharata.

After a career of over two decades in Magna and DNA, Kavita quit her job as assistant editor of *Times of India* to devote herself to writing novels full-time. With a post-graduate degree in English literature as well as in journalism and mass communication, the only skill she has, she confesses, is writing.

Passionate about theatre, cinema and art, she is also a columnist, a screenplay writer and a motivational speaker, having given several talks all across the country in educational and research institutes, corporate and management fora and literary festivals.

Born in Mumbai, with a childhood spent largely in Patna and Delhi, she currently lives in Pune with her mariner husband, Prakash, their two daughters, Kimaya and Amiya, two dogs, Chic and Beau, and Cotton, the uncurious cat.

Ahalya's Awakening

KAVITA KANÉ

First published by Westland Publications Private Limited in 2019

1st Floor, A Block, East Wing, Plot No. 40, SP Infocity, Dr MGR Salai, Perungudi, Kandanchavadi, Chennai 600096

Westland and the Westland logo are the trademarks of Westland Publications Private Limited, or its affiliates.

ISBN: 9789388754293

10 9 8 7 6 5 4 3 2 1

Typeset by Jojy Philip, New Delhi - 110015
Printed at Thomson Press (India) Ltd

MIX
Paper
FSC FSC® C010615

For my friends Niloufer and Priya
Without whom my books would have remained unfinished

Contents

Prologue

Indra
The Heavens

King Nahusha touched his crown gently. It felt strangely heavy.

'I have to warn you that you are making the same mistake the previous Indra made.' The rishi Brihaspati did not attempt to hide the disapproval in his voice. 'The king of gods chased a married woman—that was his downfall. He lost it all: his virility, his looks, his kingdom, this throne ...'

'And his wife,' declared Nahusha triumphantly. 'So, she is mine now.'

'And now, O king of the Devas, you too are about to do the same,' admonished the rishi.

Nahusha raised an eyebrow. 'I am Indra now, and so Sachi becomes my wife.'

'Indra is a title,' Brihaspati said icily. 'The position is temporary, based on conduct, karma and punya. One Indra leaves and another replaces him. There have been many Indras before you. It is a perfect system: If another Deva does greater tapas than the reigning Indra, he will take over the position. And if an Indra corrupts himself by committing a wrong, he will be deposed from his position—like Shakra was.'

'But the queen remains the same,' Nahusha interrupted, his tone brusque. 'Indrani is Indra's—whichever Indra rules as the king of Heaven.'

Brihaspati's eyes hardened. 'No, she is *not*! Sachi is Indra Shakra's wife. You have a wife, Lord. Why covet another's? You were made Indra—the king of gods—because of your righteousness, King Nahusha. But beware your downfall. Even the king of the Devas is not impervious to this.'

'All I want is a queen—Indra's queen, Sachi, my Indrani. That should not be difficult,' Nahusha said smoothly, his sharp eyes scanning the tense court of Indralok.

'She is Indra Shakra's wife,' repeated the rishi. 'Moreover, she considers Shakra her husband. You cannot have her,' stated Brihaspati, his eyes flinty.

'I can and I shall,' answered Nahusha equably.

'Don't!' warned a soft voice from the court.

Nahusha turned his head swiftly, immediately recognising the dulcet voice of Menaka; she was purportedly Indra's favourite apsara. Nahusha's eyes narrowed as he took in her breath-taking loveliness. Her beauty was lethal, known as she was to be as tantalising as she was clever.

'Ah, the exquisite Menaka. Was it not you who predicted Indra Shakra's downfall?' he asked warily.

Menaka took him in with one quick glance. He was tall, wiry and tough-looking, with a lined, sun-tanned face and clear grey eyes. His face had a stubborn, arrogant air, and his jawline was aggressive.

Menaka answered with a slight smile. 'It was his arrogance—and his committing of adultery with a married woman—that led him where he is now, hiding himself in ignominy, it seems, in a lotus stem.' Her full scarlet lips curled in open contempt.

'Castrated, I hear,' Nahusha said, and sniggered maliciously.

'So, you know the story,' she said. 'Indra's downfall began when he seduced Ahalya, the wife of the famous and powerful Rishi Gautam.'

Nahusha laughed out loud. 'He got caught! Rishi Gautam, the cuckolded husband, cursed Indra to have a thousand vulvas all over his body and to lose his testicles!'

'And more,' affirmed Menaka, irony heavy in her voice. 'He was made completely powerless. Rishi Gautam's curse also determined that his throne would be forever insecure, always susceptible to attacks. For that one transgression of Shakra, Indralok, too, had to pay a heavy price, exposed to assault and wars. Till you arrived ...'

Nahusha's eyes glittered. 'Yes, and I am grateful I was made king,' he murmured, smiling.

Menaka returned his smile, but it did not reach her eyes. 'After Shakra had to relinquish his throne in disgrace, the gods and the rishis together decided to make you—the noble son of Ayusha—the king of the three worlds. For the first time, a mortal has been crowned Indra.'

Her ice-blue eyes were directed at the king, with that disconcerting stare she was well known for.

'You have, since then, been blessed with divine effulgence, which can destroy every creature of energy. You have proved your worth by restoring peace, glory and harmony to the three worlds. Do not throw away all that you have gained with one transgression—just because of your desire for Sachi. Don't fall into the same trap that ensnared Indra Shakra.'

The king flinched; his face was flushed. 'You just said that I am a better person than Shakra. I am!'

'You are, but *show* that you are. Treat Sachi with respect.'

'I do, and that's why I want to wed her!' he argued.

'But she is already married; she is someone else's wife,' reasoned Menaka. 'She cannot be yours—unless she wishes it. But she is clearly mourning Indra's absence.'

'Is she? How can she mourn a husband who cheated and chased another man's wife?' demanded Nahusha. 'That coward left her for another woman! I am not as selfish or shallow as Shakra. I am the Indra who loves her and wishes to marry her. What is so wrong with that?'

'What is wrong is that *she* doesn't want *you*,' retorted Menaka. 'You cannot force yourself on her! She continues to love her husband; she is the one person who stood by Shakra through his darkest times.'

'How can she forget—or forgive—that he was unfaithful to her with Ahalya?' Nahusha said, exploding.

'Just as you intend to be unfaithful. Or have you forgotten that you have a wife yourself,' said Menaka tartly. Her voice softening, she continued, her tone persuasive. 'Forget her, O king. Sachi can never be yours.'

Nahusha threw Menaka a long, probing look.

'Did you warn Shakra with the same words when he chased Ahalya?' he asked.

Menaka nodded sadly. 'We all did. But he was too stubborn. And see what happened to him.'

'And you fear I am treading the same path of self-destruction?'

Again, Menaka nodded.

An uneasy silence settled in the court of Indralok, the high ceiling of the hall echoing the tension.

'Ahalya,' murmured Nahusha. 'She was born to break Urvashi's vanity, isn't that so? And she was supposedly so beautiful that Lord Brahma developed his three heads while turning his head to look at her. Is that true or is it just a fable?'

'Ahalya was the most beautiful woman on earth and in the three heavens,' concurred Menaka.

'And what about her?' frowned Nahusha. 'Indra got his punishment, but what happened to this lovely lady?'

'Do you want to know her story, King? And that of her husband, Rishi Gautam, ... and Indra?' she added after a shrewd pause.

Nahusha nodded impatiently.

Menaka smiled. 'I will tell you ...'

1

The Twins

'Ahalya *is* the most beautiful girl in the world,' King Mudgal whispered as he bent forward to kiss his baby daughter on the forehead. She was magnificent, delicate and glowing with life.

'All new fathers say that!' laughed Nalayani, amused by her husband's reaction.

King Mudgal could not take his eyes off the two babies placed together in a large, ornate cradle. 'I am indeed fortunate,' he said, sighing happily. He cast an affectionate glance at his smiling wife.

'Now we need not quarrel over whether we should have a son or a daughter,' chuckled Nalayani, her face tired but radiant. 'We have both! The prince and princess of Panchal.'

'Twins seem to run in your family. You and your twin brother, Indrasen, and now these two—Ahalya and Divodas,' said her husband, glancing down at the gurgling infants.

Nalayani settled herself contentedly against the pillows. 'Names heavy enough to suit the weighty legacy of our families—from both sides,' she said matter-of-factly.

'How can I ever forget that you are the daughter of the famous Emperor Nala of Nishad and Queen Damayanti of Vidarbha?' he teased.

Nalayani frowned prettily. 'But of course, and it's evident in my name itself—Nalayani has both Nala and Damayanti in it,' she said, not for the first time. 'They were less creative while naming my brother, Indrasen, though ...'

'Well, he is a part of Indra's coterie,' remarked Mudgal thoughtfully. 'As your family has always been.'

'It pays off well,' she said, shrugging. 'Better to have Indra as a friend than an enemy. Naming my brother after him is a mark of respect. It is something we might have to do sometime, someday.'

'We may not need to—the line of Indra kings has always been close to our family,' said Mudgal, frowning.

'But we have a daughter now. And such a precious, beautiful daughter ... She is meant for someone special—someone like Indra, the king of gods.'

'Stop it, Nalayani!' he said sharply. 'Don't make plans for your children; that's a mistake parents often make to fulfil their own ambitions.'

'But she deserves the best!' protested his wife. 'This girl of ours is not just pretty.' Nalayani picked up her daughter from the cradle. She gazed down at the small, fair, serene face. 'She is simply ... oh, so, so beautiful.' She let out a breath in awe. 'And it's not a fond mother saying this,' she continued. 'I am not gushing about our son, am I? But this girl, well, there's something so divine, so ethereal about her. Don't you agree, Mudgal?'

Mollified, her husband said, 'Yes, there is. And something so ... mature!'

Nalayani nodded vigorously. 'Yes, that's what I mean—odd, isn't it? She looks so grown-up, so wise and solemn. Nothing babyish about her. Look at her eyes!'

The parents gazed down at their daughter as their infant son cried in protest. 'She does not cry much, either. She has that sensible, curious look, as if she knows everything and yet wants to learn more. Oh dear, hold her, Mudgal, while I see to our prince,' she said, sighing and handing the girl to her father.

'On Lord Brahma's suggestion, Rishi Vashisht decided to name her Ahalya—the beautiful one without blemishes,' said Mudgal. 'But for us, cattle herders who became kings, Ahalya means something deeper, something related to the earth, the soil. Ahalya means the plough, too, when broken into two parts—a-halya, as related to ploughing.' He looked thoughtfully at the baby girl in his arms.

Nalayani sniffed. 'That sounds mundane. I prefer the people's praises. Everyone says that Lord Brahma took special care in creating our daughter; that he extracted the beauty of all creation and expressed it in every part of her, making her the loveliest girl on earth!'

King Mudgal gave a hearty laugh. 'Singing paeans about a new born is just respect given to the royals by the public!'

'But I love them. That's how legends are created. Look at the stories around my parents, and your grandfather Brahmavasya. Like the one about how he created Panchal—the land of the five—by distributing his kingdom between his five versatile sons,' said Nalayani. 'From the great King Puru and King Bharat and Arka, right down to you, the legend lives.'

Mudgal shrugged his slight shoulders. 'That's a heavy weight to carry.'

'Humble, as always,' observed Nalayani with a slight smile. 'You come from the Bharat clan, one of the most ancient families in the land, and that is why songs are written about you.' She glanced at her daughter, who stared back with bright, alert eyes. 'And now it's Ahalya's turn. People are claiming that Lord Brahma himself attended the naming ceremony to witness what he had so carefully created.'

'That is very unfair to our son!' protested Mudgal, but he smiled jovially. 'He is a healthy, good-looking lad too, our Divodas, but the attention is all on our girl.' He gently caressed his son's ruddy cheeks. 'Divodas, the servant of God.'

'The one who serves God,' repeated his wife thoughtfully. 'Why did you choose that name? Do you want him to be a saint and not a king?'

'A king, too, can serve God by serving the people and his subjects,' Mudgal reminded her gently. 'A king conquers not only land but also the hearts of the people.'

'Sometimes, I think you are more a seer than a king!' said Nalayani lightly. 'Like my father—a hopeless idealist.'

'A royal or a rishi, it doesn't matter,' murmured the king. 'Only one's deeds do.'

'They are our children,' scoffed his wife. 'They will both be famous.'

Ahalya looked towards her teacher and opened her small rosebud mouth. To her young eyes, the rishi was an old man; so old he seemed to have outlived time and change and death. His parrot face and parrot voice were dry, like his wrinkled, thickly veined hands. His simple white garments clashed with the opulence of the palace. And he had a stiff, odd way of squatting. He could sit for days, be it in the cold or the sun, under the palace banyan tree or on an opulent couch at court. He never showed any sign of fatigue. Or impatience at her incessant queries. When he spoke to her, his voice was unfailingly kind.

'Hmm, another question from our dear princess,' said Rishi Vashisht. 'Now, pray, what do you want to know?'

'Why is the earth called a mother and not a father?' asked Ahalya eagerly, heaving a silent sigh of relief that she had been given yet another chance to voice her question.

She heard her brother chuckle. 'What a silly question— and really, what difference does it make, sister?' asked Divodas impatiently. 'I need to finish this lesson and go to archery class. You can stay on here and drive the guru crazy with all your questions.'

'Yes, I will,' she retorted. 'And it's not a silly question, it's pertinent. I simply want to know why.'

'Your whys,' sighed her brother, throwing her an affectionate punch, which she deftly avoided.

'Stay still,' ordered the guru, staring sternly at the ten-year-old twins, thinking how dissimilar they were in looks, mood and manner.

The girl was delicate and always quiet, except when she popped up with her sudden questions, her fair face suffused with colour and glowing with curiosity, her soft eyes shining. She was exceptionally lovely, with her tumble of wavy hair tied neatly in a thick plait, each feature on her heart-shaped face perfectly matching the others. She had a wide forehead with delicately carved eyebrows arching over a pair of wide-set doe eyes, a small, sharp nose, a soft mouth, and a chin with a cleft in it. It was the determined chin—a contrast to the placidity of her face and frame—that gave the girl away. Her ethereality made her appear deceptively frail, her strength more quiet than shown.

The boy was tall and lean, boisterous and amiable. Ahalya was the more beautiful of the two, but the boy, with his ready smile and twinkling eyes, was more popular with everyone— the royals, the nobles, the soldiers and the people. His sister rarely smiled, but when she did, it was so shy, it was endearing.

And there was one huge truth that the guru allowed only himself to know: Ahalya was far more intelligent than her brother. The girl was brilliant, and she displayed that brilliance quietly, as was her nature, but Vashisht wondered whether her parents would be able to handle her extraordinariness; they were more fascinated by her beauty than her intelligence.

Ahalya was speaking in complete sentences by the age of two. She brought an astonishingly precise logic to bear on the world around her, and the intensity of her presence, that indescribable inner radiance and clarity, drew people to her— whether it was the king himself or the courtiers. In spite of this undeniable uniqueness, her childhood was for the most part normal. She spent her days like the princess she was: eating the best, living in the best and learning from the best.

'I am sure you will bless Ahalya and Divodas with your immense knowledge and scholarship. We could start with some serious reading material to direct their learning,' the king had remarked when he requested Rishi Vashisht and Rishi Bharadwaj to be his children's gurus.

It was in the spring before their sixth birthday, by which time Ahalya had learned the basics of grammar tolerably well, that the king suggested they might proceed with her academic education. And so, they had begun that very morning with the first lesson. By lunch, Ahalya had mastered the alphabet, the special shape of each letter and the various ways of pronouncing them. By evening, she had memorised her first lesson, a discourse on the good habit of cleanliness, and with her hands clasped in front of her, she had repeated the essay in its entirety for her parents.

'Was that correct?' she had asked, glancing at the king and then her mother, who had been following along in the reader.

Nalayani's face was the pale colour of astonishment. 'Precisely.'

Mudgal examined his daughter curiously. 'When did you learn that lesson, Ahalya?'

'Just today, Father, after dinner.'

'It doesn't make sense,' Nalayani said. 'This should have taken a month, perhaps two weeks, for a particularly bright child like Divodas.'

The king drew in his breath deeply. 'Tell us how you did it.'

'Once I heard the words in my head, the lesson was easy,' the little girl explained.

'Do I have permission to take leave, Guruji?' The boy's restless voice broke into Rishi Vashisht's thoughts. 'I have to collect my bow and arrows from the armoury.'

Vashisht nodded, knowing it would be futile to restrain the prince any longer. He was too distracted, as he often was while studying philosophy and theology. Divodas had adventure in his blood and was a born warrior; he would certainly do his father and the royal family of Panchal proud one day.

The old sage clasped his hands one over the other upon the notes Ahalya had neatly written down on parchment and leaned forward. He knew she had it all in her head; she always had a firm hold of the work assigned to her. He was surprised when the girl got up too.

'Where are *you* going, Ahalya?'

'I want to try the bow and arrows today,' she announced, her tone soft.

Her brother guffawed loudly and Vashisht raised an eyebrow. 'But why? You have never shown any interest in archery before.'

'But I have to know! Why is it that a prince is taught archery and not a princess? Besides, Ma said I should!' There was a stubbornness in the soft tone. 'She told me a princess, too, should be a warrior. What if there's a war? How will I defend myself?'

'Girls don't fight wars, men do!' retorted Divodas gruffly.

Vashisht shook his head. 'No, prince, women have fought wars. When it comes to self-preservation, pride and valour, there is no distinction between the genders. One fights for survival, remember. So, princess, should we abandon our discussion and handle the bow this morning?' he asked, smiling.

'Yes,' she said, nodding sweetly.

'Sir, you pamper her,' complained the boy as his sister walked away. 'Now my time will be wasted; I'm sure she'll take ages just learning how to hold the bow, forget stringing it.'

'You might be surprised, prince. She has great will and patience,' said Vashisht mildly.

'It's quite likely the fascination will last only for a day,' grumbled the boy. 'She wants to hold it just because Father

t to. That's so typical of Ahalya—she always wants
she is not permitted to.'

Vashisht was surprised at the little boy's perspicacity.
His guileless observation had revealed more than the prince
realised. Ahalya, he had noticed, liked to dare the impossible
because the forbidden was a constant temptation: she had
a deep desire to do something different prompted solely
by curiosity. And yet, nearly all the time, she was the most
obedient and passive child.

Clearly not so obedient today, the rishi thought, sighing.

He could see the twins at a distance, where Rishi Payu
Bharadwaj was teaching them archery. Divodas showed signs
of being a great archer, stringing the bow with ease. Ahalya
was struggling, but she was not one to give up easily. He could
almost feel Bharadwaj's amusement. But the young rishi knew
the princess as well as he did: she would not let this opportunity
slip by; she would make the most of it.

The Bharadwajs had always been closely associated with the
Puru and Bharat clans, which had been further splintered into
the Panchals by King Brahmavasya, King Mudgal's grandfather.
Their association with the Bharats was particularly close, with
several instances of the adoption of a Bharadwaj by the Bharat
family, starting with Bhumanyu—popularly known as Vithath—
by King Bharat. A member of the Bharat family had also chosen
a life of priesthood to become part of the Bharadwajs.

Vashisht grew thoughtful. King Mudgal seemed to be
showing signs of leaning towards the life of a scholar these
days, rather than monarchical thinking.

He was interrupted by an unexpected shout. It was the
prince, and he could hear the raw panic in his raised voice.

'Ahalya! We can't find her, sir!'

His heart jolted as he went up to where Divodas was standing. 'Were you not training together?' he asked, frowning.

'She got bored after ten rounds, and I got busy shooting arrows at the target,' said the boy, almost in tears. 'No one noticed her slinking away ...'

'The hand maids? The guards?' Vashisht asked urgently.

'She gave them the slip too. They are searching for her.' Divodas's voice broke. 'How will I face Father? I should have been looking after her.'

'You were,' Vashisht said, taking the boy's hand. 'Let's search for her. Try your hunting skills,' he said lightly.

Divodas gave his teacher a weak smile.

They searched the palace grounds swiftly and thoroughly. She was not in the palace either. *She is just a child, how far could she have gone,* wondered Vashisht, feeling the first prick of anxiety. It was so unlike her.

'Sir! We found her!' cried a soldier.

The prince pushed past and ran towards the approaching figure of a soldier carrying the little girl in his arms. Vashisht increased his pace too.

He felt the cold hand of the prince slipping into his.

'Is she alive?' Divodas asked fearfully, his eyes wide.

'Yes, of course,' assured Vashisht.

And sure enough, the slight figure of the princess moved and then wriggled away from the guard's protective arms. Ahalya had the quiet dignity required of a princess, sedate and graceful as the soldier led her towards the rishi and her brother.

'Where did you disappear?!' Divodas pounced on her as soon as she was close.

She looked surprised at the anger in her brother's voice; he rarely scolded her. 'But I was simply following the arrow. I wanted to know where it had fallen!'

'What?' cried the prince. 'You were chasing an errant arrow?' He looked more incredulous than furious.

'Yes. I missed the target and it swept over the trees and beyond. I wanted to know where it had landed.'

Divodas was speechless, his mouth hanging open.

Vashisht's experienced eyes were searching the tall trees that bordered the high walls of the palace. He turned to her with a long, probing look, trying to understand her actions. He could not be annoyed at her for very long. She was barely ten years old, but the spark in the quiet girl had flared. Vitality had blossomed early in this little lady, clearly evident now, shimmering through her thin frame like a glow.

He took the girl gently by the shoulder. 'Princess, you know you cannot roam around without your maids or guards,' he admonished gently. 'You are from a royal house and in danger of being kidnapped. You are the daughter of an important king, and he has enemies who may not wish you well. That is why your father has appointed these guards to protect you. You know that.'

'I know my way around,' she said quietly. 'I did not get lost.'

Vashisht sighed. 'Not this time, young lady. You were thoughtless, and I always considered you a wise, responsible girl.'

Ahalya recognised the stern rebuke in her guru's voice. She opened her eyes wide. 'But I did not mean to be irresponsible,' she said, her face contrite, her eyes troubled. 'I had to know what happened to that arrow.'

'Dear child, what would have happened to *you*?' he said. 'Your curiosity is laudable and I have always appreciated it. Perhaps I was wrong to encourage it. I should have taught you instead that caution is the other side of curiosity.' He paused, throwing her a reproachful glance. 'You might be clever, princess, but prudence and discretion sharpen wisdom and prevent it from going wild. I hope you have learnt your lesson today.'

Ahalya nodded meekly, wondering what she had done wrong.

'You are a fool,' said Divodas under his breath, giving her a quick, hard hug, but not before she caught the look of stark anxiousness on his face. Suddenly, he did not look like a boy: he had grown to be a man, as he placed his hands protectively around her slight shoulders.

Ahalya gave a rapturous smile; her brother had forgiven her.

2

The Education

'Have you made all the arrangements, Ahalya?'

Ahalya nodded absently without raising her head from her book. This was the fifth time her mother had asked her the same question.

'Ahalya, your brother is coming home victorious from a long war with those bloodthirsty Dasas, and you are busy with some book!' snapped Nalayani. Her daughter's placidity often unnerved her.

Ahalya sighed and looked at her mother.

Nalayani was a petite, bird-like woman, with bright, dark eyes. She made no attempt to conceal her age; her beauty was still intact, her fair skin still smooth and unlined—but she was confident that any wrinkles she might get later in life would not bother her. She loved her diamonds: her long fingers displayed several flashing rings and her slim wrists were adorned with gold and diamond bracelets. As a child, Ahalya had loved watching her mother putting on her jewellery. Ahalya also knew that when she was nervous, her mother fidgeted with

her bracelets and hummed under her breath. She wa
so now. When her mother was in this mood, Ahalya had
realised it was best to go along with anything she said and no
argue or try and dissuade her.

'Everything's done, Ma. Don't be tense. You shall see your
son soon, and I will be the first one to welcome him,' she said,
her voice reassuring, her eyes softening. 'I am proud of him
too, you know.'

Nalayani gave a short laugh. 'Yes, I know I am nervous.
But it's only to you I can show my fear and apprehensions,
isn't it? A queen is not supposed to reveal her feelings when
her husband or son go to war. She just has to wait with
dignity, never showing the fear she may feel, or the worry, or
the sadness ...'

Ahalya got up and gave her mother a quick hug. 'Divodas
should be here by noon. Now put on your best silks and smile!'
she urged.

Nalayani immediately brightened up. 'He is a hero! He
defeated the mighty Kirat king Shambar!' she said, beaming.
'He's just sixteen and he's won a war for his father. I wish your
father would show more enthusiasm.'

Ahalya detected the accusation in her mother's voice.

'Father does not like war,' she said simply.

'He used to; he has won many wars himself,' Nalayani
retorted. 'He comes from a family of conquerors, and he was
one himself. But recently, all he has been keen on is poring
over books of philosophy and listening to the seers he invites
to court from across the land. He ... he has changed. He seems
to be so disenchanted with everything—it's worrying!' she
said, her brow pleated in a frown. 'It's like he is just waiting to

...bilities on to young Divodas's shoulders.

...he's too young!'

...be young in age, but he is wise beyond

...lwaj says so. Father has seen this in him,

...rages him so ...'

...sending a child to war?' said Nalayani, fear and annoyance clouding her face. 'What if Divodas had been hurt? Or worse, killed?' she whispered tremulously, wringing her hands. 'I would never have forgiven myself! What would happen to Panchal? To us?'

'Ma, in war, all live in fear, don't they?' Ahalya recalled the thick fog of dread that smothered her every time her father or brother went to war. 'Be it the king's or the soldier's wife. We have won; let's halt the worries and savour the victory and the moment. Why, you were just now beaming with pride—it's not unjustified. Divodas is an exceptional prince! He is a hero. He is a victor!'

'That he is,' said her mother, forcing a broad smile, wide enough to push away any sad thoughts. 'But what about you?'

'Me?' asked Ahalya, her serene face showing surprise. 'I thought we were talking about Divodas, not me!'

'Yes, you. Your brother is already famous for his feats. Now having trounced that dreadful Shambar, he will become a legend ...'

'Is not one famous child enough for you, Ma?' Ahalya asked dryly.

'Oh, stop being ironic. How you love to run yourself down!' her mother said, sniffing. 'You know you are very beautiful.'

'But where is my achievement in that?' Ahalya asked, with genuine puzzlement. 'It's not my talent; it's God's gift.'

It was Nalayani's turn to look amazed. 'Ahalya, you are said to be the loveliest princess, someone gods and kings from far and near are eager to marry,' her mother said, her voice slightly sharp. 'You are the daughter of King Mudgal of Panchal, a Puru princess—'

'And?' asked Ahalya blandly. 'I am proud of my family, but that legacy, again, has been bestowed on me. It's a privilege, not a consequence of my personal abilities.'

'I know what you are trying to imply. That I am ignoring *your* talent. Yes, you are a very bright girl, but honestly, intelligence too is a gift, isn't it?' observed her mother, her thin lips curled. 'Not all people have intelligence.'

'But no!' exclaimed Ahalya. 'All people have been blessed with intelligence—but *employing* those brains is what makes you intelligent. It's neither heredity nor hereditary.'

'Yes, I understand; for that, you need knowledge as a tool for thought,' commented Nalayani, realising that the conversation was leading to a disagreement that had been arising frequently in the last few months. She would have liked to change the subject, but her daughter, Nalayani knew, would not remain quiet for long. Ahalya was unassuming and usually placid, but she could also be exasperatingly obstinate.

'Yes, and you know I want to study further,' started Ahalya, a slight assertiveness in her soft voice. 'I want to learn at Guru Vashisht's ashram.'

'Why at the ashram?' her mother demanded. 'He is our royal priest, and he has been teaching you here. Why go somewhere else?'

Ahalya heaved a deep sigh of frustration. She recalled all those years ago when she had read out her first lesson to her parents. That same night she had overheard her father and mother quarrelling. She couldn't hear exactly what was being said, but the next morning her father had announced that Rishi Vashisht and Rishi Bharadwaj would be taking over her academic education. After the first few lessons, she had quickly graduated to writing, arithmetic and the rudiments of the Vedas. Through the years, as her mind and hunger for knowledge expanded, she mastered each new subject with astonishing ease.

As she approached the age of sixteen, the fate of Ahalya's lessons had been a matter of debate. While her mother had come around to the idea of her studying further, till she married, she would not agree to sending her daughter to an ashram. No amount of reasoning or pleading would convince her mother to relent.

'An ashram is meant for higher learning,' Ahalya reasoned. 'I can't remain in the palace and acquire the knowledge of the world. I don't want to be some cloistered princess who just looks pretty and does nothing! I want to study. If you think that is my gift, Ma, allow me to use it the way I want.'

'No. If you want to study further, it will be here in this palace,' snapped Nalayani. 'Meanwhile, as you well know, I shall be searching for a suitor for you, after which we can hold your swayamwar. That's what is done for girls who have come of age.'

They were interrupted by the sound of elephants trumpeting in the distance, announcing the arrival of the victors. Ahalya set aside her disappointment and rushed to the window to catch a glimpse of her brother. Nalayani followed her warily, sure the argument would resurface later, possibly more heatedly.

Ahalya peered over the balustrade for a clearer view. Some way away, she could see the golden flag of their family flapping.

'They're here!' she exclaimed.

'Yes, and I hope you are ready to welcome them,' said King Mudgal from behind her. Aged prematurely but regally, King Mudgal was tall, lean and stately, his thick hair the colour of burnished silver. His benign expression, his quiet dignity, his mild manners and his hair made him appear more like a scholar than a king. 'Ahalya, is the puja thali ready for them?' he asked as he led his wife and daughter to the palace entrance, where they would receive Divodas.

'Them?' she asked, taken aback.

'Divodas and Indra Shakra,' her father said.

'It was because of Indra that Divodas won against the Dasas,' he said.

'Oh, I thought it was Rishi Bharadwaj who was the guiding force,' said Ahalya, surprised.

'Yes, but Indra helped him with his army and expertise,' said Mudgal. 'When will these skirmishes between the Bharat clan and other tribes, like the Dasas and the Panis, ever end?' she added, visibly vexed. 'My father was exhausted fighting them.'

Mudgal looked grave. 'So am I. I have fought them all my life, as did my ancestors. We are from the Arya tribe of the Trtsu dynasty, Nalayani, and as our Puru–Bharat clan has increased its domination over the other tribes, the power struggles have become more frequent and ferocious. That is natural,' he added after a short pause. 'No one wants their lands to be taken.'

'Wars, my dear, have always been fought over land and water,' his wife said tartly.

'It is more greed and bruised pride now,' rued the king.

'It could well be the start of the consolidation of power of our Puru–Bharat dynasty, Father,' remarked Ahalya quietly, the puja thali in her hand and a frown on her brow. 'You may have grown weary of this, but for Divodas, this is just the beginning. Thankfully, we have royal priests like Rishi Vashisht and Rishi Bharadwaj on our side.'

'I'm surprised that you're aware of politics, too, besides philosophy, Ahalya,' her father said, his silver-grey eyebrows lifted.

'Politics is a subject as well,' she said demurely but with smiling eyes. 'And we are subjected to it every day.'

'Yes, and it makes sense to have someone as powerful as Indra as our ally,' interjected Nalayani.

Mudgal nodded. 'Indra is said to have vanquished several Dasa kings—Cumuri, Dhuni, Pipru, Susna ... That's why he helped Divodas in this war too.'

Nalayani looked miffed. 'That is all very well, but Divodas held his own,' she said, sounding disgruntled. 'Don't take the credit away from him!'

'I am not, my dear. I cherish my son too,' said Mudgal, his tone instantly conciliatory. 'He is a fine warrior and is already showing signs of being a master strategist as well. But I wonder why he did not kill King Shambar on the battlefield. Someone like Shambar is sure not to take his defeat lightly. He will strike back some day.'

'Perhaps Divodas is a pacifist like you, Father,' joked Ahalya, noting the worried frown on her father's lined face. 'He is not yet bloodthirsty enough.'

'He will be,' assured Nalayani swiftly. 'He is a Puru!'

'Yes,' said Ahalya, nodding. 'And there will be Indra around, too, to help him become more vicious. But they make a fine pair, he and Indra,' she remarked thoughtfully. 'They will win wars together.'

'It's the first time Indra is coming here, so let's give him a grand welcome,' said Mudgal. 'I shall ask him to stay over for a few days.'

Nalayani agreed instantly. 'But of course, that is our duty as hosts. We need to keep Indra on our side. Though my Divodas remains the hero of the hour and the hero of our hearts!'

Ahalya could not help smiling at her mother's open adoration of her son.

'And the people's as well,' Mudgal added, smiling.

They were now outside the palace, and Ahalya saw two men clambering down from their chariots and entering the palace gates. Her eyes were only on her twin brother.

Divodas was a tall, athletically built boy, unaware of his good looks and always amiable, with a ready grin. He was big and strong and strapping, as a warrior should be, though he was just sixteen years old. His eyes were black and were quick to reveal his flashes of temper. His hair was thick and dark, rather long and curled a little near his temples and neck. His skin was creamy and rosy, like their mother's, which he secretly detested and was wickedly teased about. He really *was* handsome, Ahalya thought proudly.

He was grinning at her widely, as usual, ignoring the formal decorum expected of him. But he was a reckless rather than a staid prince. If he could have his way, she was certain he would have rushed and picked her up, as he would do when they were children.

He bowed to his parents with a flourish. 'Your blessings, Ma,' he said flamboyantly.

'Always,' Nalayani murmured with delight, throwing her arms around him to give him a hug. He hugged her back, almost lifting her.

Divodas looked a little subdued as he approached his father, slightly wary. But his father was far from displeased.

'Well done, son,' he said. 'The time has arrived when the son has far exceeded the father. You did what I could not in all these years! You vanquished the Dasas.'

'Once and for all, I hope,' said Divodas fervently.

'If you had killed Shambar, it could have been so,' said his father.

Divodas looked surprised. 'You wanted for me to kill him? But you were always against unnecessary bloodshed.'

'That was my mistake,' said Mudgal quietly. 'Perhaps that's why I could never end the war. Now it's a wounded enemy you have, more angry than before. He *will* retaliate.'

The smile was wiped off his beaming face, and Divodas suddenly looked grim and old beyond his years. His face tightened and his eyes turned steely. Suddenly this was the face not of a prince but of a ruthless warrior.

'Then I will not spare him the next time, Father,' he vowed. 'I shall kill him.'

Ahalya felt her nerve ends prickle, and watched with concern as the expressions on her brother's face shifted.

'Let's not talk about death and bloodshed. Haven't we had enough?' interrupted Nalayani and turned to Indra. 'I should thank you, for being with my little son and protecting him.'

'He doesn't need protection. He is not little, he's a lion!' Indra said quickly, only giving the queen half his attention. The other half was reeling under the impact of the girl standing in front of him. She had stopped him mid-stride.

It was a curious day, Indra thought, filled with fleeting, unfamiliar impressions. One minute he had the sense of being a hero, and the next he felt like a trespasser.

It was the girl. As she held the puja plate loosely in her hand, Indra could not take his eyes off her. Her pale blue garments accentuated her fair skin and made her look ethereal. She was as arrestingly beautiful as he had been told she was. His gaze had flooded her cheeks with colour, and he felt a hot spark singeing him as well. The warmth of her blush and the slight tremble of her rosebud lips as she tried to hide her confusion imprinted on his mind an impression of quiet flux, of a strange intensity, of passionate vitality tempered by the quietude in her doe eyes.

He swallowed, hoping to break the sense of bewitchment.

Ahalya noticed that the man who had helped her brother in the war was barely listening to her mother's words; he looked utterly transfixed. He was staring unabashedly at her, as if in a trance. But it was she who felt disconcerted and embarrassed. She felt a flush rise hotly up her neck and her face. She was used to appreciative looks, but his was burning through her.

She had a good look at him through lowered eyes. He had everything a man could want in the way of good looks. He was tall, fair and had broad shoulders. His grey eyes, sharply chiselled nose and glossy hair matched perfectly with his ready smile. That he was too handsome, too perfect, was her first thought.

He was not distracting enough, however, to make her stop ruminating over the unfinished argument she had had with her mother. She had to convince all of them somehow ...

The occasion came soon enough, after lunch, when Indra had retired to the other wing of the palace. He would be staying over, and Ahalya was not too pleased. There was no need for a stranger to have knowledge of her future plans. But Ahalya quickly realised that for her brother, Indra was more than just an ally. He was his friend, though Indra was senior to him in years and status. She observed him as discreetly as he did blatantly, but she wished him gone as she had more pressing matters to attend to.

They were all sitting together in the morning room, tucking into the sweets her mother had made for Divodas. She was wondering how she would broach the subject. Nalayani had already noticed the troubled look on her daughter's face and knew what was coming.

'Father, Divodas, Ma, since we are all together after a long time, I need to talk about something important,' declared Ahalya in a rush, her heart fluttering, holding on to all the courage she could muster. 'My education,' she said more strongly.

'Need to?' enquired her mother, raising an eyebrow, fixing her for a moment with a cold eye and then returning her gaze to King Mudgal. 'No, you don't *need to*, Ahalya, your formal education is done. You don't *need to* continue studying. You turned sixteen last month and you *need to* get married.'

Ahalya pursed her lips and clutched her hands together. 'No, Ma, not yet!' she pleaded, her tone again plaintive. 'I know that's expected of me, but I don't want to get married. I really want to study further. Guru Vashisht agrees with me,' she said, throwing her teacher an imploring look. She was grateful he had agreed to remain in the room.

'I know, I heard him. And your father as well,' replied Nalayani dismissively. 'But I don't agree. You have finished your formal education ...'

'Education is never finished, Ma,' Ahalya said, her voice firmer, her composure seemingly unruffled.

Her mother seemed to get more irked by her serenity: it hinted at a manner of control that came naturally to Ahalya.

'Ahalya, don't argue,' snapped Nalayani with unusual acidity, throwing all those in the room an exasperated look. King Mudgal looked distressed. He had confidence in both his wife's judgement and his daughter's abilities, and felt shaken and torn. His daughter, surprisingly, was looking as adamant as his wife was.

Nalayani sensed the mood in the room. It was thick with hesitancy and uncertainty of what the outcome of this argument would be. But that was often the case: her husband and the twins often ganged up against her, even if it was just a game of chess. But this was a round from which Nalayani was not ready to back down. Nor was Ahalya, she realised, noting her daughter's raised chin, her assertive tone and stance.

'Ma, let her study,' began Divodas. 'She's a brilliant student. And if I have excelled as a warrior, why can she not study what she wants?'

Nalayani was hurt at her son's accusation.

'I am not against her—or her wishes! It is all of you who are against me and what I have to say,' she said bitterly. 'It should have been your father discussing this, not me. The stubborn girl wants to study and not marry! What foolishness is this to be encouraged by both father and brother?'

'I didn't encourage anything,' protested King Mudgal quickly. 'Believe me or not, I refrained from so much as lifting an eyebrow.'

His wit did not lighten the atmosphere, as he had hoped. He threw his wife a despairing glance and then looked at his daughter, helplessly.

Ahalya gave him an almost imperceptible nod, registering his plight. Her father, unlike her mother, had readily agreed when she had confided in him her desire to study more, as soon as she had completed her last term with Rishi Vashisht and Rishi Bharadwaj. She had hesitantly put forth her idea to him.

'It's not just about higher studies, Ahalya,' he had remarked in his cautious manner. 'All this time you studied under Rishi Vashisht in the comfortable confines of the palace. To learn more, you would have to go and live in their ashram, in a forest, in modest, austere conditions. Will you be able to take it?'

Ahalya had stared back at her father steadfastly, not blinking from the hard truth.

'You know I can do it, Father,' she had said simply.

King Mudgal had nodded slowly, seeing that beneath that apparent mildness and fragility lay the fire of determination. 'Yes, I believe you can.'

Ahalya had smiled that shy smile of hers. 'Oh, Father, I knew you would not refuse me!'

Nothing was too much trouble for her, thought Mudgal indulgently. And when she got what she had wished for, she accepted it with a quiet, kindly dignity.

She had also managed to have a quick conversation with her brother after Indra had left, hoping that any supportive words from him would convince her mother.

'I know you like studies more than playing princess or queen,' he had initially bantered, his tone light.

'Oh, be serious,' she begged. 'I know Ma will refuse, and I need your help.'

'Hmm, so you are building your army of supporters like a clever commander,' he teased. 'I am sure you have convinced Father by now.'

She nodded. 'Will you persuade Ma? She tends to listen to you.'

'Because I am often right!' he said with feigned haughtiness. His grin slipped a little and he continued solemnly, 'But in this case, I'm not sure it will work. I honestly don't know how you will manage Ma. I have a suggestion: why don't you marry a rishi instead of some young prince? You will be happy, and so will Ma!'

'No, she won't! She wants me to marry ... someone like your friend Indra!' she replied crossly. 'I saw it in her eyes the moment she saw him!'

And I saw it in his *eyes*, Ahalya thought but did not say aloud.

Divodas had been too stunned to react to this observation. Even now in the chamber, he looked slightly confused and remained silent, though Ahalya knew he was trying to give her his full support. It was her mother who was obdurate. But she would not give up either, Ahalya thought with sudden determination; not this time. One look at her father, however, and she knew she had to rein in the argument, which was fast growing unpleasant.

Her expression still calm, but her smoky black eyes dulled and her shoulders slumped in resignation, she murmured, 'I will marry, Ma, but not so soon. Please let me study a bit longer.'

'May I intervene,' said Vashisht. He stood up slowly and bowed to the indignant queen.

His patient old eyes seemed to take stock of the family in front of him. The queen had been arguing more than usual, he thought, and as she spoke, her eyes had wandered to her husband, with a kind of anxiety that was unusual in her.

It was Ahalya who did not take her earnest eyes from Vashisht's face. Her steady gaze was unnerving. He did not look at her as he spoke, but the princess continued to look at him. Her eyes suddenly seemed equally fearless and full of hope.

'Until marriage plans for the princess are fixed, I am happy to teach Ahalya in my ashram.'

'No!' Nalayani flared up. 'Ahalya needs to get married— she's a princess, not a scholar, Guruji! A quick wedding is the best choice. She is a most eligible princess, and any king would be willing to marry her.'

'But *I* should be willing to marry!' Ahalya interposed, her voice a little louder than she had intended. Still, she told herself, she needed to be heard over her mother's obstinacy.

'Any king would gladly agree, Mudgal. Please, we could have a quick wedding,' Nalayani said insistently, looking pleadingly at her husband.

Why the needless hurry, wondered Ahalya, her mounting panic galvanising her into a reaction.

'You mean Indra, Ma! You have been keen on him since you saw him here!' said Ahalya, her fair face flushed.

The moment she uttered the words, Nalayani looked mortified at being caught.

'Our daughter is extraordinarily intelligent,' King Mudgal had once said to his wife. She remembered it now as he said,

'Let us do her justice. We are kings after all; we can make and break the rules.'

'No, we cannot,' argued Nalayani. 'My father did that when he lost everything in that game of dice, and my mother had to suffer for it—and so did we, as children. Indrasen and I were twelve by the time we got to see our father again ...' she trailed off dully. 'Please, Mudgal, you can't encourage such wild thoughts in our daughter. She is destined for better things.'

Her husband's expression told her she would not receive support from him.

'You are called a raj-rishi now, but you are all but ready to be a full rishi yourself!' she accused him bitterly. 'Still, right now it is not you but Ahalya I am worried about! I shall not allow my daughter to make the wrong decision. She is young and gullible; we are not, Mudgal.'

Met with silence, Nalayani concluded that her husband was against her and so were her children. She squared her shoulders. 'There's a guest in this house right now, so I will not argue further about this,' she announced, her tone flat and final.

Becoming aware of her mother's probing stare, the soft, gentle expression returned to Ahalya's face. Once more, she was the efficient, obedient daughter. But this debate was clearly not over, Nalayani knew; she could see a quiet rebellion building in Ahalya's smoky eyes.

3

Indra

Ahalya. She was like mist merging with the skies ... like an apsara. Indra gave a start. He knew apsaras. He lived with them, and they served him. But none was like Ahalya. Not even Menaka.

Indra had accepted King Mudgal's invitation to stay in the palace. Not for the warm hospitality displayed by Queen Nalayani, nor even his affection for his young friend Divodas. It was not for the sake of diplomatic ties with King Mudgal either. It was for Ahalya. It was the daughter's fault, or rather, that of her bewitching beauty.

Even as she had glided in front of him as she led the way up the marbled stairs into the palace, he had not been able to tear his eyes from her. She had the most alluring walk he had ever seen. Her small, rounded hips were sheathed in sky-blue silk, draped loosely but allowing light to ripple through the fabric as she moved, so that it flowed sinuously like a thick, sensuous liquid.

He had been so instantly smitten that he needed a physical nudge from his friend to bring him back to reality.

'Indra?' Divodas prodded him, studying him carefully.

Indra flushed under his friend's scrutiny. He was sure that were it not for his status, he would not have been forgiven his impertinence. Indra had to struggle to take his besotted eyes off Ahalya.

It was so that he could see her, have her close to him, that Indra accepted the invitation to stay at King Mudgal's palace. The mere sight of her precipitated a sort of ecstasy in him, and it was with that ecstasy that he viewed what was happening to him now. It was as if he was in a blissful stupor, a mood of intense elation, an exhilarating sense that, for once, he was magnificently attuned to love and to life. Everything about him was radiating a brightness and a bliss he might never know again.

Just watching her gave him great joy, but the fact that he had not got a chance to talk to her caused him intense angst. As the days passed, he felt his elation dissipating swiftly. One evening, he waited for her to come downstairs, determined to speak to her. He moved to a large window that overlooked the vast palace gardens; he gazed at it and at the grey, rain-swollen clouds which seemed to mirror his dark mood. He had tried to have a word with her whenever he could, but she had been politely indifferent, regarding him steadily, her chin up, her dark eyes remote.

Indra impatiently peeped into the sunporch in the summer room, where he could see King Mudgal reading, scrolls heaped on the marble-topped table beside him. They were marriage proposals for Ahalya, Divodas had revealed, communicating the desires of all the young men who wanted to marry her.

Raw jealousy clutched Indra's heart. He knew the sort of men they were: ambitious kings, eager princes, men who were young, good-looking, rich and powerful, with graceful garments and expensive gems and deep tans from healthy summers. But he prided himself on being better than these men: he was Indra, the king of the gods, stronger, more handsome and more powerful.

He watched her move down the wide carved staircase, elegant and exquisite, and it did not escape his notice that she chose to sit down on the seat farthest from him. Her movements were unhurried, and calm. She was petite, unlike her brother, but carried herself with her shoulders square and straight, her neck stiff. There was a compelling grace about her, and he found himself staring again at her large eyes and full, firm mouth. But that was not what sent a hot wave of blood through him. The girl exuded a magnetic sensuality that burned through her frosty façade, like a flaring oil lamp flimsily concealed by a shawl. He could sense this, and yet from her calmness and the way she looked directly at him without any sign of self-consciousness, he couldn't be sure if she was aware of it or not; this intrigued him.

'Father and Ma won't be joining us,' she informed him, her tone low. She absentmindedly contemplated her tiny, well-shaped hands, folded neatly in her lap, then looked up, meeting his gaze, her eyes dark and aloof. 'Father is busy with some work and Ma is attending to dinner. But Divodas should be here soon,' she murmured stiffly.

Hoping fervently that Divodas would take his time, Indra looked at her as he sat down, drinking her in. He was used to beautiful women fawning over him. Her iciness irked him. He stared down at the marble floor to stop himself from looking at her. Her small, delicately shaped feet, adorned with gold anklets, came into view. He gazed at them until he abruptly realised his examination was causing an awkward pause and jerked his mind back to the present.

Ahalya wished her brother would join them soon. She had a suspicion that Divodas and her mother had set this meeting up; the excuses for their absence had been too convenient.

Indra attempted to alleviate the awkwardness by starting a conversation: he spoke of Indralok, his palace, his capital, Amravati, even his wars, but he soon found that he was doing all the talking. She was listening politely, with that steady look of hers but—to his chagrin—did not appear particularly impressed by his descriptions of victories and grandeur.

'Enough of me,' he said finally. 'How does it feel to be known as the most beautiful girl in the world?' he asked, determined to provoke her into dialogue.

Any other girl would have taken it as a compliment and blushed in response. Ahalya merely looked at him with a faint, quizzical expression in her eyes.

'I'm not sure I can give you an intelligent answer to that question,' she said at last, in the curiously deep voice that he had noticed when she first greeted him at the palace steps.

Indra was taken aback by her response.

'You *are* the most beautiful woman in the world,' he commended, floundering in the face of her brusqueness. He sat for a moment, looking at her, collecting his thoughts and composure. He had himself under control again, and his warm, charming smile returned. 'You are more than your brother's sister or your father's daughter.'

'I *am* my brother's sister and my father's daughter—as well as my mother's,' she reminded him gently. 'And I am privileged to be so—without conceit or guilt.'

'But soon you will be more than that,' he said delicately. 'Beautiful girls do get married quickly.'

Ahalya was surprised by his overfamiliarity. His bluntness, she suspected, was more out of genuine interest than inappropriate informality.

'And a girl needs to get married?' she asked wryly.

He squirmed. Somehow, this was not going the way he had wanted it to.

'You must have thousands of suitors,' he hastened to amend.

'If that's what you want to believe,' she said curtly.

Indra felt uneasy.

'You are not interested?' he said ingratiatingly.

'No,' she said, shrugging.

'Why not? Don't you want to marry?' he asked.

'I have to, but I don't want to, not yet,' she said without hesitation. 'Does marriage always validate a woman? Or her future?' she asked instead, throwing him a telling look.

'Does it not? You are born your father's daughter and then you marry and become your husband's wife ...'

Ahalya, who had been sitting stiffly, frowned, and an expression of distaste came into her eyes.

'And then the child's mother, and so on and so forth. Is that all there is to a woman?' she said sardonically, her eyes openly scornful. 'You should know better, sir. As Indra, the king of gods, you are surrounded by so many women!'

For a second, Indra preened, but then he realised it was not praise and his smile slipped. A faint sparkle came into those remote eyes and her lips curved into something Indra thought was a smile; whatever it was, he liked it.

'There are devis, there are apsaras, there are dancers, there are musicians, teachers who instruct, cooks who prepare your meals, masseuses who relax you when you are tired. Do you see them as just objects of beauty and desire and not as women, as people engaged in specific occupations? Women as individuals learned in their respective fields?'

She looked steadily at him. Her smoky black eyes opened a little and he found her even more exciting.

'They are all lovely creatures,' he managed to murmur, his breathing uneven.

'Exactly,' she said sharply, and for the first time he saw fire in the ice, the passion raw in her voice. But not for him.

'Just lovely creatures,' she repeated his words, her lips curling in contempt. 'Prejudiced and patronising. That says it all: a woman as a mere object.' She paused, but he had heard the quiet sneer in her voice. 'And not as a person of intellect and emotions, capable of choices and opinions.'

Indra knew he had displeased her. He wished she would smile again.

'And so you want to be—what, not just a daughter or a wife?' he said, hoping he had used the right words.

But she was not so easily beguiled. 'It's not about me; it's about you,' she replied. 'Or rather, how men like you view us,' she said. 'That is often more galling.'

Indra was intrigued by her argument. He leaned towards her, his expression frank and open, hoping his warm smile was enveloping her.

'But ... does it not please you at all that you are viewed as the most beautiful woman in the world?' he asked. 'Does that not make you happy?'

'Should it?' Ahalya lifted her elegant shoulders, bare and creamy, making him tremble. 'Besides beauty of the body, there is in women beauty of the heart and beauty of the brain, too,' she said. 'But how many see that? Kindness is ignored and intelligence is dismissed. Most would not recognise or acknowledge the wisdom behind loveliness, the wit behind the appealing beauty of a woman.'

Indra felt inadequate. He fidgeted and, after a moment, said, 'But women are considered to be more pleasing to the eye than men. Why not enjoy the attention and the flattery that comes with that?'

Her eyes opened a trifle wider. She appeared to hesitate, then she nodded.

'We do; we have our vanity,' she said. 'But would you like it if we viewed men only for their, say, physical strength?'

'That would be short-sighted,' he said instantly, glancing at his slim hands. 'Men are more than just muscle!'

'Agreed. And that's what I mean,' she said, her voice containing a hint of condescension. 'Women are, likewise, more than just lovely creatures.'

'Touché,' Indra said and smiled. 'I see your point.'

'At long last.' She suddenly smiled back. 'Hopefully you will not forget it and return to viewing us as just lovely creatures,' she said.

It was the first real smile he had had from her, and, in spite of the reprimand in her voice, it made her even more attractive to him.

Indra leaned back and grinned. He looked very pleased with himself. 'I would be honoured to be enlightened by you.'

'But I am not your teacher,' she said with a smirk—even that twist of her mouth was beautiful. 'In fact, you are probably my brother's tutor, and you have coached him well.' Her smile expanded.

'He is an excellent student.'

'You would be visiting here more often then, wouldn't you, to meet your pupil?' she said guilelessly, and the moment she uttered the words, Ahalya knew she had made a mistake. Her careless question had come out as an invitation.

Indra's heart turned over, and he even imagined there was a sensual caress in her voice. In the first of many instances to come, her casual words gave new direction to his life.

He wanted her; he wanted to marry Ahalya.

4

The Proposal

Why did she not fall in love with him?

It had been a couple of months since he had last met Ahalya, but she showed no signs of warming to him. Indra knew he could not hurry her. It was a novel experience: no woman had thwarted him before. He felt restless. He moved impatiently even as he thought of her cold response. She was cool, indifferent to his efforts. His smile, his looks, his status, his power had gained him so many easy conquests in the past ... but not Ahalya.

Indra knew he had won her mother's heart: Nalayani adored him. She regarded Indra as their own, welcoming him warmly each time he visited them. So did Divodas; they were close friends now. It was King Mudgal who had been wary, almost reluctant. Indra knew he would have to work fast: if not the girl's, he needed the parents' approval at least.

Discussing his feelings with her brother would not be a smart move, he decided. He would have to talk to her father first.

Indra took the first opportunity he got to broach the subject when he visited Panchal next.

King Mudgal was a little wary of Indra, but he was philosophical enough to know that a good artisan made good use of inferior tools if he had to. As a king, he regarded Indra as a strong ally; someone whom he and his son needed. But as a father, he did not wish the association to turn into a marriage alliance with his daughter.

'Ahalya is too young,' he demurred diplomatically.

'I am ready to wait, sir,' said Indra evenly, though he hated saying those words. He wanted to rush into her room, grab her by the hands and marry her.

As soon as he said those words, King Mudgal, who had been eyeing him with doubt, looked more cheerful.

'Yes, it's better to wait,' he said instantly. 'She wishes to study, and I am all for it. Ahalya is a bright girl and—'

'That she is,' said Indra smoothly. 'That is why I wish her to be the queen of Indralok.'

A veil seem to fall over the old man's face again. 'She is a mortal, Indra,' he said gently. 'Will she be able to handle the celestial demands of being the queen of the Devas? I am not too sure ... that's why the hesitancy.'

'As I said before, I shall wait,' repeated Indra, with a fawning smile.

The old king did not return the smile. A worried look passed over his lined face. 'I shall speak to her,' he said finally, but he knew what his daughter's answer would be.

In a moment of uncharacteristic candour, she had admitted to him that even though Indra was really the most attractive man she had known, he was not more appealing than her desire to study. His warmth, his handsomeness and his easy manner delighted her. But that was it: no more, no less. She had no powerful feelings that could translate into marriage.

King Mudgal was in a quandary. He didn't wish to strong-arm Ahalya into marriage against her wishes. And his daughter's potential refusal was very likely to hurt this powerful man's pride. King Mudgal greatly needed Indra in their armed campaigns against the Dasas. He was faced with two choices: coerce his daughter into marrying Indra, or manage without this man's military help. He wished for neither, and the perplexity showed on his face.

Mudgal glanced at Indra; his mouth, pursed thin like a knife, moved slightly into what might be mistaken for a smile.

'I shall talk to her,' he said again faintly.

Indra got to his feet. He felt uneasy and frustrated. He had not even found a pretext to see Ahalya. As he walked out of the palace and down the marble steps into the sunshine, he hoped he would see her in the gazebo by the garden pond— her favourite haunt. He saw Divodas instead, standing by the steps, his face breaking into a wide smile. But his eyes were worried.

'I hope you are not leaving soon? I have much to discuss with you,' said Divodas.

Indra grabbed at the chance to remain longer at the palace. 'It's about Shambar again, isn't it? He has been gathering an army.'

Divodas nodded, his brow furrowed. 'I had hoped that would be the last of him, but I was wrong. I should have killed him when I had the chance in the last battle. But I did not; that was my mistake and we suffer still ...'

Indra shrugged. 'It can be rectified. We need to counter his attack. And we shall teach that wily king a lesson he will remember as long as he lives.'

'No, he won't live; this time I *shall* kill him.' Divodas sounded ruthless. 'That man is a reminder of my one big mistake.'

Indra nodded, patting his friend on his back. 'We shall,' he assured him with his beautiful smile.

Indra consequently remained at the palace for a day more, much to his satisfaction and the queen's delight.

'Indra!' she said, extending her beautiful hand, which flashed with diamonds. 'What a wonderful surprise, as always!'

'I cannot have enough of this palace!' he said, grinning.

'Be honest, is it the palace or the princess?' she teased.

The mischievous note in her voice made Indra smile. 'Just some discussion with Divodas,' he said, seating himself beside her, but not before bowing low and touching her feet, a gesture he knew pleased her and something he had cultivated to charm.

'The wretched war again? But I can't complain if you are there with Divodas. Together you will win again! You look after my son so well. I can't thank you enough for safeguarding him for me,' she said gratefully, clasping his hands in hers. The sparkle of the diamonds struck flashes of light on the carved ceiling.

'But please give me a chance to look after your daughter too,' said Indra immediately, not one to allow an opportunity to slide by. 'You know how much I want to marry her.'

'Yes, I do; and I wish it too,' she said, but the sparkle in her eyes died.

'Then ... can we have the wedding soon?' he cried, not believing his ears and his good luck.

She eyed him uneasily. 'No, I am afraid we can't. I would love it if you were to marry Ahalya but ...'

'But what? Aren't I eligible enough?' he bantered, forcing a grin, but his heart thudded with a certain trepidation.

'Of course you are! But it's not about you; it's Ahalya. She has no desire to marry right away—she wants to study instead. She has got it into her head to go to an ashram for higher studies.'

'Why, does she want to be a rishika?' joked Indra.

Nalayani's face fell, and he saw that he had touched a raw nerve.

'I am so afraid that she wants to!' cried Nalayani, visibly agitated.

'Then all the more reason for you to get Ahalya married fast,' said Indra smoothly.

'Do you think I haven't tried? But that stubborn girl refuses to listen,' she said, throwing her hands up.

She looked at him, hope flaring in her eyes. 'But if you try, Indra ... will you be able to convince her yourself?' she murmured, throwing him a wavering smile. 'I have tried telling her several times, but she can be very adamant in her own quiet way.'

So Ahalya had not submitted to persuasion or pressure. Indra gave a tight smile and said in his beautiful voice, 'I shall try as well.'

And right away, Indra promised himself fiercely as he left the hall. He was greeted by Divodas on the way, and it took all his will to control his impatience as he spoke briefly with his friend. Finally taking his leave, Indra left the palace to look for Ahalya. He glimpsed her at a distance, in the gazebo, sitting on the bench by the creeper of wild roses.

Nalayani was watching from above. This was no accidental meeting. She had arranged it, and her timing had been perfect. Overhearing Indra chatting with Divodas in the hallway, she had asked Ahalya to fetch her some flowers from the garden. The unsuspecting girl had obediently gone down to the gazebo. She was glancing through the bright shrubs, wondering which flowers her mother would like, when she saw, to her consternation, that Indra was approaching the gazebo with quick, purposeful strides.

'Ahalya!' he called.

She gave him the ghost of a smile.

He ran up the short steps. 'I was hoping to see you.'

She was warmer to him now than she had been when he first met her. But she still kept her distance from him, more from shyness than dislike, he soon realised. Her reticence came from her innate reserve. Even as she stood silent now, he felt his heartbeat quicken. He couldn't judge from her expression whether he had been successful or not in making some impression on her. She always looked the same: calm, quiet and remote, and this often infuriated him.

'See me? Why?' she said.

He moved closer to her, his breathing uneven.

She immediately stepped back, her eyes widening.

He gazed at her, trying to see any sign of promise, but the calm face only presented a baffling barrier to him. Still, he was sure that if he pressed more ardently, he could have her.

'I wanted to talk to you about something ... er ... something important ...'

'Oh?' Her brow furrowed. 'About war? Then I am not the right person. I know nothing about warfare,' she said, spreading her hands helplessly.

'No, it's about *you*.'

She stiffened, her face a mask again. 'Me?' she repeated through pursed lips, her neck strained. Even now, as she moved her slim, slender neck, the line of her throat stirred him. He imagined holding her, his mouth pressed against that lovely firm flesh. From past experiences, he knew women reacted violently when he kissed their throats.

He blinked. He was going crazy; this woman was slowly driving him insane.

'Yes, I wanted to talk about you.'

There was a long pause while he waited hopefully, but he realised she wasn't going to help with a rejoinder.

'I want to marry you. I love you.'

For the first time since he could remember, Indra felt embarrassed. And vulnerable. His mouth went dry, waiting for her next words.

Ahalya had seen it coming. His unbridled interest in her, his furtive attempts to meet her, his feverish glances ... she had noted it all with mounting apprehension. Warding him off was how she spent her energy and effort. But when she heard the words, she could not help but look surprised.

'Oh,' she muttered, dismayed that she had not prepared an adequate response. For a moment, she looked flustered and then murmured incoherently, 'Thank you. That's ... that is very kind. I am flattered ...'

Ahalya felt foolish; could she not have said something more intelligent? More honest? But how could she refuse him point-blank, she thought desperately. How could she wriggle out of this situation without hurting his feelings and damaging her future?

Indra had hoped for a more positive response. He clenched his fists and waited. Would she say yes?

She regarded him. The probing stare made him feel uncomfortable.

'I was just wondering if—'

'You can take your time,' he said hastily.

'No.' She shook her head, her face bent low. 'I was wondering if it was about convenience,' she said and looked up at him. She seemed remote again, not nervous like before.

'What, my proposal?' he asked quickly. He felt his heartbeat quicken. 'How is it convenient? It's straight from my heart.'

There was a pause, then Ahalya said, 'I am flattered, sir. You have, of course, an irresistible appeal to women.'

Indra was pleased. Praise to him was like water to a plant, and coming from her, it meant something. He shifted his weight from one foot to another and gave her a boyish smile.

'I don't care about that ...' He waved a deprecating hand. 'But what about you?' Trying to keep his voice casual, he continued, 'I feel there's a barrier between us ... you're so distant.'

'Indra—' She paused as she stroked the flowers thoughtfully, the gesture strangely arousing him. She looked up and her lips moved into a half smile. 'I believe in paying my debts, but not this way.'

'Paying your debts?' he repeated, confused.

She nodded.

It took him a moment for it to sink in.

'Ahalya!' he muttered. He looked stunned, bewilderment and embarrassment suffusing his face deep red. He was baffled by this woman. Was she serious or was she taunting him now? How had she realised that his entire effort, everything he had been doing just to woo her, was to be repaid by her getting into his bed, even if it meant a wedding bed?

There was a slight pause, then Ahalya turned and looked pointedly at him. Indra found it difficult to hold her gaze. His heart racing, he said, 'I want to marry you. It means everything to me ... there are no strings ... I wouldn't want you ... what did you think?' he demanded furiously.

'Please!' She held up her hand, her voice low but unexpectedly firm. She didn't look like the shy, taciturn, aloof girl anymore.

'I know what I am saying,' she continued calmly. 'I know you have done great favours for my brother, my family, our prestige. You have saved us from defeat and dishonour and even death.' She gave him her soft glance. 'You have saved my brother's life. And you wish for a return of all those favours.'

Indra flinched. But before he could protest, she resumed relentlessly, 'I take love seriously. I think it is the most God-given experience, one that should never be abused. Love to me is not offering myself as a gift or a trophy or as a barter in exchange for favours.'

Indra saw the disdainful look on her face. He had never felt more humiliated. He also knew he was flushing and sweat beads had broken out on his forehead. He was disconcerted with the way she was controlling not only the conversation but the very moment, him and his future.

'You don't have to talk like that,' he said unsteadily. 'I don't want you to get the wrong idea ...'

'Am I not right? Did you not expect something in return? Do you not want me to say yes to you, with the burden of your favours crushing me, crushing us?' she persisted, her gentle eyes now fierce. 'I know you have asked my parents, individually and insistently, pressuring them to make me acquiesce to your wishes. Or should I say it was a subtle demand? But yes, am I to pay our debt to you?'

He had never believed it would be an easy conquest, but this open insult made him bristle; yet, he sensed the veiled promise of a future payment, which left him breathless.

'Do you realise what you are saying?' he said, sounding indignant.

He knew this was no ordinary woman and that his charm was a blunted weapon. But he wanted her as he had never wanted any other woman. He was shrewd enough to know that he had to give her free rein. Is she to pay her debts?! *Patience*, he told himself.

'I have no intention of forcing this marriage on you. That was not my intent when I requested your parents for your hand. As I said, I love you, and I want to marry you. Is that so difficult to believe?' he said, trying to sound hurt, hoping it would pierce her cold heart.

'I had a doubt and I wanted to clear it,' she said straightforwardly. 'I think by relaying how you feel to my parents first, you were, of course, following procedure. But by doing so, you not only pressured them, you also put that pressure on me through them. They were cornered; you knew that. My agreement to your proposal would be the only escape, the solution, the answer you so desire.'

Indra made an impatient movement.

Ahalya looked unfazed. 'So, I am asking you now, frankly.' She paused deliberately, giving him time to think. 'If I say no, would you still be a loyal friend to my brother?'

Indra tried not to let his emotions show on his face. So she *was* refusing him. A white-cold ungovernable fury slithered through him, and it took all his control to not unleash it. He lowered his eyes to hide his confusion, his humiliation and his rage. Why, *why* did she not want him?

And what rankled him further was that she had been in control the whole time; this, he wasn't used to. It infuriated him.

I believe in paying my debts ... That must mean that in her own time, when she was ready, she was prepared to be with him. What else could it mean?

But she did not want to be in his debt—*If I say no, would you be still be a loyal friend to my brother?*

And with that question, she was testing him: his patience and his loyalty. She had seen through his motives; yes, he had used her parents to put pressure on her, to lower her defences and to surrender to him. She had not bowed down—not to her parents, not to him, not against her principles. She not only was refusing him but also had the temerity to demand his continuing loyalty and allegiance to her brother and family. But if he wanted to remain in her good graces, he had no choice but to be nice.

He would have to tell her what he had said to her father. He would have to.

'You misunderstand, Ahalya; the situation, my proposal and me. I love you, Ahalya, and that is why I want to marry you. Not because of Divodas, despite or in spite of him. Or your family. And fear not, your response will in no way affect my relation with your dear brother—I remain his friend and his ally always. That's a warrior's word of honour. You should know that,' he said, a slight note of reprimand in his voice, hoping it would make her feel guilty.

'Of course,' she said in that quiet, controlled voice that had slowly started exasperating him. 'I understand. But I wanted to be transparent—and honest. I hope I have made myself clear. And cleared all doubts, whatsoever,' she added softly.

'Yes, Ahalya, it's my turn to understand.'

'And now it's my turn to explain,' she said. 'I cannot accept because I do not wish to marry so soon. I want to study, and I hope to go to Rishi Vashisht's ashram for further studies. Marriage does not interest me, learning and knowledge do. Because of which I cannot accept your proposal.'

Each word was succinct, sharp in its crispness and clear in its brevity. But her lovely face wore a perplexed look. She was standing with the light against her; he could see her long, shapely legs and the curve of her rounded hips through the diaphanous silk. This sight always affected him. And though this was not the time for such feelings, his eyes glazed over, drinking her in like a thirsty man. He loved every inch of her— the shape of her face, her body, her gait, her elegant passivity, the way she smiled, her soft laugh and how she threw her head back daintily to expose her long, white neck.

Indra clenched his fist. Would she ever be his?

Something moved in her opaque eyes: she looked troubled, yet there was a cold fire in her. She was never rude, and the moment she had said it, Ahalya was filled with remorse, watching Indra's handsome face crumble. 'I mean ... I ... it is about my studies first,' she said lamely, horrified that she had unwittingly hurt him. 'Please, understand, sir. I do not want to marry now. Not you or anyone else.'

Indra's wretched heart thumped wildly and he was wondering what to say next when Ahalya turned to him, her eyes distraught.

'I have to clear this,' she said hesitantly. 'I get the feeling you might wait for me ...'

'Yes, you know I will,' he said sincerely.

'I don't want you to,' she said desperately. 'You can't wait for anything to happen, Indra. I don't want to rush myself, either. That is not how I am: I have to think, probe and move carefully. Can you try and understand?'

His blood on fire, Indra nodded.

'But anything could happen tomorrow ...' Ahalya murmured. *I don't want to marry you today, but I may want to marry you when I return*, she thought wildly, wondering if she should say more.

Hope stabbed him deep in his heart.

'Yes, anything could happen tomorrow,' he agreed with a sharp intake of breath.

She continued, more at ease. 'It's the pattern of things. For me, life is urgent, as it should be for you. I believe I should do everything I want to do now, grab every opportunity. I don't know my future, but I know by now that I would rather study than marry. Don't you believe in destiny? What is to be ... will be?'

Indra moved impatiently. 'I don't believe in waiting. Yes, I believe in destiny, but I also believe I can cheat destiny by not waiting!' he said with a gruff laugh. 'But then, as I said before, I will wait for you.'

She hesitated, then nodded slowly, biting her lips, still refusing to commit to the man who had professed his love for her. He sounded hurt, and she again felt a stab of remorse, but that terrifying thought left her trembling: *whom* would she marry? She dared not look at Indra.

There was that mask again. Ahalya was an enigma to him, and mysteries worried him. The indifference in her eyes warned Indra he could lose her, and he felt suddenly scared and insecure. Knowing it would be useless to try to persuade her further, Indra decided a retreat would be best.

'Let's hope it will work out ... someday,' he said tremulously. He remembered her tone when she had said anything could happen tomorrow. It had been almost gentle, kind. It gave him sudden strength. 'But you shall agree to marriage once you are back, won't you?' he asked hopefully.

Her shoulders drooped slightly. 'I'll have to,' she said. She looked up, straight at him, and said again, 'But please don't expect too much from me so quickly.'

'I shall never say goodbye, Ahalya. Good day, and good wishes,' he said, and bowed low.

As he walked slowly away, Indra could feel her gaze boring into him. He was still thinking of what she had said. *I take love seriously. I think it is a God-given experience.*

In later days, and on longer nights, he asked himself again and again why this woman set him on fire. It wasn't that she was the only beautiful woman he knew. He could not understand it. Yet, he was obsessed with her: the thought of her lying by his side made him sick with desire. This urgency was something that he had not experienced before. He had lusted after many women but not in this gut-tearing, all-consuming way. There was something special about her that sparked this violent desire that half-frightened, half-elated him.

What was it, damn it? What was it?

5

The Decision

Ahalya tucked a tendril of hair behind her small ears, unknowingly revealing her anxiety: why had her father called for all of them to gather in his inner chamber? Her parents were there, as were Rishi Vashisht and her brother. She threw her brother a questioning glance; Divodas was quick to notice her nervousness but kept silent. He was worried himself, and wondered how his sister intended to fight her battle today. It was going to be her battlefield, her war.

'It's about your education, Ahalya,' King Mudgal started hesitantly, casting a cautious look at his wife.

Ahalya caught the exchange and turned to her mother, immediately wary. 'Ma, please, let's not start another argument to convince you to let me study further,' implored Ahalya in a voice stronger than she felt.

'Yes, we have had enough disagreements these past few months. We have finally come to a decision,' interrupted her father swiftly.

At this point, Nalayani blurted, 'Ahalya why don't you just agree to marry Indra? It would save us so many—'

'You want me to marry him because we can't do without him? Because we owe him for all his help?' Ahalya shot back, suddenly more angry than anxious. She did not care if she sounded disrespectful. 'I will not marry him as a way out, Ma. It is not fair!'

Nalayani reddened, but before she could utter another word, an audible exhalation from the prince tautened the tension in the room. Divodas controlled himself and replied in a voice struggling for temperance.

'Indra is going to get busy with war, Ma,' he said shortly, his usually affable face tense. 'The wedding, however much you want it, cannot happen so soon. We discussed this—' He stopped short, but Ahalya realised they had been discussing this prickly topic between themselves in private.

Divodas continued. 'Besides, that's no solution. Enemies don't spare the wife either—it might only endanger Ahalya further.' He stopped abruptly, pursing his lips tight.

There was a sudden stillness in the room. Ahalya was puzzled: why were they suddenly talking about war when they were supposed to be discussing her studies?

'No one is forcing you to do anything, Ahalya,' Mudgal said gently. 'With regard to your studies, I have another arrangement in mind, and I hope it will suit all of us.'

Rishi Vashisht leaned forward then and said, 'We want to send you to the ashram of Rishi Gautam for your studies, Ahalya. That is an amicable solution, I think, for everyone?' He gave Ahalya a questioning look.

Ahalya drew in a deep breath, briefly perplexed. Confusion soon gave way to comprehension and then awe. Rishi Gautam! He was the best among the best, considered to be one of the great Saptarishis—the exalted sages with the highest creative intelligence, Parmatma. These seven seers—in whose ranks their royal priests Rishi Vashisht and Rishi Bharadwaj were included—were supposed to be the most evolved 'light beings' in creation. And as the guardians of the divine laws, they were believed to have descended on earth to spread knowledge and energies.

Rishi Gautam, the favourite of Lord Brahma, had gained a formidable reputation for being the most prolific mantra-drashta—a seer of thought—and was said to be currently working on the Gautam Smruti while compiling the Dharmasutras—the laws and duties of man in society, describing everyone from a king to a cobbler.

Ahalya had long yearned to join Rishi Vashisht's ashram—he was the founder of the Vedanta philosophy after all, and she was eager to master it, though she knew it would take years. But to be given the opportunity to study at the gurukul of the great Rishi Gautam was an immense privilege.

She asked, 'Is Rishi Gautam not from the lineage of Angiras, the sage credited as the author of some hymns in the Rig Veda, and followed by Rishi Bharadwaj as well? I am aware that Rishi Gautam is an expert on law, especially women's laws, and is constructing the Nyay Sutras for them as well.'

'Yes, exactly!' nodded Vashisht. 'You seem to be familiar with his body of work. Did Bharadwaj teach you?' His aged eyes twinkled knowingly. 'Gautam gave us the Jyotishshastra Grantham, or the Gautam Samhita, as it is popularly known among us rishis. Don't you want to know more about it, Ahalya? Besides, you need to know the other point of view too,' smiled Vashisht. 'Being contrary does not necessarily mean being wrong or incorrect. It is another perspective which you need to comprehend as well.'

'Yes, it would be an honour to be his student,' she acknowledged slowly, breaking into a small but sparkling smile. 'I shall be glad to go to Rishi Gautam's ashram.'

No sooner had she said it than the words seemed to percolate into her senses, her mind, through her skin into her blood, making her heart race, filling her with an exhilaration. She was going to study in a gurukul! Even in her moment of delight, Ahalya was quick to notice the veil of sadness on her parents' faces ... why? It must be tearing at their hearts to let her go. She felt a momentary twinge of hesitancy, but she brushed it off hurriedly before she was weakened by it.

Smiling gratefully, she said, hoping to reassure her despondent parents, 'As the guru says, I shall go to Rishi Gautam's ashram till you, Ma, decide on my marriage—and the suitors,' Ahalya added, though she knew they had already decided on Indra.

Nalayani nodded. Her face was drawn and she seemed unusually unhappy. Ahalya again wondered why: was her grief to part with her daughter so acute? 'I shall make arrangements for you to go to the ashram,' she heard her mother say in a resigned voice.

Ahalya saw that her father was smiling. He was clearly a much relieved man. But her mother looked grim. She wondered what had made her mother finally agree to her request. All these months Ahalya had pleaded, threatened, argued with her, but to no avail. This had made the usually mild-mannered Ahalya more resolved, even truculent: she would *not* marry if she was not allowed to study. But why had her mother acquiesced now? Why the sudden change of mood and manner? Had her father managed to persuade her mother?

Ahalya got up restlessly: she did not want to give it any further thought. She hated any sort of acrimony in the family, and this had been a long-drawn, acerbic debate. It was finally over. She still could not believe her good fortune.

'Then it's settled. I shall ask Rishi Gautam if Ahalya can come to his ashram to study,' Vashisht said.

'I am sure he will not refuse your request, Guruji,' said Nalayani in her usual direct manner. 'Ahalya is, after all, an extraordinary student.'

Ahalya felt an uneasy stirring again: her mother *was* behaving oddly.

The queen fidgeted, her eyes anxious. 'I have heard Rishi Gautam is an overbearing person ...' She glanced desperately at King Mudgal, who sat with his head bowed and his hands tightly clasped. 'If we had a choice, I'm not sure we would have agreed to send my daughter to such a strange man.'

Vashisht waved his hand and said, his tone placatory, 'Yes, he is eccentric, as most brilliant people are, but Gautam is one of the most gifted rishis of our times.' Coming from a brahmarishi like Guru Vashisht, this was high praise indeed. 'He is essentially a philosopher but also, interestingly, a logician who is currently working on law.'

'I am not interested in his brilliance. I am worried about whether he can look after my daughter!' snapped Nalayani.

'You have no choice, Ma,' Divodas said, with suppressed ferocity.

Ahalya was surprised; her brother seemed to be in a strange, anomalous mood as well. She could not figure it out. She felt the air freeze around her.

Afraid that the arrangements might collapse, Ahalya turned to the guru and said, 'Law, logic and philosophy—what an unusual synthesis! That is path breaking, is it not?'

'Yes, and I predict that, one day, he will become a maharishi,' stated Vashisht. 'So, take the opportunity, dear girl, and glean all the knowledge you can from him. Be his best disciple.'

Ahalya felt her heart soar, like the ascending arrow she had chased years ago. She recalled that moment. She had been so fascinated by the arrow: the quick, sharp flight, the neat curve as it rose higher and higher, like her mind right now, eating the miles, piercing the skies, conquering every inch as it blazed forward.

Ahalya snapped back to attention, aware that all eyes were on her again.

'Yes, I shall. I promise,' she said, nodding.

Her mother sighed and sketched a gesture of finality by extending her beautiful bejewelled hand.

'So you did not allow yourself to get married off—again?' said Divodas, his face thoughtful.

Ahalya grinned at him cheerfully, happy that she had got her way and ready to take on even her brother's pensive mood. They were in her favourite spot in the palace garden— the gazebo by the pond—away from her mother's alert ears and eyes. 'I'm just surprised that Ma agreed to send me to the ashram.'

'You cannot hold off Ma for long,' he said, his eyes still serious. 'She has agreed to send you to that ashram only on the condition that you will return once she finalises your marriage plans. I wouldn't be surprised if you are married by the end of this year.'

'Hmm, we'll see,' Ahalya said with a nonchalant shrug. 'For the moment, I am too excited to allow that thought to deflate my mood. I have always wanted to leave this palace, to travel to different places, to study, to—'

'You wish to be what—a scholar or a wandering mendicant?' asked Divodas, a laugh in his voice. His smile dimmed as he continued soberly, 'But seriously, are you really sure? Or are you doing this for the novelty it assures? Or for the challenge of defying Ma?'

Ahalya looked aggrieved. 'I thought you knew me better!'

He gave her a hard look. 'I do. That is why I am asking. Not that you are much of a rebel, but you do tend to be overcurious! Or get goaded by the challenge to attempt the impossible. It's always either of the two. Which one is it now?'

'I simply want to learn,' she sighed. 'I hadn't thought it would be so difficult. I still can't believe they finally agreed.'

'It was just the right time,' remarked Divodas cryptically, his face distracted. 'The fact that Father was on your side helped of course.... And we all want you to be safe at the ashram!' he muttered abruptly.

'Safe?' she asked, puzzled. 'Of course I shall be safe! It's a rishi's ashram. Even the fiercest armies think twice before attacking an ashram.'

'Yes, that's true ...' responded Divodas, a brooding expression on his face.

She looked at him curiously. 'You are being overly protective as always. Is that why you are in such a strange temper today?'

Divodas forced a smile. 'I guess so. I'm worried about how you will manage in the wild jungles—you jump at the smallest sound in the wilderness.'

Ahalya blushed. 'I will be braver. And I think Father has more faith in me than you or Ma!' she said crossly.

'Yes, that's because Father is a thinker and less of a worrier!'

She smiled. 'Yes, more a rishi himself than a king—certainly not a bloodthirsty warrior like you! He is being hailed as a raj-rishi these days, by seers and the people alike.'

'That's because of his generosity and his philanthropy. But I wouldn't be surprised if Father gives up his throne soon to retire to the forest and devote his life to being a rishi.'

'Oh, no. Ma would never allow it!' said Ahalya with an emphatic shake of her head. 'She is dead against shirking away from one's responsibilities—that fear comes from what her father, King Nala, did when he lost his kingdom to gambling.'

'Father is not gambling!' argued Divodas. 'He just wishes to retire soon.'

'By placing the full responsibility of the throne and kingdom on you,' said Ahalya quietly. 'Ma resents that.'

'What she resents more is his philosophical bent of mind,' said Divodas.

'Ma wants a king to behave like a king, a princess like a princess!' said Ahalya. 'She doesn't want Father to become a rishi or me, a rishika.'

'Rishika! That is very ambitious!'

'Is it the right of just kings to be ambitious?' she asked primly. 'Or is it only allowed in the way that Ma has ambitions for me?'

'I was joking,' Divodas said mildly. 'And as for Mother, she's worried about you just as she is about Father—and me. That's fair enough, isn't it?'

'But she has this irrational wariness of rishis and gurukuls and the like. Probably, for her, wealth and one's status in the world are the most important things.'

'She lost it all as a child and she fears it still—for all of us. It doesn't take long to lose a kingdom ... just one war!' he said, a suddenly angry look on his face.

Ahalya looked at him sharply. 'But her father was a good king and a very learned man who patronised gurus, scholars and educators, like Father does.'

'They did not get King Nala back the throne. A war did,' retorted Divodas.

'War! Is it a solution to all our problems or the reason for it?'

'You are right, Ahalya,' her brother said bitterly. 'War is not a game—like dice. But then, like a game of dice, war does decide the future of kings and kingdoms.' He expelled a long breath. 'That's why Ma believes more in the sword than the pen, war over words!'

'You sound like Ma!' accused Ahalya. 'Or are you plain bloodthirsty?'

'I am a realist,' he replied tersely.

'I would rather be a scholar,' she said with determination.

'You will be one, if you stay long enough at Rishi Gautam's ashram,' Divodas said, smiling.

'But will I ever actually get to be one?' she asked pensively, playing with a stray tendril of hair. 'It will take years—and Ma is reluctant to give me even a couple of months. All she really wants is that I marry Indra.'

Divodas's face cleared. 'And why not? Indra would make an ideal husband: rich, handsome, powerful. What more does a girl want?' he teased, watching his sister's face darken. 'And yes, I know for a fact that he is deeply in love with you. Surely you've noticed! It's so obvious.'

Ahalya coloured, recalling Indra's confession, his marriage proposal and, more vividly, his gaze on her. She recalled him leaning forward and gazing at her, his eyes smouldering with open passion. He really was the most attractive man she had known, she thought. His warmth, his handsomeness and his easy manner had delighted her, but she was wary. She did not trust him with her heart or mind.

'I think he's too fond of women. He's a charming flirt, a confirmed womaniser, Divodas, and he cannot be taken seriously,' she said, giving an impatient shrug of her shoulders, slightly annoyed that this man was, even now, distracting them from their topic of conversation. 'He's in love with all the pretty women he meets.'

'Till he met you,' commented Divodas wryly. Indra was so completely besotted with his sister, Divodas noted, that it made him feel uneasy ...

'He is a facetious man who claims to love women, yet is so prejudiced against them,' she remarked tartly.

Divodas contemplated her words for a moment. 'Yes, you are probably right. He needs to be given time to test how long this infatuation lasts.'

Ahalya giggled. 'Oh, how serious and grown-up you are, Divodas! What do you know of love and infatuation?' she said, smiling.

'I don't tell you all my secrets,' he said, shrugging.

Her eyes widened. 'You mean you are in love?'

'I am married to war,' he said gruffly.

'Oh, war again!' she groaned, looking bored. 'What a mess it is!'

'Yes, a bloody mess.'

Ahalya glanced at him uncertainly; the last battle with King Shambar seemed to have affected him badly. He was abnormally sensitive and obsessive, and always looked worried and tense. Like her mother. Ahalya frowned, reminded of that anxious, almost frightened look that had clouded the queen's eyes.

Before she could voice her misgivings, Divodas placed a reassuring hand on her shoulder. 'You leave tomorrow. You should get ready, dear. And make the most of your experience.'

Ahalya looked up at him, discerning a change in the tone of his voice.

'We shan't see you for a long time, I think,' he said, his smile forced. 'But come home soon and safe ...'

They looked at each other. She suddenly found herself assailed by an unmistakable emotion: it was fear.

6

Gautam

The ashram was as Ahalya had expected: bare and austere huts standing amidst thick foliage, a courtyard with a large banyan tree in the middle. Yet its wildness came as a jolt to her; she was used to the sylvan ashram of Rishi Vashisht, forested with fruit trees and flower beds and pretty bushes. Ahalya got down hesitantly from the chariot, her heart hammering, throat dry.

Divodas had offered to come with her, but she had refused, wanting to start her new journey alone. This was her first taste of freedom. She was now on her own.

She had cherished the long journey of almost a week from the capital city of Kampala to the ashram, located south of the city of Vaijayanti in the kingdom of Videha. From the very first moment till now, standing at the doorstep of the ashram, she had been nervous with excitement, a bursting eagerness that she could not still. The feeling dried up as she regarded the silent ashram.

'Where is everyone?' she asked one student passing by.

The young boy looked at her as if she were demented. 'It is the meditation hours. The guru won't meet anyone now,' he said briefly. 'But you are the princess who was to arrive today, aren't you?' he said, glancing at her bejewelled attire.

Ahalya nodded self-consciously. Was she supposed to wear clothes of bark as did the rishis, she thought in dismay. How foolish of her not to have checked with Rishi Vashisht; but then he had better things to do than let her know how to be suitably dressed for a stay at an ashram!

'So I won't meet the guru today?' she asked uncertainly, as the boy led her to the rear of one of the huts.

He shook his head and pointed to a small room. 'That is your place of residence,' he stated, his tone matter-of-fact and slightly impatient.

'What's your name?' she asked politely.

'Uttank,' said the boy. 'I shall bring you your supper soon. We have our dinner early here,' he added pointedly, as if he was familiar with the ways of the palace. She was slightly amused by his haughtiness.

'We have our meals early at the palace too,' she supplied, observing him.

Despite his attempts to appear older, she could tell he was around twelve years old. Slim of build, his eyes were small, dark grey and restless; his mouth was thin, his nose short and blunt. He looked satisfied with his way of life, serene and serious, sure of himself but with a latent impatience that could slip out should he encounter any kind of opposition or criticism.

Uttank stared at her. 'We don't talk much here,' he said, clearly disapproving of her attempt at conversation. This was ironic, since she was fairly reticent herself. Yet here she was trying to get a little boy to talk to her. It must be the woods, she thought, as she dumped her bag on the floor and looked around the small room. It was bare, with not even a cot.

She recalled Rishi Vashisht's words to her before she had left.

'Rishi Gautam is your guru, Ahalya, for the time being, but you are *not* his student,' Rishi Vashisht had said. 'Gautam will not take on an older student. You are to serve him and try to glean whatever knowledge you can at the classes you attend.'

'He won't teach me?' she repeated, her heart sinking.

Vashisht smiled. 'He will. But yours is not a guru-shishya relationship. There is a lot of practice involved, and one has to be initiated very early.'

'Oh, why can't I go to your ashram?' she had begged, already feeling unwelcome.

'Because I have taught you all you have to know. If you want to widen your horizon, you need to learn from a different teacher.'

Ahalya settled down to sleep early, as soon as she had finished her evening meal of lentils and boiled yam brought to her by a punctual Uttank.

It was a warm night. There were stars, but it was pitch-dark in the woods. Since she had never in her cloistered life been in such surroundings, the starry night seemed to her inhospitable, and darker than it was. The silhouettes of the trees, the flat tops of the mud huts in which the disciples lived—all this, tinted by the darkness, gave this world a strange, wild aspect that suggested chaos to her, not the peace that it was supposed to convey. There was so little order in all that lay before her that in the midst of the stillness and silence, it was somehow strange to hear the last movements of the students retiring for the day. Everything seemed to belong to a different world. Soon it was quiet, and the only sounds came from the swaying of branches, droning their wearisome refrain somewhere very high above her head. She was lulled by it and soon found herself falling asleep.

The day at the ashram started before dawn, as she rudely found out when Uttank came to wake her up.

'Princess!' he hissed. 'You are going to be late!'

'But studies start at six ...!' she started, but gave up. She had made a fool of herself again.

She rushed out to bathe, shivering, in the cold stream. Her teeth still chattering, she tried to quickly dress in the simplest clothes she had, and barely managed to reach the banyan tree where the early morning prayers were being held. Catching her breath and trying to calm her thudding heart, she shut her eyes in meditation. It worked, and soon she was mesmerised by the hymns echoing all around her, echoed by Rishi Gautam's gravelly baritone. It was his voice that first caught her attention: the baritone had a strange effect, almost hypnotic in its resonance.

It was only at noon that she got to meet the rishi, when he sent a message through Uttank.

'Guruji will meet you after lunch,' he said. 'Be punctual.'

She hurried through her lunch, scarcely tasting a morsel. As she hastily washed her hands, a tall, lean shadow fell across the grass at her feet. She looked up, startled, her eyes huge and alarmed. Rishi Gautam stood over her, his face calm, coal-black eyes burning through her.

'Welcome to the ashram, princess,' he said, unsmiling.

She nodded mutely and folded her hands in a namaste.

'Do you know why you are here?' he asked the moment she looked up. His abrupt question threw her off balance.

'To study from you?' she stuttered after a brief pause.

Gautam saw the rising panic in her eyes and softened his voice. 'No,' he said. 'You are not a regular student. You are under my protection here.'

'Protection? What do you mean?' she stammered, her voice shaky, her eyes darkening. 'I came here to study!'

Gautam frowned. 'That's not what I was told by Rishi Vashisht.'

'I don't understand!' she whispered wildly, trying to remain calm. *What was happening?* She threw Gautam a look of desperation. His eyes remained placid, calming her down, and she properly registered him for the first time. He was younger than she had thought. His eyes defined his whole face. They were good eyes: direct, honest and without guile, the eyes of a thinker; but right now, they were also slightly apprehensive, eyeing her with concern, making her feel stupid.

She tried to explain. 'I thought I had come here to be your student ... I wanted to learn from you,' she said feebly.

'No, you are not to be my student.' He shook his matted head. 'I don't want you to go through the trying daily schedule that the other students have. I noticed you attended the dawn prayers; it's not necessary to start your day so early.'

'But then, why am I here?' she asked, overwhelmed by confusion.

Gautam looked sombre. 'Have you not been told?' He frowned slightly. 'Your kingdom has been attacked by King

Shambar, forcing your father and brother to go to war. You were sent here to hide you away from the enemy. My ashram is your sanctuary for now.'

His words seemed to echo through the silence of the ashram. She could hear nothing but the murmur of the trees swaying near her and the beating of her heart, wild and hammering. Lifting her eyes to the sky, she found the sun suddenly dull and sullen, concealed briefly by clouds prowling in the sheer blue firmament. War! Her family was at war ...

The news sank into her with dawning horror; the last long conversation she'd had with her family screamed through her convoluted thoughts. So that was why her mother had unexpectedly agreed to her coming to the ashram. And why her father and Divodas had been so keen that she leave as early as possible. The sudden decision about her education had just been a pretext to get her out of the palace.

'You wouldn't have agreed had you known, would you?' guessed Gautam astutely, his tone gentle, watching the fleeting play of pain and perplexity on her pale face.

The gentleness in his voice almost broke her: she felt a sob in her throat and she swallowed convulsively. Her family was in danger; they could possibly be killed. And she was hiding here, like a coward.

'My m ... m ... mother?' she asked hoarsely.

'She is at the palace. She refuses to leave,' said Gautam. 'A queen does not run away from her palace—that's what she told Rishi Vashisht when he tried to persuade her to leave as well.'

How like Mother, she thought frantically. Imperious as always. And so brave ...

'.... besides, it's easier to hide one person than two,' he continued. 'The absence is less conspicuous.'

Ahalya nodded dazedly. 'And how long am I supposed to remain here?'

'Till the war ends,' he said. 'Till it's safe for you to leave.'

She recalled her brother's last words. *I am married to war ... I shall have to kill Shambar ...'* Would he? Or would he be killed? And her father? Fear tore through her body, grief stabbing her throat ... and here she had been, living in her dream world.

'You must drop those thoughts,' Gautam said gravely.

'Why?' she cried in despair. 'I have been inconsiderate, so self-absorbed that I didn't notice what was happening in my family ...'

'Because such thoughts are for the end of life,' he said. 'Not for the beginning of it. You are too young for them.'

Ahalya shook her head slowly. 'No, I feel like I have aged suddenly. I am no longer what I was ten minutes ago.'

'To my mind, it is better at your age to have no head on your shoulders rather than to think along these lines. Think of what you will do rather than what will happen. It is what you do that will make things happen. All these thoughts of the transitoriness, the insignificance, of life, of the inevitability of death, of violence and war, of the shadows of sorrow, all these thoughts, I tell you, my dear girl, are good and natural in old age, when they come after years of inner travail, and are won by suffering and the acquisition of intellectual riches.' He paused to think while Ahalya, mesmerised by his voice, waited, feeling a strange certainty seeping back into her, making her feel like he could solve any problem. 'Leave them for a later day. For a youthful brain on the threshold of real life, they are simply fruitless. Fruitless!' Gautam repeated with a wave of his hand.

'Why are they fruitless?' she asked, briefly forgetting her grief.

'Can you help your family right now?'

She shook her head miserably.

'No, you can't; but you *can* help yourself by not drowning in sorrow and these tears of self-pity. Possibly what you consider to be misery is but a passing phase of dolefulness. Because there is flickering hope always beckoning you even in the deepest dungeon of darkness.'

'Why are these thoughts disagreeable? Are they not natural, stemming from grief?' she asked, brushing away her tears, now quite engrossed in his novel argument.

'You ask a lot of questions, my dear girl,' Gautam remarked, with a small twinkle in his eyes.

She was already feeling a lot better, the shroud of sadness momentarily shrugged off.

Rishi Gautam was tall—so tall that he appeared thin and wiry. Judging from his words, he was every bit as intense as his deep-set flashing eyes indicated. He had a high, broad forehead, a long, narrow nose, a thin mouth and a square jutting chin that was hidden by his beard. He was not a handsome man, but the raw, pulsating energy emanating from within him was arresting, even disconcerting.

He was just at that stage that her mother described as 'being in the prime of his life'; that is, he was neither young nor old, which was a surprise, as Ahalya had expected him to be much older, considering his history of accomplishments. And neither was he as choleric as his reputation had led her to expect, for in his manner with those surrounding him he had displayed to her that imperturbable good humour which is unusual by the time seers have reached the high status of a rishi. His hair and beard were a dark raven black, but already, with a condescension of which he was unaware, he addressed young people—largely his students—as 'my dear' or 'my child'. His movements and his voice were calm, smooth, and self-confident, as they are in a man who has got his feet firmly planted on the right path.

He was unlike all the rishis Ahalya had met till now. There was a sensible earthiness about him that was immediately appealing, and not daunting. His sunburnt, thin-nosed face and lean, muscular frame amply conveyed that he was a man of rigorous hardship. Only his thick hair and beard, and, perhaps, a certain restlessness and frigidity in his features, betrayed traces of his ascent into seerhood, but everything else—his name, his ideas, his manners, and the expression of his face, were purely earthy. Perhaps that made him more amenable.

But the calmness that exuded from him was of a different kind from the usual. On his intelligent, composed face, his curious eyes glittered from under his brows, and his whole figure expressed spiritual rejuvenation and mental agility.

'Why are these ideas disagreeable, you ask. I hate melancholic thoughts with all my heart, but then, who doesn't? I was infected by them too in my youth, when my father passed away,' he said, almost nonchalantly. 'They did me nothing but harm. Grief is like a mire bringing you down, sucking you into its darkness. It is cheer and hope that save you. But ironically, it's these contemplative thoughts of the aimlessness of life, of the insignificance of the ephemeral visible world, that are to this day considered the highest and final stage in the realm of thought. The thinker reaches that phase and then comes to a halt! There is nowhere further to go. The mind stops functioning, overridden by emotion, as is natural and in the order of things.'

'What normal people end with, you begin with,' she said, gathering courage to reply.

'Sadly, we have been taught since childhood to want to climb the very top rung of the spiritual ladder first, and without knowing anything about the steps below,' he said quietly, his dark eyes unfathomable. 'The whole long ladder of life, with its rainbow of emotions and experiences and thoughts, loses meaning on the top rung. You have to find that meaning, those missing steps.'

'It is going to be difficult,' she murmured, wondering what she would do if her brother and father got killed in battle. Could she ever survive without them?

'Thus, at your age, such reflections are harmful and absurd,' said Gautam. 'Let us suppose I ask you to read the Vedas now and you have scarcely read a page before you get distracted by the intrusion of your own thoughts and you believe you are wasting time and life, and the Vedas to be nonsense. But that does not take away the importance of the Vedas: it shows your ignorance or rather your reluctance to seek truth and knowledge. But if life is deprived of meaning in that way, all science, poetry, and exalted thoughts seem only like useless diversions, and you set them aside, feeling disillusioned, if not stupid.'

That is exactly how she had felt, trapped in the palace—but how had he known?

'Now, suppose you are asked if you think war is desirable. You, as the daughter of a king and sister of a warrior, may claim it to be morally justifiable, but for others—the soldiers who do not receive coins or kingdoms or glory; or the people killed in plunder—for them it is ashes and oblivion.'

'I *hate* war!' she said.

'But your brother cannot afford to,' Rishi Gautam said calmly. 'He has to protect himself and his family. It is his only means of preservation and survival. But his enemies see him not as a brave prince but a plunderer, who loots the Dasas for horses, foodgrains and gems.'

'No!' she cried in horror. 'Divodas is nothing of that sort, he's not a pillager! He is fighting this war to protect us, our kingdom! It is Shambar, that powerful king of the hills: he has blocked the river water by building a hundred dams and placing huge armies there. My father has requested him, several times, to release the water because of drought in the low-lying areas. People and animals were dying, the crops were drying ... Even during my grandfather's time, another hill king, Vritra, made use of his vantage position and strong-armed the kings in the plains by blocking the river ...' she said hotly.

'And yet that's how the Dasas see your brother: he is the invader attacking the older inhabitants of the land,' said the rishi gravely. 'For water, and for land—that's what wars are about. Though both are available in plenty, it's very bountifulness is limiting, making Man avaricious!'

Clearly this rishi knew as much about royal intrigue as he did his scriptures. 'Tell me more,' she said shakily. This was not what she had heard from her father, brother or their royal priests. Politics seemed to lie in the hands of the powerful and was contaminated by the jaundiced eyes of the beholder.

'Times were turbulent—and are still,' Rishi Gautam said, sighing. 'Turbulent and very violent. There have been battles caused by greed, for wealth, for cattle mostly, for domination in religious and social practices, for fertile lands, for offspring and, most important of all, for water. Water will have to be saved and shared, to save us from wars. It's around water that Man has to live—and for that he will fight. For each civilisation, springs and rivers and having control over the waters is paramount. The war your brother is fighting is big and bloody.'

The colour drained from her face. He continued, 'Whoever wins will be supreme, but it will sap both: the victor and the vanquished.'

His voice carried a conviction that filled her with dread. 'It won't end?' she whispered.

'This war is not new. You are a Puru princess and you know that the Purus have always fought the Dasas and the Panis. If it was over water, they fought the Dasas—or the Dasyu, as some disparagingly call them; and it was over cattle that the Purus battled with the Panis, as both consider it to be a status of wealth. Shambar's father, Kulitar, was more of a pacifist, and during his time, peace reigned between the Dasas and your Puru families. His son Shambar is different—ambitious, restless and unwilling to give up claim on the lands they lost to your ancestors. The fact that Divodas killed the hill king Sushna, a close ally of Shambar, precipitated matters, and Shambar has united all the hill kings of the Himalayas to fight your family and bring them to their knees. That is why he is fighting so hard, so bitterly.'

Ahalya stayed mute, shocked by the barbarity. Were there two truths? One the guru had told her, and the other, what she had believed?

'See how our conversation has distracted you from your grief?' he said, smiling at her startled expression. 'However much you grieve, dear, you cannot run away from the reality.' His deep, gentle voice was like a salve, soothing the sting his words carried. 'In our pessimism, we wish we could renounce life and live in a dark hole. But as the universal law goes, we have to live and love. It is better to face what is in front of you, not just with dignity, but with some humour. It makes sad, less sad and glad, more glad!'

Her lips trembled, not with unshed tears, but with a ghost of a smile. He had made her smile again. He had just taught her the first lesson in his ashram.

7

The Ashram

Gautam was immediately impressed by Ahalya. Although now, at his age and stage of life, he no longer bothered with women, he was not blind to her sensual innocence, her calmness and her efficiency.

He recalled Rishi Vashisht's words when they had met at the ashram.

'There is something I would like your advice about,' Rishi Vashisht began.

Gautam had bowed slightly. 'Of course.'

'It concerns my student.' Rishi Vashisht was silent for a moment. 'I haven't told you anything about her. She is Ahalya ...'

Gautam frowned. 'The Puru princess Ahalya?'

Rishi Vashisht stared down at his hands. 'If you met her, you might call her a genius. Or a savant. I don't know what the right word is to describe her.'

Gautam leaned forward, resting his elbows on his knees. He had encountered many extraordinary children in his teaching years, children who learned how to read early, performed difficult sums in their heads, took easily to languages. 'The subject is fascinating to me and I am often tempted to compile a compendium of such savants throughout history,' he remarked.

'You would probably head the list yourself!' laughed Vashisht. 'But I believe that with proper training and direction, Ahalya might be able to enter university, a higher academia your gurukul might provide.'

Gautam was an honest man with little pretence or pride, but it was difficult not to be sceptical of such claims: Ahalya was, after all, the daughter of a king that the guru served.

The two scholars spoke for a long while about Ahalya's many achievements, the lessons Bharadwaj had devised for her, the queen's reluctance and fears about the full extent and ambition of Ahalya's brilliance. When Gautam had finally expressed some reservation, Vashisht had shaken his head and said, 'If only you could meet her. You would know in a moment.'

And he had.

He saw how she handled herself and life at the ashram. She had a sharp brain and quick wit. She barely spoke, but her presence was intense with quiet efficiency. It had been six months since she had arrived, and the ashram seemed to have been revitalised with a fresh vigour. The barren expanses had transformed into blossoming shrubbery; flowers and bushes and grass replaced the bare ground. It was as if she had moved a magic wand. The old leaf scars of the palm trees gave way to billowing greens, the trees suddenly seemed taller and stronger, heavily laden with fruits and flowers. She changed the kitchen into a warm, hearty space, filled with the simple flavours of turmeric and the aroma of wholesome, tasty food.

When she had first arrived, she had reminded him of a frightened doe: nervous about all and anything. Her first day at class had gone badly. He realised he would be wasting time going over the different subjects with her. He wanted her to relax, to get to know him, and to stop jumping at the slightest noise in the forest. This was the acclimatisation process. Gautam recalled how he had taken special effort to speak quietly to her. He was trying to make her understand that learning could come alive in her hands, that she could embody it, and that it could be her friend and guide. He didn't articulate it in so many words, but he did try and convey this thought.

Initially, his words did not seem to penetrate. But years as an instructor had taught him that the breakthrough often came just when you despaired of success. It came soon enough in her first instance of overcoming her fear of him and those around her.

Initially, Gautam regarded her dispassionately, noting not her breath-taking beauty but the gentle, patient smile she bestowed on each and every person in the ashram. The animals were not excluded: the deer did not scuttle off in fright but drew close, daring to sit by her side and even allowing her to caress them. She seemed a mere slim, slight girl, just seventeen, but she was something created by nature especially for love. What a charming little creature she was, he thought, as time passed. Pale, fragile, light, as though a breath would send her floating like a feather to the skies. With her serene face, her slender white hands, her waist-length hair—she was altogether something ethereal, transparent like moonshine, illuminating all with happiness. Even from the point of view of a hardened seer, she was a peerless beauty, her heart as beautiful as her mind was brilliant. She was flawless.

When leaning against a tree and talking to him one evening as usual, she had confessed, 'I don't know what's the matter with me. I had always been so excited to come here, and tonight and every day I am more excited to be with you!' she had gushed, without tact or thought.

It seemed to him a beautiful thing to say. He was glad that she had been so transparent with him. Her candour had an exquisite excitability. But a week later he was compelled to view this same quality of her honesty in a different light. She had quickly made friends with the other young students, mostly young men, and had invited him for what she called a picnic lunch, for which she had prepared dal, rice and vegetables. They all ate under the open sky, on the grass, and not in the long corridor near the kitchen. After lunch, she disappeared with the young girls and boys, who helped her clear up. Gautam, to his absolute consternation, found himself enormously upset and was scarcely able to be civil to the other pupils present. He was jealous, he realised, mortified. But he knew he had no reason to be. She spent all her time with him.

'I have heard you are working on women's laws,' she had asked him one day. 'Do women need special laws?'

He nodded, wondering what the girl wanted to know. 'I am not interested in the rules of rituals and yagnas, but in the rules that should govern us, men and women, as individuals in society. For that, we need laws. Laws are meant to protect and serve justice to the weak—'

'You think women are weak, is that why you are outlining new laws for them?' she asked instantly.

'No, they are *not* weak; women have been made weak, their strength undermined if not underestimated,' he said, smiling. 'That is why we need laws to empower them. There is no limit to Vedic laws. The Vedas teach you to question and discuss. Law-making is one way of doing that, like in the Upanishad and Aranyakas.'

'But a law by definition is something that you don't question, simply obey,' refuted Ahalya. 'Is this not a contradiction?'

Gautam's eyes glinted. 'Yes, you have a point, but then that is exactly my job—to make rules that are just, that will help people. Not harsh ones that weaken them!'

'But then the purpose, is it not lost? If laws are not rigid, no one will follow them; people will break the rules instead,' she argued, twirling a tendril of her hair absently. She was in the habit of doing that when thoughtful or tense, he had noticed.

'You're thinking about the implementation of the law, not the drafting of them. I am the law maker, while you, your father and brother are the law givers; you enforce the law for people,' he said. 'I am trying to make laws that all are happy with, to protect. It is like an armour, a shield against injustice and violence and crime.'

'Laws then serve as a restraint rather than remedy,' she concluded, pensive. 'I think I need to start studying the basics right away,' she muttered under her breath. 'Instead of debating.'

'Yes, and I have been meaning to speak to you about your oratory skills for a long time, for I noticed from the very first moment of our acquaintance your partiality for eloquence when debating!'

He would watch her as she studied through the day and, often, at night, in her little room. She pored over books she had requested for with her usual tremulous smile and her large, questioning eyes. Sometimes in the evenings she would sit on a rock in the woods while the other students of the ashram crowded round her, gazing reverently as she recounted some tale or joke—the only time she actually spoke at length. Her voice was soft and soothing, yet carried an underlying firmness and strength. He could not believe she was the same taciturn girl who had come to his ashram all those months back.

Whenever they got into a discussion about philosophy and nature, she was immensely delighted. She hated politics, and one word about war or statecraft would make her an indifferent student.

'You cannot be good at one subject at the expense of another,' he warned her gravely one day after their lessons were over and the others had dispersed to do their chores. 'Especially subjects like political science and economics. You are a princess, you will need to look after your kingdom someday.'

A cold fear instantly gripped her heart. She had not experienced that emotion for a long time, had almost forgotten it. Her family: the war was not over. Where were her father and brother?

She turned away, walked to a nearby tree and sat down. She did not want to show her fear or pain to this man or anyone else. She was a princess; she had been taught to hide her emotions from a very young age. *But it's unbearable. When will I find out how and where they are?* she asked herself. *And do I want to know, to face the fact that they might possibly be dead?*

The only one who could help her—and was helping her—was the man standing by her side. She blinked back unshed tears. She looked up at Gautam and forced herself to return to their conversation.

'Not all princesses become queens,' she said. 'Is it a rule for princesses to marry only kings? In fact, can she not do anything else besides getting married?'

Gautam detected the discontent in her voice.

'You do not want to marry?' he asked, his tone curious and doubtful.

'No,' she said tonelessly. 'But no one understands. Especially my parents. Is it something odd?'

'Not at all. Is there something else you want to do?'

'I want to study. I want to learn more; I want to enter the bottomless realm of wisdom and knowledge,' she said, her eyes suddenly blazing with passion. 'I want to be a scholar. I want to not just be "good", but excel at *something*!' She paused, her face flushed, her chin raised. 'Even a fool can marry,' she added contemptuously. 'A woman is like a slave.'

'That *is* extreme!' remarked Gautam, regarding her closely.

'Yes, like a slave. We are nothing but the legal property of our fathers or husbands or brothers, and are forced to obey them. And when a woman has to marry against her wishes, it is slavery. She is not free to choose. She has to submit.'

'Is that why you wanted to go to an ashram. To escape? Or to be a student?'

'I wanted to escape from the palace, and be a student. But I wasn't allowed,' she said, forlorn again, the fire in her extinguished as quickly as it had flared. 'They finally only sent me because of the war,' she said with a bitter smile. 'But would you accept me as your student? Guru Vashisht said you don't take older students, but I shall work hard, I promise. Allow me to remain here as your shishya, not as someone seeking shelter. I shall do whatever is expected of me!'

'I can't, dear,' said Gautam, averting his gaze from her beseeching eyes.

'But why? I just want to learn ... I have proved myself. I shall prove myself more,' she cried, panic rising in her throat. 'You are a guru, you can't turn away a student!' she accused desperately.

She saw him turn his face away, and was filled with desperation. 'You can't refuse, you are a *teacher*! Your job is to teach!' she said with all her royal imperiousness. '*That* is your duty, your dharma!'

So, she has a temper too, Gautam could not but observe with detached amusement.

'I know my duty, princess, and I will forgive your rudeness,' he replied coolly. 'I am teaching you, am I not? It is just that you haven't realised it,' he said, with his small, lopsided smile. 'You *are* learning here in the ashram. But as much as I can and as little as you can take,' he added cryptically.

And from that day onwards, she saw the ashram in a new light. It was no longer a shelter but a school of learning. She was a quick, keen learner, and Gautam was surprised to find that Rishi Vashisht had taught her more than he had expected.

'You are a very good student,' he said after a week of rigorous training in law and philosophy. 'You excel in all subjects—but for politics!' he said, smiling.

'Am I? Actually, Guru Vashisht has said the same thing, but I needed it to be acknowledged by you as well.'

His face shuttered, Gautam drawled, 'Why? Because he's your teacher at the palace? Just because he is your royal priest, do not undervalue him. He is a brahmarishi, the greatest of them all, and you should consider yourself extremely fortunate—and blessed—to have been his student. And it is because you are a true scholar that he agreed to send you to me, or he would not have wasted my time and your efforts,' said Gautam gravely.

'You have been his student for the past ten years and more—that's a lifetime,' Gautam continued. 'He trained you; he taught you. You are *his* disciple. He recognised and respected that spark in you and that thirst for knowledge that still remains unsated in you. That is why you were sent here. And now, you are on your way to becoming a rishika.'

'Really?' she said, overwhelmed. 'I have always yearned to be a rishika. I know I am still raw and there's a long way to go ...'

Gautam nodded. 'Yes, you are just starting off on the journey to be a rishika. To be a gargi or a maitreyi, you need to devote an entire lifetime—' He stopped abruptly, realising he was showing her a mirage, an impossible dream.

'Why did you stop? Can a princess not become a rishika?' she asked astutely.

Gautam considered this, then nodded. 'Yes, she can. Lopamudra was the daughter of the king of Vidarbha and married Rishi Agastya. Likewise, Shashvati Angiras was the wife of the Yadav king Asanga Playogi.'

Ahalya had heard of the philosopher Lopamudra Vaidarbhi. She was the princess of Vidarbha, and had married Rishi Agastya. His austere penance was said to have upset Lopamudra. She wrote a hymn, which appeared in the Rig Veda, asking for his attention and love. This hymn, detailing the relations between a husband and wife, made Rishi Agastya realise his duties towards his wife.

'But these princesses became seers *after* marrying rishis,' said Ahalya.

Gautam nodded. She, like himself, had a naturally analytical mind, he noted.

'Can the daughter of a king, given a choice, not become a rishika—without marriage?' she asked wryly.

He thought about this. 'Given a choice,' he said quietly, 'would she be able to devote her life to seeking and imparting knowledge—that is her decision to make.

'People often assume that the most famous figures of ancient times were men. Be it rishis or rulers. But there have been several women seers who have excelled equally. Learning, my dear, has no gender or caste or class. You worship knowledge and you are blessed with wisdom.

'My young niece, Ghosha Kakshivati, is one such seer. She suffered from an incurable disease—it was later diagnosed as leprosy—because of which she wasn't able to get married. The Ashvini physician twins treated her with their medicines. They were so impressed with her intelligence that they taught her the Madhu Vidya—the supreme bliss of the self.'

'Like Rishi Dadhichi received from Indra?' she asked with open awe.

'Yes. My cousin Ratri Bharadwaji, Rishi Bharadwaj's daughter, has also received it. She has composed some hymns in the Rig Veda, with Kushika Saubhari, another scholar.'

'There are a lot of women in your family who are rishikas,' Ahalya said, visibly impressed.

'Not nepotism, I assure you,' laughed Gautam. 'It started with my grandmother Mamata. She had exceptional sons: Kacha and my father, Dirghatmas. As you may have heard, my father was born blind. Like my grandmother, my mother, Pradveshi, was an accomplished woman of great learning; she was pious and an intellectual, and also the greatest support and inspiration to my blind father in all his work.'

'And to this remarkable Dirghatmas was born Gautam, meaning the one who dispels darkness and ignorance by his brilliance of light, which is spiritual knowledge,' said Ahalya. 'It is the opposite of blindness, is it not?'

'Yes, it is ironical,' Gautam said with a smile. 'My grandmother named me Gautam, the son of Dirghatmas, the one enveloped in perpetual darkness. He was very proud of his mother; she was one of his gurus. Just as I am a disciple of my mother.'

Ahalya had heard so much about the great and wise Dirghatmas. This extraordinary rishi, the raj-purohit of Emperor Bharat, was renowned for his paradoxical apophthegms and philosophical verses in the Rig Veda, and was the author of the Suktas, the highly enigmatic and brilliant hymns. She recalled what Rishi Vashisht had told her: in one of his ambiguous hymns, Rishi Dirghatmas had mentioned the zodiac signs with a clear reference to a chakra or wheel of 360 spokes placed in the sky. It was one of the earliest mentions of the zodiac signs. And Gautam was his eldest son—the illustrious son of an illustrious father in an illustrious family that boasted several women rishikas.

'It is often wrongly assumed that we are patriarchal in our teaching and education,' he said thoughtfully. 'Women have always been included in almost all aspects of Vedic teachings. My students have become panditas, priests, rishikas, scientists and teachers. There is so much to say about women's spiritual leadership. In today's fragmented and noxious culture of not just war and violence but worse—ignorance and discrimination—we have forgotten our legacy of knowledge. Many don't even know that there are as many priestesses who lead rituals as there are women in power and politics.'

'My mother is certainly one of the latter!' Ahalya said, smiling. 'She is more keen on me mastering the martial arts than the scriptures.'

'Smart lady,' smiled Gautam.

'It was my father who was a little sceptical, but perhaps he was just being protective—he always insisted that I be as well taught as my brother,' Ahalya said, in quick defence of her father.

Gautam nodded. 'I strongly believe a woman is able to do more jobs simultaneously. Planning, strategizing, taking risks, moving forward, retracting when needed—these are all part of a woman's daily life. A man tends to categorise his life, day and relationships very simply: into discrete divisions! But yes, we need to acknowledge intellect and that passion for knowledge without prejudice, as your parents did.'

Ahalya winced. Were they as fair as they claimed to be?

'Education sees no gender, no bias,' continued Gautam. 'If the Upanishads clearly declare that individual souls are neither male nor female, who are we to discriminate when educating men and women?'

A thought struck her and she blurted it out. 'You come from the family of Angiras, like Rishi Bhardwaj does, do you not?' she asked.

'Yes, we are related. We both descend from my great grandfather Rishi Angiras, and are bracketed under the name Angirasa. Rishi Bharadwaj is Rishi Brihaspati's son and my uncle.'

'But was he not also your disciple?!' she said in astonishment. A nephew was his uncle's tutor!

'There's no hierarchy, my dear. One should glean knowledge from wherever one can: be it from a parent, sister, brother, friend or stranger. Anyone can become your guru, your teacher.'

'Rishi Angiras was not just a legendary rishi, he was a lawgiver and astronomer. He is credited with introducing fire-worship, along with Sage Bhrigu, is he not?' she said. 'And yet, it is said that you—his descendant—do not believe in rituals and yagnas. You firmly believe in scientific reasoning and logic and have mastered law and philosophy along those lines.'

'You seem to know a lot about the ancient sages and their families,' Gautam said with a smile.

'I *am* interested in the different schools of thought,' admitted Ahalya shyly.

'Yes, that is important,' he agreed thoughtfully. 'Despite the differences between us seers and scholars, we need to discuss and debate ideas.'

'Is that why I was sent here? To master the art of your famous logical reasoning?' she said playfully, surprised by her own boldness.

'Perhaps. Though not many agree with my logic,' he said dryly. 'And I am not sure how well I can teach you the "art", as you call it.'

'But you are said to be a great teacher too! You are known as "Akshapaad", for having mentored great disciples like Praachina-yogya, Shaandilya, Gaargya and Bharadwaj. How wise all of them are,' she said, looking animatedly into his face. 'Of all the students educated here, not one has been a failure. One a seer; another a doctor; another, they say, is a celebrated scientist ...'

'That says more about them than me,' he said, laughing.

'No,' she said, her eyes serious. 'It says a lot about you as a teacher. Teaching is not just about imparting knowledge; it is also about enabling a student to understand their own potential for learning. *You* made them understand and realise their own abilities.'

Gautam wore a thoughtful look as he watched Ahalya's eyes shine with genuine goodwill and gladness. She was admiring him and his past students like an overawed child, but there was an inherent truth in her observation. She was innately wise, and as he looked at her sweet face, he thought, *She is blessed who is happy in seeing others happy.*

It was difficult to ignore her. Or *not* like her. She was not someone who could be wooed or won over in the usual way— she was averse to over-familiarity, she was proof against praise or swaggering cleverness, she was proof against superficial charm; if any of these assailed her too strongly she would immediately retreat into her well-spun cocoon, shutting out the person responsible. She was entertained only by the gratification of her intellect and curiosity. Though Ahalya, he soon noticed, could never be rude or injure anyone's feelings. Besides her loveliness, she had a natural charisma—of innate goodness. It glowed through her face, her small smile, her soft eyes, her kind thoughts and gentle manner.

Gautam slowly found himself surrendering a part of himself to her. Ahalya had become an intrinsic part of his world. The day always began with, as she bashfully put it, 'A tumbler of milk for the meditation.' He could tell that she more than admired him: he could see it in her luminous eyes. Her initial wariness had almost disappeared, replaced by an amiable level of comfort between them. And the more they chatted and the more often they laughed together, the stronger was his conviction that he should send her away before the situation became complicated. But he did not have the heart or will to betray her trust: she looked upon him as her saviour.

Gautam was not just an astute teacher, he was also perceptive in matters concerning emotions as well. His thirty years on earth and all his experiences had helped him. And when he saw the blind adoration in the girl's eyes, he felt both fear and excitement. He had never been married and had escaped the impediments of romantic felicity; he had no desire for romantic love. He did not want to encourage unnecessary emotions in either of them, or make a fool of himself over a woman who was probably just on a lookout for new experiences. Love was an adventure he did not want to undertake.

But Gautam could no longer deny the truth: with each passing day, Ahalya meant more and more to him. And her open adoration for him made it more difficult for him to stay aloof from her. He was only held back by his sense of duty, and that painful twinge of conscience.

One evening, as they walked through the groves and talked, she said, 'You know, the war my family is fighting did not just help put me on the path to learning.'

'What do you mean?' he asked, turning to her.

'My mother wants me to marry Indra,' she said. 'And Indra wishes it too; he even proposed to me. Had it not been for the war,' Ahalya continued with a frown, 'I might have been married to him by now.'

Gautam felt his heart contract painfully.

'But I don't want to ...' she added desolately.

'Then you should refuse,' he said evenly, his face composed.

'Can I?' she said and sighed.

'Yes. You are still young. Experience, not emotions, will teach you not to condemn or judge so easily. Even marriage is not as sacred as one would like to believe: more than love, a couple needs to respect each other. Most, if not all, don't.'

'If that is so, why get married?'

'Because it is the most exquisite, meaningful relationship between a man and a woman: but only when it is a marriage of two hearts, two bodies, two minds, two souls and two friends. Then, it is happy companionship,' he said. 'Otherwise, life can be horrid. An unhappy marriage can be stifling.'

Was that a warning for her, Ahalya wondered.

'Is that why you have not married?' she asked, and could have bit her tongue. She had overstepped a line; she was getting dangerously personal. She knew this rishi was vowed into celibacy—brahmacharya. Gautam was famously known to be a samyami, and his mind and soul were always with Brahma—the mind—that was why he was a brahmachari. No woman could tempt him nor ever break that self-control.

Gautam let out a short laugh. 'I am married to my work. I'm afraid if I ever were to marry, I would end up neglecting my poor bride. And I am a wanderer. I don't stay put in my own ashram. I like to travel all over the country and teach. That's my life.'

'That is why your ashrams are scattered all over the country and your disciples are everywhere,' said Ahalya. '*That's* your family!'

Gautam noticed her change of tone and what it implied. She was infatuated with him. His heart sank. He had seen hints of it: in her faint blush, her self-consciousness, her little smile ...

Seeing her standing so close to him, the open happiness on her face, the gentle smile, the stray tendril that had escaped from under her loose bun—it reminded Gautam of what he meant to her and she to him.

8

The Departure

Ahalya had always thought she was a practical person, someone who was ruled by her mind; but now, she found herself imagining a man whisking her away to a life of love, happiness and knowledge. She hated to admit it, but perhaps she was essentially a romantic.

It was Gautam's kindness and respectfulness that had made her melt. He had given her this unbelievable confidence, offering her advice, listening to her. He had saved her, taken her into his home without forcing her to tell him who she was, and had been kind about her timidity and ignorance. He had never laughed at her.

At first, she had been suspicious of this kindness, but now she was free of panic and could think clearly, she began to wonder if he reciprocated her feelings. Was that the explanation for his generosity and obvious desire to protect her? Surely no man would invest so much time in a woman unless he held certain strong emotions? No, she was being silly. Gautam would have helped any person in need, not just her.

She sighed, closed her eyes and, for a time, allowed her mind to swim in a sea of romantic sentimentality.

It was three o'clock in the morning. Through her window, she could see the clear night sky. Ahalya smiled softly. She could not sleep; she was too excited, too happy. She was enjoying every moment in the ashram. Whether it was engaging in hard chores or in philosophical debates, which Ahalya found, to her utter astonishment, could last for days.

'But there are two kinds of debates,' Gautam had elucidated in his deep baritone. 'The free, unrestrained one, and the other, which is more a volley of words, a tussle of power play, one-upmanship. It fuels the ego, not intellect. A true scholar would not get upset if defeated by another in a debate. That maturity is not something a king—or a fool—would be capable of! I remember hearing about a king who invited a monk for a debate. The monk accepted on the condition that the king would debate as a scholar and not as a ruler, as anyone daring to disagree with a king is likely to invite not praise, but punishment. It is not debate at all but acquiescing to what the king decrees.'

'You have much contempt for royals,' Ahalya had remarked.

'No, I simply avoid them,' he said briefly but with such undiluted derision that she looked up quickly at him.

'Is your dislike for them, or what they stand for?'

He looked at her expressionlessly. 'For all of it—the king, the warrior, war and violence. War is a whim, not of soldiers, but of kings. And there is no victor or victory, just destruction and death, so needless and mindless. War *is* violence and the king has to be a warrior, an invader, and nothing has ever been won, no victory declared without one or the other being destroyed.'

'Because you are a pacifist?' she asked inquisitively.

'As a seer, I am expected to be one.' He smiled unexpectedly, and his hard features softened.

Her heart instantly melted.

'I am a teacher, and for me, imparting education is enlightenment. Education and knowledge, if made into weapons, will also lead to war—an intellectual war of ideas,' he said. 'Like you, I think, I do not enjoy politics nor am I a very political person.'

'Yes, I realised that,' she said slowly. 'But then perhaps you are not in support of having royal priests, or the custom of having a raj-purohit at court?'

She saw him pause; neither giving a nod or a shake of his head.

She persisted, now intrigued, wanting to know more about what he thought, what he believed. 'But your father was the royal priest of Emperor Bharat. And your uncle Rishi Bharadwaj is at our court, as is Rishi Vashisht. Do you see them as rishis blindly carrying out royal orders? Are they all wrong?'

'It is not so simple. It's not about being politically right and morally wrong. Each has a way of spreading knowledge— through the king or through his ashrams. I chose the latter,' he said, shrugging.

He narrowed his eyes and said, 'See, we are arguing again ... can we ever not contradict each other?'

'I call it debating,' she said without hesitating, returning his words neatly.

Amused, he said, 'Ah, but it happens too often! Are you implying our discussions drift more towards the second category of debates—more a word play?'

'But ours is not an ego clash,' she said meekly, though a small smile danced in her eyes. 'Indeed, if debates are often the preferred mode of teaching in most gurukuls, and this intellectual tradition is encouraged at your ashram too, then I am not contradicting you; this is just a wholesome debate! You did teach us how to value discussion, deliberation and questioning.'

His face broke into his rare, lopsided smile. 'You are turning my words against me, young lady!' he said mock-sternly. 'And debates can get bloody—spilling into the public arena too.'

'This is a private discussion,' she said, smiling.

'We have to agree to disagree. That is why there are different schools of thought, dear.'

She warmed instantly when he called her 'dear'. But, she reminded herself, he called everyone 'dear'.

'Maybe our conversation will become as famous as the philosophical dialogues between, say, Yama and Nachiket?' he teased. 'The Upanishads delight in dialectics: like the discussions between Rishi Yajnavalkya, King Janak and Rishika Gargi. Or Rishi Uddalaka Aruni and his son Shvetaketu. Or twelve-year-old Ashtavakra's debate with Rishi Vandin, whom he defeated to avenge his father Kahod's defeat and death?'

'Please don't mock me,' she muttered, the colour rising hotly up her neck and face. 'I know these are legendary debates in the Upanishads. I was simply practising your art of dialogue. But you haven't answered my query—*why* are you so critical about the royals?'

'I don't consider myself a philosopher or a scientist. I am a teacher first—I prefer teaching students to advising powerful kings,' he said with a sardonic twist of a smile. '*That* is why I prefer the forest to the palace.'

'Probably because a king or prince would not listen as obediently as we students in the ashram,' she mocked, taking up his tone.

He threw her a questioning look. 'Is that how you feel? That you are being forced to obey the orders of a tyrant?'

'Not a tyrant, but yes, you are certainly as autocratic as a king!' she riposted, refusing to cower.

'The fact that you have turned from a mouse to a tigress means I am not a tyrant,' he stated, his sombre eyes crinkling with amusement.

She turned indignant, piqued at his description. 'I am your student,' she reminded him. 'And I have learned a lot. Perhaps in the process, I grew braver.'

She had. The gurukul tradition encouraged intellectual self-confidence; there was a freedom to challenge, question and even dissent. She found this exhilarating.

'Life around us is a dispute,' he said, smiling. 'Keep asking yourself questions, and you will find yourself debating yourself a lot more! Here in the ashram, perhaps you get a subconscious glance at the spiritual and the philosophical. But I have seen that ideas sometimes run their course too soon. That does not happen to you, though—you are brimming with them. Use your abilities to reflect and reason. It is not me or a guru that your mind needs, Ahalya. You will have to sustain your own spirit of free enquiry and confident engagement.'

Ahalya was overwhelmed by happiness; she knew he meant the compliment this time.

His words continued to resonate in her brain, his gravelly voice rumbling through her wakeful mind and her dreams. Her whole being throbbed with a strange, incomprehensible feeling; her mind was a constant churn of tumultuous thoughts. She could not analyse it, she simply knew it. She felt resurrected. Rejuvenated. No, she thought wildly, resuscitated. She had been reborn in this ashram ...

She was living the life she had yearned for since becoming self-aware. She was studying in an ashram under a rishi who was one of the most prolific scholars of the times. She pulled up the thin quilt and snuggled into the coir cot, happy with the knowledge that as soon as she woke up in the morning, she would be engulfed by memories of the previous day. Never had she got up so excited and eager to face the day; never before had she looked forward to the next day so much—just to be with *him*. He was her everything: her teacher, her mentor, her guide, her friend, her hero ...

Her day started early. She tried to be with Uttank as much as possible: he was Gautam's favourite disciple amongst all the boys and girls there. Uttank had joined the ashram at five and clearly held a deep reverence for Gautam. He served his guru with almost single-minded devotion: he kept hot water ready for his bath, prepared his bed and massaged his legs. Outside of these duties, he would collect firewood, herd the cattle and kept a sharp eye on the vegetable patch as well. Whatever free time he had, he spent on his classmates. He often cleaned their rooms, prepared beds for the unwell, helped Ahalya water the flowerbeds and even mended clothes for his guru and his other classmates.

But it was not just Uttank: all his students clearly adored Rishi Gautam.

'I shall never forget your kindness and how ... how good you have been to me!' Ahalya said one day, a shy smile on her lips. 'You are so honest, generous and clever.'

Gautam stiffened as she sat at his feet, her head close to his knees, looking at him with shining, adoring eyes. 'How do you do it? How did you make my world suddenly so wonderful?' she continued, not noticing that his face had suddenly become drawn and pale. When he was quiet, she said, 'Do you consider my words too sentimental, affected and bereft of "depth of thought",' she said, laughing self-consciously.

She looked into his remarkable eyes: black and pure, the most beautiful eyes she had ever seen. He did not move. Nor could she. They continued to gaze at each other until she began to feel the same tightness in her chest that she felt each time she was near him. These days the atmosphere crackled each time she and Gautam made eye contact. When she was near him, only the strongest act of will kept her from touching him.

She saw his face turn grim, and then it flooded with bafflement. He got up abruptly, in one quick movement, and stepped back. Still silent, he gazed down at her with wide-open, tortured eyes. She was utterly overwhelmed, staring up at him in rising confusion, her trepidation mounting as he turned around and strode away, each step furious and deliberate as he moved away from her.

After that episode, Gautam changed. He now treated her with a cold indifference. No longer did they have their long, lingering conversations about every topic under the sun. Had it all been a performance to make her feel less lonely, less unhappy?

Gautam's changed demeanour forced her to think about who she was, where she was ... and the fact that she would have to return to her home someday. Gautam had kept her posted on how her family was doing, but there had been no news for a few days. There was now a constant coil of fear twisted inside of her; a churn of anxiety and the agony of waiting for news. She was not bothered about victory or defeat: were her brother and father safe? Alive or wounded or ...? And her mother? What was she doing alone, so brave in their huge, empty palace: waiting for the enemies at the gate or welcoming the victors' return?

Ahalya moved restlessly. She did not want to go back to the palace, she wanted to be here, with *him*, learning, reading, discussing. Just being near him filled her with a completeness that she had never experienced before.

But then she recalled his behaviour towards her now. Early in their acquaintance, it had seemed that there was a deep and spontaneous mutual attraction—she had been sure of it. He had been so gentle and caring, not how he was now: cold, almost intimidating.

She watched as he picked up a book, sat down facing the students, and start moving his beautiful lips, ignoring her the entire time. She looked at him and sank into thought. *I am nothing to him*, she reflected dolefully, her heart contracting.

One week, a fortnight, a month, a season, another month—so long she had been here, so long she had devoted her active life, mind and soul to him. He had treated her with interest, with tenderness, even. Now there was sometimes malice, some indifference, much contempt. He inflicted on her innumerable little slights and indignities, as if punishing her for caring for him. He had done everything except disparage her, and it seemed to her that he held back in this because it might have contradicted the utter indifference he sincerely felt towards her.

Over the months she had spent at the ashram, he had been the cause of an ecstasy of hope and an intolerable agony of spirit within her.

And then the day she had dreaded for long arrived with the appearance of a messenger bringing news from Kampilya.

'It's good news,' Gautam said shortly. 'Your brother has won the war and Shambar has been killed at Udvraj.'

His expressionless eyes refused to meet her suddenly dilated ones.

'Which means I need to leave the ashram,' she said shakily. He did not want her around anymore.

'Yes. And I see no reason to delay your return,' he said curtly. 'You have to go back to your family. Your world,' he added deliberately.

Her heart beating fast, she pulled herself up proudly and nodded. 'Then I shall leave immediately with the messenger ...'

'No!' he said roughly. 'It might not be safe. I am sure your father will come himself or send some soldiers to escort you back home. Please wait for further news. I came to give you the good tidings as I know how miserable you were about your family—and the war.'

The war which had imposed her on him, she thought bitterly.

'And so, princess, you shall be leaving soon. What will you be giving: daan or dakshina?' he said with forced geniality. 'You know the difference between the two.'

He was teasing her again, she cried silently. He *was* cruel!

'My memory, I hope,' she said flatly. 'For I shall never forget you!' she blurted in anguished innocence.

The colour drained from his face, and his eyes filled with an undecipherable emotion.

She swallowed convulsively, and hastened to add, 'You have been my guru, my teacher, my guide ...' She felt a dry sob in her throat, but continued in a tight voice, '... my everything. You taught me well and made me discover a new world and myself.'

'Ahalya,' he began and stopped. His dark eyes searched hers. 'Bless you, dear ...' he murmured in a soft, strangled voice. She hated it now when he called her 'dear'—he did not mean it; it was not even an endearment but a casual, patronising sobriquet.

With a slow shake of his head, he left the room, leaving her to ride a new wave of anguish. She was going to have to leave this ashram and him.

The next day, early in the morning, she left as she had arrived—in his absence. He had not been there to receive her; he saw to it that he was not there to bid her farewell.

The sight of her brother—alive and well and smiling—made up for a thousand pains inflicted by Gautam and his marked absence. She flung herself into his arms and allowed the tears to flow uninhibited.

'You lied to me,' she sobbed. 'You left me here while you went to war! You—' she choked, happiness and grief, anger and relief, mingling in a fresh bout of tears streaming down her face. 'I could have lost you! I ... how could you?!' she cried furiously.

'Shh, I am back, everything is fine now,' he said soothingly, running his hand over her hair. 'We are going home!'

She nodded weepily. 'Yes, take me home!'

Divodas looked around the quiet ashram. It was still very early hours; the purple shadows of the night were only just lightening with the rising dawn. Everyone must be at their prayers, he presumed.

'I would have liked to meet and thank Rishi Gautam for looking after you,' Divodas said, his eyes scanning the ashram. He was a little perturbed both by the rishi's conspicuous absence and his sister's unnaturally wan face. She seemed to have suddenly grown up: she was certainly not the girl he had seen off at the palace. In front of him was a mature woman he did not recognise.

'He must be deep in his meditation,' she mumbled, suddenly wanting to leave this place she had grown to love. She felt like a stranger, an unwanted guest who had overstayed her visit.

'Are you sure?' he asked doubtfully. 'I am happy to wait. After all, we owe him a lot. Though he hates getting dragged into political situations, he agreed in your case.'

She nodded. 'He is kind, very kind ...' she said, a catch in her throat.

Divodas cast her a sharp glance, but only said, 'Yes, he must be. But then, he is known to protect and fight for the underdog.'

Ahalya let out a small hysterical laugh. 'You make me sound like a lost animal!'

'Weren't you?' asked Divodas quietly.

Yes, she had been lost, but she had found her way, she thought as she hurried inside her hut and packed the few things she could call her own. When she met her brother outside a little later, she was pleasantly surprised to see that everyone had come to bid her goodbye, but for *him*. As she walked out of the ashram, her eyes darted about nervously, hoping to spot the familiar silhouette of his tall, lean frame. But Gautam did not emerge from his hut.

Uttank was by her side as always, and walked with her up to her brother's chariot.

She pressed his hand and said, 'Look after this ashram. Look after him.'

As the chariot drove away, she heard nothing but the murmur of the river and the thudding of her heart, one beat more painful than the other. Lifting her dry eyes to the sky, she saw that the sun was hidden behind thick clouds.

She felt the prick of tears. She had been so foolish. She had gained so much knowledge but no wisdom. Gautam had tutored her to become a rishika, but she had little control over her emotions and desires. But was it a sin to fall in love with the man who was her god—her very spirit, her divinity, her idol?

After a few hours, she glimpsed the outline of the palace in the distance.

She was back home, but her heart was lost forever.

9

The Dilemma

A short spell of rain was followed by another long day at the palace, and it occurred to Ahalya at last that she was far, far away from Gautam. She could not be his. She could never be his. He did not love her. And she could not love him. He was a celibate sage. She only had to hammer this into her mind and her heart.

She lay awake at night, gazing up at the intricately carved ceiling of her opulent bed chamber, which seemed to mock the humble hut she had resided in for the last few months. She had repeatedly rationalised the whole thing with herself over and over again: that he was not worth her love anyway, given the amount of pain he had caused her. She enumerated his glaring deficiencies as a man: he might be a scholar, a visionary, the brightest, most brilliant mind, but he was heartless. He could talk of love and beauty but was incapable of loving.

She *had* to forget him. She had to erase the imprint of his smile, the memory of his forehead and lips, his baritone, his hot, coal-black eyes ... She tried to lose herself in books, studying hard and late. Each restless night she went to her bed chamber only to have her fatigued mind immediately move to the ashram, and Gautam.

She remembered how she had treated Indra, how quickly she had rejected him. Now she forgave him everything. The beseeching words, the incoherent passion, his flirting, the desire to make small talk. She understood it all now, since Indra's blunders were her own, and many things that would have made her wince back then moved her now to sympathy and even a certain acceptance. Her love for Gautam was inexplicable, even to herself. She wanted his hand holding hers, his gravelly voice calling to her and their children in the little patch of garden in the ashram...

Ahalya blinked. She was being foolish and self-indulgent, she thought. There was no point in her dreaming of those things anymore. But she could not help it. His image was imprinted deep inside her. And she was too strong, too alive, to allow it to die so easily.

Her mother's voice interrupted her thoughts.

'You have gone quiet again, Ahalya. Aren't you happy we are back together?' said Nalayani, her face soft with the memory of pain. 'We have gone through a lot, and it is such a relief that our warriors are back and we are all safe together again,' she murmured, throwing her daughter a worried frown.

Ahalya had always been quiet, but since her return from Rishi Gautam's ashram, the girl seemed like a pale glimmer of herself.

'War makes warriors out of all of us, forcing us to be brave,' Ahalya said softly. 'Ma, you were so valiant yourself. You stood strong here, alone in the palace, while you sent me away to a safe place. Was that fair?'

'It was not about fairness, dear, it was about being safe,' replied Nalayani, relieved Ahalya was engaging in the conversation.

'What would have happened if I had lost all of you?' she cried suddenly, more in enraged resentment than grief.

Nalayani was taken aback by her daughter's sudden vehemence.

'Indra would have married you,' she said swiftly.

Ahalya looked incredulous. 'Is that your solution to everything?' she demanded, her eyes narrowing at her mother's flushed face. 'Or was it so planned?' Her eyes widened in disbelief.

'Yes,' said Nalayani. 'You could not have remained at Rishi Gautam's ashram forever, could you?'

She saw her daughter wince, her delicate features twist in a flash of pain.

'Why this sham of a swayamwar, Ma?' Ahalya said finally with a shrug. 'If you have decided on Indra as my husband, then why the charade of me choosing some suitor? All I need to do is marry Indra once you fix the day and date!'

'I would prefer it to be so, but your father won't allow it,' retorted Nalayani. 'He wants *you* to choose your husband. He insists there should be a swayamwar. It seems he had a dream in which Lord Brahma instructed him that this is the way it should be done.'

'A dream?' repeated Ahalya, puzzled.

'Don't you know, child, that your father believes you are a special gift from Lord Brahma to us, that you are his precious creation?' said her mother.

'Those are just ballads sung by minstrels to flatter a princess,' said Ahalya dismissively.

Nalayani shrugged. 'In any case, he believes Brahma wishes that a swayamwar be held,' she said, her tone making it clear that she was not pleased.

Ahalya smiled mirthlessly. *If only I could marry the man I want, if only the man I loved, loved me ...* Ahalya got up abruptly.

'Is my marriage the only path that you can think of for me, Ma?' she asked.

'What do you mean, Ahalya?' asked her mother quietly.

Ahalya whirled around to stare at Nalayani. 'I *don't* want to marry, Ma, you know that!'

'That's not a choice!' shot back her mother. 'You can't remain unmarried!'

'Why not?' Ahalya said. 'Why can I not do what I want? I don't want to marry. I want no swayamwar.' Her voice rose slightly. 'I just want to be left alone! I want to be me! I want to become a rishika!'

A tense silence followed her words. Ahalya felt a sob of frustration in her throat; oh, she wished she could go back to the ashram! She felt like a prisoner in this palace, trapped in its sprawling opulence, its falseness, its procedures

'What are you saying?' barked Nalayani, frightened out of her wits. 'I knew it was a mistake sending you to that ashram. I have always known—'

'It's ... it's not just about my recent time in an ashram,' cried Ahalya in exasperation. 'You know I am not interested in marrying Indra or any king or some darned prince! You know it.'

'I thought you would have outgrown this madness,' snapped her mother angrily. 'You are no longer a child; you know you need to marry—'

'*Need* to?' Ahalya said, mimicking her mother's characteristic sarcasm. 'No, I *need* to be at peace with myself, and I find peace in books and scriptures and sutras! Why can I not focus on that?'

'Ahalya, you promised,' said Nalayani, her voice now soft and dangerous. 'I shan't allow any more of your tantrums.'

'They are not tantrums, Ma,' Ahalya said tearfully. 'It's *me*! I am telling you, I am begging you—it's a plea, an outpouring of my heart and my tormented mind. I can't be Indra's wife or anyone else's! Please understand that!'

Nalayani looked at the woebegone, wan face of her daughter; she saw that it did not diminish her loveliness—it heightened it. Since her return, Ahalya *had* changed, but Nalayani had not been able to determine just *how*, leaving her with a strong sense of trepidation. A quick sliver of fear ran through Nalayani—had Ahalya's heart as well as her mind remained in that ashram?

'Nothing can be done now, Ahalya. Your father shall soon announce your swayyamwar,' stated Nalayani, hardening her heart and desperate to end the argument. 'The man who circumambulates the earth the fastest shall be your husband.'

Ahalya sank into a chair. 'So I don't get to choose after all—it's hardly a swayamwar,' she whispered bitterly. 'I will have to be won. I am the prize trophy to be gifted to the winner of this senseless contest!' A slow anger building up inside her made her head throb. 'How could Father do this to me? He did not even bother to ask me!' she burst out, her face flushed with rage.

She wanted answers and her mother was not going to give them. She stood up and swept out of the room. Her throat hurt with dry sobs, her breath coming in painful gasps. Her mother, father, brother—why were they betraying her?

She rushed into the morning room, which her father favoured at this time of the day.

'You decided on my swayamwar without letting me know?' she demanded, her voice unusually forceful.

Divodas raised his eyebrows at her tone. 'Ahalya,' he warned softly.

'The last time we discussed this, you assured us you would be ready once you were back from the ashram,' King Mudgal reminded her gently. 'In any case, we are still discussing the details; nothing is confirmed—'

'You are planning my wedding so furtively, just like you sent me to the ashram under false pretences!' she accused angrily.

'Ahalya!' rebuked Divodas, more sharply now. 'We sent you for your safety, your own good!'

'All of you plotted! Like you are doing now,' she persisted. 'Why do you insist on keeping me in the dark about decisions about *my* life?'

Mudgal looked at her with a soft, steady gaze. 'Ahalya, it's been more than a month since you have come back. Your marriage *needs* to be settled. We *were* going to discuss it with you,' he continued before she could interrupt. 'But you have been so distant, so quiet—we were wondering how to go about it ...' he said, giving her a quick, worried look.

She brushed his words aside with a wave of her hand. 'No, Father, you didn't consider informing me, neither now nor then,' she said angrily, biting her lip. 'You saw to my safety— but did you not consider, even once, that I deserved to know the truth?' Her voice shook slightly. 'How was I to face this great lie?'

'It was for your good. What else could we have done?' he asked, sighing. He could see that she was furious with them, hurt by their duplicity.

'I would have been better prepared. I am no longer a child,' she said quietly. 'And you are doing the same thing now—with my marriage. Could we not have discussed it as we always do?'

'Yes, as we used to,' agreed her father thoughtfully. 'But are you what you were? You have barely spoken to any of us, shutting yourself in the room or poring over your books. What are *you* running away from, Ahalya?' he prodded gently.

His gentleness broke her. She grasped his hands tightly and brought it to her weeping face. 'Oh, Father, you have made me a stranger in my own home! We went through the worst crisis but you kept me away ... Am I not family?' she sobbed, her tears flowing freely at last. Her long pent-up anger boiled over, allowing her to grieve for what she could have lost. The fear in the early days, her imagined horrors, came rushing back. She had felt like an orphan in the ashram at first, a waif bereft. How could she explain all this to her parents and her brother?

She shuddered and Mudgal gently held her in his arms. She sobbed harder. 'Silly child, so brave yet so fragile,' he murmured. 'You are a princess; you know how to hide your emotions, even your vulnerability. I know you too well, dear, and I didn't have the heart to tell you the truth. I should have. It would have prepared you ... I think I have sheltered you too long here,' he said, his eyes moist.

Even as he lay wounded on the battlefield, his thoughts had been with her, not even on his unconscious son lying cold and bleeding beside him on the dusty ground. He had presumed Divodas to be dead, and the grief had numbed him; but he had consoled himself with the relief of knowing that his daughter was safe in Rishi Gautam's ashram.

Ahalya smiled through her tears. 'No, I am not as weak and vulnerable as you think I am. But yes, I was hurt and angry and worried and terrified.'

'Next time, we shall seek your permission before we go to war,' Divodas said with a grin, easing the tension. 'But you have been secretive too, Ahalya. You haven't told us anything about your time in the ashram.'

'I couldn't bear to leave it!' she said spontaneously, and Divodas was quick to notice her blush.

He grinned. 'You didn't speak much on our way back. You looked so despondent that I was not too sure if you were happy to see me again!'

She bit her lip and remained silent.

'Oh, so you couldn't bear to leave it and wouldn't have come back had we not survived?' Mudgal said, laughing.

'Don't joke about death, Father!' she scolded, wiping her tears, the light banter bringing a small smile to her face. Then her tone turned serious. 'But I do wish to go back to the ashram. As a student, not a refugee. I want to spend my life studying the Vedas. I ... I want to be a rishika!' she said softly, in a low but firm tone.

'You know that is not possible, Ahalya,' Mudgal said evenly.

She raised her chin. 'Why not? Because I am to wed? Father, don't force me into a marriage I don't want,' she pleaded.

'Are you studying to escape marriage?' her father asked bluntly. She floundered.

'Would you agree, if you can marry the man you want?' he persisted, observing her closely.

Confused, Ahalya lowered her head. It was impossible; she could never marry Rishi Gautam ...

'Ahalya, I just want you to marry the best person,' Mudgal said.

'The best man or best for me?' she asked cynically. 'They may not be the same.'

Mudgal sighed. 'Lord Brahma considers you special, and that is probably why he has come up with this odd competition for your swayamwar—that the first person who goes around the three worlds shall win your hand. It will be an open contest.'

Ahalya gave a wry smile. 'Which Indra is sure to win with his super powers!'

'Why do you assume he will be the winner? There are other good men as well,' her father said.

'But what is the problem if Indra wins your hand?' interrupted Divodas, his tone slightly belligerent. 'You refused him on account of you not being sure of his feelings. But now you know—'

'You are defending your friend!' she accused.

'Yes,' agreed Divodas. 'He is a very good friend. What's wrong with him? He is good, kind, rich, handsome and powerful. Above all, he loves you! You have tested his love—he waited for you. He still loves you.'

'But I don't feel the same way about him!' she cried.

Divodas looked taken aback. There was an awkward pause.

'Do you love someone else?' asked Mudgal quietly.

Ahalya wanted to nod her head in affirmation but she stopped. What could she say? That she loved a man who had devoted himself to celibacy and meditation? She could confess her love to no one. Her unrequited feelings would remain hidden from all but her, she realised with a sinking heart.

Her shoulders slumped in dejection, she murmured, 'I didn't mean it that way. It is just that I do not wish to marry; I want to study,' she said weakly.

'Why should marriage stop your pursuit of education? You can become a rishika, dear, even after your marriage,' he said. 'You are known as a scholar already.'

Ahalya shook her head. 'I want to single-mindedly pursue my field of interest, not be saddled by marital responsibilities. Gargi and Sulabha did not marry and they are the foremost rishikas and panditas.'

'Arundhati, Lopamudra and Maitreyi are all married women who are rishikas,' her father reminded her gently.

'That's because they married rishis and—' she began, but then stopped abruptly.

What was she saying, she thought miserably. She could never marry a rishi. She could not marry Gautam.

There was a taut pause.

'Ahalya?' Divodas sounded startled.

She saw the expressions on both men. They must never guess the truth, she thought. So soon, with so little done, all the joy had gone from her. She knew that Indra or any other man would be no more than a miasma of the real thing she wanted.

She rose slowly. 'All right, I agree,' she said. 'I agree to this swayamwar. I shall marry the man who wins this impossible challenge.'

10

The Friendship

Ahalya almost collided into Indra coming down the hallway.

No, not him, she thought miserably. She had avoided meeting him ever since she had returned to the palace.

'So, at last I get to see you!' he said, and the joyful surprise in his voice made her wince.

'I was unwell,' she mumbled weakly, horrified that she had lied so easily. She cleared her throat, forcing a stiff smile and moving away.

The familiar, quiet voice sent a stab of longing through him, and he stared after her as she walked away. She was as beautiful as he remembered. She was ablaze in gold—gold sparkled in a band on her head, gold glinted round her slender neck and her slim ankles, which peeped out from below her antariya's golden hem—but he could see that there was no fire in her. There was a deep despondency writ in her large eyes.

She walked through a doorway and he hurried after her, gazing at the long, straight back, the curve of her hips and the slim legs. He had frantically been trying to meet her since her return but to no avail. In the time since they had last met, she had constantly passed through his crazed dreams and frenzied thoughts. And now, he could have wept at the wonder of her return.

She stopped suddenly and turned around to say, 'I should be thanking you again for saving my brother's life.' She paused, and then said, 'Because you came to Divodas's aid, Shambar has been vanquished at last. It seems you and Divodas managed to destroy all his fortresses, and that the last one fell when you killed him.'

'But I didn't kill him! It was Divodas!' Indra said, astonished.

'Oh, but ...' She looked confused. For some reason, she had assumed it was Indra who had finally killed their enemy.

'What happened?' Ahalya asked earnestly. 'I don't know much.'

'But you should, shouldn't you?' said Indra sardonically, and for the first time she heard a note of quiet remonstration in his voice. 'You are now the sister of the finest warrior this country has right now. Divodas won an impossible war. Don't undervalue him just because he's your brother,' he said. 'Even though Divodas was dangerously wounded when we attacked his fortresses, he managed to kill Shambar with his bare hands.'

Ahalya was overcome by mixed feelings. Pride for her brother and relief that she need not feel obligated to Indra anymore. Each time she met Indra, she felt crushed by the need to be grateful for all he had done for her family.

'Battles quickly become legends through ballads and tales of heroic deeds,' Indra said.

'I often wonder what is so heroic about war,' she started, but seeing the incredulous look on Indra's face, hastily stopped. She had no wish to argue and spend time with him.

'Anyway this war has finally ended!' she murmured gratefully.

'Yes, it has changed the equation once and for all,' responded Indra, rubbing his jaw thoughtfully. 'There's been such a long history of skirmishes, which escalated into this terrible bloody war. Earlier, the battles between the Purus and the Dasyus were always over water. But these Dasyus were always different from the Purus. They have never got along, and not just because of political ambitions. They have a belief system at odds with that of the Purus, and despite the efforts of the Purus, they have refused to give up those beliefs.'

'But naturally, why would and should they?' she said. 'Of course they would rebel.'

Indra's eyes narrowed. 'Rebellions often become wars. There have been instances when the Dasyus have incited people and emboldened them to even stand up to me!'

'Is that why you are siding with Divodas?' she asked shrewdly, finally understanding why Indra favoured Divodas. Indra needed him—it was not the other way round! Relief overwhelmed her, as if the shackles had at last fallen off.

'Yes,' admitted Indra frankly. 'The Dasyus do not respect me. They don't believe in rites and rituals like the Purus.'

'And that's why they are branded as doubters,' said Ahalya, recalling the conversation with Gautam in which he had detailed the long-standing feud between the two clans. It was more than politics; it was, as Gautam had warned, the social beliefs of the Purus that the Dasas were at odds with.

Indra looked visibly surprised. 'So you do know quite a bit of our history with the Dasas!' he remarked, his eyes alive with curiosity. 'The glory days of your family have begun, Ahalya. The two tribes have agreed on a truce and Divodas's vanquishing of Shambar heralds the dominance of the Purus over the Dasas from now on.'

'But is Divodas powerful enough to maintain peace?'

'Well, however much he may want it, it is not up to him. Divodas has stamped his domination over all the other clans but it is bound to start a new power struggle with neighbouring kingdoms.'

'You mean, there might be wars between our Puru clans in the future?'

'Yes ... in fact, it seems to have begun.'

Gautam's warning rang in her ears. Would the wars never end?

She said restlessly, 'We haven't recovered from one, and soon might start another.' A sense of dread settled in her bones again.

'I am there,' he said softly. 'Don't worry, Divodas will never come to any harm—ever. That's my promise to you.'

She swallowed, a warm flush rising up her cheeks. His words touched her deeply. She nodded, her throat thick with emotion.

He tilted his golden head to appraise her. She looked at him searchingly.

A light, warm breeze wafted in through a window. He caught a whiff of the scent of her body and his hands tightened spasmodically. Indra was filled with a sudden excitement.

There was a pause.

He imagined an almost imperceptible sway bringing her closer to him as she looked up into his eyes. A dry lump rose in Indra's throat, and he waited breathless for the words he was sure would emerge from those luscious lips, half parted now, a sigh escaping them; he ached to kiss them, savour their mystery.

He stirred—he was dreaming, as he always did when he saw her.

'Have you missed me?' he asked suddenly, wondering how to broach the topic he so desperately wanted to talk about—not wars but their wedding. 'I missed you. Everybody missed you,' he added.

She stiffened; she knew where the conversation was heading.

'I can't say that,' Ahalya said with such acute sadness that Indra felt his heart contract. 'I seemed to have missed a lot here,' she mumbled, looking vaguely around her till her eyes settled steadily on his. 'But you're looking thinner than before,' she said, floundering, trying to figure out a way to change the conversation.

'Don't! You always took some pleasure in teasing me, Ahalya!' he said with an injured look and tone.

'I'm not teasing you, Indra,' she retorted, something snapping in her. 'I am just awfully tired of everything. I wish my family would stop trying to marry me off!'

'I thought there was going to be a swayamwar,' he said weakly.

'Yes. But I don't want to get married,' she said, her tone flat and final.

It threw him. 'Still? But you will have to marry someone, someday. Why not me?' he said wildly.

'I was hoping you would have forgotten me and fallen in love with another girl,' she said, so openly that it was cruel.

Indra winced.

'I hear there is this princess, Sachi, who is besotted with you?' Ahalya asked, hoping to lighten the mood.

Indra laughed. 'Nonsense. Sachi is someone I met recently. She is an Asura princess and I am a Deva king.'

'Which makes it more interesting!' smiled Ahalya. 'You'll have to fight for her.'

Again, Indra felt unreasonably hurt by her banter. He gave a small smile and said, 'She isn't the kind of girl to fall in love with anyone.'

'There's never been a girl who wouldn't fall in love if she's given the chance,' Ahalya said quietly. 'I should have thought you would be more perceptive about these things, Indra.'

Was she mocking him? It hurt. Was she honestly pushing him towards some other woman?

'Never mind Sachi,' he said a little impatiently. 'I am not interested in her.'

As he said her name, Indra was suddenly ashamed of his callousness. He had met Sachi during one of his tours. She was the daughter of Emperor Puloman, a powerful Asura who was very pious and encouraged several rishis and scholars in his kingdom. He was said to have supported Shukracharya, the priest of the Danavas and Asuras, to take up research on immortality. This bit of news had flustered him when Sachi revealed it to him ... but Ahalya's unexpected return had distracted him from his worries.

Ahalya frowned before saying, 'But then she *is* in love with you. Or she would not pursue you so openly.'

Startled, Indra stared at her. Then he realised she was stating a fact and he smiled, passing his hand over his immaculately groomed hair.

'Not quite, but perhaps something like that,' he conceded. 'If she was you, I would have to be careful.' He laughed nervously.

There was a pause, then Ahalya said, 'I am not her. Nor is she me. Don't take her so lightly, Indra. Sachi is in love with you and from what I have heard, her father is ready to marry her off to his most trusted general, Vrut, who is madly in love with her. You might lose your admirer.'

Indra felt a surge of irritation. He shrugged. 'It is up to Sachi ...'

Ahalya shook her head. 'She won't give up on you, that's what they say. And you have, of course, an irresistible appeal to women.'

Was it compliment or censure?

'You know I could never love anybody but you,' he said simply.

Ahalya continued, restlessly shaking her head, 'Have you forgotten what I said last year?'

'No, not you or your words. But I like the way you do not love me,' he whispered thickly, his tone passionate.

His words seemed to make love to her; his passion aroused her. She could hear her heart beat rapidly. Was she sincerely moved, or was she feeling sorry for him? Or was she being carried along by the wave of her own emotions? How was it that she could make this man love her so ardently and not that man whom she loved?

In a swift flash, Ahalya became remote to him. Her quiet, calm expression had returned, and he realised her barrier had come up. For no reason he could quite put his finger on, he began to feel uneasy.

'What is the matter, Ahalya?'

He recognised the same wretchedness in her eyes that he often saw reflected in his own eyes. She *was* unhappy.

He stood perfectly still, his nerves in wild clamour, afraid that if he moved he would pull her into his arms.

'I cannot marry you,' she said finally. Flatly.

Indra felt his nerve ends prickle.

'Why?!' he cried, erupting in volcanic rage. Ahalya stepped back. 'I suppose you think I'm not worth having, but I would be so suitable for you, Ahalya!'

'I don't love *you*, you know that!' she cried, her eyes frantic.

A thousand words of fury, pride, passion, hate, tenderness, bitterness wrestled on his lips. A wave of emotion washed over him, carrying with it the last residue of patience, perseverance and honour.

His voice altered, dropping dangerously. 'You don't love *me*,' he said slowly. 'I hoped you would someday. And I waited. I am still ready to wait for you, but not for a lifetime.' He exhaled sharply. 'But for the first time, I hear decisiveness in your voice.' He paused, controlling himself. 'Is there someone else?' he asked, his eyes glinting.

A cold fear sliced through her; Indra seemed so different suddenly.

She remained silent, too terrified to let him know the whole truth.

'I *shall* win you, I *shall* woo you, Ahalya. You shall be *mine*!' he said savagely, his beautiful face twisted with rage.

His golden eyes blazed down with a fire that Ahalya thought would consume her. And for the first time since she had known him, Indra slid out of character. His thin face tightened, the anger taut on his chiselled features, his eyes slowly froze into chips of grey ice. Suddenly, this was a face of utter ruthlessness … a predator's face; it sent a chill through Ahalya.

'Do you hear?' There was a harsh note in his voice she had never heard before. He paused, regaining his breath. 'I had come to let you and your father know that—that I accept the challenge,' he said. 'I shall go round the world and come back a victor, winning you at your swayamwar, and we shall wed in front of all the three worlds I will have travelled for you. You cannot refuse me then. And thus, I shall have you. It is just a matter of time.'

11

The Assessment

From his vantage point atop the thatched roof he was repairing, Gautam spotted the slight figure of Rishi Narad approaching his ashram. He was not surprised to see his friend: they were working together on the Dharmasutras and he assumed the rishi had come to visit him in this regard.

'Oh, esteemed journalist, what news do you have today?' Gautam called out, smiling.

Narad was a young man with light coloured hair, a fair, almost pink face, and quick, smooth movements. He was looking the worse for wear at the moment: he was panting for breath after the long walk.

'So you agree I am a journalist!'

'And more! You claim to be a "divine messenger", but you are nothing less or better than a gossip!' Gautam said, laughing. It was good to see his old friend again.

Catching his breath, Narad looked up at Gautam and responded with a broader grin. 'I *am* a journalist, the very first. I observe, I write and I inform! I let people know what's happening where! And please don't disparage it as gossip, it *is* news, my friend.'

'Hmm, just information of the unconfirmed kind,' said Gautam, grinning. 'So what have you got to tell me today?'

'The biggest news going around is Ahalya's swayamwar,' announced Narad brightly.

Gautam stiffened and his smile became fixed as he pretended to rearrange straw on the roof.

'King Mudgal has come up with an incredible condition: the one who travels fastest round the three worlds will gain the hand of his daughter,' informed Narad, observing Gautam's taut face.

Gautam refrained from responding. He jumped down smoothly from the roof and walked up to his friend. Narad felt immediately dwarfed. He noticed a fresh streak of grey in his hair since he had last seen the rishi—it helped to soften his face.

Narad looked at him closely. 'You remember Ahalya, don't you?' he enquired innocently. 'She studied here—'

'No, she was just given shelter,' Gautam corrected. 'She wasn't my student.'

'Nor were you her guru, agreed,' Narad said, nodding knowingly. 'You gave her refuge when she needed it.'

Gautam merely shrugged at that; his face remained expressionless though a vein pounded at the temple.

'So that same Ahalya is soon to get wedded,' continued Narad, his manner typically effusive. 'It's touted to be the biggest wedding in the kingdom—and why not, she *is* the most beautiful princess in the country!' Narad added, throwing his friend a sidelong glance.

Gautam's face remained inscrutable.

'In the past, Lord Brahma has created several beautiful women, but legend goes that Ahalya surpasses all—she has been blessed by Brahma to make even the apsara Urvashi jealous!' Narad said with a sigh. His voice dropped to a conspiratorial whisper. 'Is she that beautiful, Gautam? I did not get to see her when she was here ...' he grumbled. 'Is she as ethereal as everyone has said?'

'Yes she is,' Gautam interrupted tightly.

'And she's supposed to be brilliant too, is she not? You yourself mentioned it once.'

Gautam stood on the balls of his feet and looked down at Narad, his eyes brooding. 'I thought you had come here to continue our work on the Dharmsutras,' he said, frowning. 'The last time we met, we were checking on the references of previous authorities on individual and social behaviour defining personal and criminal law—'

'That's your field entirely,' groaned Narad, placing his mahathi, his special veena, down. 'I am more interested in constructing a concise format for the sutras, to match your terse sentence structure—which, I personally feel, should remain ambiguous.'

'But that would make it difficult for the reader to comprehend the sutras,' Gautam said, scowling.

'My dear friend, those who read our texts are supposed to be intelligent enough to understand what we write!' riposted Narad, clapping his khartal as if to emphasise his point.

'I disagree,' said Gautam. 'Being obscure does not mean being erudite. The communication between the writer and the reader has to have a certain clarity, not arrogant assumption.'

'I thought you'd want to see what I had done till now,' Narad said. 'I did want to ask, though—the sutras you have composed so far are essentially commentaries on personal and social ethics. Do you have any new ideas? Perhaps on the rules for love and marriage?' Narad teased, his eyes sparkling with mischief. 'But then, what would you know, you are a confirmed celibate ...' he said slyly, '... who can never fall in love or marry.'

'Get serious,' snapped Gautam. The muscles on either side of his jaw stood out suddenly.

'I *am* very serious,' announced Narad, his face solemn. 'I am telling you the biggest news everyone is seriously talking about: Ahalya's wedding and how Indra is sure to win her in this unusual contest. He is her brother's close friend as well, you know.'

'So?' asked Gautam coldly.

'So, Indra is probably the favoured suitor anyway,' supplied Narad succinctly. 'I have heard Queen Nalayani strongly favours him as well. But in any case, right now, all the kings and nobles, even some revered rishis—' He paused here pointedly. '—have embarked on the remarkable journey that this swayamwar demands. The country suddenly seems to be depleted of kings: they are all busy going round the world!' The young sage sniggered.

'How, pray, does this affect our work?' barked Gautam.

'Why are you so irritable?' asked Narad curiously. 'I am just letting you know about Ahalya as she studied here; and I heard she was quite taken with you—and the ashram,' he said suavely, ignoring Gautam's dark look.

'You seem to be hearing a lot of nonsense! As I said, Ahalya was a guest, not my student,' he said tersely.

'Whom you looked after so well,' said Narad, nodding thoughtfully.

Gautam gave him a sharp look, but before he could respond, an unusual sound interrupted them.

Narad looked bewildered. 'What was that?'

'It's the cry of a new-born calf,' replied Gautam excitedly, nimbly stepping over a rock as he quickened his pace.

Narad followed the long strides of his friend, who was rushing towards the shed across the courtyard. He was led to a small barn, the morning light streaming in, spotlighting a white cow in the process of giving birth to a calf, now almost completely out.

Gautam carefully checked both the mother, Surabhi, and her calf, and heaved a sigh of relief. 'They are both healthy!'

He folded his hands and reverentially circumambulated them thrice. Then, he went out and repeated the process around a Shivling placed in the courtyard. Gautam was a known Shiva devotee.

Narad watched his friend, an idea slowly stirring in his quick mind.

'You have received the Lord's blessings,' he murmured as his friend returned to the shed.

Gautam noticed the change in Narad's tone.

'Do you realise what you have done?' asked Narad, his small, light eyes glinting.

Gautam frowned, puzzled.

'By circumambulating the cow and calf and the Shivling, you have travelled round the three worlds!'

'I did it out of respect,' said Gautam, his eyes soft as he gazed at the suckling calf and the mother. 'Is it not the most moving sight?'

'Gautam, Gautam, realise what you have done!' repeated Narad. There was an excited urgency in his tone. 'You have unwittingly participated in Ahalya's swayamwar!'

Gautam's head shot up, and for the first time the articulate rishi looked bewildered, finding himself at a loss for words.

'You have travelled the three worlds!' Narad said, gleefully. 'By circumambulating the birthing cow, you have won the contest Lord Brahma and King Mudgal put forth! You know that as per the Vedas, the cow at the time of bearing a calf is equal to the three worlds. By saying your prayers just now and paying them respect, you have fulfilled the swayamwar's condition ... unintentionally. Or was it intentional?' Narad teased. 'Oh, I always knew Lord Brahma had a hand in this! He always considered you the best! You are his favourite, you know; he sees in you the most profound intelligence. I suspect he had already selected you for Ahalya!'

A dark flush washed over Gautam's craggy face. He turned on his heel angrily and crossed the long courtyard. Narad followed him anxiously, but there was a smile on his face.

'What is there to be so furious about?' he exclaimed. 'I say what I observe—'

'These are just wild contentions! What do you see?' growled Gautam.

'A man who does not want me to voice his thoughts,' replied Narad, his voice unusually soft. '... his desires, his longing.'

'Have you gone crazy?!' There was a harsh note in Gautam's voice. Narad felt a shiver; was he crossing the line of cordiality and friendship?

Narad decided to persist. 'Not me, Gautam, *you* have gone crazy—well, almost,' he accused bravely. 'Since Ahalya left the ashram, you have been singularly morose and moody. Why do you not admit it, friend? You *are* in love with Ahalya!' he announced with a deadpan face, but trembling inside.

'Don't call me a love-lost fool!' Gautam said in a strangled voice, his jaw clenched.

There was a deliberate pause, an uneasy stillness that Narad refused to break, allowing the older man to collect his composure.

Gautam wished to hear no more, but he could not silence the roar in his heart. Had he fallen in love with the girl? Always analytical of his own feelings, he had pondered over this question, the answer to which he knew but did not wish to acknowledge. He had tried to be indifferent to Ahalya, to his raging feelings for her. And in his fear of this knowledge, he had lashed out at her. He had treated her cruelly, even hated her for what she was doing to him. It was an odd sensation for a man of his spiritual prominence to be moved just by the heady whiff of a girl like Ahalya, and yet he was shaken; he could not deny it. It would be nice, he thought achingly, if she were here and could come in now and be kind to him as she was to all. He would have liked her to sit by the window and talk to him as they used to. He wanted to hear the sound of her voice, to look at her, to have her near him.

Ahalya suited him. Oddly enough, he decided, she was his type of person. He hadn't ever thought of being with a woman before, to love, to live with her, to cherish, but now his heart kept prodding, while his mind resisted ... Was Ahalya the one for him? Or more importantly, was he the one for her?

'Why do you keep denying it?' demanded Narad. 'Why don't you take this as a sign—even fate and destiny are with you, Gautam! Indra may well consider himself the best suitor and the only one who can win the challenge, but you did it right here! I say it's you who have won her while he is still at it! You love Ahalya, Gautam, now go marry her!'

Gautam looked away, awkward and uncertain.

'But does *she* love me?' he asked with a small grimace, staring abstractedly at his reflection in the small pond. He was only too aware of his lean, reedy physique, his narrow chest and the coarse dark hair that covered his long limbs. This was no body for a woman to fall in love with. Yet, he had glimpsed the look of adoration in her eyes. Or was it infatuation? But not love for a man of his courage, vision and ambition, he thought bitterly. He exhaled a long sigh. He might not be physically the most attractive, but there was nothing the matter with his brain. He had every confidence in his mental alertness, his ingenuity, his clear-sightedness. It was ridiculous for a man of his abilities and mental equipment to be crippled with such feeble thoughts— it was as ridiculous as expecting a princess to fall in love with a sage. But he had been over this argument so often before that he was sick of it ...

'Why do you presume she prefers Indra to you?' chided Narad. 'Ahalya is a clever girl who respects intelligence more than looks, I'm sure.'

Gautam regarded his reflection again. Till he had met her, he had not been acquainted with the incredible power of beauty and the possibility for shape and form to have the ability to instantly please the aesthetic sense. But her beauty transcended the corporeal; it was a combination of virtues that appealed to the intellect and moral sense as well. The sallow-complexioned, craggy face he saw reflected in the pond taunted him. But for the eyes, it was the face of any average person. His eyes were the only true indication of his worth, he decided: soot-black eyes, alert, passionate. He would simply have to make do with what nature had given him.

Narad had been watching his friend's face, astutely deducing the doubts clamouring through his mind. He had known Gautam now for more than five years, having first met him after he had just started this ashram. Gautam had engaged him for help with the rhyming and grammatical structure of his works, but soon, over time, they had become friends.

The enterprise that Gautam had taken on was a hard one, and there had been difficulties, but Narad had quickly learned that difficulties and disappointments only made Gautam work harder. He discovered that Gautam had an indefatigable spirit. Often, he had gone without rest and food as they worked together tirelessly for weeks. Narad had found strength in Gautam's daunting perseverance. His optimism and determination had been infectious. Narad knew he must succeed in whatever he sought to do. No one who worked as hard as he did, even in the face of constant setbacks, could fail to succeed.

Looking at Gautam now, Narad realised just how far he had come and what an authority he had become, so much so that he was no longer of real use to Gautam; he was just one of many who considered it a privilege to serve him. Gautam, in his unassuming way, did not realise how extraordinary he was, and Narad was secretly shocked that such a gifted personality could harbour any doubts about himself.

'Go to King Mudgal's court, Gautam, and claim her before it's too late,' coaxed Narad, hoping his words would propel Gautam into action.

'She's no prize to be claimed. She's a woman to be cherished!' exclaimed Gautam.

'That sounds very poetic!' Narad said, smiling. 'Philosopher that you are, use your logic but follow your heart for once.'

Hesitation flickered in the shadowy eyes.

'How can I claim her against her wishes? Why would she choose to marry me over the handsome Indra? He is the king of gods, not a poor, old mendicant.'

Narad's amazement turned swiftly to indignance. 'When did you start floundering in self-pity? You are known to be an intellectual giant—how can you entertain such trivial thoughts,' he remonstrated. 'I have seen how love weakens one with desire, but here it's weakening your very thinking! These are but inane self-doubts! Are you going to allow Indra to win the contest just because you are assailed with some irrational self-doubt?' demanded Narad, scowling into his friend's face. 'Are you allowing him to have her?'

Gautam hesitated again. He remembered Ahalya as he first saw her. He had been in the midst of his work and had heard the soft tinkle of her anklets as she followed Uttank, who was leading her to her hut. He had caught a glimpse of her slim figure in gossamer silk, the long, diaphanous angavastra and her fragrance trailing entrancingly. He had unconsciously strained further, curious to see what the girl looked like, but had caught himself, feeling foolish. Somehow, it had felt like it was just the two of them alone in this big, silent ashram, and the only sound that came to him was the hard thudding of his heart.

It was only the next morning that he had been able to see her, though not yet her face. The girl was standing at one of the partitions, her back to him. He stared at her, wishing to see her face, but as she did not look round, he had to be content to eye her slim shoulders, her straight back. He had always prided himself on being invulnerable to feminine beauty. He was surprised to find that she interested him. It was an odd sensation. This girl had instantly attracted him, probably because he had never seen such loveliness before. And perhaps the fact that she was helpless and needed protection had instantly forged an intangible bond between them.

All right, admit it, he thought savagely. *You* are *in love with the girl.* For the first time in his life, he had discovered someone he wanted to care for. He did not want to get hurt, but even more than that, he did not want her to get hurt; she was so fragile. It was ironic given the way he had hurt her himself in the past, after the beastly things he had said to her to push her away from his growing feelings for her. He had seen the naked adoration on her face, yet he had been unsure, fearful. He desired no complications. And he had turned her away ...

Now, so many months after her departure, he found himself still struggling with the emotions she evoked in him, and however much he denied it, they had only grown stronger. He knew that unless he took action, he would lose her. The thought threw him into a new panic. He would do anything to keep her ...

Gautam shut his eyes and opened them after a pause; there was a new glint in them. His heart began to beat unevenly. He knew then that his destiny was to be linked with this girl's. He had helped her and taken her in, but what he had not known was that she, in return, would have a hold on him; that it was he who would come to be grateful. He went over to Narad and tapped his friend's arm.

Fear and an intensity of emotion drove his decision.

12

The Choice

'Has any contender returned?' asked Ahalya dully. She could not bear to utter the name Indra, though she knew, as everyone else did, that only he could be the winner.

There was a long pause.

'What is it?' she asked, her uneasy eyes searching Divodas's face. She had expected him to be happier than he seemed now, but his handsome face wore a worried frown.

'Indra has not yet returned ...' he said.

'You want him to win, don't you?' she said bitterly.

'Yes,' he replied. 'It will do all of us good.'

She was too dejected to argue.

'Indra *is* the best,' her brother said more kindly.

She shrugged.

'Any other girl would be glad!' A peevishness crept into his otherwise mild tone. 'Why do you insist on being so unhappy about your wedding?'

She bristled. 'Would it mean anything to you if I said I *cannot* love Indra, but love someone else?' she said, wanting to wipe the virtuous look off her brother's face.

Divodas was momentarily stunned, his eyebrows shooting up in shock. 'You are in love with someone else? But why did you not say so?' he demanded.

She bit her lip. 'What could I have said? Besides, the man I love does not love me ...'

'Who is he?' her brother asked.

'It does not matter, not now anyway,' she said.

Divodas glanced at his sister. She sat on the edge of the couch, clearly unhappy, not like a bride-to-be. Her face was pale, and her red-rimmed eyes were glassy with unshed tears.

His heart contracted. Divodas stood by the window, looking through the sheer muslin curtains into the palace grounds below. He had not expected this. His eyes desperately scanned the courtyard below, willing Indra to pull up in his chariot. But his sister did not love Indra, he thought bleakly, her heart belonged to someone else.

'You can't be unhappy all your married life,' he muttered to his sister, helplessly. But he wasn't looking at Ahalya; he felt too wretched to face her. 'Has that man you talk of participated in the contest?' he asked finally.

'He does not love me, brother, why then would he partake in the contest?' she said.

'*Who* is he? Who is this unusual man who does not love you? You, whom everyone wishes to marry?'

Ahalya remained silent.

Divodas reluctantly left the window and stood over her.

'This mystery man seems to have made a philosopher out of you, I see,' he remarked cynically, racking his brain furiously, wondering who this man might be; he, who had the power to break his sister's heart. She barely knew anyone. She had always lived in this palace but for that one instance when she had gone to Rishi Gautam's ashram. She had not been the same since then. Had she met this man at the ashram? Some disciple of the rishi? Or was it Rishi Gautam himself? Divodas's heart vaulted in sudden trepidation.

'He's a rishi, isn't he?' he asked suddenly, crystallising his wild guess.

He noticed her stiffen. He was right!

He persisted. 'That's why he has not reciprocated.'

She stared at him, vulnerable and trapped, reading the words as they formed on his lips, her own white and trembling, the words frozen inside her.

'A rishi can marry if he wants; he does not have to remain celibate,' said Divodas, his tone reassuring, but he was thinking furiously. 'There are rishis participating in this contest too. He too could be—'

She shook her head, cutting him off.

'Then are you going to waste yourself pining for a man you cannot have? Or rather, one who does *not* want you?' he demanded harshly.

Ahalya flinched.

'Pull yourself together,' he said sternly. 'You have got to think rationally. And are you sure *you* love him?' he asked suddenly, fixing her with a solemn stare. 'From what I can surmise, he is a rishi. Are you in love with the man or just attracted to his mind?'

'No, do not think that I am confused,' she said fiercely. 'I know I love him. And I know I *don't* love Indra!'

Divodas gave an impatient shake of his head. 'This man, whoever he is, is clearly not for you. So why not marry Indra—

happily? He is in love with you, that's what matters! Is it not better to live with a man who loves you, than one who does not?'

She got up slowly and shakily.

'Please!' she whispered.

'No, Ahalya, don't run away from the situation you have created for yourself!' snapped Divodas angrily.

She turned to him, surprised at his harsh tone.

'Why did you not let us know of this sooner?' he demanded. 'Why did you allow the swayamwar to happen?'

'I tried, but ... but does it matter?' she asked desperately.

'Yes, it does, because I cannot bear to see you so wretched, Ahalya!' he blurted. 'This wedding is meant for *your* happiness; it's a decision that affects your *life*.' His hands balled into fists. 'Now it's too late to withdraw the swayamwar: you will have to marry whoever wins this darned contest!' He threw his hands up in frustrated fury. 'And it will be Indra,' he ended flatly.

She looked into his eyes and then covered her face with trembling hands. Divodas made no attempt to comfort her. He stood back and watched her sink slowly back on to the couch. She looked like a broken doll that has been tossed into a corner.

'Why did you not speak out when needed?' he asked, his tone gentler. 'If you had just told us before, we could have halted the swayamwar, if nothing else!'

She continued to sob quietly. 'I would have to marry someone someday, wouldn't I?' she said. 'For how long could I have pushed it?'

'You should have let us know the truth, instead of keeping quiet as is your habit.' He drew back exasperated. 'Silence can be interpreted as complicity, but it's not acquiescence, Ahalya. You avoid confrontation, that's your weakness, not wisdom!'

'I did what I thought would be best!' she said tremulously. She dropped back against the settee, an arm across her eyes. The white column of her throat jerked spasmodically as she struggled with her tears.

'I am doing what I have to,' she said, and slow tears began to run down her face. 'Oh, I have to, I have to, what else can I do?!'

It was the anguished cry of a child and it disturbed Divodas. He put his hand gently on her shoulder, but she threw it off so violently that he stepped back, startled.

'Pull yourself together,' Divodas said, now equally furious. 'You've got to think of others, not just yourself!'

'But that's what I have been doing all along, haven't I?' Her eyes flashed bright.

'By keeping silent?' he asked sardonically. 'If you had let us know before, we wouldn't be in this place at all! What about Father? By holding your swayamwar, he has invited all the kings of the world to participate. With what face can he now say that his daughter does not wish to marry anyone as she is in love with some man who does not return her feelings!' he exploded.

Then, seeing that she was getting consumed by her own misery, he caught hold of her roughly and pulled her up. His fingers circled her arm. 'Come on. Pull yourself together,' he repeated when he was sure she was looking at him.

Her face creased tearfully. 'Please, I can't go on. I can't stand it any longer!' she whimpered, gripping his wrists tightly. He could see she was desperate to avoid any responsibility or to have to make any decision.

'It is too late,' she muttered brokenly.

'I don't care,' he said, controlling his voice with an effort. 'And yes, it *is* too late now. You've got to go ahead with this—with a smile, not tears!' he said brutally as he held her rigidly, dragging her to her feet.

She twisted away from him and folding her arms defensively, she hugged herself tightly and nodded miserably. 'I'm sorry,' she said. 'Yes, I shall go ahead with it, of course ... !'

'Look more happy than you feel,' he said roughly.

Divodas knew he was being harsh on his sister. But he knew the realisation that her own reticence and her misplaced naiveté were partly the cause of her current unhappiness had shocked her. He guessed that the moment he left the chamber, she would collapse, and he was reluctant to leave her alone.

There was the sound of hurried footsteps. It was their mother. Her face was white, and she was breathless. She swayed slightly as she stood at the door. Then she swallowed and said: 'The winner has been announced!'

The moment Narad entered the court, King Mudgal knew something was amiss. Narad always arrived with intent, never by chance. What was he going to say now, Mudgal thought with rising trepidation, as he rose to his feet and bowed to the young seer.

'I have just met Lord Brahma,' Narad started in explanation for his presence at the royal court.

'Has he sent a message for me?' asked King Mudgal politely. 'Is it about the swayamwar—none of the contestants have returned yet.'

'But there is someone who has already gone around the three worlds—heaven, earth and the underworld. There is someone who can claim victory,' proclaimed Narad.

There was a collective gasp of surprise in the court.

'What, when?' Mudgal stammered. 'And why is it that he has not come here?'

'I am telling you what I conveyed to Lord Brahma,' said Narad mysteriously. 'That a man has already accomplished the impossible.'

'But Indra hasn't returned yet,' interrupted Queen Nalayani coldly.

Narad bowed to the regal lady. He had heard a lot about her. She was regarding him unsmilingly, with an aloofness that made him feel unwelcome. But no one could deter the irrepressible Narad.

'Who said it was Indra?' returned Narad, equally frosty. 'He may be using all his magical powers to win, but he has lost this time!'

There was unsuppressed glee in his voice. The animosity between Narad and Indra was legendary. Mudgal sighed. Both were egotistic, both trying to prove that they were the best at what they did, he thought wryly.

'Who is this secret winner, Narad? Don't talk in riddles as you always do,' pleaded Mudgal. 'Where is the winner? Let him present himself!'

'Don't you want to know how he won?' asked Narad.

'I am more keen to know who he is!' retorted the queen imperiously.

'It was Lord Brahma who came up with this challenge, and it is to him I went when I realised that the conditions have been met and the contest has its winner,' started Narad, knowing he was building up the tension. 'When I explained the situation, Lord Brahma agreed that this man had won the contest—and that he is worthy of marrying your daughter,' he said.

Narad was an incorrigible exhibitionist and was clearly enjoying being the centre of attention. He was happy to milk the moment.

'Lord Brahma declared that the first person to go around the three worlds—swarga, prithvi and pataal—shall win the hand of your daughter, Ahalya,' Narad said, dramatically. There was absolute silence in the court and his voice carried clearly. Each word was making Nalayani more nervous, and she clutched her silk stole.

'Kings and princes, gods and rishis, Devas and Daityas— they all made a mad scramble to compete in the challenge. Each wanted to win the fair hand of the most beautiful woman in the country! Of course, King Indra tried his hardest, employing all his super powers to meet the challenge,' Narad said, his lips curled in contempt. 'Meanwhile, as all of them raced around the world, there was one man who managed the feat right in his very backyard!'

'Who is this man?' demanded a pale Nalayani.

'And how is he the winner?' added Mudgal anxiously.

Narada gave a slow, benevolent smile. 'This man performed a pradakshina: he circumambulated Surabhi, the wish-bearing cow, while she gave birth, which denotes the panch bhuta— the five elements—as well as purity and fertility, Mother and Nature and the sustenance of human and cosmic life. Pradakshina is a form of meditation, a worship performed with utmost humility and devotion. It is a mark of respect, obeisance while bowing to the supreme divinity within us—'

'Everyone knows that,' interrupted Nalayani impatiently. 'The cow is a divine being so primordial that it is a symbol of the power of focus and manifestation.'

'Yes, and being a representative of a spectrum of diffused powers, the cow forms a link between the realms of all powers, gods and nature. According to the Vedas, through the solemn ritual of go-pradakshina, the sacred cow is equal to the three worlds, by identifying the four key elements of destination, movement, magnitude and motivation.'

'So say the Vedas, those ancient books of knowledge.' The queen smiled mirthlessly.

'The Vedas contain the revelations of sages enlightened after intense meditation. The texts have been preserved and revered for a long time. The Vedas are profound; they are the sruti literature, not the smriti! Each word and hymn has been carefully composed by rishis after inspired creativity, just as a potter moulds his pot and the sculptor hews rock!'

Mudgal had noted the change in Narad's tone; it contained a stinging reprimand for his wife. 'Yes, I know and I agree,' he said hastily. 'This man certainly has accomplished the condition that Lord Brahma told me to place for Ahalya's swayamwar.'

'Yes, and Brahma too concurs,' announced Narad grandly. 'He has agreed that this great man should marry Ahalya.'

'*Who* is he?' asked the queen.

Narad decided to finally reveal the mystery. He took a deep breath and said, 'Rishi Gautam.'

The silence that pervaded the court hall was loud and thunderous. Nalayani could almost hear her screaming heartbeats.

'No!' she whispered. But no one heard her; it was a silent scream only she could hear.

Mudgal's lined face broke into a genial, wide smile. 'Rishi Gautam!' he said warmly, awe in his voice.

Nalayani sat frozen on the throne.

'Yes, my dear king, and he has even deigned to come here to formally ask for your daughter's hand in marriage,' informed Narad.

Nalayani felt the world rushing by; everything was crumbling ...

Her eyes swivelled to the man who had just entered the hall. Rishi Gautam! She stifled a gasp of horror. Her Ahalya would be marrying *this* man? Her heart sank as the man approached them, walking confidently, almost arrogantly down the long hall.

Gautam was unfazed by the splendour of the palace and barely glanced at the ornate pillars and polished marble floor. He had never thought he would enter a palace again, not after his childhood days when his father, as the royal priest of King Bharat, resided in such luxurious mansions. Not that he had unhappy memories, but they had soon blurred with a contempt for royalty and all that it represented: power, politics, war and violence. As he walked towards the elaborately carved throne—which was as grandiose as expected—he was struck by a sudden thought. He was now going to bow to the very symbolic figure he despised, the king, whose daughter he wanted to marry.

Gautam was used to being looked at, but today he felt the stares were coming from more than mere curiosity about his reputation as a seer, or his shabby looks. It was because he had dared to woo, win and would wed the loveliest princess in the land.

The atmosphere was as warm and festive as a funeral. The queen regarded him stonily as he stood straight and tall in front of her and the king. She lifted her eyebrows as her icy eyes scrutinised him in a way that she hoped would unnerve him. But it had no such effect on the unsmiling man in front of her. He met her eyes with a steady scrutiny of his own.

Looking at her, Gautam thought how very different she was from Ahalya. There was definitely a physical resemblance between mother and daughter, yet how much more beauty, how much more character, was in Ahalya's face. He had met the queen now and he didn't think much of her, but was prepared to admit prejudice. She was as a queen would be—predictably haughty.

Mudgal had quickly got up to greet the rishi. He bowed low and moved forward to touch the man's feet. Nalayani's heart squeezed with rage. They would have to pay obeisance to *this* man, she acknowledged bitterly, rising stiffly and following suit.

'I owe you a lot,' started Mudgal. 'You saved my daughter's life,' he said with thick emotion.

'I did nothing of the sort,' said the rishi.

'You are being humble, sir, but I am forever indebted,' said Mudgal.

Gautam shook his head. '*I* come here asking today, not you, O king.'

Nalayani flinched. *Ahalya, my poor girl! She will have to marry this man!*

Mudgal nodded his head gratefully. 'I shall be honoured to serve you.'

'You are greeting your son-in-law, king,' interrupted Narad. 'As I said, it is he who has won your daughter's hand in this swayamwar.'

'And I am honoured,' replied the king, his hands folded.

'But your daughter,' said Gautam tersely. 'Does she want to marry me?'

Mudgal looked momentarily taken aback. Nalayani grabbed her chance, seeing a sliver of hope.

'I shall let my daughter know the news, sir,' she said, her hands folded but head held proud and straight. 'But if she refuses, will you agree with her decision?'

'She cannot refuse,' reminded Narad softly. 'It is her swayamwar and the rules were set. Gautam is the winner, whom she has to marry!'

Gautam ignored him.

'Yes, I shall respect her decision,' he said without hesitation. 'I do not wish to marry a reluctant princess.'

Nalayani could barely suppress her relief: this scruffy rishi would not be able to wed her daughter after all!

She smiled suddenly; it wasn't a pleasant smile.

'I shall get Ahalya and she will announce her decision herself.'

13

The Swayamwar

'The winner has been announced, and is here in court!'

Ahalya lifted her shoulders in an indifferent shrug. But one look at her mother's alarmed expression and she knew something was amiss. Her mother looked as if she had seen a ghost—Ahalya had never seen her in such a state.

'Is Indra back already?' asked Divodas.

'It's not Indra!' exclaimed his mother harshly.

Ahalya felt a weight lift off her heavy heart.

'Then ... who is it?' Divodas asked, puzzled.

'Rishi Gautam!' spat her mother.

Ahalya sat down suddenly as if the strength had gone out of her legs, and her face went white. Then she felt the gush of blood and bliss rushing in, making her heart race erratically.

She stared at her mother, her eyes glistening, her smile dazzling.

Nalayani could see at once Ahalya's physical transformation on hearing the news. Her lovely face seemed stunned, then suffused with unrestrained joy. Nalayani sucked in her breath; her daughter looked elated!

Confused, Nalayani dropped back against the couch, her hand held at her quivering chin, looking from her son to daughter. Divodas had an expression of sudden comprehension, as if some truth had dawned upon him. He glanced at his sister, his eyes narrowed and knowing.

'Is he the man, Ahalya?' he asked softly.

Ahalya nodded beatifically.

'What is it that I don't know?' demanded Nalayani. 'I came here to let you know that Rishi Gautam has won your hand by circumambulating a cow. *That*—' She paused and then said bitterly, '—is supposed to be translated into going around the three worlds! But I won't have it, it's preposterous—a sage marrying a princess!'

'It's happened before, Ma,' remarked Divodas laconically.

'What's preposterous about it, Ma?' asked Ahalya and turned to her brother, her face awash with shimmering happiness. '*He* loves me, Divodas, he loves *me*!' she cried.

'Are you mad, child?' interposed Nalayani wildly. 'What are you saying?'

'That I love him and he loves me; that's why he came here!' wept Ahalya, tears of relief coursing down her pale cheeks. 'That's why he is here,' she repeated thickly, her hands trembling at her white throat.

'*You* are in love with *him*?' repeated Nalayani dully.

But one look at her daughter and she had her answer.

She covered her face with shaking hands. Why had she not seen the truth earlier, she thought, throwing her daughter a despairing glance.

'He is *old*, Ahalya,' she argued desperately.

'He's kind,' Ahalya said. 'That's something you wouldn't understand.'

Nalayani snorted. 'Kind? My dear, you sound as if you were raised without love, imprisoned in this palace by us tyrants!'

Ahalya smiled. It was a secret, complacent smile that startled her mother. 'You judge others by yourself,' she said softly. 'He's kind. That's why he helped us in the first place and gave me refuge in the ashram.'

'Don't talk like a fool,' Nalayani said. 'He helped you because rishis are meant to help kings when they are in need—after all, we give them protection! He's got a plan. There's something behind it all. He's not in love with you! Nor you with him, you fool! You are simply enamoured of the novelty he represents. He is *different*, that's why ...'

But her words seemed to harden her daughter's resolve; Nalayani could see it in her eyes, which glinted with a sudden fierceness, her expression changing from obstinacy to hostility.

'He is wise and good and kind,' she repeated stubbornly.

'Stop saying he's been kind. No one's kind these days unless they have an iron in the fire. You've got to be realistic, Ahalya!'

'I do know I love him,' Ahalya said firmly, aware that at the back of her mind, doubt was assailing her. She remembered the look of hesitancy on Gautam's face when he had chatted with her on her last night at the ashram. She had thought it was indifference ... Was it? What had changed his feelings? Well, she wasn't going to tell her mother that, but her mind was troubled. She chewed her lower lip, thinking. She was learning more about her mother than her feelings for Gautam.

'You are a princess, my dear, you *cannot* marry a seer! He's old, he's poor, he can't keep you in the luxury you are used to, he ...' Nalayani realised she was rambling wildly. She was desperate to rip at the blindfold of sentimentality that draped her daughter's mind and foolish heart. How could her mild daughter turn so militant? The meek don't become rebels, she thought dismally. First her insistence to study, now this man ...

'You wouldn't be happy, dear,' she pleaded, probing, trying to find a weakness in Ahalya's armour. 'It might be all right for a year or so, but you'll regret it, that's what I fear. Oh dear, can't you see? He's not good for you! Worse, what if he wears you down? You are beautiful now but beauty wanes. Then how do you think he will like you?'

It was a shot in the dark, but it brought a deep flush to Ahalya's face. 'I am sure he is not in love with me for my beauty,' she said in consternation.

'Then what?' said Nalayani, with a snort. 'He's supposed to be a genius. You are bright, Ahalya, but not a brain that a man would be attracted to. If he wants you at all, it is for your looks! Just as you want him for his intelligence and not his looks. But you will regret this. Don't be under this misapprehension or you'll disgrace him some day,' Nalayani said, feeling that she had gained a point and pressing her advantage. 'He has nothing to offer but his brains and you have nothing to offer but your beauty.'

'I won't listen to you!' Ahalya burst out. 'You're unkind, and what you are insinuating is untrue. We love each other, and nothing you say will make any difference.'

Ahalya folded her arms in front of her, and fixed her mother with a belligerent gaze.

'You are a cruel person, I know, and you can hurl the cruellest words at me, it won't hurt. But, Ma, why? Isn't loving each other enough?'

'Love!' scoffed Nalayani, trying to keep the edge of her temper out of her voice. 'Love can't feed a hungry stomach or swathe your body in silk!'

'I don't need to eat much, and I don't need to wear silk,' said Ahalya, her smile mocking.

If only she could reach her, Nalayani thought, livid. She controlled herself with difficulty. It was no use showing her anger; Ahalya would only move further away. She had to talk to her, reason with her. She had disliked Gautam even without knowing him; she distrusted him more now. But the more she said anything about him, the more it was bound to be taken wrongly by her love-addled daughter. Anything she said would be useless, but she *had* to try.

She threw her son a look of appeal.

'Let her marry him, Ma,' he said curtly. 'It is her decision.'

'But it is wrong! She doesn't know anything about life!' cried Nalayani. 'She's lived cloistered in a palace till now, and you expect me to send her off to a jungle with an old, mad man?!'

'But she will be happy with him, not Indra,' broke in Divodas gently.

'How can you, too, say that?' Nalayani said.

'Ahalya would have been miserable with Indra, Ma. We didn't know she was in love with Gautam. And he with her. Or he wouldn't be here. You can't stop her, you can't stop this wedding. Give them your blessings, Ma.'

'*No!*' The despairing sob tore her throat.

Her frustration abruptly dissolved into grief: she did not have the power to provide the happy fate she had intended for her child. The sorrow was overwhelming; that her daughter would not have the future she had dreamt of—as the queen of Indra, reigning over Indralok—but instead toil mercilessly at some decrepit ashram with a rishi. She recoiled in horror, hoping desperately for some miracle to halt this madness.

There was a crashing thunderbolt. Divodas knew what it was even before he rushed to the window.

'It's Indra, isn't it?' Nalayani said eagerly. 'He has arrived!'

'Too late,' said Ahalya happily, as she peered over her brother's shoulder.

Down below, at the porch of the palace, Matali, Indra's charioteer, drew short and halted the resplendent chariot of the king of gods. It was a sight to see, and every time Indra visited them, Ahalya could not help but admire this gorgeous vehicle, which was said to be the envy of even Surya, the Sun God, and Agni, the God of Fire, both owners of flamboyant chariots themselves. With flecks of gold, a thick flagstaff encrusted with gems—most of them were flaming cat's eye, Ahalya guessed correctly—and tinkling with a hundred fitted bells, the chariot looked glorious in the hot afternoon sun. It was yoked to a long fleet of magnificent tawny horses, tossing their handsome heads and flowing manes.

'I think we need to be in court,' said Divodas, his lips compressed in a grim line.

'Yes,' said her mother with a nod, collecting her composure. She held the folds of her angavastra and, with impeccable bearing, walked towards the door. 'I had promised that Ahalya would announce her decision herself at court,' she said coldly.

Ahalya flinched, her heart quaking. She fervidly wanted to meet Gautam again and declare to the world that she was ready to marry him. But for one daunting thought—she would have to face Indra as well.

She allowed herself to be led by her mother, her happiness curdled by her churning thoughts. She felt a knot of fear that seemed to tighten at every step, rising to suffocate her as she drew closer to the royal assembly hall.

The first person her eyes fell on was Gautam. Parched, she drank in the sight of him. He was leaning slightly forward, as if observing everything intently. His thick, dark hair was smoothed away from his face. He seemed leaner, his cheekbones more pronounced, his face taut and tanned and unsmiling, without the wry amusement lurking in his dark eyes, his lips straight and stern; his eyebrows, dark like a raven's wings, were furrowed.

But everything changed the moment he saw her: the thin line of his lips widened into a glorious smile, his dark eyes lit up, ablaze with an intensity that made her heart somersault, and she felt oddly weak at the knees. She wanted to run and fling her arms around him. Discretion halted her ... that, and the white-hot wrath on Indra's face. He was not addressing the king, not Narad, not Gautam. He was looking at her, his eyes crazed with fury.

The pink-hued light streaming in through a window accentuated the faint flush on her face. Her eyes were bright, and there was a radiance on her face that transfigured her and made her look even more beautiful, if that was possible. Her beauty enraged him.

'How did this happen?' Indra shouted. 'How did this rishi manage to win you? You are *mine*!'

The raw hurt and anger unnerved her. She could say nothing, shocked by his frenzied eyes and the wild despair on his face. Indra gazed back at her, plunging into sorrow, swept up by a wave of hungry longing for her. The Lord help him, he was her slave!

He scarcely recognised the forlorn girl of the last few months. The blazing red silk she was wearing set off her figure and her complexion; her bejewelled hair had golden tints in it. He was certain now that she had fallen for this rishi, and the hot flame of jealousy flared again.

Ahalya had once offered him a little hope, and he had lived on it. But now ... Indra raised his clenched fists, his face contracted with fury. She had made him look like a stupid little lovelorn fool, while she had fallen for another man instead. It was Gautam she loved! Gautam she was thinking about now. He had been such a fool. She had humiliated him in front of all; the world would laugh at him.

'You were to be mine!' he repeated thickly.

Ahalya looked beseechingly at him, imploring him to keep calm. 'No, I never was,' she said, her hands unconsciously going to her thudding heart.

Divodas stepped between the two. His eyes darkened in warning. 'There's no need to get excited about this, Indra. Please. I know you are disappointed—so are we—but I care more for my sister's happiness than our hopes for her future. The rishi has won the challenge and won my sister's hand—and heart,' he said, glancing at Ahalya. 'And she has agreed to marry Rishi Gautam.'

'She cannot!' Indra thundered. 'I am the only god worthy of her! She was promised to me!'

'Promised?' Divodas asked, surprised. 'By whom?'

Indra glanced at Nalayani, and his glance was followed by all. Nalayani could feel all eyes on her in the room.

'Yes, I wanted Indra to be my son-in-law, and if I had my way, I would still want it to happen,' she said assertively. 'I am so sorry, Indra, but I tried as much as I could. I wanted you to wed her but ...' Her voice trailed away as she furiously clenched her hands under her husband's glare.

'I recall what you said to me out here, in this very palace,' Indra said. 'That Ahalya could and would one day be mine. That I would marry her eventually!'

'But then there was the contest,' intervened Divodas firmly. 'And Rishi Gautam has been declared the winner.'

Indra snarled at him. 'By doing a pradakshina?'

'That notwithstanding,' said Divodas quietly, 'it is also Ahalya's choice.'

'You well know the importance of a parikrama around a cow,' interrupted Narad, his tone severe.

'Yes, of course I know that, but it is not fair,' snapped Indra, beside himself with rage, one clenched fist beating his right thigh. 'It is *not* fair!'

'Yes, you would feel it is unfair that you spent so many days and so much time and effort travelling around the world, while the rishi did it within a few minutes!' remarked Narad cruelly. 'But then that's the difference between bravado and intelligent thought and action, yes? You must be tired, Indra, why don't you rest?'

Indra made a slight movement towards Narad, but then controlled himself. His eyes narrowed, now fully focused not on Ahalya but on the smirking Narad.

A note of doubt crept into his voice. 'Was this planned? It was Lord Brahma who came up with this strange contest. Is it just a coincidence that it is Lord Brahma's favourite person, Rishi Gautam, who has won it? Is that how it was to be? Ahalya was meant for Gautam?' he spat.

'Yes, for once, you are right,' said Narad happily. 'Lord Brahma wished it so. And it happened. Brahmadev created Ahalya—the girl who lacked nothing—and made her a divya soundarya murti: the epitome of beauty. And since then, Brahmadev has wondered who deserves to be the perfect companion for this perfect woman,' explained Narad, glancing at a bewildered Ahalya. 'He decided that only a person with immense self-possession, self-command and self-restraint—with akhanda, teevra, nishtha—could be hers. And in his eyes, only Gautam fit this description.'

Noticing the look of shock on Gautam's face, Narad remarked, 'The test for you, O great rishi, was not this challenge at all. It was the time when Ahalya was sent to your ashram ...'

Ahalya held her breath; Gautam went still.

'... and how you responded to her,' Narad continued gravely. 'Brahmadev decided to test you then, Gautam. When Ahalya was opportunely sent to your ashram as planned by him and King Mudgal ...'

Ahalya threw her father a bewildered look; a sanguine smile lit King Mudgal's face.

'... Ahalya was meant to stay at your ashram long enough to see if you—'

'You mean she was sent to test him?' interrupted Indra contemptuously. 'And our righteous rishi here didn't fall into the temptation of lust, is that what you mean, Narad? That he showed no such weakness, but a commendable strength of character—was that the grand plan?' His voice dripped cold derision.

Narad nodded happily. 'Yes,' he said, chortling.

Gautam still looked stunned. Narad turned to him and said, gently, 'And as expected you behaved with respect and restraint, despite your dilemma. You won her then, not now.'

Indra flushed, and his face was contorted with fury. 'It was all an ingenious scheme; it was decided well beforehand that Gautam would get Ahalya eventually!'

'No, Gautam had to prove himself too, Indra,' replied Narad gravely. 'Gautam is a great samyami with immense self-control, and his manas—his mind—is always with Brahma, hence he is the most loyal brahmachari! Gautam did not ever entertain thoughts like yours, Indra!'

Indra scoffed loudly. 'Who are you to judge what I feel for Ahalya? I love her!' he declared fervidly, the raw passion in his voice making Ahalya pale and Gautam go still. 'More than this rishi ever can.'

'It is not a contest, and above all, Ahalya does not love you. She has chosen Gautam,' said Narad pointedly. 'Gautam, as a devotee of Shiva, as the param Shivabhakt, easily passed Brahmadev's test. And what you witness today, Indra, is Brahmadev himself blessing them! Gautam and Ahalya are the perfect couple—the aadarsh daapatyam. And as a gift, there is an ashram at Brahmagiri waiting for the two of them.'

'All so perfectly set. Go on—glorify him,' Indra said with a sneer. 'Try to make the rishi out as a saint! But this is nothing but subterfuge! It was a unholy trick!' he thundered. He whipped around and turned on Ahalya savagely. 'And you, you

Ahalya, you led me on, making me hope, knowing I was in love with you all the time.' Indra had the pleasure of watching her lovely face crumple. 'You prevaricated each time, you deceived me, you are a liar!' he said viciously.

Ahalya blanched. Indra's coarse, petty words revolted her; she felt humiliated.

But for Indra, it was a delicious moment—to be able to puncture her new-found happiness. He would teach her the bitter lesson she had inflicted on him. He would make her suffer the same agony she had made him writhe in.

King Mudgal rose to his feet. 'Indra, please mind your words, you are talking about my daughter,' he said heatedly. 'I sympathise with you, and if my wife misled you, I apologise for her blunder and her maternal ambition,' he continued with undisguised sarcasm.

'I asked you, too, for Ahalya's hand in marriage, sir,' reminded Indra savagely.

'Yes. And I told you that it was up to my daughter,' the king replied evenly. 'She has declared her decision, and I go by it.'

'She led me astray as did all of you! Ask her how often I begged her to marry me!'

Gautam stood still, his head slightly to one side, his eyes dark. There was a long pause, then he said to Ahalya, 'Is that true?'

She began to quiver helplessly, but she shook her head.

'Of course it's true,' Indra said. 'She knew how I felt, she knew her mother wanted us to be married, she knew—'

'—that I never loved you!' she cried, holding her body stiff to stop it from trembling. 'Even before I met Gautam, I told you so!'

Gautam ignored Indra. He took Ahalya's hands in his, much to Indra's jealousy.

'It's your word against mine!' jeered Indra, his lips drawn back.

'Indra!' warned Divodas.

Indra choked back his rage. There was something in the other man's calm eyes that startled him.

The warmth and firmness of Gautam's hands holding hers comforted Ahalya. She nodded, and her breath caught in a rasping sob. 'Yes, it's true, I knew about all that he said ... but I was honest with him, I *was*! I made it plain that I was never interested in him ... oh, I said so, so many times!'

'And I waited for you!' roared Indra. 'You knew that!' Indra was shouting, beside himself with rage.

'Stop it,' Gautam said fiercely, his eyes glittering. 'How dare you?!'

Narad took a quick step forward, coming between the two men.

'I know what you are trying to do, Indra!' Narad said. 'Don't plant doubts and sow suspicion in either of their minds—that is something you were always good at. Is that how you win your wars?' he taunted.

'Do you want war, Narad?' Indra asked, his voice dangerously soft, his eyes wild. 'Do you want me to war with a rishi?'

'You already lost that war, Indra!' snorted Narad contemptuously. 'Brains, not brawn, remember?'

Gautam laid a warning hand on Narad's thin shoulders. He laughed lightly, now completely at ease.

'Well, there is no need to be that bloody. You know how I detest war, Narad,' he said, turning his calm gaze to Indra.

'We mustn't keep you, Indra. No doubt you have things to do besides duelling with me,' he said, and smiled again.

Indra felt a grudging admiration for this man, who could carry his ill-humour with such dignity. But in spite of his smoothness and his easy laugh, Indra had a feeling that he was jeering at him. Gautam's self-assurance ignited a spark of fury in Indra again.

'I don't wish to argue with you, rishi,' he said contemptuously. 'But I haven't finished with her,' he said, moving menacingly towards Ahalya.

She stepped back, her eyes dark with alarm, her face white.

Gautam stepped forward and moved Indra's arm away. 'Stop that. Don't try my patience. I am trying to be nice to you,' he said sharply. 'Leave her alone,' he warned and something in his deep voice stopped Indra in his stride.

There was something about Indra that Gautam didn't like. It was not just that he was so obsessively besotted with Ahalya. He had heard a lot about the king of the Devas. On the surface, he seemed a handsome, likeable fellow. He was charming, intelligent and powerful. But there was something about him ... He was two-faced, perhaps. Gautam got the sense that he would be pleasant not because he liked you, but because he thought it might pay to be nice to you.

He was said to be a bit too free with women as well: not just apsaras, but any beautiful girl was his prey. It had worried Gautam when Ahalya mentioned how often Indra was at the palace. He hadn't liked it.

'What an odd word to use—finished, that you haven't *finished* with her,' Gautam said, looking coolly at Indra, who glared back at him. 'Yes, you are finished, Indra. She is finished with you. Please don't frighten my bride.'

He put his hand protectively around her bare waist and stood beside Ahalya who looked up at him. 'She has said what she wanted to say to you, haven't you, Ahalya?' he went on, smiling at her.

Watching them, Indra saw Ahalya's face light up when Gautam smiled at her, and how the worried expression left her eyes.

Gautam turned his eyes on him again.

'I don't want you to come near her again,' he said silkily. '*Ever*. She has said what she wanted to. Hear it well.'

Indra gritted his teeth. An intense hatred for this lanky man boiled up inside him. He could think of nothing to say, and after throwing them one last glance, he could no longer bear to look at them. He stared out of the window, his fists clenched, his face a hard mask of misery.

Indra knew he had lost: lost her, his pride, his love, his dignity. Lost his all. He cast a last glance at her. Ahalya moved closer to Gautam, and held his hand.

Snarling silently with disappointed fury, he watched them together—happy, smiling slightly, their eyes locking often, absorbed in their own private world ...

He moved restlessly. She was in love with Gautam. Anyone with half an eye could see that. Gautam with wealth of knowledge, his air of intellectualism and suave manners was just the kind of man a girl like Ahalya would fall for. It was natural.

But Gautam ... Why would a rishi want to marry a princess like Ahalya? Suppose Gautam was one of those heartless husbands who want to take on a girl as innocent and naive as Ahalya for a wife? There were many such men. Suppose Gautam was one of them? Indra felt himself sweating. He'd kill him if he ever hurt her! He clenched his fists in a gesture of frustrated fury.

He was about to shout his ire again, but the angry, bitter words died in his throat. He scarcely recognised her as she stood close to Gautam, their hands touching, her face flushed, her eyes bright with suppressed excitement. She was every inch the glowing bride.

He felt a bleakness overwhelm him. There was something about this tall, lean man that Indra could not fathom. He was so quiet, calm, assured, and yet every now and then, Indra could see an indecipherable emotion on his face when he glanced at his bride-to-be ... Was it anxiety? Or was it the kind of fear that Indra understood well, that furtive, painfully concealed fear that only betrayed itself by the quiver of his hands, the darkening of his eyes. Of a man lost in love, afraid of losing ...

Why was he frightened? If Indra could find that out, he would have a weapon with which he could win back his Ahalya. Had Gautam committed some wrong? If only the rishi had done something wrong, he could find out what it was, and he would then hold the upper hand ... and get back his Ahalya.

Indra stood pale, and his eyes showed his suppressed fury.

'A war is never won until the last battle, Gautam,' he said, his voice unsteady but ringing out in the hall.

Gautam looked at him and made a grimace of disgust. Indra stared at Ahalya for the last time, his eyes narrowed, his lips scowling. He stalked out of the hall.

14

The Consummation

The six-horse-drawn chariot waited for them in front of the great white palace. The courtyard was drenched in the splendour of silver moonlight. The chariot's solidity startled Gautam. The strong sides, the strength of the girders, the breadth and ostentation of it.

'It's time to leave,' he murmured, as Ahalya climbed up and sat beside him in the chariot. She nodded, glancing backwards for a last look at her brother and parents clustered against the palace doors. She did not look back long. She swivelled around sharply to blot out the lingering image of her family and turned her face firmly towards the road ahead. She was leaving for their ashram. It would be a new day soon.

The dark road lay before them. The dwellings in passing villages loomed up around them as they travelled, mostly in silence. Ahalya was confused. It was odd, meeting Gautam, wedding him, and yet have nothing to say to him now when they were allowed some time of their own. In the whirlwind of a quick but big wedding, they had barely had time for themselves.

After a few hours, Gautam decided it would be best to rest at an ashram. It was more of an inn than a school—a collection of small huts owned by one of his students. It was tiny yet cosy, and Ahalya was again reminded of the sprawling emptiness of her palace.

'Now let's talk,' Gautam said. 'Shall we go into the inner room?'

He walked ahead of her, and they sat down cross-legged opposite each other on rough mats.

'You know nothing about me, do you?' Gautam said, leaning back against the mud wall. 'And yet I feel you don't dislike me.'

'Dislike you? You *know* it's the opposite,' she said, surprised, only to realise he was teasing her.

He continued to look at her, his winged eyebrows arched with interest.

Ahalya looked down, cursing the hot blush suffusing her face. Why was she so pathetically awkward around him, she thought, annoyed with herself. She was nervous, too, and her heart fluttered against her ribs, her mouth was dry and her hands unpleasantly clammy. Probably because this was the first time they were talking at a very personal, intimate level. As they should be, she thought; they were married now, she was his wife. Gautam was her husband. It was a strangely uplifting emotion.

'I—I'm very grateful to you …' Ahalya stammered.

'It gets worse—only grateful?' he said in mock dismay. There was an encouraging smile in his eyes. 'Nothing more than gratitude? You know, I hate gratitude; it's like pity. And I have done nothing for you to be grateful for.'

'Oh, but you have, you don't know how much!' she cried. 'You've been so kind to me,' she said, her face scarlet. 'I—I—of course I like you.'

'Only because I've been kind to you? Not for myself? But I'm glad you said that,' he said, grinning, his teeth even and white against his tanned skin. 'Now I feel I can talk to you not as a stranger but as a friend.'

'Friend?' she mimicked, pleased to get her turn to tease him. 'I thought I was your wife!'

'A wife needs to be her husband's friend as well,' he said, smiling. 'I shan't say you are more than a friend. A friend is a more difficult role.'

'Then I am honoured to be your friend,' she said shyly.

He made a sudden movement, offering her his hand.

She sat still, staring at the big, calloused hand, anxious and yet weak with physical excitement. She slid her hand into his. The heat of his hand was like fire, enflaming her, spreading wildly all over her body.

'I believe you have enormous courage and a strength that I think even you—and your parents—do not realise you are capable of.' He stroked her with his caressing gaze. 'Your keen sense of curiosity allows you that expansive hunger for knowledge, that eagerness to know, to enquire. To debate, to argue,' he said and smiled, making her heart race again. 'And besides, you're delightfully pretty!' he teased, touching her cheek, a smile in his voice as he took in her breath-taking loveliness, silhouetted against the moonlight. 'I like the way you talk, speak out, the way you walk, the way you hold your head, the way you look at me ...'

Her breath caught, and she felt herself going warm and red. She covered her shyness by quickly lowering her eyes. She did not dare look up, but if she had, she would have glimpsed a tenderness in his eyes that she had never witnessed before, one he had never experienced before.

He paused, breathing deeply, his thumb lightly outlining her delicate jawline. She gave a start. His touch was feather-light but it electrified her very being. Her throat became taut.

She heard him murmur, 'It's extraordinary. The moment I saw you ... frightened ... alone in the ashram ... so lost yet eager and curious ... it's a strange blend. You interested me very, very much.'

The naked passion in his silky voice overwhelmed her.

'Oh ... I didn't know,' she stammered. 'I never thought ...' She gulped and tightened her clasp over his hand. She scarcely knew what she was doing. The warm, strong hand pressed hers back, the other moving closer to touch the bare skin of her back. It was happening, as she had hoped it would happen. He was making love to her.

She looked away from his hungry gaze, a dark flood of colour rising in her face.

'I couldn't have those feelings, could I?' he whispered in a tortured tone. 'You were my protégé, I was to protect you, not make love to you ...'

His candour made him acutely vulnerable, his admission sounding strangely erotic coming from his beautifully shaped lips, his almost ascetic face.

'But I always liked you,' she said faintly, luxuriating in the warm, heady waves his touch was causing and unconsciously leaning into him.

172 / Kavita Kané

'Good.' She could hear the smile in his voice. 'I want you to like me,' he said gently. 'Because I love you.'

She sat up and faced him. Her eyes anxiously searched his face as if to read what was going on in his mind. Her ears were hearing what she had wanted to hear all these months, what her mind wanted to believe, and now he had said it.

'Do you really love me?' she murmured in dazed wonderment.

'Yes, so madly, so surely,' he said hoarsely, gripping her waist, pulling her closer. 'There's nothing I want more than you. The moment I saw you ...'

She watched his beautiful lips move, mouthing those lovely words. 'I still can't really believe it. I've been going mad, thinking ... I—why did you come to the palace?' she asked.

'To bring you back with me as my wife,' he said succinctly. 'I had to have you! You don't believe me?' he asked, watching the range of expressions flitting across her bewildered face.

'I hoped for so long, so hard, that I can't believe that this is happening! My brother says I am a bit of a romantic fool; I know I am. I've no experience, no knowledge ...'

'Nor do I,' he said thickly. 'But I know I love you, Ahalya.'

She shivered with joy. 'You do?' she whispered in awe, her eyes still uncertain. 'But ... but I do know that you didn't always want to marry—' She broke off and looked away.

Gautam tightened his clasp, then took hold of her chin, turned her face so she had to look at him.

'Go on, tell me,' he said 'Please tell me. If I don't really love you ... what then?'

'It's just that I find it hard to believe. You've been good and kind and also mean and nasty to me ... I–I just don't know why and what made you come to me ...'

'What makes you think I don't love you?' he repeated softly, shifting closer to her, so their thighs touched.

She felt like she was on fire, the heat consuming her. But the gnawing pain in her heart prompted her to say more.

'My mother,' she said desperately. 'She said I would disgrace you, that I would not make you a good wife and you'd regret marrying me. Just like I would regret it too one day ... I—' She choked.

The long, slim fingers closed over her wrist, his thumb rubbing it reassuringly. There was warmth and strength in the fingers, restoring her confidence.

'You should be sorry for your mother, for she doesn't know what an exceptional daughter she has,' Gautam said gently. He leaned forward, brushed her cheek with his lips, singeing her. 'She is worried about you, that's why her harsh words. And yes, I agree with her that I am not the perfect suitor for you, the son-in-law anybody would want,' he said with a soft chuckle. 'It was her concern for you that made her so hard and say those things. We are often cruellest to the those whom we love most.'

'But *am* I good enough for you?' Ahalya asked earnestly.

'So that is what's troubling you,' he said, looking down and stroking her wrist sensuously, causing new tingling sensations, dispelling her doubts with desire. 'Can you not believe that I fell in love with you?' he said thickly, his dark eyes blazing. 'I have fought against my own feelings, those mad, raging emotions, before finally acknowledging that what I feel for you is love and not some transitory passion,' he said as he cupped her face between his hands. He leaned forward, his warm breath fanning her flushed face. 'I went through what you are going through now. I could ask you the same question: what is in me that made you love me? You had Indra pining for you; he was a better choice, a worthier one! Don't let's start with doubts, Ahalya. Trust is deeper than love. And more difficult. Trust me—I love you.'

She looked into his face, saw only kindness and tenderness there, and she urgently grabbed his hand, her eyes wide with delight. 'Oh, yes,' she smiled. 'So do I, I love you, I love you madly!'

'I know,' he said, but there was no smugness in his admission. The euphoria dissipated as fast as it had surged.

'You knew?' she asked incredulously. 'Then why did you not say so? Why did you make me suffer all these months?' she cried, moving away, snatching her hands away from his warm clasp. She was about to get up, when he gripped her wrist, willing her to remain close to him.

'You are so young, so naïve, so unexposed ... It was unbelievable,' he said, his eyes scanning her face anxiously. 'How was I to believe what was happening—to both of us?' He exhaled a long breath. 'It was new to me too. I have never felt like for this for any woman. I'm sorry if I hurt you. No matter what, Ahalya, I love you.'

She remained mute in silent hurt.

'I'll remember this confession of love, and I'll forgive you if you ever hurt me.'

It was almost like a vow: to himself and to her. She saw him looking down at her with an intent expression, as if he were seeing right into her soul, as if she was the one person for him, making her aware of herself.

She moved closer, and their bodies touched more intimately.

'So how do I know it's not a passing infatuation for you, but actually love?' she teased, getting braver.

His confession had oddly freed her from her own inhibitions.

'I gave myself a lot of time,' he said, his tone serious, his brown hand slid over her shoulder and his fingers gently stroked her silken throat. 'I was in denial for a long, long time.' He smiled his slow, lazy smile again.

'And?' she murmured blissfully, again feeling blood rising to her face, feeling beatific and powerful at the same time: she had no idea she had affected him in any way. She did have some power over him ...

'And? And now we are here. Together. Man and wife,' he said with a grin.

He leaned forward. She saw her name Ahalya form on his beautiful lips but she barely heard it, blood drumming in her ears.

She was seized by a sudden shyness, barely able to breathe, trying to make out his shape in the darkness. But when he reached for her and pulled her to him, her timidity dissolved. Softly he placed each of his big hands on either side of her face, curving them to fit her face. Mesmerised, she saw his head swoop down, first feeling his warm breath on her face and then tasting the smile on his lips as he kissed her softly on the mouth. Her breath caught. For a second or so her mind exploded. She closed her eyes, savouring each new spiralling sensation. She felt his fingers sliding down her arched spine, resting tantalisingly on her hips. The hard lips crushed hers, drawing the strength out of her. Then, vanquished, she let herself go, became limp in his arms, throwing her head back, exposing her throat to his seeking lips. He was holding her tightly now, one hand on her knee, moving slowly upwards as the other pressed firmly against the small of her back.

'I think this is the first time and the last time I am in love, Ahalya,' he whispered, his lips on the white softness of her throat.

Her heart was bursting, as were her mind and her senses. She was helpless, yielding to his strength, not knowing what he was going to do next, but instinctively feeling that this was only the beginning of a moment of supreme rapture ...

He ran his eyes over her as she stood before him. Sachi had long, glossy brown hair with a hint of red, magnificent grey eyes that seemed to change colour with her moods and a lively, almost mischievous smile. She was just the way Indra liked his women: voluptuous and vivacious.

He stretched on the bed, his head against the pillows, watching her. It fascinated him to see how seductively she undressed. She pulled a string here and a knot there, and in a moment she was standing before in all her dusky, naked loveliness.

'Sachi, you are the most beautiful woman,' he said, his voice catching.

'Only you can say that to me, Shakra, and make me believe it,' she said with a smile.

Shakra. Sachi was the only one who called him by that name. It carried an intimacy which 'Indra', his more hailed appellation, did not have.

He had met Sachi by chance. He was roaming the skies and spotted her in her personal garden, which—over time—had become their favourite meeting place. They met often, not because he liked her that much, but because he felt lonely after the war with Shambar. He did not visit the palace in Kampilya, the capital of Panchal, as often as he used to: Ahalya's absence was too hard to bear. Now, there would be no Ahalya for him at all; there never would be ... The thought of her made the dull ache in his heart more pronounced, and memories of that last meeting in the palace came rushing back.

In anguished frenzy, he had turned to Sachi, rushing into her waiting arms the very same day Ahalya had spurned him publicly in the royal hall. In his intoxicated, depressed state, he had seduced Sachi, a virgin. He had literally demanded that they be lovers that night—not that it had taken much persuasion. Sachi had yielded willingly. Since then, they had continued their secret trysts, and Indra found himself visiting her more and more often. Soon they were together almost every day, and then for days together.

This was her personal garden, with a fountain and a gazebo, all gifted by her indulgent father because she loved flowers and the sound of gurgling water. *Like Ahalya does*, he thought ... Whenever he visited Sachi here, he felt like he was in a haven, where no one could hurt him, and certainly not Sachi, who loved him madly. He needed a place to get away from those marauding memories of Ahalya.

Their meetings had gone on for some months when they both realised Sachi really was in love with him. As the king of gods, Indra had had a score of women pursue him, but it was only Sachi who could make him forget Ahalya, however momentarily. At that moment, Sachi meant more to him than any other woman.

She had recently suggested that it could be a good idea for them to get married, displaying her mischievous smile, stroking his arm.

He had shook his head. The desire to marry had died down with Ahalya's brutal rejection. 'Not yet, Sachi,' he had said. 'I like the idea, but I am going to be involved in a series of war campaigns—'

'Again?' she had interrupted worriedly.

'With the Asuras, yes. And I know that they are being secretly supported by your father and his general Vrita ...'

'I am an Asura, Shakra, and I am my father's daughter. We are Asuras and we will always help each other,' Sachi said defensively.

'Even against me?' he said and raised an eyebrow.

'Especially against you,' she had responded, her tone cutting. 'You are our most hated enemy.'

'And yet you are here with me,' he had said, grinning unabashedly. 'With the enemy.'

'Because I love you,' she said, almost sadly. His heart jolted; not out of elation but a certain unease. 'And it would work better if we got married—it might just end all this war and animosity, would it not?' she suggested with a wry smile.

Indra had been shocked more at the open confession than the depth of her emotions.

'I shall carry your love as a talisman when I go to war now,' he had said, trying lighten the situation. 'Anyway, if I married you, I would have to first fight your father face-to-face. Not yet, my love, but later. When I am back and all this is over! For all you know, your father may start liking me!' he had joked.

She had looked at him with hurt, reproachful eyes.

'Shakra, if my father comes to know ...' she said hesitantly, fear creeping into her voice.

Indra threw back his head and laughed. 'He wouldn't dare cross paths with me, however powerful a king he is.'

'It is not as a king but as an angry father that h confront you,' Sachi had retorted spiritedly.

He had shrugged away her words, and a few weeks later, h found himself in her luxurious mansion again, on her huge bed.

Indra lay limp and satiated. His mind dwelt on the past half hour. This beautiful woman lying by his side had been everything he had hoped for. No ... that wasn't true; she had been better than his most sensual expectations. This was a woman in love who knew how to give and receive pleasure. Nothing he had known could be compared with the time he spent with her. Sachi was his. Like Ahalya would have been ... In a drowsy stupor, he thought back on his many sexual encounters, even the imagined ones with Ahalya, but suddenly all he could conjure was an image of her and Gautam. It made Indra rigid with fury.

Sachi sensed something was wrong. She peered anxiously at him as he rolled away from her. She waited until his breathing became steady and heavy, then reached for him, but he lay still.

Sachi knew there would be no post-coital affection and she felt used, as she always did after their love-making. Shakra was so selfish and egotistic, once satisfied, he wanted only to sleep and go into his dream world.

'Are you drunk?' she asked curiously, sniffing the stale stench of wine on him.

Why must she talk at a moment like this, Indra thought, annoyed. She always did. She never seemed to know when to stop talking. After a body-shattering experience like the one he had just had, he wanted to doze and dream it all over again, with the vision of Ahalya clouding his befuddled mind.

'I have to leave before dawn,' he mumbled.

...n time,' she said, stroking his back. They
...urs before he would have to leave.

...felt Sachi rest her head gently against his

..., his eyes closed.

'It's Father. He knows about us,' she said.

'So the worst is done.' He shrugged nonchalantly. 'What does he think—that I deflowered you before marriage?' He grinned in the darkness, but Sachi could sense the malice in his voice. 'Now, since he knows, he knows. He can't do anything about it.'

'He can't, but you can,' she said calmly. 'I want you to marry me.'

Indra turned then, suddenly alert. She seemed different. Why was he feeling uneasy?

'Marry?' he repeated, incredulous. 'We discussed this before.'

'Yes,' she said shortly. 'The war's over, you won and it's time we wed.'

There was a set look on her face which Indra had never seen before. He became conscious of the fact that he was lying exposed and felt vulnerable on the big bed. He shifted a little and pulled the sheet across him. Instinctively, he felt that there would be no more love-making.

'Marry?' he repeated foolishly. 'Are you voicing your father's words?' he asked sharply. 'He doesn't mind his daughter marrying his worst enemy?'

'But it's my wish,' she retorted, flushed. 'I want to marry you because I love you, Indra.'

He began to get angry. There was a snap in his voice when he said, 'Of course I know that ... and I love you too. Come here, darling. We're wasting time.'

'Yes, time we need to spend talking,' she said, still in bed but keeping a distance from him.

He gazed at her as he contemplated what he should do next. Sachi was the first woman he could call his own. She was complicated, of course, but he had come to accept that all women could be difficult. There were times when she was cold when hurt or deliciously warm when they made love. But she had never been contemptuous of him as she was now.

This he could not accept, though he was contemptuous of himself. If he was asked why this tempestuous girl should have such a hold on him, he would have been hard pressed to explain. The ultimate thing, he thought, was that when they were together, she gave herself in such a way that he knew he owned her, and he had never felt that way with any other woman.

Ahalya and Sachi were unlike each other. Ahalya was ice, Sachi all fire; if Ahalya was like a calm, placid lake, serene and ethereal, Sachi was like a bubbling stream, effervescent and sparkling ...

But not today; today, she was in one of her black moods. He knew that once Sachi was in the mood for lovemaking, he would get her back. She was exciting; to him, being with her was like rolling dice. You never knew what would come up. And after the way Ahalya had treated him, this way of life was important to him. He hated women whining. He liked compliant women. Sachi was like that, and she was able to draw from his body a kind of explosion that no woman had ever been able to before. Would it have been the same with Ahalya ...?

Damn her, why could he not stop thinking of her, even when there was this ravishing woman by his side?

He gave a start. Sachi was talking to him, a mutinous expression on her face.

'You claim you love me but not enough to marry me?' Sachi was asking him sharply.

Indra's face hardened. He swung his legs off the vast bed and sat upright and looked directly at her.

'Why this sudden urge to get married?' he asked, glaring at her.

'I am a princess, Indra, not one of your apsaras that you can have fun with and leave,' she said calmly, but he heard the simmer of discontent in her voice. 'How long did you think you could play around with me?' she asked, her lips twisted in a bitter smile.

'This is your father speaking, not you!' Indra countered furiously, feeling trapped.

'Yes, my father is definitely not pleased that a sexually vigorous but duty-shirking god has ravished his daughter!' she said. 'He will punish you for what you have done if you don't mend your ways!'

'What? Mend *my* ways? Sachi, you should mind yours, virgin princess!' Indra said with a scowl.

Sachi went white with anger. 'How dare you!'

Indra was unmoved. 'If I recall, you didn't protest too much, did you?'

'Yes, I agreed,' she said, her face flaming red. 'Because I love you!' She drew a deep breath. 'But right now, forget my father, *I* am asking you,' she continued evenly. 'Will you marry me?'

He continued to stare at her, his mind busy. He had to give her an answer: she wanted it and he owed her one. But he could neither commit with a yes nor refuse directly.

Sachi studied him. She knew she had to be careful with him. She could goad him only so far, and no further. He wasn't like other men, like her father's army general, Vrita, who was deeply in love with her. This man was a shrewd, nimble-minded philanderer and experienced in the most complicated love liaisons—and she was hopelessly in love with him and wanted him at whatever cost. She felt this was the moment to sink in the gaff.

'I am waiting, Shakra,' she said, her tone openly sardonic.

There was a slight pause, then she said, 'Incidentally, my father has asked you to come and visit him at his palace.'

Indra drew in a hiss of breath and his hands turned into fists. 'The king of the Devas going to an Asura king?' he said. 'Never!'

'You have to. You need to formally ask the father for the daughter's hand in marriage. You should know, you have done it before,' she added cattily.

Indra blanched, speechless with rage.

'Why do you hesitate, Shakra? Is it Ahalya?' she openly taunted. 'Is she still haunting you?'

Her cold, undisguised sarcasm fired a white fury in him. 'Don't get her into this. This is between you and me and yes, your father,' he said scornfully.

'Is it?' she asked insistently, her tone flat. 'Is it Ahalya?'

He made an impatient movement. 'She's now married to another man, Sachi,' he said bleakly.

Sachi felt an agonising flare of jealousy burn through her. It always did; that was why she never broached the topic with him. But today she had to have her answers.

'But that does not mean you have stopped loving her,' Sachi said quietly. 'You pine for her still!' she said.

'I lost at her swayamwar, that's all,' he snapped.

'Did she hurt your pride—as I assumed all this while—or your heart, Shakra? I really wonder,' Sachi said, her lips pursed.

Indra inhaled sharply. 'It's done and over with. She, I have heard, is very happy in her new world,' he said, forcing the words out with a tight smile, his heart weeping.

'But are you ready to begin afresh yourself?' demanded Sachi. 'You are not! That's why you are so averse to the idea of our marriage!' she said.

He made a movement of impatience.

'If you cannot give me marriage, Shakra,' she paused, looking straight into his troubled eyes, 'then I cannot be with you,' she said.

He could not believe his ears. He whistled. 'Oh? And where will you go?' he said. 'To that servile Vrita whom your father wishes you to marry?'

Her grey eyes were chips of ice. 'I might. He loves and respects me.'

A cold stab of jealous rage assaulted him. 'And here I thought you considered him just an able commander-in-chief, a mere servant of your father!' he said, his lips curled contemptuously.

He realised that he hated the thought of her with that dark, handsome army general. It made him uneasy, that she apparently meant so much to him. Now the interfering father and that ardent lover Vrita were about to snatch Sachi away, just as that rascal Gautam had taken Ahalya from him. His heart churned in fear and fury.

Sachi shrugged. 'Yes, I do think he is an able commander, and he wants to marry me. I might just accept,' she said frostily.

He regarded the calm, remote face and the certitude on her face startled Indra. Was she arm-twisting him, using extortion in order to make him comply? Indra stiffened with helpless frustration. He had underestimated her, underrated his importance. She *could* live without him. She could leave him...

The thought sobered his rage abruptly. He *was* scared and insecure. Blind panic hit him. For a long moment, he sat motionless, his hand like a claw, gripping the edge of the bed. He might lose her as he had lost Ahalya ... Terror seized his heart but he willed himself to think. He knew he had to win her back, regain her trust. She couldn't leave him!

He forced a smile.

'What is wrong with you, Sachi? You know I love you,' he said, his tone conciliatory, trying to be assuring.

She shook her head, her eyes dull, and moved away. 'As you said, you should leave,' she said tersely. 'It will be morning soon.'

He stared after her, seeing the long, straight back, the bare curve of her flaring hips and the long, slim legs, remembering each moment he had been with her since Ahalya had left ... No! Now she would go too. She was telling him to leave; *she* was leaving him ...!

He got up quickly, his heart hammering. He came to her and put his arms around her, pulling her close to him. She stood stiff and cold but she did not shrug off his arm. He rested his face against hers, his lips brushing her cool forehead.

'Don't. Please, don't,' he whispered, his tone imploring. The arrogance had dried up, the pride wiped out.

She put her arms around him and her face against his. They stood for some moments holding on to each other, then she felt a pang of desire run through her and he tightened his grip.

'I know I'm selfish,' he said, his hands sliding down her back. 'I know it, but you *are* the best thing that has ever happened to me. You want marriage. Okay, so you want marriage ... marriage to me means nothing but trouble. I don't want trouble ... I want *you*. I need you!'

She felt her heart contract. Although she was aching for him, hurting and torn inside, a warm surge of hope filled her heart; that was the nicest thing he had ever said to her. '*I want you, I need you.*' No other man had said this to her. Not even Vrita. 'I love you.' Many, many times ... but what did that mean? Love? Nothing! But I *want* you ... I need you—*that* was something. It meant a lot.

'I can't do without you. I am yours, Sachi,' he murmured, his voice husky. 'Don't leave me,' he begged.

She had never heard this tone in his voice before. But she would *not* succumb, she told herself fiercely. She stood stiff, her hands clenched.

Indra felt her resistance. How could he soften her? This wasn't the time for this kind of talk. He pressed his lips urgently on her brow, but her skin felt cold. Her quiet, calm expression reminded him of Ahalya's almost dispassionate, faintly contemptuous look ...

That familiar, unforgotten look was now on Sachi's face and he realised that she had put a barrier between them.

'What's the matter, Sachi? Don't you believe me?' he entreated, feeling a little panic-stricken.

He was met with silence. He cupped her cold face with hot, feverish hands.

She could hear his breathing, quick, short and uneven.

'I *want* to marry you,' he blurted. 'I will, I promise! Just don't go, please!'

Her flinty eyes flickered. There was a thaw: he detected an undecipherable emotion in them.

He grabbed the moment like a drowning man struggling with a floating raft. 'And I will go to your father,' he whispered hoarsely.

She noted the desperation and fear in his voice, and it was that and the sensual caress in his throaty voice that had an effect on her as always.

He heard her draw in a sharp breath.

'You really mean that?' she said after a long, excruciating pause. 'Shakra, please don't lie.'

It hit him hard. He was not lying. That was his new truth. He could not lose Sachi.

He deliberately paused, thinking of a life without her. 'Yes,' he said finally. 'Let's get married.'

15

Love and Marriage

Every morning, she woke up in his arms. It had been a beautiful, satiating way to start the new day for the past one year, Ahalya thought, as she revelled in the feel of her husband against her.

She snuggled closer against his chest and woke him.

'It's going to be dawn soon, I should get up,' Gautam groaned in protest, but she could hear the smile in his voice.

'So should I,' she said lazily. 'Fortunately the baby slept through the night peacefully.'

Gautam threw a quick glance at his infant son, Vama, lying in a cradle by their side.

'Yes, he is a good baby.'

Ahalya got up, but not before planting a kiss on his lips.

'I shall wind up my chores quickly and join the class on Vedanta philosophy. It's a new chapter you are starting today, aren't you? I prepared the notes and memorised the required hymns.'

'Oh, you did? When?' he asked, astonished.

'While you and Vama were asleep,' she said, grinning. 'I'm less distracted then.'

'Are you sure you should be staying up so late?' Gautam said, frowning and peering up at her face. 'You have just given birth to a child ...'

She quickly passed her hand over her hair and gave her head a vigorous shake. 'No, I won't compromise on my studies—ever!' she said, her face fierce. 'Don't worry, I shall manage. You just teach me!'

'That I shall,' he said. 'I am a teacher, after all! And you are a very good student,' he added fondly.

'Am I not? I don't make you repeat what you have told me—not even once. Nor have I ever wriggled out of my commitments.'

A couple of hours later, sitting in the bright summer morning sunshine, a breeze fanning the tall trees, the sun hot, both of them were at work: he teaching, she learning from him, the baby chortling by her side.

Ahalya was still nervous of Gautam as a teacher, but she enjoyed her lessons with him and took in all his instructions with ease. She could recall the exact wording of a passage read a week before, she followed complex philosophical texts with dogged tenacity, and she saw connections even Gautam had not considered, composing her own rebuttals. He was most impressed, however, with her capacity for numericals; it was little more than filling in a series of blanks to her.

Much had changed in Ahalya's daily routine, but she never missed a class or chance to pore over her books, alternating between the books of her interest and the ones assigned by Gautam.

'Take a break,' he said at last after three gruelling hours. 'We shall start again after half an hour.'

'Yes, I need to check on the students' lunch,' she said, nodding. 'And yours. And nurse Vama, of course.'

The first shock Ahalya got when she stepped into the ashram was how little time she had to pursue her studies—instead, she had to begin her first lessons in housekeeping. The work was boring but not especially difficult. Ahalya helped Gautam around the house, peeling vegetables, dusting, scrubbing floors, cleaning the courtyard, washing clothes by the river and drawing water from the well. But no matter what she had to do, Ahalya would always look forward to the time the sun set, when, without fail, she heard the clank of the garden gate and the hard step of her husband's feet on the threshold. Running to him, she would bury her face in his chest. In those moments, she knew everything would be fine ...

Now a year later, she was a master at housekeeping and cooking. She finished the last of the lunch preparations and walked back to their hut, where Gautam was sitting. She watched as Gautam went through piles of palm-leaf parchments. He gestured for her to sit.

'Uttank was relating what happened once when was studying at Rishi Veda's ashram,' Ahalya began, her voice hesitant. She wondered if she should go on.

Gautam noticed her reluctance and his eyes narrowed, but he gave her a gentle smile. 'Yes?' he said encouragingly.

'He recounted how, once, Rishi Veda's wife asked him ... er ... to ...' She floundered, the colour deepening in her face.

'To sleep with him?' supplied Gautam bluntly.

She nodded, mortified.

Reading her thoughts, he gave a faint smile.

'Why are you embarrassed, Ahalya?' he asked. 'Her husband had been in meditation for the past five months, the wife had a sexual need, which her husband could not provide, so she asked one of the students she liked. She was honest and upfront—to herself and the student.'

'And the husband?' asked Ahalya, affronted. 'She cheated on him!'

'The rishi knew about it too. He allowed her to do so; he was equally calm and practical about it. He admired the student for refusing the offer but did not see the need to chastise his wife. The matter was resolved with no emotion or drama.'

'What are you saying?' she asked aghast. 'It was disloyal, wasn't it? It is depraved!' she said a little heatedly. 'Tell me, please, don't you find anything wrong with this? You, as a teacher, should be more morally upright.'

'It is not up to me,' he said gently. 'Every situation is a test, an examination of the self, and how you react is like writing an exam.'

'Oh, you are being obscure again,' she said. 'What has happened to the morals and values we were taught? What is the matter with us as humans in the sacred bond of marriage? In the old days, all were so moral and virtuous, and now if one asks about anyone, one is told such things that one is quite shocked at human nature!' she continued, her cheeks flushed.

'What old days are you talking about?' he asked coolly. 'By using words like moral and virtuous, you sound not like a girl open to see the world but a prude ready to judge and not think and learn!' he chided.

She cast hurt eyes on him. 'But that's how marriage is, is it not?'

'No, sex and marriage change as per social construct. Did you know that women, like men, were free to choose their sex partners outside marriage?' he asked, looking faintly amused at Ahalya's evident surprise. 'There was a time when there was no concept of marriage. Women as well as men were free to go to anyone until patriarchy seeped in to establish the concept of fatherhood, describing not just the ownership of the offspring but the ownership of the woman, the wife, as well, cleverly linking it to the new notion of fidelity.'

Ahalya frowned as she considered what he had said.

'Of course, the thought that men are superior to women was clearly invented by men themselves. It was Rishi Shvetaketu—the grandson of Rishi Aruni and nephew of Rishi Ashtavakra—who on seeing another man holding his mother's hand in the presence of his father, believed that a woman should be confined to one man—her husband—for life. He thereupon insisted on fidelity from women so that children knew who their biological fathers were. It was he who introduced the law of marriage, making it a legitimate form of relationship for a man and woman based on gender. We largely practise monogamy today, but our society is still mature enough to know and tolerate polygamy—and polyandry as well.'

'A woman could legally have more than one husband?' Ahalya asked, incredulous.

Gautam nodded. 'Polyandry is uncommon but not unknown and not against the law,' he corrected. 'Of course, it was more prevalent amongst the royals, but there is no Vedic law which denounces polyandry. The Aranyakas—which explain the philosophy behind rituals in the Vedas—mention polyandry. There are several instances: Queen Sussondi, King Brahmadatta's daughter, had four husbands, while the Queen of Trigarta had at least six. A woman called Bhadra is said to have had seven ...'

'Are these stories true?' asked Ahalya, still amazed.

'They are true. Most are exaggerated versions or gossip, of course. But then you must have heard my scandalous story too. There was polyandry in my family as well,' he said, chuckling softly. 'My grandmother Mamata, the wife of Rishi Uttathya, gave birth to my father with him and also bore two other sons—Kacha and Bharadwaj—from my grandfather's brother, Rishi Brihaspati.'

'Rishi Brihaspati, the priest of the Devas?' she echoed, dazed, pulling thoughtfully at a curling tendril. It seemed she was walking into a new world.

He nodded. 'Yes, the very one who taught you in your palace. Your royal priest.'

Ahalya remained silent, still too stunned at the revelation, though he had once cursorily mentioned it before. Gautam saw her confused face and said, 'Of course, you think this is "wrong" ... But everyone ought to bear the lot that their own doing has laid on them. It is not upon us to condemn or blame. Circumstances are sometimes too strong and ambiguous and ...'

'Are you talking about Rishi Brihaspati or Rishi Veda's wife? What circumstances can produce such decisions?'

'It's very simple,' replied Gautam, raising his eyebrows. 'It is the latent power of desire which overrides reason and scruples. It has always happened with Man, though we have tried to shackle him with moral values and laws of the world.

Brihaspati got a taste of his own medicine: his wife, Tara, left him for Chandra and had a child with him, Buddh, whom Brihaspati later accepted as his own.'

Ahalya sighed. 'What goes around comes around,' she said.

'But we *are* a complex family,' said Gautam, grinning.

Ahalya stared at him. 'Are you too good or am I too critical?'

'Your feelings probably arise from the aversion of thinking about women as sexual beings,' he said. 'But it is a righteousness that is an oversimplification of emotions and desires.'

'Possibly, but I stand by my argument. It *is* cheating and nothing, *nothing* can justify it!' she said hotly. 'Infidelity is dangerous and revolting.'

'It can be potentially healing and transformative too.'

'Healing?' she exploded.

'Yes, it can sometimes mend a bad marriage, or even an indifferent one. It is transformative in the sense that each partner views the situation they are in from a different perspective.'

She eyed him over. Her dark eyes were thoughtful.

'Would you approve of it if I did the same?' she challenged.

Gautam raised an eyebrow. 'You wouldn't,' he said simply.

'That's no answer! And why do you say that?' she demanded.

'Because you are too upright,' he said with a smile.

She flared. 'You mean too *uptight*, and that I wouldn't ever dare to stray? Don't make fun of virtuosity!'

'No, no one has the right to laugh—or condemn. That is exactly what I am trying to say. But you wouldn't do it because that's how you are, those are your beliefs. I trust that,' he said.

'Exactly, it *is* about trust. Betraying a trust is the wrong part of it.'

'You are still young,' he said with a sigh. 'You make presumptions too easily!' He said this with a dismissive wave of his hand. His face was completely relaxed, but his patronising tone irked Ahalya.

She tossed her head crossly, and the rich colour of her hair glistened in the light of the hut. 'You're making fun of me. Don't dismiss me so casually, Gautam. I am not so young or impressionable anymore!' she said. 'I am your wife. And the mother of a son now!'

'Yes, I know,' he murmured silkily, taking her hand in his. 'And I am a father.'

She looked at his big hands on her thigh and her body melted with desire for him. Her breath caught.

'Undoubtedly,' she replied saucily.

He looked at her for a long moment. It took him a second or so to realise what she was saying, then he gave a short laugh and grabbed her, whisking her to her feet and carrying her into the inner room.

'Gautam! What are you doing?!' She tried to wriggle out of his grip. 'There's lunch to get ready! Gautam, put me down at once! Oh, what will the students say?!'

She bit her lip and turned her head a little and looked at him. Then she lowered her lashes and slowly raised them again, like a darkened veil.

'You are a witch, wife,' he muttered savagely as he put her down and drew her to him, one hand tugging at her waist and the other sliding up her smooth back, deftly untying the knot behind.

She was protesting, but laughing at the same time.

'Undoubtedly is it, you say?' he said with a grin. 'Let me prove again ...' he murmured before his lips swooped on hers.

It was after some immeasurable time that she opened her eyes and stared up at the thatched ceiling with its patterns of late afternoon sunlight, then turned on her side to look at him. She felt languorous and could barely manage to lift her head. Her lips against his broad, sweating shoulders, she murmured impishly, 'Gautam ... you could have given me another baby.' She touched his hand. 'Would you like to be a father again?'

'Yes,' he said, taking a strand of her hair. 'But only if it's a girl: then I could teach her to be nice, kind, understanding and as clever as you are.'

She snuggled into his chest, content and happy.

Her home had changed forever: it wasn't hers anymore, Sachi thought swallowing a lump in her throat.

'How does it feel to be married to the killer of our father?'

Sachi looked up at her sister. Fury glittered in the grey eyes of Sivasri.

'It was self-defence,' said Sachi feebly.

'Self-defence for the mighty Indra?' Sivasri said scornfully. 'He is said to be immortal, the king of the Devas. Yet he used the most dastardly ways to fight both Vrita and our father. He got rid of the two Asuras who did not bow to him.'

'It was a duel,' argued Sachi. 'It was a fair fight.'

'Is that how you have convinced yourself?' sneered her sister. 'You would take anything, do anything, to be his wife. You are his slave, Sachi! Even the fact that he killed our father does not revolt you ... *You* disgust me, Sachi!

Sachi flinched. Her thoughts went back to the moment Shakra had arrived to ask for her hand.

Things had not panned out as she would have wished. She had not anticipated her father's wrath.

'So, the great king of the Devas has deigned to meet a Danav king,' her father had said, his voice loud and dripping with open contempt as Indra entered the royal court. He did not stand up from his golden throne to greet him.

'I would like to marry your daughter Sachi,' Indra had stated stiffly, his face as insolent as that of the king facing him.

King Puloman was an old man, his face was large and heavily scarred. He had a straggly moustache that hid his top lip and eyes that conveyed suspicion and cruelty. Yet she had seen them kind and soft. Her father was the kindest man she and the kingdom knew.

King Puloman glanced at his daughter, his eyes questioning. Sachi was not looking at him but at Indra, round-eyed, too shy to welcome him. It enraged the king further.

'I do not respect a man who has seduced my daughter before marriage,' the Danav king said, scowling.

Indra flushed. 'That is why I wish to marry her,' he said, keeping his temper in check, his voice even.

'Oh, you have scruples too, you mean to say?'

The sarcasm was not lost on Indra. He clenched his jaw.

'So, after chasing Ahalya and not getting her, you turn your attention on my hapless daughter,' accused Puloman.

'I, the king of the Devas, am requesting you, a Danav king, for his daughter's hand in marriage. Is that not scrupulous enough?' Indra said, his lips twisted in disdain. 'Yet here I am.'

Puloman made a dismissive gesture with his small, fat hand. 'Perhaps. But Sachi shall be marrying Vrita, it's been so decided. You asked, I refuse and you may leave now.'

For a moment Indra could not believe his ears.

'Father, no, please!' cried Sachi, jumping to her feet. 'I will *not* marry Vrita. I have explained everything to you!'

Puloman had lost the benign expression he reserved for his daughters and looked like what Indra knew he must be: a shrewd, tough father.

'Let there be a duel; it will decide the outcome and our fate,' interrupted a quiet voice. It was Vrita.

'You dare!' Sachi snapped, her eyes flashing.

Indra turned and looked the army general over. Vrita had everything in the way of good looks a man could want: he was tall and broad-shouldered. He looked strong—almost unpleasantly so—and had a reputation for being as lithe as a jungle cat and twice as dangerous. His brown, lean face was coldly savage, and there was a chilling expression in his eyes. His skin was a smooth ebony. He was truly handsome and made a formidable rival. Unlike Gautam, Indra thought wryly, yet he had lost to that unattractive rishi ...

Indra found himself nodding. The time had come when words would not work, swords would.

After this, things had moved so swiftly that Sachi could barely register it all. All she knew was that Shakra had killed the unconquerable Vrita in spite of the latter being blessed with a boon that stated that he would not be killed by any weapon. It had been a long and terrible fight. Desperate, fighting more for his throne and life than his love, Indra had been forced to create a special weapon—the Vajrayudh, made out of the bones of Rishi Dadhichi, the only rishi who knew the secret of the Madhuvidya, the knowledge of immortality. It was only because of his vajra that Shakra had finally been able to kill Vrita.

Her father had been shattered, and in anguished frenzy, had decided to face Indra himself on the battlefield.

'Father, please don't!' she had implored, for the first time frightened for her father's life. Never in her wildest imagination would she have believed she would be responsible for such calamity. 'Vrita is dead, Father, and everyone knows he was practically invincible. Shakra will kill you too; please don't duel with him!'

'I would rather die than agree to have you marry him!'

'But why?' she sobbed. 'I love him ...'

'He can never love you. He is a selfish debauch who parades as the king of Devlok!' he thundered. 'He used you to get to me, Sachi! And he is using you right now to get rid of us. He killed Vrita and now he will try and kill me!'

'I can't have you die because of me, Father, please, no!' she cried. 'I take back my words. I shan't marry him, I promise, I shall forget him! But please don't war with him!'

'It's too late now, the word is out,' her father said grimly. 'Why do you think he agreed to meet me? Not for your supposed love, you silly girl, but as a pretext to challenge us—the Asuras—and destroy us forever. Till now, he has never directly confronted us and you provided him with a reason to do so.'

Sachi looked at her father and then at her clenched fists. Would Shakra be so devious, she thought. She remembered Shakra's reluctance to meet her father, his reluctance to commit to her, his reluctance to marry her.

Sachi blinked, rushing back to the present. She had lost her father, her family, her respect ... Her sister and her mother hated her.

'Don't make me feel worse than I do! I didn't know ... I had no idea ...' She turned her face away from the condemning glare in Sivasri's eyes, feeling wretched.

'You forgot you are an Asura-putri who is now the queen of the Devas,' Sivasri said, her face contorted in a grimace of hate. 'You are our enemy now, as was Indra. We loathe you! Your husband killed Father!' She glared at Sachi. 'And now you dare come here to tell us we can stay put at the palace? To "allow" us to stay in our home?'

'That is not what I meant. And where will you go?' pleaded Sachi. 'Shakra does not seek vengeance, Sivasri. He sent me here to convince you of the same. Remain in the palace. It is yours. And mother's.'

Sivasri did not look at her, but her nose was pinched and her eyes were like holes in a mask. She prowled around the large chamber. Her eyes roved around the room, lingering on each piece of furniture, then came back to Sachi.

'It *was* ours, Sachi,' she hissed. 'Always. But no longer. You took our everything to have that damned Indra! And all he wanted was to get rid of Father and Vrita.'

'What makes you think you're so right?' Sachi snapped. 'If that were so, he didn't have to marry me after killing Father, but he kept his word. He loves me!'

'If you insist.' Sivasri shrugged dismissively. 'But by marrying him, you haven't got his loyalty,' she continued contemptuously. 'You are the trophy he got for defeating the Asuras, but will it stop him from going after other women? He says he loved Ahalya, but he seduced you the very night she got married to Rishi Gautam—that is the depth of his love.'

Sachi's mouth tightened. 'He was a broken man ...' But she stopped short, the doubts milling in her mind again.

'I am his wife now; he is mine,' she said finally, trying to convince her sister as well as herself. She was still saying it to herself much later, when she was back at Amravati, back in his ornate chamber, back in his ornate bed, back in Shakra's arms.

'Did you manage to persuade them?' he murmured, his hands moving down her silky curves, his lips on her bared neck. He vaguely recalled Sachi's sister as a trifle heavy in the bottom but boasting of a long-limbed, voluptuous figure. She had a wide, glistening mouth, he remembered—and an utterly disdainful expression on her face every time she looked at him, as if she could see all the sins that lurked in his past.

Sachi struggled to answer.

'Does it matter?' she said bleakly. 'They said you were ruthless, and now that I've seen what you did to Father, I believe it. I have lost them forever. They will never forgive me and they hate me now, as they hate you. Now I am your companion in crime,' she said.

'I am not a monster,' he said, caressing the inside of her thigh. She trembled. He felt the muscles in her back stiffen, but she made no attempt to break away from him. Instead, she shifted closer. She looked at him and then leaned against him. Her back was warm, but the tiny drops of perspiration on her skin felt cold. He put his arm around her. She leaned against his chest, her hair, damp and perfumed, against his cheek.

'Make me forget them, Shakra,' she murmured hoarsely, sliding her arms around his neck. 'Make me forget everything.'

He took her chin between his finger and thumb and raised her face. She closed her eyes. She looked pale, like a beautiful porcelain sculpture, in the moonlight. He looked down at her, then he kissed her long and deep. Her lips tasted salty, from her tears.

They were kissing, holding each other, their mouths seeking and getting what each wanted from the other. When their lips met, her fear seemed to dissolve as she was carried on the crest of desire. Each touch of his lips drew hungry moans from her. She wanted to stay like that for eternity: loving him, he loving her, while they rode the waves of desire. At that moment, she didn't care what was going to happen, even though she was sure that *something* was going to happen. Till a small sound parted them.

'Ahalya ...'

Sachi froze. Had she heard right?

His face was above hers, beautiful and tortured, suffused with a strong, uncontrollable emotion; she could barely see through her own haze of heightened ecstasy.

No, she had not heard right. It could not possibly be. She had only imagined it in her grief, because of her father's warning words: *He loved only Ahalya ...*

Shakra had never taken *her* name while they were in the throes of passion. The pain slicing through her was as intense and violent as the passion convulsing through him.

Grief overcame her, but she dared not allow a sob to escape. She closed her eyes, trying to stem tears that felt very wet, very hot, very heavy behind her eyelids ...

An hour later, she stood gazing outside the palace windows, watching the opalescent seawaters changing hues as clouds moved overhead. Scattered green islands gleamed like emeralds. On the distant horizon, the sky traced a line of pink and orange, the sun rose over the golden sands, the ocean sparkled and the palms nodded their heads in the lazy breeze. Indralok looked wonderful, but Sachi, now dry-eyed, was beginning to wonder if it was too good to be true ...

16

New World

Gautam was with the students, while Ahalya was working in the cowshed; their two little boys played in a haystack nearby. They had been at it since dawn, with a break for the early meditation and another break for a morning meal. Ahalya was carrying a bucket of milk out of the shed when she saw a small boy come up the dirt road that led to the ashram.

Ahalya put down the bucket, stood up and wiped her hands. She watched the boy curiously, and a glance revealed that Gautam was doing the same. He, too, was looking at the tiny fellow as he came slowly up the path, absently kicking at pebbles and scattering sand.

As he approached, she saw that the boy was barely seven; he had dark, tousled hair and wore shabby but clean clothes. His eyes—so alert—looked huge on his thin face. Her heart instantly melted.

'Are you hungry?' she asked. The boys, Vama and Shatanand, had followed her out. She picked up the younger toddler, Shatanand, and placed him comfortably on her hip.

The visitor shook his head, keeping his eyes averted from the bucket of milk but not before she had glimpsed a swift look of longing in them.

'Here, have some. It's fresh,' she said, thrusting a big tumbler in his scrawny hands.

He hesitated and then, looking at her warm smile, he gulped it up hungrily.

'I want to meet the guru,' he said shyly, wiping his mouth with the back of his hand, glancing curiously at Vama, who was tugging at his mother's sari.

'You may, soon. What is your name?'

'Jabaali.'

'That's a lovely name. What does it mean?'

He gave her a blank look. 'I don't know. But my mother is called Jabaal and I am Jabaali, her son.'

'Oh, that's beautiful—to have your mother's name!' said Ahalya, genuinely moved. 'Come, I shall take you to the guru. You have come here to study, have you?'

He nodded his little head vigorously.

'But why alone? Where is your father?' she asked, looking down the road to catch sight of an adult.

'I don't have a father,' he said matter-of-factly.

'Your mother?' she questioned a little anxiously. Had this child run away from home?

'She is busy. She works through the day and can't get away from work to have me admitted to this school. She told me to go on my own.'

'And that's why you are here,' she said. She led him to the hut and placed a bowl of grapes in his lap, Shatanand still chortling at her hip. 'Have these till the guru comes. He is busy taking a class right now.'

'I shall wait,' he said, smiling diffidently.

They did not have to wait long. Gautam walked in to see his wife chatting with the boy and his two little sons trying to be friends with him.

'You are my new student, I hope?' he asked cheerfully with a smile.

The smile put the boy immediately at ease. He smiled back shyly, his eyes getting bigger in his small face, the awe obvious.

'I want to learn from you. My mother sent me here,' he stammered.

He reminded Ahalya of herself: scared and unsure the first time she had arrived at the ashram.

'His name is Jabaali,' said Ahalya. 'Is that not an unusual name?'

'And your father's?' questioned Gautam.

The boy looked fearful again. He shook his head. 'I don't know,' he whispered.

'Is he dead?' Gautam asked, his tone more gentle now.

'I don't know,' repeated the boy.

Gautam gave the boy a searching look.

'And your mother?'

'Her name is Jabaal,' supplied the boy. 'She works in the town. Mostly at night. During the day, she cooks for me and takes care of me,' he said.

He paused and then continued, 'My mother said that if I were asked about my father, to let you know that neither she nor I know who my father is ...'

The pause was short but heavy. He was an abandoned child, Ahalya realised.

'Can I join the school?' he asked Gautam tentatively, his large eyes earnest and eager.

'Yes, of course, you may!' Gautam gave the boy a reassuring smile. 'Aha, Jabaali, the son of Jabaal, that is good. You can start coming to class from tomorrow itself. This lady here is now your mother in the ashram. She will look after you, and you can only go home when it is a holiday.'

'Can I?' the boy said. 'I miss my mother already. I have never been away from her. But she said that if I wanted to be a scholar, I would have to stay away from her and study hard here ...' he stuttered, his voice thick with tears.

Ahalya touched his shoulder gently and drew him close to her. 'Yes, now you stay here and study hard, and she will be happy. But first, tell me, what are the sweets you like. I shall prepare some for you.'

Jabaali smiled through his tears. 'I haven't had sweets before—we can't afford them. But I love dal with vegetables.'

'You will have it tonight for dinner,' she promised. 'Now go and have a quick bath. I shall take you to the river. Let's go. Come, Vama, join us!'

The four-year-old solemnly followed his mother and his new friend as they walked together towards the riverbank.

It was only an hour later, after she had settled in the new boy, that Ahalya got to speak with Gautam again.

'How did you take him in without knowing his background?' she asked curiously.

'His background is his mother,' Gautam said shortly.

'Exactly. We don't know who the father is, the name nor family.'

'That is because he doesn't know who his father is, he said so himself, and—'

'He has been abandoned?' she asked, her heart contracting.

'Or worse,' Gautam said with a sigh.

'He is illegitimate?'

'Ahalya, the boy is a prostitute's son.'

Ahalya was taken aback. 'How do you know?'

'I recognised the mother's name. Anyway, the boy said it himself, in no uncertain way. The mother sent the message through her son. He is Jabaal's Jabaali. That is all I need to know of the boy. Nothing else matters.'

But, for some, that was evidently not the case. The next week, Ahalya was surprised to see a crowd of elderly people from the village and the nearby town arriving at the ashram.

Gautam greeted them in the assembly room, but she was surprised when he lead them into the inner room. What were they discussing that Gautam did not want the others in the ashram to hear or know?

Within half an hour, they left, angry and red-faced, their lips compressed into tight, furious lines, as if they wished to argue no further.

Gautam hesitated, wondering whether to tell Ahalya what had happened in the room inside. For a few brief moments, he considered not telling her, then he changed his mind. She would have to know. She would hear it from someone else anyway. So he told her.

'They were the priests and local heads of the adjoining village. They want me to throw out Jabaali,' he started.

She sat motionless, her hands between her knees, her eyes a little wide, listening.

'Because he is a prostitute's son?'

Gautam nodded. 'They had come to inform me about that. I told them I was aware of who his mother is and assured them that it does not matter; the boy stays here. They clearly did not like that, and threatened to withdraw the other students. I remained adamant—I refused to send Jabaali away.'

'So this makes for complications,' she said. 'From now on, we mustn't say a word about Jabaali or his mother to anyone?'

'There is no need to explain anything to anyone,' Gautam stated firmly. 'The boy remains here in this ashram. And he remains under my protection.'

'Could those people make trouble for us and the ashram? Because you are teaching a boy they don't consider worthwhile?'

'Who decides that?' he said angrily. 'These are the people who make up rules to distinguish and discriminate, to exploit and subjugate. In my ashram, all are welcome. I will never say no to anyone who has the yearning and will to study.'

'But what if they carry out their threat and take away the other students?'

'I cannot do anything about that,' he said with a shrug. 'But I shall not forsake the child to appease these people. He is my responsibility.'

The next day, it got worse.

A few young men arrived, but Gautam refused to let them inside the ashram. He and Uttank walked up to the gate to address them.

'This is an ashram meant for those who want to learn and study,' Gautam said, his tone terse. 'Do you?'

'Get that boy out!' said one man rudely.

'Get yourself out!' Gautam barked at him, using his teacher's voice that could carry a quarter of a mile. 'What are you hanging around here for, troubling the students during their study hour?'

If Gautam had hit him across the face, the youth couldn't have looked more startled. But only for a moment; then he stiffened. His face turned vicious and hard, and his eyes glittered with rage as he glared at Gautam.

'And don't ever try and step in here again!' roared Gautam, his voice quivering with fury.

There was a long explosive pause. The lad seemed unable to make up his mind about whether to attack Gautam or give up. Finally, the lad forced a vicious grin on his face, and then walked slowly to the other waiting men.

'Go ahead, children, go back to your studies,' Gautam ordered, softening his tone. He walked over to the hut where Ahalya was standing in the veranda. He knew she had seen and heard what had happened. He wanted to reassure her.

'Don't let my big teacher's voice scare you!' he said with grin, trying to be reassuring. But she stared at him, bewildered and a little dazed. 'It's a trick. You just shout back at the bullies, louder and clearer, and you get things done.'

She made an effort to pull herself together. 'I've never heard a voice like that. I couldn't believe it was coming from you!'

And then she smiled radiantly, her eyes shining. 'I was not scared, Gautam. I am proud of you!'

She reached for his hands and held them in a warm grasp.

Sachi sat on the balcony that ran the length of Indra's palace and watched the city of Amravati sparkling below her. The wonder city was built along blue waters with miles of golden sand and palm trees. The palaces were exquisite, with high domes and white marble. Tree-lined avenues led into Amravati from all four directions. Flowerbeds decorated the winding pathways. Every exotic flower, tree and plant blossomed around her, and the effect was like a dream. The colours hurt her eyes.

But right now, Sachi barely noticed what was in front of her. From time to time she glanced towards the doorway with an impatient frown. Indra had not returned since the previous day. It was now late afternoon and there was still no sign of him.

Then she spotted him walking down the wide porch and she felt her heartbeat quicken. He looked inordinately pleased, and she could judge from his expression where he had been ...

He was always the same when he had been with the apsaras—happy and garrulous—and it infuriated her. It infuriated her even more that he was so blasé about it. Even while she ranted, he remained annoyingly unrepentant; the tone of his voice would sharpen and his golden eyes became like molten fire.

'Where have you been?!' Sachi asked peremptorily.

Indra raised an eyebrow. 'Sachi, I am a busy person. I can't stay at the palace resting with you the whole day!'

'You have been gone the whole of yesterday and half of today!' she snapped. 'You were with your apsaras!'

He exhaled exaggeratedly. 'If you know, why are you asking me?' he said. 'Yes, there was a dance recital by Urvashi and Menaka, a sort of competition between them. It was thoroughly entertaining!'

She gave him a thoughtful look. 'You *would* find it fun. Pitting one against the other is your favourite past time,' she said with a sneer. 'Your divide and conquer rule works with the apsaras and gandharvas; they all seem to be at loggerheads with each other.'

'That's how peace reigns in paradise,' he said with a grin that he hoped was disarming enough to calm Sachi down.

'And that's how you rule ... How stupid can you be?' she said quietly.

Indra flushed red. Only Sachi could dare talk to him in that manner. She crossed her long legs, the folds of her silk parting to show the silken length of her thigh. Indra felt his blood rush.

'The apsaras might prance around you, but they don't love you as you think they do. Menaka loves Vishwavasu, Urvashi cannot get over Pururav, and Rambha is crazy about Tumburu, the celestial musician and your best singer. Women like the apsaras want to be the centre of attraction, always,' she said, smiling mirthlessly. 'If they fuss around you, it's to make you feel good, nothing else. It only makes you look foolish that you believe otherwise.'

'Why are you jealous of them, then?' he asked, smiling back, but the smile did not reach his eyes. 'You could have joined us. It was a beautiful dance and music show.'

'Us?' she said. 'You mean you and your best friend, Vrishakapi, your partner in crime? I will not attend your private shows. If there is an honorary guest, I shall join you, as a good host should,' she said with a careless lift of her shoulders. '... as the queen of the gods and goddesses.'

'No,' Indra shook his head and said softly. 'As my consort. You are *not* the queen of the Devas and Devis.'

'No?' she said, smiling frostily. 'Then what is my status here?'

'As I said, my consort. The wife of Indra. You are Indrani.'

'Like I was Paulomi, the daughter of Puloman, the Asura king?' she asked insolently.

Indra glowered. 'No one knows you as Paulomi here! You are Indrani, my wife, who has been granted immortality, thanks to *me*. Remember, I chose you over all of the other Devis because of your, ah, magnetic beauty.'

He gave her a lascivious smirk.

Sachi was standing before the open window. She was in shimmering sheer silk. With the light against her, he could see her long, shapely legs and the curve of her firm breasts and flaring hips through the flimsy material. This sight always affected him, but Sachi's mood made it impossible to sustain such feelings.

Without hurrying, he entered the chamber and went past her without looking at her. She felt a surge of exasperated rage rush through her, and she had to restrain herself from jumping to her feet and going after him. He was incorrigible, she thought. Nothing ever moved him! He must know how the past hours had dragged for her, waiting for him. Couldn't he have given her just a slight hint of affection?

She persisted, her eyes flaring. 'Each one at Indralok has a purpose and designation. What is mine, Shakra, besides being your wife?'

'Sachi, I have chosen you, amongst all women ...' Indra started impatiently.

'Yes, despite being an Asura princess,' she said wryly. 'I know just how welcome I am here in Indralok because of who I am. I am considered an evil spirit! Some call me the goddess of wrath behind my back. Some sneeringly refer to me as a devi of jealousy.'

'Sachi, your constant fighting has become so well known that they think you are nothing but a jealous shrew,' said Indra in exasperation.

'*I* am a shrew?' she cried shrilly. 'And what do they call you? A philanderer, a womaniser. What's more insulting?'

She jumped to her feet. 'Your good friend Vrishakapi does not approve of me. You are all in cahoots. They despise me for what I am—an Asura in Devlok, and worse, an Asura who has married the king of the Devas. Do you know that, Shakra? Have you ever noticed it?'

'How does it matter? You are my wife,' he said flatly.

'And I am supposed to feel honoured?' she said.

The quiet rage in her voice made him look sharply at her.

'Why are you so angry, Sachi?' he demanded. 'And so unhappy? You don't like it here, you don't like the apsaras, you don't like my friends—'

'I don't mind your friends—but for Divodas, Ahalya's brother,' she said. 'And I would prefer if you spent less time with your "soulmate" Vrishakapi. You spend more time with him than me!' she said, irate. 'But then, I can understand. He's your oldest friend. How can you still be friends with Divodas, after your humiliation at their court?'

Indra clenched his hands into fists. Why did Sachi insist on raking up memories? He gave an exasperated sigh. It was best not to talk of it further.

'What do you want, Sachi?' he asked helplessly. 'I have given you my all!'

'All?' she said. '*I* have given my *all*, Shakra. And I lost my all for you. As your wife, can't you dignify me with the respect I deserve? Even the apsaras pay me no attention!'

'Because you resent them,' he said impatiently. 'They are the heart and soul of Devlok. As are the gandharvas. You have riled them all since your arrival. *You* give them respect, and it shall be returned.'

'I was born a princess,' she muttered through clenched teeth. 'For me, they are entertainers, and I give them the respect they deserve.'

'This is not prithvi, with its rules and values. This is Indralok—the heaven all want to live in after they die. You have been given the gift of immortality to live here. Live in peace and love.'

'I seem to be having it in excess all around me,' she said testily.

Indra sighed. 'What's troubling you? Why are you looking so unhappy?'

She stared sullenly at him as he moved to the doorway.

'Sometimes I think I'm crazy in the head to have ever loved you,' she said savagely. 'Do you have to be so coldblooded ... like ... like ... that Ahalya?'

'Please, not Ahalya again! What do you know of her? You seem to be obsessed ... !'

'Am I or are *you*?' Sachi shouted, jumping to her feet, her face flushed with fury. 'You moan her name when we are in the throes of lovemaking, you mutter her name in your sleep and fantasise about her with your eyes wide open all through the day! *That* is obsession!'

Indra went a waxen white.

'Whatever I say won't convince you otherwise. Pardon me and my obsessions, Sachi,' he said with a shrug. 'I am going to bathe now,' he added dismissively after staring at her for a brief moment. He moved past her and walked towards the pool in the garden.

She listened as he stamped down the corridor. When his footsteps faded away, she sat on the edge of the chair, surrounded by the chests of gems and jewellery he had given her the day before, and pressed her hands to her eyes. Another day, another quarrel. But what was constant was Ahalya, always Ahalya!

17

Uttank

Gautam woke up at dawn, and almost immediately began to feel that sense of restlessness again. It was something he had been experiencing for the past few months: a restiveness that he could not explain.

Ever since he had got married, he had looked forward to waking up with Ahalya and seeing her sleeping form nestled on his chest. It had brought him a feeling of contentment and pleasure. These last few months, though, he seemed to derive no pleasure from it—only resentment. For the past five years, he had been getting up late because of his late nights, and the thought of the lost hours irritated him now.

He was thinking: *Of course I am in a rut. I've been in a rut ever since I married. I don't suppose I shall ever get back to the routine of endless hours of work and meditation and research.*

He could hear Ahalya in his study. Was she studying? He frowned. She should be resting; she was pregnant and close to the delivery date of their third child.

He cursed himself for not being up and about before her. He had slept badly, and that made his mood worse. He walked to his study and saw Ahalya not poring over her books but clearing up the room. His room was a mess: books lay about in disarray, and his desk was covered with a dozen stacks of parchments, each of which warranted careful study before placing them where they belonged. Ahalya, heavy in her last month of pregnancy, was perusing them, a slight frown pleating her smooth forehead, absently trying to smooth back strands of hair that had shaken loose from her bun as she went steadily through the pile.

Dipping a pen in the inkstand, she paused when she noticed him standing in the doorway.

'I'm drawing out a list of tasks that you need to get done in the next three days,' she said.

He nodded.

'You're late; you go join the students. I shall clear this room later,' she said with a quick smile before she hurried to prepare breakfast for everyone.

Gautam had work ahead of him, and usually, he was in a good frame of mind when he was working. But during the past few months, he seemed unable to handle his workload. That worried him. He stayed up nights thinking about sutras that he had not been able to finish, and worrying about what was pending only made him more irritable. The only consolation was Ahalya, and he felt guilty about her too; he barely gave her any time, and when he did, he ended up venting his temper on her. Even now he had worked himself into a vicious mood. Exasperated with himself, he started across to the kitchen.

He could hear Ahalya's voice as he approached. She sounded animated. He slowed, then stopped in the shadow of the thin wall and listened.

'I was like you before I met the guru,' she was saying. 'You may not believe it, but I was. I'm still nervous sometimes, of course, but I am better ...'

Gautam frowned. Who was she talking to?

'... before I met Gautam, I was so mixed up, so unsure, just looking in a mirror made me jump. I guess it was my own silly fears ...' A long pause, then she went on. 'They say that most kids blame their parents when they are in a mess. What do you think?'

Gautam was surprised. She was chatting as she had not spoken with him recently: they barely had time together these days. He rubbed his face and edged closer. This was something he wanted to hear.

'It's as good an excuse as any.' Gautam scarcely recognised Uttank's voice. The boy was actually talking in sentences! He, too, sounded animated.

'We are all looking for excuses,' Uttank said solemnly, sounding so wise for his years. 'Maybe our parents are to blame, but we're to blame too. It is merely a consoling thought to wish our parents had only been different. There are special cases, of course, but I think we just have to help ourselves.'

'You're lucky to be able to think like that,' Ahalya said. 'I realise it too. I am the odd one in my family.'

'Odd? In what way?' he asked curiously.

'I think that I am ... hmm ... maybe a disappointment. My twin brother is an achiever: he is handsome, confident, affable—everything my parents could have hoped for him to be. I simply wasn't.'

'But you are so beautiful!' Uttank said with obvious awe.

'Beauty doesn't help face daily parental expectations. I seem to do nothing right,' she said with a sigh. 'My father hoped I would be a scholar, my mother wanted me to marry a powerful, handsome, wealthy man—like Indra—and be queen of the celestials. Instead, I am here,' she said with a laugh.

'But Rishi Gautam *is* the most powerful man,' frowned Uttank.

Ahalya smiled. 'It's not him; it's about me. You see, my mother had great expectations from me. I think I spent a lot of time trying to get some attention and love from her. To me, love is important.' A long pause, then she asked, 'Don't you think so?'

'I wouldn't know, but I reckon it's important to all.' Uttank's voice was suddenly flat. 'I've been brought up in a different way. I am an orphan. But I know my guru loves me. He is the only one who does. But why do you say you are a disappointment: you are so loving and clever and lovely. You are a mother to all of us here at the ashram.'

'I have no confidence in myself. I feel inadequate. I scare easily. I almost faint if there's a thunderstorm. I was much worse before I met your guru. You mustn't think because he shouts and scowls that he isn't kind and understanding.'

There was no response from Uttank.

'I don't know why I'm talking like this.' Ahalya's laugh was self-conscious. 'You looked so depressed and worried, the same way I know I look sometimes, I guess I couldn't help it.'

Gautam decided it was time to walk in on the scene. He backed away silently, then started for the kitchen, treading hard to herald his approach.

He entered the kitchen. The moment he walked in, he felt the relaxed atmosphere change. Uttank was holding a ladle. At the sight of Gautam, he stood as if transfixed. Fear jumped into his eyes and he looked like a dog expecting to be kicked. Ahalya was sitting on one of the benches, her face a little flushed, her eyes sparkling. When she saw him, the sparkle died and she looked at him apprehensively.

Uttank was quick to notice her nervousness. 'I ... I was h–helping with the heavy utensils—she sh–shouldn't be carrying them anymore,' he stammered, paling at the sight of his guru's tense face. 'I shall collect the firewood from the forest,' he said hurriedly and rushed out.

Both waited for him to leave the room. 'I am surprised you are indulging in this kind of chat with a student. He's a kid—what are you filling his head with?' Gautam said, his face as stern as his tone. There was a snap in his voice. He hadn't meant to speak so sharply, but he was already upset.

She gave him a startled look.

'He's petrified of you. I was just trying to make him feel better after the shouting you gave him last evening,' she said, biting her lip.

'Uttank—scared of me? What nonsense! He's like a son to me!' It was not just the hotness outside which made his mouth feel dry and his throat constricted; it was the rising heat of his temper.

'A son who is terrified of his father,' she said sardonically. 'And a father who takes his son for granted.'

Despite the scowl on her husband's face, she went on, her fingers weaving nervously. 'He is obedient, he is respectful, he is efficient, he is hardworking, but that is not an indication that he is not scared of you. These are *his* qualities, not yours,' she said, smiling diffidently.

'Am I a fiend?' Gautam demanded, his tone sharp.

She flinched away from him. She hesitated for a brief moment. They looked at each other, then she nodded.

'When you shout and rant, you are like a fiend, though you don't seem to realise it,' she said. 'You don't seem to know it! There's something wrong with you these days. All that temper! That frustration! You must know there's something wrong.'

He pulled himself together and gave her a close look.

'What is it, Ahalya? What's on your mind?'

She bit her lip and pulled hard at a lock of her hair.

'I don't know what's troubling you these days,' she began hesitantly. 'I think you are pushing yourself too much with your writing ...'

His scowl deepened. 'For God's sake! Don't be a typical complaining wife!'

'Am I?' she demanded, sitting forward and staring at him. 'I am simply letting you know that you are tense and worried and angry. And I want to know why.'

'It's work, you know that!' he said impatiently.

'See, that's what I mean. I can't seem to get through to you when you are in one of your moods. And you frighten everybody, especially the students,' she said. 'Otherwise, you are a saint,' she said more gently. 'Or who else could have been so kind to Jabaali?' she said.

Gautam gave an unexpected small smile, easing the tension. 'He is a bright boy. You can see he's doing so brilliantly. He deserves a good education.'

'Most wouldn't agree,' she said dryly. 'Not many ashrams would have taken in a child of dubious parentage.'

'But that is exactly what I get angered by—the discrimination in education. Every child, every person, has a right to knowledge, a right to education. Who are we to deny it? As teachers, if we discriminate, that *is* a sin!'

'Is that what is causing the anger in you?' she said. 'I love you like this, when you are so kind and concerned,' she said softly, slowly slipping her hand into his. It calmed him immediately.

'But you say I am a monster,' he said grimly.

'Most of the time, these days,' she said. 'That's why I had to make Uttank feel comfortable. He is now grown-up—a man. I know he is very dear to you, but Uttank has completed his education. You need to let him go. He is too scared of you to say so.'

Gautam looked perplexed—the thought had never struck him.

'Uttank might be a learned rishi, but he still needs to become more confident,' said Ahalya.

'And you can help with that by feeding him some tall stories about yourself?' scoffed Gautam. 'From what I overheard, let me assure you that you are nothing like him.'

Ahalya slowly shook her head. 'I was, and I think I still am. We are rather alike,' she said.

'You're not!' he said, feeling a flash of irrational annoyance again. 'Don't compare yourself with him, Ahalya. I don't like it. He's my student, you are my wife.'

'We think alike.'

'How so? Like both of you are scared of me?' he said in disbelief. 'I'm asking you: Why are you being so overprotective of Uttank? What does he mean to you?'

She looked at him, her face crimson, her eyes shocked. 'What are you saying?!' she cried. 'He's like a brother to me—the first friend I made when I came to the ashram. That's what he means to me! He's frightened, and I felt sorry for him.'

'Well ... Fine ... though I think you protect him too much. In any case, please stop casting aspersions about me! I have enough to handle without you insinuating that there's something wrong with me.'

'Gautam, you don't seem to realise that you *do* frighten people,' she said gently.

'Now you're going to tell me I frighten you too, aren't you?'

She nodded. Her hands turned into fists. She looked very young, scared and vulnerable.

'Yes. These last few months you've become someone I don't know. Yes, you frighten me.'

Gautam slapped his hands down hard on his knees. The sound made her start.

There was a long, tense pause. He looked around for a second, and then said, 'I'm sorry. I don't want to frighten you or anybody. I am simply overworked and worried. I really am a boor these days, am I not?' he sighed, expelling a long breath. He forced a smile on his face.

She hesitated, then nodded.

'Yes, sometimes,' she said. 'Especially when you get agitated and shout.'

He shook his head. 'But that's because I get impatient when I teach—you know that!'

She pressed her hands together. 'No, you never did, you never were like that. You were a kind, patient teacher. But these days, you are so jumpy and irascible. You get so angry with the students—and us,' she said. 'You shout at us so often; Vama and Shatanand are afraid of you too—have you not noticed?'

When he remained silent, she continued. 'Is it the teaching or the additional work that has changed you?' she asked in a low voice. 'Or your own expectations of yourself? Because you *have* changed, Gautam,' she repeated, looking up and forcing a smile. 'When you told me the first time we met that you were essentially a teacher, I found it hard to believe. You weren't like any other rishi ... You were so kind, so understanding—and not just to me. I couldn't believe how well you handled the students and the ashram. It puzzled me.' She paused. 'I see now how and why you teach, but there's some latent anger in you now—it is a little scary ...'

He stared at her. It was the second time she had said that. Those words brought him down to earth. During all the time he had known her, Gautam knew Ahalya scared easily: he had never left her on her own in the ashram. He was annoyed with himself for frightening her.

He took her hands in his, and realised that his hands were shaking.

'I do see you have to be rough and hard sometimes if you are to succeed, but please try not to be that way with me,' she said.

Gautam sighed. He took her face gently in his hands.

'No matter what, Ahalya, remember this: I love you. I am the luckiest man alive to have found you. But bear with me.

I am a difficult person to live with. All this is getting to me now—the work, the ashram, the students, my new book ...'

'Our little boys and me,' she finished quietly.

He shook his head and hugged her to him.

'No, no. Please bear with it for a few more days, Ahalya; it will change soon. You'll look back on this and you'll forgive me if I've hurt you. Or frightened you.'

'I've never seen you like this ... Suddenly, you're so hard and tough ...' She was speaking with her mouth against his neck and he could feel her trembling.

He pulled her hard against him. 'I love you,' he repeated huskily to reassure her and, also, to bolster himself.

He touched her lips softly with his, tender and tantalising, and soon they were kissing, holding each other and she was forgetting everything else ...

Uttank stood with his head bowed, his hands folded and his tone respectful.

'What would you like as gurudakshina, Guruji?'

Gautam shook his head absently. 'Nothing, Uttank, nothing.'

'But, you must ...' Uttank said sincerely.

'There is no must,' said Gautam gently.

'But I wish to give you something,' said Uttank, his face earnest.

Gautam smiled. 'That you are such a fine young man and a brilliant scholar is my gurudakshina.'

'If I am, it is because you made me so,' replied Uttank humbly.

Again, Gautam gave a slight shake of his head. 'I am a teacher, Uttank, I did what I have to do: it is my duty to impart not just knowledge but also values. It is an education in values, not information, that makes a better man, a better world.'

'And I am a better person now,' said Uttank, nodding.

'*That* is my gurudakshina, Uttank. You have made me happy and proud. I wouldn't wish for anything else but your prosperity.'

Uttank fumbled, his fingers clasped nervously. He licked his dry lips and said, 'But, I would like to give something ...'

Gautam sighed. His tone resigned, he said, 'Why don't you ask Ahalya? She has also been your guru. She has taught you subjects like history and geography and the arts.'

'And so much more!' gushed Uttank, his eyes glistening.

Gautam watched him thoughtfully. 'Yes, she loves you as much as you love her. Giving her something is like giving me my gurudakshina.'

Uttank nodded eagerly and left the room. Gautam stared after him, a solemn look on his face.

Uttank found Ahalya sitting by their hut, poring over books while the new-born baby kicked his little legs and watched the sun come up behind the trees.

'Does little Nodha not disturb you while studying?' he asked.

'That is a woman's special ability: to perform more than one task!' Ahalya said with a laugh.

Uttank watched the smile light up her face as he recalled the shy, reserved girl she was when she first arrived at the ashram, and how it had been easy to bully her. But that had been just for a few days, after which Rishi Gautam had taken her under his wing, like he had taken him in as an orphaned child.

'Yes, I can see that! Besides the baby, there's a pile of the students' clothes you intend to mend,' he said, picking up a singlet and starting to patch up the tiny tear in it.

'But you are leaving now, Uttank, you don't have to do these chores anymore,' she teased.

'I have trained Jabaali; he'll do it henceforth,' he said.

She laughed. 'But he's not as good as you!'

Uttank flushed. 'I am a better worker, but he's smarter,' he said with a wide grin.

The sudden whimpering cry of her son brought Ahalya to her feet. She picked him up and hurried back inside the hut to nurse him. After he was done, she resettled the baby in his cradle and he fell asleep. She remained kneeling beside his cradle, gazing into his sweet face. When her knees began to ache, she kissed him softly on the cheek. She listened for any signs of him stirring as she cleared the parchments Gautam had strewn around the room. It was late in the afternoon when she made her last inspection of the kitchen and shut the kitchen door. Her neck and shoulders burned with fatigue as she moved down the sunny veranda.

She was surprised to find Uttank still waiting for her on the porch; he was sewing swiftly, the needle flying fast. She had completely forgotten that she had left him there.

'Oh, I didn't realise you were still here,' she said. 'I see you have finished the pile of clothes,' she said.

'Yes, one less chore for you,' he said without looking up.

She looked at him tenderly. Uttank always fussed over her, trying to take on whatever he could to help ease her load of work. He was like Divodas, whom she missed acutely, shouldering the burden and worry with a winning smile and attitude bordering on the protective.

'What will I do without you?' she teased, but she was already feeling the sorrow of his departure.

Uttank looked solemn. 'You will take care of yourself, won't you?' his brow furrowed. 'Especially with the baby and the two boys and all this work and, of course, your studies, which you refuse to give up!'

She gave him a quick, reassuring smile. 'I don't mind the hardship,' she said, shrugging her delicate shoulders.

'What would *you* like as gurudakshina?' he said. 'Guruji said he does not want anything and suggested that I ask you. What would you like?'

'Nothing,' she said simply, stacking the books neatly. 'I have everything, don't I? But yes, without you, it will be difficult out here—what with you not hovering around to make things easy for me,' she said with her sweet smile.

There was a pensive note in her voice. Uttank knew Ahalya to be an emotional person, reacting intensely to situations and people.

'But that is why I want to give you something—something you will remember me by.'

'Isn't your absence strong enough to remind us of you?' she said brokenly.

'Don't get maudlin on me,' he said with mock sternness. His brows knitted together in thought and then his expression suddenly changed. 'How about the gem earrings you wanted?' he said with a bright smile. 'You once told me about them!'

Ahalya flushed in embarrassment. 'I said that in jest. Queen Madayanti's earrings are too precious for her—she won't ever part with them!'

'I can try,' he said earnestly.

'Don't be foolish, I have heard the earrings are special, that they are protected by the Nagas. They won't allow you to take them.'

Uttank rose. 'Good, you have given me a mission,' he said, grinning.

As he started towards the gate of the ashram, Ahalya called after him, 'Uttank ... please, stop.'

'What is it?' he said.

'Are you sure you want to get mixed up in this? I–I have a feeling ...'

'You are being nervous as usual! Leave it to me. This is a chance in a lifetime for me to prove myself.'

And with those words, Uttank left the ashram, leaving her with a nagging unease.

It was during dinner that Gautam broached the subject.

'Did Uttank meet you before leaving the gurukul?' he asked.

She nodded, absentmindedly stirring a pot, watching the curry simmer.

'He is a most obstinate fellow,' Gautam said with a fond smile. 'He insisted on giving gurudakshina despite my saying it was not required. He didn't take no for an answer. That was when I suggested he ask you. Did he?'

Again, Ahalya nodded.

'And what did you ask for?' he said, baffled by his wife's reticence.

'I told him to get me Queen Madayanti's earrings,' she mumbled, and hurriedly explained. 'I once mentioned to him that these earrings were so unusual that everyone aspired for them—even the Devas and the Daivas. I had wondered aloud what made them special. Clearly this conversation stuck in his head, and Uttank insisted that he would get them for me. He ... he said it would be his mission. Why "mission"? Is it so difficult to get them? Are the stories true?'

Gautam drew in a sharp breath. 'Do you realise what you asked for?'

She felt a prickle of apprehension crawl up her spine. 'Oh, why did I blurt it out in that moment of confession?' she cried, frightened now. 'It was self-indulgence, stupid me!'

'It is far worse,' Gautam said, his face and tone grim.

Her hand flew to her mouth; that niggling fear had a reason after all, she thought despairingly.

'What?' she murmured, in a stricken whisper.

'You sent him to bring you the precious earrings of King Saudasa's wife, Madayanti. Saudasa was cursed by Rishi Vashisht to become Kalmashpada—a roaming rakshas, a cannibal. It is impossible that Madayanti will give the earrings without her husband's permission, and meeting the king in his current form means certain death for Uttank.'

'No, *no*!'

Ahalya stood up, white, her face stiff with fear. 'Oh, what have I done?!' she whispered through bloodless lips. 'I have sent him to his death!'

Gautam looked down at her and put his arm round her. 'No, he can look after himself. I have not trained him to be pushed around. He is clever and will get out of any crisis, come what may. Be assured.'

'Will he?' she asked tremulously.

'He is my best student, and if I have taught him well, he won't come to harm,' he promised.

She allowed herself to be persuaded. She nodded weakly. Faith replaced fear.

It was Gautam's reassuring words that allowed her to hope that Uttank would return to the ashram soon. Till then, she had not realised how intense an emotion was regret. It nibbled ravenous through the mind and the heart and finally the soul. Why had she mentioned those damned earrings to him? Why had she allowed him to persuade her? Why had she not stopped him from this mad pursuit? Why had she ...? The whys tormented her silently, and it was only the memory of Gautam's words and the prayer on her lips that kept her in her senses to be able to go through the days, the weeks .... Uttank did not return.

Gautam, she knew, was trying to conceal his anxiety. His thin, craggy face remained expressionless, but Ahalya knew he was worrying himself to distraction.

One evening, she sat next to Gautam, who was looking out the open window as the darkness slowly settled over the ashram.

'I'm worried, Gautam. Can't we search for him?' she asked quietly.

'No, we can't,' he said shortly. 'I don't know where he has gone. All I know is that the queen did hand him the earrings.'

'Oh ... how did you find that out?' she asked, her face still tense.

'I have been trying to track him down,' he said. 'But after visiting the queen, he seems to have disappeared.'

Naked fear grabbed at her throat. Had he been robbed or worse, killed for those precious earrings? She found herself shaking, her mouth dry.

'He will come back,' she said with a conviction she did not feel.

She waited each day, every day. Weeks swiftly turned to months and the months expanded into a year. Yet, he did not come ...

It was an unusually sultry day. The stale, baked air coming in from the river, the stillness of the trees, the hot, sweating faces of the students and her children—all of these annoyed her. *A storm is probably about to come*, she thought, as she picked up an irritable Nodha in her arms. The air was claustrophobic, and she went to throw open the windows. It was then that she spotted him.

'Uttank!' she whispered in relief and delight.

No sight had ever gladdened her as the sight of him walking slowly towards the hut. She rushed out.

'Where were you?!' she asked unsteadily, choking back a sob of relief.

'All over the world!' he said weakly before settling down on the kitchen floor. 'Oh, the baby has grown into a big, bonny boy!' he said, taking Nodha in his arms. 'See, I got you these!'

His hand snaked into the sack he was holding on to and pulled out a pouch. He opened it with swift fingers, unfolding a sight to behold. As the multicoloured gems flashed and glittered against the shining gold, their brilliance seemed to taunt her.

'Were they worth it?' she asked, her voice dull. 'Uttank, you could have got killed and ... and ...' There was a catch in her voice. 'Gautam would not have ever forgiven me. Nor I myself.'

'Yes, it was dangerous,' Uttank admitted. 'But it was an adventure! As the queen rightly said, they are well deserving of the effort.'

Ahalya looked enquiringly at Uttank, her face still wan.

'Queen Madayanti handed me those earrings once I got permission from her husband—'

'I did not know he had been cursed to be a cannibal,' she broke in urgently.

'Well, I managed to convince him, telling him that I want them for my guru's wife. Later, I went to the palace, and she grudgingly gave them away, only because it would redeem her husband, I guess, and lessen the curse,' Uttank said gravely. 'She told me why they are so extraordinary. You were right. She, too, warned me that they have been coveted by the Nagas, the Yakshas, the gods and the rakshasas, who would try their hardest to steal them from me. "It is best you keep them close to you and do not allow them to touch the ground to prevent the snakes from seizing them," she cautioned me. Apparently, they produce gold! And the wearer is immune to disease, poison, thirst and hunger, fire and wild animals. That should keep you supremely safe in the forest from now on,' he said, happily. 'Now you need not fear the beasts in the jungle!'

'But the gold?' Ahalya's eyes widened. 'I thought that was just a legend! Do they actually produce gold?'

'Apparently so. You can check,' he said cheekily. 'They are like the earrings of the mother of the gods, Aditi, which were coveted by all and got stolen by Narkasura. They were gold-producing too.'

'What do I need gold for?' she sniffed daintily. 'I wonder why I even yearned for them: where and when would I wear them at the ashram?'

'But you have to, after all that I went through! I escaped being gobbled by a man-eating rakshas, cajoled a queen into parting with them, then lost them to a snake of the Airavata family and managed to recover them, thanks to Agni and Indra—'

'Indra?' Ahalya said quickly, with a sharp intake of breath. 'What was *he* doing there?'

'It's a long story, but without him, I wouldn't have been able to retrieve the earrings. On my way back from the palace, I had tied the earrings to a deerskin at my waist. I was feeling hungry, so I climbed a tree to pick some fruits. While doing so, the earrings fell to the ground, and before I could climb down, they were grabbed by Nagas, who hid them in an ant hill. For a month, I tried to dig through the enormous anthill but in vain. The Nagas kept them hidden deep inside it. Fortunately, Indra was riding by in his magnificent chariot, and he stopped to ask me why I was ploughing through an anthill. I told him my plight and how I badly wanted to gift you the earrings.'

Uttank paused, and Ahalya could feel her heart thudding, her throat dry with rising consternation. *Indra* ...

'Indra was very keen to help out after hearing my story. He offered me his new weapon, the vajra, to shatter the anthill. I finally entered Naglok,' Uttank said, his eyes shining. 'It was a fascinating, hypnotic world. And then I noticed an unusual horse—effulgent with copper eyes and muzzle, and a black-and-white tail. The horse was Agni: Indra had called for his brother to help. Agni willingly agreed, as the Fire God is the guru of our Guru Gautam.'

Ahalya sat motionless, listening, her hands between her knees and her dark eyes wide.

'I followed Indra's and Agni's instructions to blow hard on the hill from behind. The flames and smoke emerging from the horse spread to the anthill, choking the snakes and forcing them out, the culprit Takshak included. They were led by Vasuki, the Naga king himself. Takshak surrendered, proffered me the earrings and asked for pardon. I took them and hastily made my way to the ashram, clutching them close to my heart! And so here I am, and here they are!' he finished grandly.

A long pause, then she looked at him, her eyes inquiring.

'And what did Indra have to say?' she asked, her tone dipping low to a whisper.

'He said he was pleased he had been of some help to get you the earrings as gurudakshina. He sent his greetings,' replied Uttank sunnily. 'He truly was a huge help, and it was very kind of him to take the time to help a stranger on the road. He is the king of gods, and I did not expect him to even stop and ask. But the moment he heard I intended to gift you the earrings, he seemed more than eager to help. He—' Uttank stopped short as slowly a dim realisation dawned upon him. He stared at Ahalya. 'He did it for *you*, not me ...' he muttered.

Blood rushed into her pale face, and, to hide her confusion, Ahalya glanced down at the earrings, blazing against the deerskin. They seemed to mock her, each glint reminding her of Indra ...

'Please don't say no,' begged Uttank, seeing the change of expression on Ahalya's face. 'It is gurudakshina—you are not just my guru's wife, you are the mother I never had, the sister in whom I could confide, the friend with whom I could chat, the guru who taught me my first lessons in life. Please, please accept them on my behalf, with all my love and devotion to you—and to Guru Gautam.'

With an unsteady hand, Ahalya delicately touched the glittering gems. They flashed seductively. She shut her eyes, and an image of Indra came to her: beckoning her, teasing her, mocking her ... Her eyes flew open in shock.

'No, I can't,' she said helplessly.

'Please don't refuse after all I have gone through to get them!' he said again, his eyes distressed. 'You deserve them—they are meant to be worn by someone special.'

Trembling, she picked them up and fastened them in her ears. Uttank gazed at the sight before him: the earrings were as dazzling as her luminous loveliness.

'Don't ever take them off,' he breathed, mesmerised.

'I won't,' she promised, forcing a small laugh. 'For you.'

How could she tell him that the earrings were no longer dear to her? That they were no longer just a gift from him, something he went through so much trouble for?

Ahalya was aware of the slight tug of the earrings each time she moved: it was a reminder of the man she had spurned, the man who had loved her.

Indra.

18

Disappointments

Indra could not believe his eyes.

'What in hell are you doing in my wife's chamber?' he roared.

They both looked surprised at seeing him, Vrishakapi's hand quickly falling from Sachi's shoulder. Indra looked as if he had gone out of his mind: there was a wild, crazy glint in his eyes, his mouth was working hard, the muscles in his neck were standing out like knotted ropes and his lips were drawn back in a snarl.

'It's not what you think, Indra,' Vrishakapi said urgently.

Indra stormed into the room, reaching Vrishakapi in two quick strides. His fist slammed against the side of Vrishakapi's head with the force of a thunderbolt. Vrishakapi's knees buckled, and dimly he saw a fist coming in again towards his face. There was nothing he could do about it. He felt the shock, then a white flash of light scorched his eyes. He heard Sachi scream.

'What are you doing?' cried Sachi in rage and horror. She jumped back against the wall, her face furious.

The lash in her voice brought Indra to his senses. He stood for a long moment, looking down at the stunned form of his friend, and then made to turn around and leave the room, not trusting his ungovernable fury.

'Wait, Shakra.' The coldness in Sachi's voice made Indra stop in his tracks. 'You have no right to hit your friend or cast aspersions against your wife!'

'Don't, Sachi, don't try me now,' warned Indra, his tone dangerously soft.

She looked back at him defiantly.

'But you would like to know what we were doing?' she said mockingly.

His face went white.

Sachi felt a thrill jolt through her: she was enjoying her husband's jealous rage.

He leaned forward, the blood rising to his face. 'I am going to throw him out of Indralok, and you as well!'

Sachi raised an eyebrow. 'On what grounds? That he was in my room ... *our* room? But we were standing at an arm's distance from each other, like two decent people.'

'Is that right? His hand was on your shoulder!'

'Indra, it was a spontaneous gesture, I was consoling her,' interjected Vrishakapi.

Indra glared at his friend. For the first time he saw him as his rival. He had assumed that after killing Vrita, there would be no contender for Sachi's attention or affection.

But now he was seeing his friend with new eyes. The thought made him sick. Standing tall at the far end of the room, Vrishakapi was running his hand through his thick hair, as was his habit. His brown hair was tousled and shone like burnished gold. His handsome face was heavily sunburned and his eyes, now troubled, were the most startling green he had ever seen.

Indra remembered how Vrishakapi had been created, to help him out of a very difficult situation.

Mahashani, Indra's fiercest enemy and the son of the Asura Hiranya had defeated him ignominiously and worse, imprisoned him in his deepest dungeon. Indra shuddered in recollection. It was only because of the Rain God Varun's personal intervention that Indra was freed. Mahashani, who was also Varun's son-in-law, would taunt Indra in his court and had made his life hell in his heaven. The only recourse was to kill Mahashani, but no one was able to do this, and thus Vrishakapi was created. He was born out of water after Indra did a penance to both Shiva and Vishnu. Indra recalled how Vrishakapi had emerged from the waters with Shiva's trishul and Vishnu's sudarshan chakra in his hand, the two mightiest weapons. It was with these that he had killed Mahashani, and the two had become more brothers than friends.

This was the same man now, standing near his wife. His instinct was to kick him out of the chamber, out of heaven, out of his life—and Sachi's. But something in his friend's eyes told him to rein in his wrath for another moment.

'It is not what you think it is,' repeated Vrishakapi. 'Sachi called me to check if you were using my home as a rendezvous for *your* affair,' he blurted.

Sachi's face went red, but she held her ground. 'Yes. We are not having an affair as your muddy mind assumed, but I suspect that *you* are having one!' she spat. 'With whom this time, Shakra? And why are you cowardly enough to make your friend's house your boudoir!'

Indra looked thunderstruck.

'Are you crazy?!' he said incredulously. 'I go to Vrishakapi's place because I have always done so, from before I met and married you!'

'That's exactly what I was saying to her,' explained Vrishakapi, his tone perturbed. He turned to Sachi. 'I said it then and I say it now, in his presence, that he is not involved with any other woman besides—'

'Ahalya?' Sachi's full lips curled.

Vrishakapi flushed. 'No, *you*.'

'Why are you dragging him into our daily fight?' Indra said with an exaggerated sigh. He felt relieved; Sachi was back to her jealous self and it appeared that he had no reason to be jealous.

'You give me enough reason, Shakra!' she said. 'And anyway, it was *you* who jumped to conclusions ...' She left her statement unfinished with deliberate artfulness.

Indra stared at her. He could see she was no longer anxious.

'Agreed, I got caught in the same trap,' he admitted sheepishly. 'My apologies,' he said, looking not at her but at his friend with mixed feelings.

'I think I should take my leave, since I have played my role and am no longer needed,' Vrishakapi remarked.

Sachi looked at Indra as Vrishakapi left the room. Her eyes were expectant, bright.

'Come here,' she said.

Indra crossed the room and put his hands on the curves of her hips. He smiled at her.

'Hold me close,' she said and swayed towards him.

He laughed and put his arms around her. Her hair was scented and soft against his face. He tightened his arms and

242 / Kavita Kané

pulled her against him. Her mouth felt hard against his, resisting yet teasing, but after a while her lips opened. She was shivering.

'You drive me crazy—either you are jealous or making me jealous!' he said, grinning.

'Tough man,' she said softly, breathing into his mouth. 'But I like you jealous; it's a good feeling,' she whispered, so close that he could feel her breath on his face. 'It shows you care.'

'But I do,' he muttered. 'You are *mine*, Indrani.'

Yes, but you *are not mine*, thought Sachi, her despair momentarily overshadowing her rising desire.

Ahalya got up with a start. Her hand went instinctively to her side: Gautam was not there. He was already up; she could hear him moving outside as he finished his morning rituals. She saw the first sliver of dawn through the window and she groaned inwardly. She was late again. She must have overslept. The baby had given her a hard time at night. This girl was not like her brothers, Ahalya thought wearily. Little Anjani was demanding.

Ahalya got out of bed and walked to the window. She liked hearing the sound of the river—that gurgling sound made her feel happy. But even the sight of the river did not lighten her heavy heart. She wished she hadn't been too tired to make love—not that Gautam had been too eager either.

It was her own fault, she told herself. She hadn't given him the slightest hint that she wanted him to come to her room. But where had he gone? She dropped down on to the bed and stared up at the ceiling. Had he spent another entire night busy with his books? Had he got that urge he had told her about—

his mad passion for work and his long spells of meditation; the urge that was now torturing her?

She lay there, her mind tormented. The silence and the darkness weighed down on her. After a while, she began to weep.

She got up a few minutes later, spotted the dark stain of tears on her pillow and brushed at her wet cheeks angrily. She was being silly and selfish. Gautam had not woken her because she was fatigued. She ought to be touched by his gesture, not so irrationally hurt. But she knew she was upset with herself too. For not waking up on time, for not having finished her studies the previous night, for the grogginess in her head right now, and the sinking feeling that she would miss her class yet again. This was the third time in a week, and it had been happening for over a month.

She frowned at the infant girl. Anjani was sleeping peacefully now, oblivious to the tumult in her mother's mind and life. She dragged herself out of bed. This was the start of what was going to be another disappointing day, she thought.

She was right. She received a quick dose of it at breakfast itself.

Gautam was with a student, a new arrival who was being coached extra hours to catch up on what he had missed. He was sitting by the little boy's side, explaining the parts of a hymn to him when Ahalya appeared in the doorway.

'You can come inside,' she called out loudly. 'Breakfast is ready. He must be hungry.'

She saw him give a slight shrug as he returned to his coaching. She was exasperated: she could see him scowl even from a distance. He had that look he reserved for when someone had done something injudicious. It had clearly irritated Gautam that she had come to him just when he was probably making a little headway with the boy.

'I'm sorry,' she said instinctively. 'I didn't mean to disturb you ...'

Gautam knew he was devoting a lot of time on this student, but he wanted him to relax, to learn with a clear head. He was trying to help him extract the meaning of the hymn he was reciting, for it to come alive in his mind. Ahalya's appearance had broken his concentration and it sent a rush of blood to his head. But what she said was also true: you could not study on an empty stomach.

'Coming!'

The snap in his voice made the student stiffen. It also made Ahalya take a step back inside the hut.

Minutes later, they came inside and sat down for the meal: boiled daal and roasted brinjals, perfectly cooked and flavoured with a light seasoning. The only thing missing was conversation.

'You go ahead and join the other boys. I shall come later,' Gautam said to his pupil when he had finished eating.

The student hurried away, hearing the change in his guru's voice. Ahalya moved back, giving him room to pass. She looked at her husband. He was frowning darkly. Although she was anxious, she also felt defiant.

She asked, almost wearily, 'Do you intend to teach *me* the Bhadra hymn you scripted in the Sama Veda?'

Gautam drew in a breath. Her tone annoyed him: there was a hint of complaint and censure in it. He could feel a vein in his forehead beginning to pound. He felt resentful that her interruption had undone the work of an hour on that boy. He made an effort to hold down a burst of temper and succeeded, but only just.

'Don't you need to check on the new students arriving for this term?' he said tersely.

'Yes. I'll look into that as well. But you had promised we would begin with the Sama Veda soon,' she said, her face pinched. 'There's nothing else to do in the morning. I have taken out time to study all that I missed last week.'

'But *I* don't have time!' he said, his tone impatient. 'I have to start the curriculum with the new batch of students today. Besides, Narad will be coming here to help out with the grammatical structuring of what I have written till now ... Oh, there is too much work.' He paused, noting her pale face and the dark circles around her eyes. 'Anyway, I think you need to rest a bit,' he said, his tone softening. 'You need it.'

'I have rested enough,' she said stubbornly. 'I am lagging behind in my studies.'

He nodded, again noting the tiredness on her face. Anxiety always takes something out of a face. For the first time since Gautam had met her, Ahalya looked a little ordinary. His heart twisted. Was that what he had done to her—taken the extraordinary out and left her with ordinariness?

'Yes, you *are* trailing behind. But that was to be expected. You require the rest now that there are four children to look after.'

'That is just an excuse,' she said, but her lips curled downwards. 'Does this mean you won't teach me? Again?'

The single word weighed heavy with accusation.

Gautam bristled. 'Will you let me handle this?' He was now using the tone he used with his duller students. 'I'm doing what is best for you and for me. Let there be no argument about this; let's finish our meals.'

She stayed where she was and stared at him, disappointment lurking in her eyes. She put down the tumbler of half-finished water that she was holding. She placed her hands on her knees and stared down as if she were seeing them for the first time.

His tone had been final; it was clear that he would not teach her, not anymore. She could study no more, no further. Her mouth trembled, hesitated, then closed. His dismissal of her was almost more difficult to withstand than a harsh rebuke, and she reacted with an unexpected rush of tears. Perhaps he saw them and wanted to spare her the embarrassment because he said no more, simply turned and walked away. She wanted to argue, shriek and shout—*No*, he could not do this to her! He had promised: he would guide her, teach her, groom her to be a rishika someday ... A day that would never dawn now.

But she *was* a rishika, a voice taunted her: she was a rishi's wife, half-learned, half-baked, a half-hewn sculpture. She was a rishika, running his ashram as his devoted companion, the mother of his children; her lips turned down with bitterness. She felt a hot, searing pain as her heart contracted agonisingly ... this was but betrayal! A breach of trust, she screamed in silent fury.

When she looked up, Gautam had long gone from the hut.

She perfunctorily went through her routine for the rest of the day, tending the garden and preparing the day's meals wordlessly, while Gautam remained at the gurukul.

At lunch, she quietly placed his food in front of him. He glanced at her, knowing she was disappointed and hurt. They began to eat. Gautam found he was not all that hungry. Ahalya merely nibbled on her food and finally, she put back her bowl.

'You do realise I have other students to teach, don't you?' he said when he could stand the silence no longer. 'You do realise that I have a responsibility towards them. I cannot neglect them.'

'I'd better get the new students' beds ready. When are they arriving?' she said. Without waiting for his reply, she got to her feet. 'Have you finished?'

He sat still, his temper rising, then he got up and followed her in.

'Ahalya! I'm telling you I have to juggle meditation and writing and teaching the students. I cannot neglect any of that!'

'But you can your wife!' she said. Her throat tightened, but she managed to say, 'It sounds noble ... but I cannot afford to neglect my duties either. You or the children or the students or the chores. But my studies,' she said intensely, looking up at him, her dark eyes blazing. 'I'm not going to ask you ever again. I'm not going to beg, Gautam.' Her eyes were bright with unshed tears, but her mouth and chin were firm. 'You once said, "No matter what, Ahalya, I love you. You'll look back on this and you'll forgive me if I've hurt you." That's what you said.'

She began to shake a little and she looked out the open window. 'You're hurting me now, but I'll look back and I'll forgive you.'

She walked away from him, away from the ensuing silence.

He saw her going over to the cradle, lifting Anjani, who immediately stopped crying at the familiar, firm touch of her mother. He watched her walk across the room and start feeding the baby. This was a sight that had once given him considerable pleasure, but he was strangely unmoved now. The same indifference he felt each time the baby bawled and broke his meditation. Or when he caught sight of her in her transparent sari that revealed her young body and her slim, lovely legs. A sight that had earlier always caused a surge of desire.

Late in the evening, he saw the light go up in the spare bedroom on her side of the adjoining huts. Ordinarily, he would have helped her make up the beds. She no longer had Uttank to help out, and he liked to share the work with her. She walked along the passage between the huts to the bedroom. Gautam knew that for the first time since they had married, she was truly unhappy. The thought nagged at him. He stood looking at his open book, the one he was supposed to have taught her from today. She had been disappointed. But she would snap out of it in time, he told himself. He had the new sutra on his mind. For the moment, she had to take second place.

Over the next few weeks, Ahalya continued to tend to the family, the gurukul and her chores without once mentioning their conversation. She no longer asked about her lessons. She did not get a chance to attend any classes: Anjani and the three boys and the students took too much of her time and energy. She tired quickly, and by the time Gautam retired for the night, she was usually asleep, a troubled look still fixed on her lovely face.

Gautam felt a pang as he glanced down at her sleeping form. Their relationship seemed to be suffering. They rarely chatted these days; they were both exceedingly polite with each other, and there were long minutes of complete silence that was completely new.

He knew she was upset and hurt, but he kept telling himself that when this frenetic phase was over, it would be forgotten and they would get along together as before.

19

The Reunion

Ahalya moved her hand and felt the other side of the bed; it was empty. As usual, she thought. She slowly opened her eyes. A delicately carved marble cornice greeted her. She stiffened: she was not in her hut getting up in a cold cot. She was in her parents' palace, back in her chamber's soft, sprawling bed. She sat up, startled and stiff, her eyes, wide open now, to be met by her reflection in a mirror. She tensed up. Was this white-faced, gaunt, desperately unhappy looking woman her?

She pressed her hands against her face. She stood in the vast room, looking around. Its hugeness and her loneliness crushed her. Aware she was trembling, she stood, drawing in slow, deep breaths until she felt steadier. She had to look happy. Today was her brother's wedding day.

Divodas was getting married to Suyasha, the princess of Kashi, and Ahalya had been surprised when she first heard the news at the ashram.

'So, he decided to get married after all!' she had exclaimed in genuine surprise. 'Ma will be hugely relieved, especially since Father has retired to the forest for his spiritual fulfilment, handing over the throne and kingdom to Divodas. He is king now and he needs his queen!' she said affectionately.

'Must be a political alliance,' Gautam had remarked dryly.

Ahalya shrugged, throwing him a mirthless smile. 'It is better than a love alliance: there are no undue expectations, only a faster acceptance of reality.'

Gautam raised an eyebrow. 'It takes courage to fall in love and choose your life partner. After all, marriage cannot be a stratagem.'

'It is, eventually, is it not?' she said. 'In any case,' she continued, wanting to change the subject, 'I presume you won't be joining us for the wedding?'

'What are you implying, Ahalya?'

'I am not implying anything. You refused every time my father invited you, so I am just stating the most likely scenario. I *know* you will not come for the wedding.'

'As it happens, I cannot attend. I am sorry,' he said, his tone not at all apologetic. 'I have to go to Godavari. There is a drought there ...'

'... and you will usher in the rains, make the land fertile and build an ashram there,' Ahalya finished his sentence with a sigh. 'As you always do. We have moved nine ashrams by now.'

'Established nine new ashrams,' he corrected tersely. 'Anyway, you should leave early as I'm sure your mother will expect you to help with the wedding.'

'I'm not going.'

He stared at her as she poured out some gravy into a pot. She finally looked up at him. 'I'm not going, Gautam, not without you. As is always the case.' Her eyes were bright with determination and her chin was raised.

'But you have to! Divodas is your brother!'

'And you are his only brother-in-law,' retorted Ahalya.

'You are his sister; you are family, Ahalya.'

'So are you, but you don't consider yourself such,' she said angrily.

'I have no time to spare,' he said.

She forced herself to stay calm. 'I knew you would make excuses not to go.' She put down the pot and pursed her lips. 'You may be difficult, Gautam, and you may be tough and sometimes unkind, but I do know for sure you're not a coward. You don't want to meet my parents, is that it?' she asked, forcing her tone to be neutral.

That was it, but he wasn't going to admit it.

'As you well know, I am uncomfortable in palaces and public events,' he said. 'The last time I was there was only for *you*,' he said, his voice cajoling, his eyes oddly tender. He placed a gentle hand on her shoulder.

That brought her up short. Her anger died.

She hesitated, then lifted her hands helplessly. 'Then come for me again, please,' she said, and he could hear the pleading tone in her voice. 'I've refused so often because you did not want to visit. That was a mistake. All it did was estrange me from my family.'

'That's why, my dear, you need to go this time,' Gautam said.

'We,' she corrected reflexively.

'I can't, dear, I have too much work here. I cannot take off a whole month for a wedding. I didn't spend that much time even over mine!' he said with forced jocularity.

'You have a legitimate excuse each time; I don't, and I invariably hurt my family—and myself. This time if I don't go, it'll be the end ...' she said, her eyes troubled.

'Go, Ahalya, please go. Don't refuse this time. I cannot, because, bluntly put, I do feel uncomfortable and like a pariah there. And as I said, I genuinely don't have the time. But it would be wonderful for both your family and the children. It's time they got to know each other properly.'

Her shoulders slumped. 'All right, Gautam, you win. As always. I'm not fighting you. I'll go alone, never mind the barbs, especially Ma's,' she said with a sigh. 'I'll tell the messenger that we will be ready to leave by the end of this week. Is that what you want?'

He nodded, secretly relieved that the disagreement had not escalated into a quarrel. 'Yes, and I am sure Divodas will send a retinue to guard his dear sister,' he teased.

She did not return his smile. 'If you are not here, and nor am I, who will look after this ashram?' she asked.

'Jabaali,' answered Gautam promptly. 'He is old enough— and wise enough—to look after a gurukul.'

Eventually, with the four children in tow, she had left for Kampilya in the north, while Gautam headed for Godavari in the south, their journeys oddly analogous to their lives: at a crossroad but both walking in opposite directions.

A strange feeling assailed her when she caught a glimpse of the palace after so many years. This had once been her home, and in spite of herself, she could not help but marvel at it—as the children loudly did. They had squealed with delight, the awe apparent on their upturned faces.

Ahalya blinked. Her mother's voice permeated her thoughts.

'I have already helped the children dress—they all look so handsome now! And I got you these silks and some jewellery too, Ahalya,' said Nalayani. 'Wear the blue for the morning function; it suits you.'

'Ma, please,' Ahalya said tiredly. They had already had this argument. 'I am going to wear what I brought with me.'

'You can't wear *that*,' Nalayani said, looking horrified as she eyed her daughter in her rumpled, rough cotton. 'A woman is complimented as much for her clothes as for herself. And one's attire reveals success and status; although it does not make success, it is a part of it.'

Ahalya sighed. 'Clothes are but costumes, Ma, and usually uncomfortable ones at that.'

Nalayani persisted. 'You forget that, besides being a *great* rishi's wife, you are a princess of this *great* kingdom as well!'

'I was going to change anyway,' Ahalya said wryly, 'but I see you have got me a whole new wardrobe.'

'Yes,' her mother said excitedly. 'It's yours! Allow me to pamper you and the children. You are here after years. And this is wonderful reason for celebration, is it not? It is your brother's wedding, after all!'

'I am happy that he is happy,' said Ahalya, recalling her own wedding, when Divodas had played a decisive role.

'And I am relieved!' cried Nalayani. 'He agreed to get married finally. He had gone to Kashi to broker peace and ended up falling in love with Suyasha!'

'Yes, Divodas in love is quite unbelievable!' Ahalya said with a fond smile on her face. '*I am married to war*,' he had once told her. He had fought many battles since and won most, but today, this emperor of many lands was going to win a bride.

'He's very earnest in whatever he does, and I am sure he'll make her happy. As you clearly are, Ma: more happy than you were for me. Suyasha is a suitable bride.'

Her mother threw her a searching look. 'Yes, she is. Getting a suitable life partner is the key to life's happiness. Let me tell you a story, Ahalya,' she said softly. 'There was this princess who was so beautiful that she had a queue of suitors. Her father, the king, was in a fix about whom to choose. But his daughter was finicky. She wanted the best: the best looking, the richest, the most learned, the most brave, the most generous, the most kind, the most healthy ...

'She was in search of the perfect husband, and she would only take the one who fit this impossible expectation of hers. When her parents could not find such a man, she decided to take upon herself this task of finding her husband. She prayed to Lord Shiva every day to get such a man—a man with all fourteen desired qualities. She persevered and wasted herself in penance, and when the lord appeared, she put forth her wish. "That ideal man," she begged. "Give me my ideal husband."

'"And who is that?" asked Lord Shiva, a smile on his lips.

'She quickly enumerated all the qualities.

'The lord threw her a dubious look. "Such a man can never exist in one mortal body."

'But the princess was adamant. "I have to have him! Or I shan't marry."

'"Well, I can bless you with your wish. You will have five husbands with all the qualities you desire ..."

'"But I don't want five husbands—I want one!" cried the princess.

'The lord smiled again and then disappeared ... much to the princess's consternation!'

'What happened?' asked Ahalya curiously. 'Did the princess eventually get her ideal husband?'

'Yes,' smiled Nalayani. 'A man who may not have had the qualities she aspired for—but one who loved her devotedly.'

Ahalya touched her mother's shoulder. 'You are recounting your own story, aren't you? The princess as stubborn as her father, Nala, and as beautiful as her mother, Damayanti.'

Nalayani gave a short laugh. 'Actually, my mother was both stubborn and beautiful! That's how she won and saved my father over and over again,' she said, her smile mirthless.

Ahalya recognised the look in her mother's eyes. 'So, you found your perfect husband in Father ...'

Nalayani nodded. 'I was foolish in asking for the impossible. The perfect man need not be perfect, but it is sufficient if he is perfectly suited for you. He was right there and I didn't see him! Just like Indra was right there but you chose Gautam instead.'

'Ma, please, not again! It's an old story! I am a mother of our four children now.'

'Exactly, nothing besides that,' Nalayani stated tartly. 'I still say that.' She pursed her lips in disapproval. 'What has it got you, Ahalya—except for these four lovely children? You had this burning will to study and be a scholar, for which you fought with me so many times! The only consolation—his single redeeming point—was that Gautam could give you that one thing: scholarship and education. I suspect that you only married him as an escape, a means to become a rishika. But did you become one?' she asked, her tone wry.

Silence followed. Ahalya walked uneasily about the room, her arms crossed and her hands clenched in tights fists.

Nalayani continued. 'No, you didn't. Instead of studies, you are poring over pots and pans!'

Ahalya flushed but she refused to get offended. 'Looking after your own home, your school, the ashram is menial?' she said mockingly. 'Yes, it is tiring, but I can't have a fleet of servants so I can indulge in scholarship,' she said with a sardonic smile.

'Gautam is doing just that, at your expense,' her mother retorted cuttingly. 'He does not need help—he has you.'

Her mother's words were cruel; it was not her words that hurt, though, but the truth in them. She was *nothing*. A failure, a painful disappointment, not just to them but—more importantly—to herself. Just as her mother had once warned her she would be: that burden of the way life had turned out was fully on her.

Ahalya saw that her mother was looking at her with unusual concern. Ahalya recognised that look of worry in her eyes; she had seen it in her father's face as well, and in Divodas's glance. They all pitied her.

Ahalya could not bear it. 'I am still a person who made an independent decision, Ma. I was convinced of my choice and I remain as convinced about the consequences of that choice. Yes, I am a help to my husband: I help him run the ashram, I help him make his decisions, I help him with his problems—'

'But what about *you*, Ahalya?' cut in a male voice. It was Divodas, as handsome as always, but that ready smile was missing. 'What about *your* dreams, *your* ambitions, Ahalya?'

Ahalya flinched.

'In helping him pursue his vision, you seem to have shut your eyes to your own,' he said, his face as grim as his tone.

Her brother's presence normally made her feel better, but today, he seemed like a formidable teacher, questioning her so closely. Worse, she had no reply to his questions, because she had realised the answer herself a long time ago ...

Overwhelmed, she looked down at her hands. She could not bring herself to meet either the distress in Divodas's face or the disdain in her mother's eyes.

It was Nalayani who broke the silence. Frowning as she suddenly thought of something, she said, 'Frankly, I am happy Gautam is not here. I don't wish for another confrontation between him and Indra.'

'Indra?! He is here?' Ahalya asked, stiffening.

'Why wouldn't he be here?' asked Nalayani coolly. 'After all, he is still a friend.'

'Still?' Ahalya was shocked.

'Surely you can't believe that silly fight between him and your husband would affect his friendship with your brother?'

Divodas gave a brief nod. 'Let bygones be bygones, Ahalya. It was an awkward episode, all of us were affected by it, the most being Indra ...'

Fury grabbed her throat. 'Indra?! It was he who was discourteous to all of us, especially me, if you recall,' said Ahalya cuttingly, her gaze accusing. 'But I was wrong to assume that your loyalty would lie with me!'

'Don't dig out old grievances, Ahalya. It won't do any good. I don't want any animosity now during this happy occasion. Indra is here with his wife,' Nalayani added with a hint of warning.

Ahalya lapsed into mutinous silence. She did not want to meet Indra. She was dreading it.

Why were they discussing that darned man again? She had wanted to have a long chat with her brother, but instead they were arguing over Indra. *Indra*. She clenched her teeth in frustration. He seemed always to come between her and her family, between her and happiness, and every time he seemed to win the round.

She dressed up obediently, as her mother wanted, too fraught for another clash. As her mother's maids helped dress her, Ahalya felt like a stranger in her own body. The silks and gems glittered, and she was a princess again in her castle, she thought mockingly as she stared through the open window at the manicured gardens outside.

When she had returned home after so long, the palace had loomed up suddenly, and her first thought was that it had assumed a strange sense of unreality. Nothing changed—and yet everything was changed. It was familiar, yet seemed larger and more opulent than before. Probably because she was not accustomed to such sprawling structures anymore.

She wet her lips nervously and walked into the hall downstairs—and the feeling of unreality increased. After all, she saw, this was only a room, not the enchanted chamber where she had passed those poignant hours years ago. She sat in a quiet corner by a large window, away from the bustle, in her favourite chair. Amazed to find it still there, a large, engraved couch, she realised that she had almost forgotten all these simple, familiar things.

'Are you hiding from the world?' a familiar voice asked her.

Her heart skipped a beat. No, not *him* ...

She turned around and looked at him.

Indra found himself breathing hard; he told himself that it was excitement, not emotion. The familiar velvet eyes found his as she looked up at him through the thick curtain of lashes, and a spasm of fright went through him at her continued power over him. She was dressed in pale blue and her attire looked like seawater sifted over with gold dust. A gold diadem bound back her dark, straight hair like a crown. She was like a goddess conferring gifts.

He had been waiting for this moment, sure he would meet her here, certain that she would not miss her brother's wedding. And when the door had opened and Ahalya had entered the room ... everything had blurred before his eyes. He had not forgotten how beautiful she was, and yet he felt his face drain of colour and his voice weaken to a sigh in his throat.

She was here—she was alone, he quickly noticed—and that was enough. He was not even sure what he had to say to her. But this was a moment in his life that he felt he could not have dispensed with. There was no triumph; he had lost her long ago. But even if he did not lay down his achievements at her feet, he could at least hold them for a passing moment before her eyes.

'You're here,' he said at last, and added, equally tritely: 'I just arrived.'

She nodded wordlessly.

He felt a familiar exasperation. She was walled up as usual, yet had the same effect on him as always. He tried to calm himself by looking everywhere but her face. The obligation to speak was on him, but, apart from rambling, it seemed that there was nothing to say. There had never been anything casual in their previous relations—and it didn't seem possible that he would suddenly be able to talk about the banal.

The flurry around them did not distract him. It was like he and Ahalya were alone in this room, which had seen the beginning of his love and the end. It seemed to him long ago and inexpressibly sad. In this hall, he had felt ecstasy and grief such as he would never feel again. He would never be so weak or so miserable and helpless. Yet he knew that he, as a person, had lost something, a trust, a warmth of personality. She had changed him inevitably. He had traded his first love for defeat and carved his happiness out of despair. But with hope, he had sustained the freshness of his love.

For years he had loved her. He wondered if, when she was sixteen, a gentle, delicate girl, so lost in thought, she had been as lovely as she was now, under this amber light of noon. From her dark eyes to her tiny feet peeping from under silken folds, she looked divine. Yet she seemed different: more earthly, more voluptuous. She seemed now to have lost her rose-coloured view of life, as though age and experience had used her up. Indra wanted to take her up in his arms, feel her skin against his, drown in her eyes, inhale the scent of her hair, and finally feel his lips on hers ...

'You look well,' he said finally, forcing some words out of his mouth. 'The years seem to have given you a ... a certain colour.'

Again, she nodded mutely, coldly acknowledging his compliment but looking at him blankly as though she had never met him before.

'Really, Ahalya!' he said, flushing angrily. 'Are you trying to pretend you don't know me? That you don't want me here?'

'Frankly yes, I wouldn't want you here, but you are at your friend's wedding. And I have come for my brother,' she said.

Indra decided that he was on dangerous ground. He had not intended to let anything spoil this meeting. It seemed to him that he was being calm and cordial and that she was deliberately misunderstanding him. With every second they were drawing further apart, and he was unable to stop himself from feeling anxious. He tried to smile, his manner jocular, but she was back in her shell, her expression distant.

'I cannot see Rishi Gautam anywhere around?' he said politely.

'He couldn't come. He is tied up with work,' she said.

'I hear he's aiming to become a maharishi now,' Indra said, a sneer in his voice. 'The great deeds that Maharishi Gautam has done for the southern parts of our country are not just immense but will be remembered forever. Using his knowledge over the shastras, he has turned many a barren land into fertile strips, undoing drought ...'

'Without your sarcasm and help,' she said icily.

Her words were like thorns piercing him.

'You mean the famine ...' he started nervously.

'I know that in spite of Gautam invoking the rains, *you* did not comply as Indra, the god of the heavens, lightning, thunder, storms and rains. You created hurdles,' she said, her face unsmiling. 'When Gautam invoked Varun, and not you, to relieve the twelve-year famine, you took offence. So, instead of the promised rains, Gautam asked for incessant water supply in the reservoir, and Varun obliged him. Saving many lives,' she added caustically. 'For your personal grievance against Gautam, you were going to let people die.'

'Isn't Gautam a man of ego too?' Indra asked nastily. 'He got his share of fame and glory for bringing water to Trymbakeshwar.'

'He would not have demurred from asking you for help, but I guess he knows you too well and knew you would refuse— or complicate matters. Let's not pretend, Indra; I have a lot of anger to declare.'

Her bearing conveyed her contempt for him.

'And I have only love and hurt to declare,' said Indra bitterly.

'Oh, yes, it shows in your malice.' She gave a derisive laugh and it made his nerves jangle. 'And love?' she queried mockingly. 'It should be reserved for your wife. You are now a married man, Indra, wedded to Sachi!' Her voice dripped ice.

Even the mention of Sachi could not rein in Indra; he was in sweet agony.

'Don't accuse me of harbouring malice towards you! I helped your disciple Uttank get the precious earrings you so coveted. If it were not for me, you wouldn't be wearing them now!'

She flushed, jerking her head, making the earrings move tantalisingly, the gems on fire in the sun. His voice had risen, and several people in the vicinity turned to look at them curiously.

'Sh!' she warned him, furious. 'You forget you have a wife who will hear you! Besides, it was Uttank's gurudakshina, not a gift from you! And I refuse to be part of a spectacle. If you want me to even look at you while I'm here, you'll have to be less aggressive.'

But Indra seemed unable to control his voice.

'You say I have malice. Do you mean to say,'—it trembled to a carrying pitch—'that I am jealous of Gautam?'

Half the guests in the room were now observing the scene, and a few others had drifted in from the garden to watch.

'Yes. And I am not asking for any explanation!' Her displeasure was increasing. 'But if you raise your voice again, I'll arrange it so that you'll have a chance to cool off! If you want a scene, I shall give you one.' She looked pointedly at the fountain in the corner of the room, in front of which he was standing.

A look of astonishment spread over Indra's handsome face. He gave a short laugh. 'You wouldn't dare!'

'Dare what?' Sachi's sultry voice brought him to his senses.

Ahalya swallowed her retort and recovered her composure. '... Dare say that we haven't met,' she said smoothly. 'I presume you are Sachi, Indra's wife.' Her eyes softened as she greeted the other woman with a smile.

Sachi was taken aback; it was a slow, gentle smile that warmed the heart, and she strangely found herself melting. No, Ahalya was her rival. She was not meant to like her. But there was something about this lovely woman that was very likeable.

Sachi's gaze moved from her husband to Ahalya. She had hated Ahalya as she didn't think it was possible to hate anyone. She blamed her for the unhappiness in her marriage. Her invisible presence in their relationship had filled her with vindictive thoughts.

A moment passed in silence. Sachi passed her tongue over her pale lips and held her breath to stop her inward trembling while Ahalya stood before her, scrutinising her with faint curiosity.

Sachi suddenly became self-conscious of her full, heavier figure, her round face, the mole on her nose and the stray curl on her forehead, which was stubborn and could never be combed back. And it seemed to her that if she had been as slim and graceful and ethereal as Ahalya, and had had no kohl in her eyes and no errant tendril on her forehead, then she could mask the reality that she was not as breathtakingly beautiful ... nor would she have felt so unsure and small facing this lovely, enigmatic lady.

'I have heard a lot about you,' began Sachi, and could have bitten her tongue for it.

She saw Ahalya blush. Even Sachi found it charming. But she wanted to wound this woman as deeply as her presence in their life had hurt her. She refrained, saying instead, 'I wanted to meet the beautiful woman whom not just the apsaras but even the goddesses are so jealous of!'

Ahalya's delicious rosiness deepened. Indra looked suddenly tense, angering Sachi.

'Every woman is beautiful,' said Ahalya quietly. 'It is up to the woman to seek and find her own beauty.'

It was Sachi's turn to flush. Ahalya's words were like a slap in the face.

'Not all are as fortunate as you,' she said sweetly. 'Born with the kind of rare beauty that drives men crazy.'

Indra made an imperceptible movement.

'But the beauty is yours, isn't it? So why does a man need to define it?' asked a surprised Ahalya. 'You are said to be a smart woman, Sachi. Do you need to a man to validate your intelligence?'

Ahalya had had no intention of engaging with Sachi's aggression. She rose now, and Sachi felt a great relief.

'I must excuse myself,' Ahalya said. 'I seem to be neglecting the other guests.'

'Yes ... yes. You have come home after a long time; everyone must be eager to meet you,' Indra said.

Ahalya nodded. She turned to Sachi and said quietly, 'Now I can leave him in your care.' She gave Indra a glare over his wife's shoulder, as if reprimanding an insolent boy.

But then a curious thing happened. A nervous Indra stepped aside to let Ahalya pass, but instead of going through, she stood still and stared at him. It was not so much the look, which was not friendly, as it was the moment of silence. They looked into each other's eyes, and both took a short, accelerated breath; then, with her heart beating wildly, Ahalya threaded her way through the milling crowd, making the half-circuit of the room. She melted away, a slim figure in shimmering blue, into the harsh sunshine of the garden outside.

Indra did not move, or think, or hope, lulled into numbness by longing and another uneasy feeling: the premonition of disaster—beyond Ahalya he saw only future despair.

Sachi recognised the stricken look; she gave him a brittle smile and said, 'Well, there are all kinds of love, but never the same love twice.'

20

Distancing

Ahalya stared blankly at the empty space beside her in the bed. It was a few hours after midnight. Had Gautam not returned from work, or had he started the day early? This was the way it had been for so many years ... yet why did she not stop hoping?

She had no answer, and knowing the explanation for her uneasiness, Ahalya made her way to the library. She knew she wouldn't be able to sleep if she remained in bed. It was too cold and lonely. It was better that she studied, use the extra time she had got.

She proceeded with her day's work, and the time passed like it did on any other day in the last few years. She worked the whole day and the nights were spent wondering when Gautam would join her in bed, hoping, aching, till her waiting eyes shut in weary sleep.

Tonight was another such night. She tried to dispel the sleep from her eyes. She gave a start when she felt the bed move. Gautam was back; she could feel the hard strength of his body against hers.

'Sorry, did I wake you? I thought you were sleeping,' he said.

'No,' she whispered in the darkness, feeling hot blood move through her. Ahalya's body ached. How she wanted him!

'I was waiting for you,' she murmured huskily in the darkness.

She touched his bare shoulders, her fingers caressing his warm skin. She felt him flinch.

'I am tired, Ahalya,' he said brusquely, and turned over.

She stared at his bare back and was struck cold.

She lay on the bed, an ache throbbing strongly within her. Her hands turned into fists as she felt another surge of hot blood move down inside her.

Gautam had rebuffed her again. Was she so undesirable? Or was there something wrong with him? Perhaps it was only his passion for work and ambition that excited him now. Hot tears rose to her eyes and spilled over. Maybe he wasn't as worldly as he had once been ...

'How long will we live like this, Gautam?' she asked. She heard him exhale sharply, felt him turning over, and then there was his warm breath against her cheek.

He got up abruptly and sat up straight.

So they were going to start this all over again, he thought. He sat there for a few seconds, feeling irritation building up.

Ahalya continued to lie on the bed, stiff and still, and his dilated eyes could make out her huddled form facing him, her clenched fists against her face.

'Ahalya, will you please try to be helpful,' he whispered through clenched teeth. 'It's tough enough to have this work piling up without you becoming so irrational. I am tired! My work is important not just to me, but to us! I'm trying to earn ...'

'Yes, *your* work. It's all about you!' Her voice was low, but her eyes, glistening in the dark, were a little wild. 'I'm not being irrational. I am simply asking you a fairly simple question—how can we go on like this?'

'What do you mean, "like this"? What is wrong now?'

'You still haven't realised?'

'Don't start with your riddles and counter-questions!' he said, and she could hear the exasperation in his voice.

She clenched her fists harder, biting her lips to stop the trembling, wondering how she could say what was on the tip of her tongue ...

'Ahalya!' His hoarse bark stopped her churning thoughts. His teacher's voice, when pitched right, could stop a storm. He was using it again on her. 'What is it with you these days? You are either morose or moody or miserable ... Why?'

'Oh, so you noticed,' she muttered.

'What are you saying?'

She jerked away from him.

'I am saying you noticed you have a wife who is morose, moody and miserable—and yet, you neglected me!'

The moon rose higher, streaming more light into the room, illuminating their faces.

She saw his eyebrows shoot up in astonishment. 'Neglected?'

Her face flushed, desire long gone, annoyance stirring within her. 'Yes!'

'Please stop imagining things. I have enough to handle without you getting—'

'Irrational?' she supplied, sarcasm dripping from her voice. 'But that doesn't answer my question, however irrational!'

He stared at her.

'If you think I am neglecting you, I am sorry.' He sighed wearily. 'My work ...'

His sigh triggered the storm raging in her. 'Again—*your* work! It means everything to you, doesn't it?' She was shocked to hear how shrill her voice sounded. She paused, then controlling herself, she went on. 'Why don't you try to understand *what* I am telling you, *why* I am saying it! Why don't you start treating me like a person? Why do you let *your* work dictate how much time we can spend together?' She got up in one fluid movement. 'I can tell you! All you think about is your work and how famous you will get when you become a maharishi!'

In the pale moonlight, she saw his face go paler. 'Are you grudging me my success?' he said in a strangled voice.

'No, never—and you know that!' she cried. 'I have been with you all along. But are *you* with me? You stopped talking, you stopped teaching, you stopped being my friend, you stopped touching me! When did we last make love?' she asked in a fierce whisper, her voice hoarse with rising frustration.

There, she had said it! She looked at him. That had got a reaction. His face was now flushed, almost red, his eyes wide with shock.

'We haven't made love since Anjani was born. And she is six years old now, Gautam.' She faltered, emptied of her anger, humiliation replacing rage. 'That's what I meant—do we go on like this? For how long?'

He opened his mouth and then shut it in a pursed line. 'I am meditating these days, Ahalya, and you, as a rishi's wife, should know what that means.'

'Yes, I know, and I understand—abstaining from physical pleasures,' she said, her lips quivering. 'But don't you have a duty towards your wife? Tending to *her* needs?'

Gautam looked flustered. 'You know I can't force myself to have those feelings, Ahalya, not when I am in the midst of penance ...'

She drew in a ragged breath. 'I am no Lopamudra, who composed a hymn for Rishi Agastya to remind him of his obligations to his wife! I am not that learned, am I?' she said bitterly. 'Nor am I Rishi Veda's wife, who sought her sexual gratification through the students in her husband's ashram,' she added mockingly.

The snap in her voice brought his head up. The anger and the frustration in her eyes alarmed him.

'Stop it, Ahalya,' he said roughly. 'This is quite unlike you!'

She shook her head, her face pale. 'What is it, Gautam? Is that shocking, or would you allow it?' she demanded, close to tears. 'When we married, I knew all this, that I would never have any other man but you. But now you simply don't care!' she said violently.

The fire of her words burned him, yet Gautam would not allow Ahalya to see the effect her words had on him. His face expressionless, he turned away.

'You know what your weakness is, Gautam?' She drew in a long, slow breath, trying to curb her spiralling fury. 'You hate even the thought of being embarrassed. Nothing should dent your status, your reputation. That is something you will not tolerate. For all your noble words, you are no Rishi Veda or Rishi Agastya. Very simply, you are too impotent to make love to your wife!'

She bit her lip so viciously that she felt the taste of her blood in her mouth.

Gautam was surprised at his calmness and how evenly his heart was beating. He had absorbed her words.

'I am celibate now,' Gautam said tonelessly. 'You knew how it would be as a rishi's wife—you had to be prepared to give up a normal life to become my wife. Remember that. You can still lead a fulfilled life. I shall give you one.'

'Will you?' she said. 'You didn't make me a scholar either!'

'You *are* a scholar. You have to aim higher in your goals, rather than be so ... so ...'

'Carnal?' she supplied. 'Don't be so polite—or are you are at a loss for words?'

He ignored her jibe. 'Yes, you are a teacher yourself, you are known as ...'

'The guru's ardhangi, the great Rishi Gautam's wife,' she interceded bitterly. 'But am I? I am neither a rishika nor a wife. A wife is also a lover!'

Gautam flinched. 'There are many other ways to lead a fulfilled life. If you are prepared to accept this situation, you will be far happier, Ahalya.'

'I am but a "normal" woman with "normal" needs, Gautam.' Her eyes were full of tears, her lips were quivering and her face was pale and distorted with anger. Gautam's indifference revolted her.

'You, as my husband, are supposed to satisfy them just as I am supposed to satiate your needs. To quote your philosopher-friend Narad, we are the perfect couple, remember?' She smiled sardonically. 'I am making you notice what you have failed to observe. Besides, it's not about making love, it's about feeling loved, Gautam. You have hardly been here these past few years, and when you are, do you even notice me—or your children? We barely talk—'

'Because you are so erratic!' There was an edge to his voice—a masculine intolerance, which indicated to her that he was getting bored with her feverishness. 'You've made your point, Ahalya. And I'm sorry you feel this way about me,' he said.

Ahalya stepped back. Again there was that impassive note in his voice, and she looked vulnerably at him. She had expected some reaction from Gautam, but his unruffled air and apparent indifference to what she had said, while baring open her heart and inhibitions, filled her with mortification.

He didn't wait for her to make a comeback; he left her like that, walking out of the room, striding purposefully away from her towards the unlit classrooms.

Ahalya felt a shudder of sobs shake her. Never had she felt so humiliated. Why had she even bothered; he couldn't care less, she thought with a shake of her head, brushing away her tears angrily.

Then she sat down on a low chair, and, leaning her head on the edge of the table in front, she wept bitterly. There was only one oil lamp burning, and the chair she was sitting on was in darkness; her head and shoulders quivered, and her hair, escaping from its bun, covered her neck, her face, her arms, cascading in chaos. Her quiet, steady weeping was not hysterical, but an expression of wounded pride, of injury, and a recognition of something helpless, hopeless, which one could not set right and to which one could not get used to.

If Gautam had been there, possibly her tears could have stirred something in his troubled and suffering heart as well.

He wasn't there, she reminded herself dully, and muttered distractedly to herself: 'Is this life? Oh, one can't go on living like this, one can't. Oh, it's madness, wickedness, not life. To live with one who smiles at me, yet feels so much contempt. I feel so burdensome, so ridiculous in his eyes! Oh, how humiliating!'

She lifted her head and looked blankly into the darkness. Finally, she passed a hand over her hair and closed her eyes wearily.

Late in the morning, when he returned to the hut, he could smell onions frying. He found Ahalya in the kitchen, preparing a curry, one of his favourites. She continued to stir the vegetables without looking up.

'Smells good,' he commented.

She looked over her shoulder, glanced unsmilingly at him, and turned back to the fire. Her neck and shoulders burned with fatigue and tension as she moved in the kitchen. He eyed her for a brief moment, feeling depressed and wanting to console her, but there was no invitation in that stiff, slim back. There was something in the way she was holding herself that warned him not to touch her.

He stood there, his head lowered, his face grey and drawn. *She's sulking*, he told himself, shrugging impatiently.

They had lunch. The curry was good, just the way he liked it, but he didn't compliment her. He did not have much of an appetite, nor did she. She moved the food about on her plate with restless fingers, silent and eyes downcast. The quiet meal was followed by another of their long, depressing silences—those long minutes of complete hush that dominated their lives these days.

She was angry; she would calm down sooner or later, he thought. But a worry niggled him all through the day while he was working—Ahalya rarely got angry. He was tormented by anxiety. He was now almost afraid of meeting her and the scene that might ensue.

In the evening, through the open window, he saw Ahalya strolling towards the river. She was going for a walk, as she often did; she would sit on a rock by the river for some time and then return home to resume her chores: it was part of her routine. He hesitated for a moment, then went after her.

Side by side, and in silence, they walked along the deserted beach. She felt the tension between them; it was so common these days, but today it carried a certain sensual undercurrent: not exciting or excitable, but loaded with anger and resentment. Why had he joined her for a walk when he had nothing to say to her? She looked around absently; there was no one on this lonely stretch of sand along the flowing river. They could have stolen a kiss right there. But the frown on his face reminded her of his cold snub the previous night, and of the many previous nights, bringing a scarlet flush to her face, the heat of shame mingling with bruised dignity.

When she thought of what she had done ... She had acted so ... so ... desperate. Desperate for his touch, his hot skin against hers, trying frantically to snatch some romance to fill in the lonely hours, to assuage her hunger, her lost ambition, her broken dreams ...

But why be ashamed, she had angrily reasoned with herself. She was his wife, she was a woman. Of course she had felt amorous, and she had done nothing to make herself feel ashamed. In fact, she told herself, she had done a good thing by bringing their problem to the fore. But to what avail, she asked herself glumly. He had rejected her, again.

She had once been his wife, his lover, his student, a seductress, but nothing seemed to draw him back to her. Certainly not her famed beauty, which seemed to mock her now. Vishwamitra was seduced by the beauteous Menaka; would she need some spell to bewitch her husband again?

He was right next to her, yet so far. Did ambition make man lose interest in a woman, in his wife? Did the desire and drive to gain more fame, wealth, respect and status become all-consuming? She had always had all this and more since she was born—was that why she failed to understand Gautam's aspirations? Just as he had failed to understand hers, a voice mocked her: what about *her* drive, *her* desires, *her* ambitions?

For how long could she keep waiting for his attention? It had become an interminable part of her life, the emotions churning up an unrest she could not handle or hold in ... Ahalya glanced at her tall, brooding husband as he walked by her side, silent and deep in his own thoughts. *It'll work out*, she told herself desperately. *It's got to work out...*

After a while, they headed back. Gautam made no attempt to reach for her hand, nor did she reach for his.

'Going for Divodas's wedding was not a mistake, as I had thought it might be,' stated Sachi, looking at Indra from the corner of her eyes. 'I quite enjoyed it.' Indra noticed that his wife appeared strangely happy. 'But you, Shakra, surprisingly didn't ...' Again, she seemed mysteriously smug. 'I thought you would be pleased to meet Ahalya again.'

Indra made an impatient gesture. Sachi was right, but he did not want to let her know that. After that one encounter, all he could see were the smoky black eyes and that firm mouth floating like a vision in front of him. All he had wanted to do was sit alone and do nothing but think of her. Most days and nights, while he was with people or immersed in work, he had asked himself again and again just why this woman would not get out of his head after all these years. He couldn't understand it. He had met her again, a meeting that had ended on an ugly note. Yet, he was obsessed with her; the thought of her naked skin against his made him sick with desire. This urgency was consuming him to near madness, a gut-tearing, obsessive passion alienating him from his wife. She inflamed in him a violent desire that terrified and elated him. *Why*?

He took a deep breath, and forced a smile. 'Sachi, let us be happy together, let us enjoy being together,' he murmured, sinking into the couch in their room and pulling her down on to his knees. She happily obliged, curling up on his lap, slipping her arm around his neck and resting her face against his.

He gripped her by the arm, began showering kisses on her face, her neck, her shoulders, and murmured promises of everlasting love. Be it affairs or marriage, he thought, promises were a necessity, however false.

Indra had long realised he was not a thinker, not a philosopher, but simply a dilettante. Ahalya had made him see that. But he had been blessed with power, handsome looks and a strong mind. He had an undisciplined heart, though, and he was completely free from principles. He had every intention of leaving Sachi if he ever had the opportunity to have Ahalya—but he knew Ahalya would never leave Gautam for him. He had seen that it was no use, that he did not possess in himself the power to change Ahalya's mind and heart fundamentally. Yet he could not hold any malice towards her. He wanted her, and he would hope to have her until the day he was too old to love.

Sachi's soft voice cut short his thoughts, even as she caressed his face and gently broke away from his embrace.

'You know ... after meeting Ahalya in person, I am no more curious—or jealous.' She gave him a quick smile, her eyes searching his. 'But I wonder—do *you* really love Ahalya as you claim?'

He raised an eyebrow. 'Are you getting analytical about a subject you detest?'

'No, I am keen to know,' she murmured. 'I love you, you don't care. You love Ahalya, she doesn't care. I realised that from what I saw at the wedding. Yet you persist and chase her ... Why?'

Indra frowned. 'I am not chasing her ...'

'Your searching eyes certainly were,' Sachi retorted, surprisingly without heat.

Again his eyebrow shot up. 'And your eyes were checking on me?' he asked sardonically.

'Yes, and what I saw was quite pathetic,' Sachi said, her eyes amused.

Indra felt a flare of irritation. He could not handle Sachi's changed demeanour. It was better when she was the jealous wife—he knew what he was getting into when she was like that. But this was a strange new confident Sachi. Her conviction, her sudden certainty about the truth of something, made him uneasy ...

'And what did you witness?' he asked.

'A little boy demanding a toy he cannot have.' She was leaning back, staring down at her long, slim fingers, laced around her knee.

She felt him stiffen.

'Is that what you think?' he said slowly. 'That I want her because I can't get her?'

'Yes,' she replied calmly. 'She is unattainable, that's why you seek her. And because she chose Gautam over you. She hurt your pride more than she broke your heart.'

Sachi put her hand on his arm, as if reassuring him.

'You can *never* have her, Shakra, not after what I saw,' she said, her eyes shining. 'Ahalya is much too into her husband— so distracted and miserable without him. It's obvious she was missing *him*. All she has for *you* is contempt,' Sachi said, almost gleefully. 'She is barely cordial to you, and all she deigns to bestow on you is her indifference.'

There was a long pause while the two looked at each other. Indra's smile was fixed now, and his eyes were uneasy.

Sachi looked triumphant. It was completely out of character. He thought, not without alarm, that perhaps he didn't know her as he thought he did. This new side of her startled him.

'Go ahead and laugh at me. Yes, I was foolish all this while,' Sachi said, smiling at him. 'I know it's funny. I laugh myself sometimes, but now that I am sure, I have lost all fear. I know what I want, and what I'm going to have. You and me. Me and you. Sounds good, doesn't it?' She chuckled softly.

Indra rubbed his jaw thoughtfully.

'I guess that's right. We will always be together,' he said with a small sigh.

'Without Ahalya,' she reminded him. 'You may keep pining, but she won't ever be yours. Now I know for sure.'

Indra blinked, and then he smiled.

'But what I saw was different,' he said with a slight twist of his beautiful lips, an enigmatic smile. 'This time I saw in Ahalya a deeply unhappy woman.'

A wary, alert expression appeared in Sachi's eyes. 'Yes, she was unhappy,' Sachi said, nodding. 'Because Gautam was not with her.'

'Was that it?' Indra said softly. There was an expression on his face that startled her. She watched him and felt a little chill of apprehension run through her. What he said next whipped the ground from under her feet.

'I wonder ...' He paused. 'Or is it that she is unhappy *with* him?'

21

The Pursuit

'Are you crazy?' demanded Vrishakapi. 'Haven't you done enough damage already? If Sachi finds out ...'

'She'll never know—as long as *you* don't tell her,' Indra said with a shrug. 'But I have to meet Ahalya again. I know there's something wrong: she seemed so different, so miserable ... I know it, and I want to know *why*.'

'Why?' Vrishakapi asked bluntly, but he knew the answer and he answered his own question. 'Because you hope that you can get a second chance?' He shook his head with rising incredulity. 'Indra, you have Sachi. Don't ruin it for yourself—and Sachi and Ahalya as well,' he warned quietly.

'I can't help it, Vrishakapi,' Indra said. 'It is as if Ahalya has some power over me—I keep getting drawn to her ...'

'Like a drowning man,' Vrishkapi said roughly. 'Stop it, friend, stop this obsession. Ahalya is married—whether happily or unhappily is not your concern. And what about Sachi? You treat her shabbily enough, but if she ever gets to know that you are attempting to seek Ahalya out again, she *will* leave you.' He paused, his eyes suddenly piercing. 'You don't care, do you? You really don't care a damn for her. You *want* her to leave you!' He sighed with anger and exasperation. 'What a cheat you are, Indra. You make a woman fall in love with you with no intention of loving her back!'

'She need never know,' Indra snapped. A frosty expression came into his eyes. Indra was not accustomed to being reprimanded by a lesser Deva, however close a friend he was. 'Don't you dare snitch on me,' he warned.

Vrishakapi was not offended, but his usual amiable expression was missing. Instead, there was a hard look of anger on his dark face.

'You know I shan't—I have never done that all this time, with all your various dalliances,' he said softly. 'But this time, it will be not for you, Indra, it will be to protect Sachi. Yes, you are right, she need not know this, she need not know what sort of a man she has married! But this time, I shan't accompany you in your escapade. I shan't say a word—but neither shall I help you,' he said, clenching his jaw. 'You are on your own. Your own way to perdition!'

His friend's hoarse words kept ringing in his mind as Indra stood in the shadows in the forest of Gautam's ashram. For the past two hours, he had been waiting hidden in the thick foliage, his eyes fixed on a lighted window in a hut in the ashram. Ahalya's house.

A few minutes after midnight, the light in the window of the hut went out and completed the darkness. For a second he wondered what Ahalya and Gautam were doing in the dark. He clenched his hand and pressed it hard against his leg to stop himself from taking an impulsive step. He had to wait and watch and observe ... and he had to check his reckless imagination as well.

The next day, his eyes and footsteps followed Ahalya as she walked to the river in the early hours of the morning while the sun was still not out. Indra leaned his broad shoulders against a tree and settled himself to gaze unashamedly on the woman as she lay, pale and lovely, in the river water, her bare white skin glistening in the darkness, unmindful of his presence and his pervading eyes.

Lying in the cool waters, Ahalya ceased to think about Gautam. She rested her head against a flat, smooth rock and surrendered herself to a feeling of lassitude. With closed eyes, she allowed her mind to remain suspended in a vacuum of sensual pleasure. In the summer, when the days became crisp and warm, and the wind blew hot, and the sun shone its hard dimensionless glare, Ahalya preferred taking a longer and more leisurely bath in the river. The soft gurgling sound of the water gave her a feeling of profound peace.

In the silence, she thought she heard a movement. She stiffened. Her hands groped for the sari she had folded neatly on the rock, snatching it as she got up and quickly got dressed. She was now sure there was someone lurking in the darkness of the breaking dawn.

A few minutes later, Ahalya moved quietly to the rocky bank and looked quickly to the right and left. The forest was deserted. Moving forward briskly, she started walking back to the ashram. The path was dark and narrow and it seemed to stretch out before her like a long, black tunnel. She ran for about twenty yards, then stopped abruptly, her nerve suddenly failing as she felt the darkness close in on her. She leaned against a tree, gasping for breath, too frightened to run back the way she had come. Too frightened even to scream. She imagined something moving near her, and stared into the darkness, her heart hammering so violently she felt suffocated. She felt a warm breath against her cheek, a breath that was so close that she did not dare move ... A cold ball of fear began to uncoil inside her, rising in her throat, but she pushed a hand to her mouth, stifling her wild, terrified scream. As she released a long breath, she turned and began to run blindly down the pathway again.

In a dark archway of entwining trees, Indra stood pressed into the thicket with his back against the tall bushes, watching her. Her wet hair, long and dark, clung to her fair, damp skin; her breasts heaved as she ran; and he could hear her rapid, alarmed breathing. He looked at the rounded, firmly built body, and again he felt the surge of blood run through him.

He wanted her. He wanted this exquisite, unattainable woman, he wanted to be bruised, violently used, even humiliated if that was what she liked, but he wanted her ... how he wanted her!

Excited, he remained hidden, watching her, feeling the stabbing need to have her. He imagined how he would have her. He had to be careful not to be too blatant, not to shock her. Or should he be brazen and bare his soul to her? Would she melt then? She would be on the bed or even right here, on this rough forest ground, so white and pure and lovely. When he came to her, she would look at him ... a long pause ... then a smile. He hoped she wouldn't turn shy. Then, when he had pulled her close, she would go to him. He was sure she would allow him to go ahead and he would take her ...

Indra blinked: he was dreaming again. He hesitated, undecided whether he should go after her. He decided to follow her and not reveal himself yet. Ahalya was walking fast and had a hundred yard start. He increased his stride. It was only when she almost reached the ashram that he ducked behind the trees. He remained in the shadows until she was out of sight, then he stepped out and walked quickly back to the river, his lips pursed in a soundless whistle.

For three days, he did this. He watched her and followed her, and he remained undetected. But then, Ahalya had always been naive, he thought with an amused grin. Apart from the brief glimpse he had got of Gautam two days earlier, teaching young disciples under the banyan tree, the rishi had been nowhere in sight.

He saw her again that evening going for her walk, but today she avoided the river, where she always sat on a rock to rest. Instead, she was strolling down the hill, near where he was hiding behind the trees. Indra decided that now would be the best time to approach her.

'I've been waiting for you,' he announced brightly as she approached.

She froze. In that long moment, her mind was paralysed by shock; then her resilience absorbed the shock and fury gripped her, sending blood to her face.

'How dare you come here!' she said furiously. 'Go away at once!'

Indra had been prepared for her wrath. 'I had to come ...'

'Do you hear me! Go!' she repeated, her voice icy.

'I thought you would come this way,' he went on, unaffected by her tone. 'So I waited.'

His unruffled stance made her more curious than angry now. 'Are you following me?' she asked. Then a thought struck her. 'You have been watching me too?' she said in a shocked whisper.

Her face reddened. Was he the one—that invisible, pressing presence she had felt this morning and for the last few days? He must have seen her having her bath. She stared up at him in horror, which was quickly replaced by embarrassment, then anger. Ahalya felt rage grip her, rage against herself. Her disgust, contempt and frustration for this man boiled over.

'What are you doing here?!' she said, her voice steady and firm and furious. 'Since when have you started stalking women, Indra?'

'What are you accusing me of now?' he asked innocently, his eyes wide and hurt. 'I came here to meet you, as I said. I could have come to the ashram, but I was not sure if Gautam would welcome me ...'

'You are *not* welcome here, Indra. Not by Gautam, not by me,' she said frostily, regaining her composure. 'I don't even want to know why you are here. Go away.'

She looked directly at him. Her eyes opened a little in anger, and he found her even more exciting.

The air was fraught with tension. But for Indra, just being near her caused everything about him to radiate with a brightness and a hope he felt he might never know again.

'If I had wanted to stalk you—as you so easily accuse me of—would I have not followed you right after your wedding, when you chose Gautam over me?' he said, trying to sound offended.

He saw the hesitation in her eyes. He pressed on.

'Why now, Ahalya, why after all these years would I try to meet you?'

When she remained silent, he continued. 'I confess, I come here for a personal reason. I came to apologise.'

He became aware of her hands as she tucked a stray strand of hair behind her ear. The long tapering fingers and the softness of the back of her hands were, to him, sensual. The thought of those hands moving over his body made him shift his feet.

He looked down, suddenly uneasy that she might read what was going through his mind from the expression in his eyes.

When he looked up, she appeared surprised but still guarded, her lips pressed in a thin, unfriendly line. 'Apologise?' she repeated.

'For my behaviour at your brother's wedding,' he said hurriedly. 'And, of course, at yours as well. I should have apologised when I met you in the palace, but again, we started on a wrong note ...'

She cut him short. 'If you wanted to apologise, you should have come to the ashram to meet me—and Gautam.'

He was momentarily flustered. Damn, she had caught him again. 'I was not sure if Gautam would be in a forgiving mood,' he said, faltering. He stood for a moment, looking at her. He had himself under control and his warm, charming smile appeared as sincere as he could manage.

'If anyone is more forgiving, it is Gautam,' said Ahalya. 'I think the way you behaved at my brother's wedding was crude and contemptible. And to see you *here* ... Please go. The sight of you sickens me.'

His heart lurched, and he could feel his heart in h mouth: *No!*

'Yes ... You have enough reasons to feel that way.' He shuffled his feet. 'Sachi told me she thought I'd acted very badly. She said if I didn't do something about this, she'd never speak to me again.'

Ahalya stiffened. 'Sachi said that? You should have apologised the very next moment!'

'I wanted to, but I couldn't get a second with you after you left the room. And then you left the very next day,' he said weakly. He cleared his throat. 'I am here because of what I did there,' he said. 'I was an embarrassment to both you and Sachi.'

'And what made you finally realise that?'

Her tone was still curt, but at least she was talking to him, he thought.

'Sachi again. She met you and made me realise what a boorish fool I had been.'

There was a change of emotion in Ahalya's shuttered eyes, but she remained silent, her head angled in a questioning gesture.

'Not only did I insult you and Divodas's hospitality, but I humiliated my wife as well,' he said, his tone low. 'She sent me here to make amends.'

Ahalya recalled that she had liked Sachi. Though she did feel sorry for anyone who was so in love with Indra.

'You needed her to get you to right your wrong?' Ahalya asked.

'Yes. I guess she made me look at what I could not see,' he said.

'Then she is wise,' murmured Ahalya.

'Yes she is. I am lucky.

'But I hope she is lucky too.'

Indra went red. 'I try,' he said awkwardly. He noticed Ahalya had thawed and her expression was not as aloof as it usually was. The mention of Sachi seemed to have ingratiated him to her momentarily, he observed with some astonishment.

He felt his heartbeat quicken.

'Am I forgiven, Ahalya?' he said, an entreaty creeping into his voice.

Ahalya eyed him suspiciously.

'I was wrong all along,' he said. 'I would like to apologise to Gautam as well. I just didn't have the courage to earlier.'

She looked up at him, a bewildered expression on her face.

'He might just curse me at sight!' explained Indra, looking sheepish. 'I have heard Gautam is so powerful that there is no one who does not quake at the mere mention of his name.'

Ahalya raised an eyebrow. 'Even the king of gods?'

'Especially the king of gods, considering my abominable conduct towards him—and you,' he added.

'And it took you more than a decade to realise that?' she said, her tone clearly disbelieving.

'It took more shoddy behaviour from me to make me realise it. I made matters worse!'

'No, you didn't; you make no difference, Indra,' Ahalya said with a shrug.

'You are unforgiving, Ahalya. I thought you would be kinder,' he said, his face still.

'Why, Indra, why should I be kind to you?' she asked, her tone glacial. 'You mean nothing to me.'

He felt rage flaring in him. He clenched his jaw.

'I see nothing I say will make you believe me,' he said flatly. 'Or make you forgive me. I take your leave.' He bowed with folded hands.

'You won't come to the ashram to visit Gautam?' she said, mockingly.

'Ahalya, don't be so cruel,' he muttered, lowering his eyes to hide the ugly fury in them. 'I bared my heart to you once, now I bared my weakness—but you are contemptuous of both! When did *you* become such a hard person?'

Ahalya was startled. She had not been expecting such a blunt, intimate query, and the familiarity of it, surprisingly, did not infuriate her as it should have. It made her feel guilty. Was she being too hard on him?

Indra stood perfectly quiet, his nerves in wild clamour. He was feeling exhausted, and his fury drained from him, leaving him weak and depressed. He noticed there was a sudden emptiness in her eyes.

'I didn't mean to be so harsh,' she said finally. She spoke without thinking, aware, with a slight feeling of shame, that she had possibly vented her own frustration on him. *It is always easy to exhaust your ire on those you don't care about*, she thought. His appearance had evoked old memories, some unpleasant, some still pleasant ...

'Don't say sorry, Ahalya, just say you forgive me!' he said, grabbing the chance as he saw her weakening, her resistance melting to reason. Or was it just compassion? 'Ahalya ... please. Won't you listen to me? I want to say I'm sorry.' He clenched his jaw, his face in despair. 'Honestly, Ahalya. I want you to believe me ... I'm sorry.'

His pleas stirred an undecipherable emotion in her. This man had loved her once and it was she who had broken his heart. Yet it was he who was asking her for forgiveness. But forgiveness for what—having falling in love with her? When did hoping to marry the person you love become a crime? Had they committed a crime, had they been too harsh on a man in love?

'If asking for forgiveness takes courage, acknowledging it is in the largesse of the heart,' she said. 'I am sorry as well, Indra, I am sorry for hurting you ...' She faltered. 'It just became too ugly and painful ... I had not expected things to go so wrong.'

'No, no, Ahalya. I was silly and immature and angry and spiteful—I could not handle that I had lost you ...' he fumbled, scared that one wrong word now would douse what he was desperately trying to reignite.

'So no apologies from both sides,' she said, her smile small but as dazzling to him as the sun rising from the darkest clouds.

'So we remain friends?' he said.

'Just as you and Divodas still are?' she teased. 'How is he?'

'Enjoying being an emperor and a husband,' Indra replied cheerfully, ecstatic to hear the responsive tone in Ahalya's voice. 'Don't you meet him often?' he asked, genuinely curious.

She flushed. 'No, not so much now at all,' she murmured, but Indra detected the defensive tone in her voice and the note of marked self-consciousness. 'Kampilya is too far from here,' she said cautiously. 'And I have been busy with the children and the ashram and ...'

'Oh, and your studies too,' he said. 'After all these years of deep studies, you must be a rishika now.'

She felt the warm colour spreading on her face. 'Do you know your way around here or did you get lost?' she asked hurriedly, and Indra was quick to notice how anxiously she had changed the subject. His eyes gleamed, his interest awakened.

He was now sure there was something amiss. He had to only wait and watch ...

'Yes, I did,' he said with a sheepish smile. 'I was heading for the ashram but somehow managed to lose my way. It was a relief to see you walking down the path.'

Ahalya bit her lip. She had misunderstood him again, assuming he had been shadowing her. She had even accused him of stalking her! She felt wretched; what a mess she was, so suspicious and surly.

'Won't you come to the ashram now?' she asked.

'Yes, of course, I shall meet Rishi Gautam,' he said, forcing a fresh cheerfulness into his grin. 'I need to ask his pardon too,' he said more soberly.

'He is not there,' she said shortly. 'He's gone to set up a new ashram near the river Krishna.'

She immediately regretted her words. *Oh, why did I reveal that,* she thought in dismay.

Indra felt his heart leap with joy. 'Is he planning to change the course of the waters of the Krishna using his tapas-shakti to make the lands fertile?'

Ahalya threw him a sharp look. Was he being sarcastic?

'But do visit the ashram,' she said. 'The students will be pleased that the great Indra paid them a visit.'

It was his turn to give her a hard look. Was she laughing at him?

'I shall come to the ashram once Rishi Gautam is back,' he said. 'When will he return?'

She shrugged. 'Possibly a week ...' she said, looking away.

Indra sensed a vague restlessness in her.

'And you stay in these dark woods all alone?' he asked, looking concerned.

Ahalya raised an eyebrow. 'I am not alone! I have my gurukul full of disciples.'

'So you cook and look after them?'

'I teach them too,' she said defensively. 'But yes, I am a mother to all of them—besides my four!'

'That's a large family,' he said with a laugh. 'No wonder you don't miss the one at Kampilya! You must be busy through the day,' he remarked, that note of concern back in his voice again. He gave her a searching look. 'Yes, you do look tired ... a little wan ...'

Ahalya felt her heart contract. 'It's the heat,' she murmured.

'Are you well, Ahalya?' Indra's voice was gentle.

She turned away from that tender look in his eyes, feeling the sudden hot sting of unshed tears burning behind her eyes. When had Gautam asked about her? And in that tone? She bit her quivering lips; why was she comparing the two men? She must be missing Gautam, she thought miserably.

She shook her head, as if to brush away her thoughts.

Indra felt his heartbeat quicken. He had been watching her for a few days and had decided to approach her today. She had looked so lost and lonely as she walked up the path, he had wanted so much to just sweep her into his arms.

She was looking over his shoulder at the green meadows ahead of them. The line of her throat stirred him. He imagined holding her, his mouth pressed against that lovely flesh.

'I know I shouldn't be asking this question, but you look so ... so ... fragile,' he said, his tone low.

'I am fine,' she said with forced brightness; it did not sound honest even to her.

'You are not,' he said, shaking his head. Indra looked at her thoughtfully, his bright eyes probing. 'You, my dear Ahalya, look miserable. I could see it when I met you at Divodas's wedding. And again last week. And now as well. You look wretched and dispirited and defeated ... Why?' He had said it so gently that it cracked her composure.

'You haven't changed, Indra, you are as impudent as ever!' she said, clearly agitated, more at the truth of his words than his temerity.

'Being honest is impudent?' he asked baldly. 'I am being honest when I say I still love you and not Sachi, though I tried very hard—'

'Stop it, Indra, don't start again,' she said, feeling the heat of his look burning into her. 'I shan't hear a word more!' She pushed past him, her face aflame.

He grabbed her wrist. 'No, please wait, listen to me—'

'Go away, Indra!' she said, and tried to jerk her arm free. He tightened his grasp, his fingers cutting into her soft flesh. 'Be careful ... you will bruise me.'

'I'll do more than that!' Indra snarled. 'What about all the pain you have inflicted on me?'

He swung her around to face him, his face looming down on hers. She stared into his blazing eyes, his lips so close she could almost taste the hot breath from them. He tightened his grip, his other hand moving to her waist, sending a hot shiver through her.

'No! This can't be happening!' she screamed silently as she felt a sudden weakness surge through her.

'Did you hear me, Ahalya? What's going to happen to *me*?' he cried in an agonised whisper, his heated breath on her flushed face.

His blood on fire, he gripped her waist. For the first time since he had known her and yearned for her, her eyes were no longer distant. Something was smouldering within, and the sight of that spark inflamed him, making his heartbeat quicken and turning his mouth dry. He ran a tongue over his lips and her eyes darted away, breaking the spell ...

Ahalya tried to draw away again. But he pulled her closer, his arms hard around her, his body against hers, their thighs touching, desire burning them ...

She could hear his breathing, quick, short and uneven. 'Did Lord Brahma create you, O my lovely Ahalya, to let you wither in this desert of Gautam's ashram?' he murmured with a soft moan.

She shut her eyes, feeling faint from the overwhelming hot rush of blood coursing through her. She forced them open and looked at him fiercely, her eyes shimmering with passion.

'I don't care!' she whispered hoarsely. 'Get this, Indra, I am never going to be yours. I don't want you ... !' Her hands trembled against his chest, feeling the wild thudding of his heart. It excited her. She curled her fingers into tight fists, pushing him away. 'I don't want to meet you. I don't want you anywhere near me or my home! You must be out of your mind to come here and ...' She pushed harder against his chest, the warm flesh scorching her fingers.

She heard him groan. 'Yes, yes—I am! This mad pain is driving me crazy ... I tried so hard to forget you ... But I *can't*. What do I do?'

She couldn't believe what she was hearing, could not believe what she was feeling, one hot wave after another crashing over her.

'Are you drunk?' she cried, unsteady with the hot pulse of blood pounding through her body, wanting again to melt against the hardness of his body. She stopped, stunned at the naked pain etched on his face.

'I've loved you too long,' he said thickly. She flinched at the rawness in his voice.

'Indra, please *go*, please,' she begged, wavering, her voice softening. 'I can't help you,' she said helplessly. *I can't help myself*, she thought wildly.

'No, you are unhappy too, Ahalya. I can see it, I can sense it, I can *feel* it,' he cried. 'Can't Gautam see it? What has he done to you?' he said roughly, trying to hold her again, his eyes raking hers hungrily.

Ahalya stepped back, confused. She had never expected perspicacity from Indra, and she could not handle his sudden acuity.

She straightened her back, collecting her thoughts and dignity, her face again a mask of composure, and regarded him as if he were a stranger.

'Goodbye,' she said, her tone even. 'Please don't meet me ever again, for both our sakes.'

22

Hesitation

Gautam stood on the porch, frowning. The hut was in darkness, and there was no one around.

'Ahalya?' he called out.

There was no answer. Taking off his sandals and putting down his bag, he walked into the sitting room. He crossed over to the bedroom, pushed open the door and turned on the oil lamps.

Ahalya was not at home. Neither were the children.

Gautam decided to have a bath—he was dusty and tired. When he was done, he returned to the sitting room and waited, his eyes brooding. Some ten minutes later, he heard Ahalya come in.

'Gautam!' she exclaimed, her face flushed, her large eyes confused. 'When did you come? I was not expecting you back so soon.'

'I just arrived,' he said. 'Where are the children?'

'They are in Kampilya,' she said, flustered. 'Ma asked for them and Divodas sent a chariot to take them. The boys were begging to go there, and Anjani pleaded too—and I admit I gave in. I didn't want to break their little hearts.' She smiled tentatively.

'That's fine, they are their family too,' Gautam said with a shrug. 'They are old enough now to travel alone, and they should know how to fend for themselves; though in the palace they will be more indulged than independent, of course!'

'When children are with their grandparents, they will get pampered, be it in a palace or in a hut,' Ahalya said, sounding defensive.

'I am not criticising,' he said mildly. 'As long as they don't neglect their studies,' he added.

'They won't. You know how earnest Vama is, and the brothers follow suit seeing their elder brother poring over his books. Anjani is, of course, a handful, but I'm sure Rishi Vashisht and Rishi Bharadwaj will know how to manage her—they handled Divodas and me after all!' she said with a laugh.

'Why, were you naughty?' Gautam asked curiously, amused at the thought of the docile Ahalya venturing into anything wayward.

'In a way. I was very curious, and if the gurus did not give me a satisfactory reply, I would go searching for it myself. In fact, it was Divodas who was always the good boy: smart and obedient, studious ...'

'But you are no rebel; you are very deferential too,' remarked Gautam. 'I can't imagine you doing anything out of place.'

'Is that you paying me a compliment?' she asked cuttingly.

'No, it's how you are,' he replied simply. 'You are a very acquiescent person, aren't you?'

'You make me sound boring.'

Then she stopped short. Yes, that was what she was. Boring, dull, dreary, unexciting ...

'But then, boring is comfortable,' he observed with a smile.

'You were to arrive last week,' she said, changing the subject. 'It's been a month since you were gone.'

'There was a lot of work to be done,' he said, rubbing his neck tiredly. 'Anything new here while I was gone?' he asked.

'Not much,' she said. 'But today—'

Ahalya stopped abruptly. Should she tell him about Indra and how she had just met him in the forest? She recalled her husband's face, frozen with anger, when he had confronted Indra. She hesitated; would he explode in fury again? He would if he knew ...

She glanced uneasily at him, sitting away from her, perusing his books. He was barely listening to her.

She pursed her lips.

'I'll get you your dinner,' she said finally. She saw him nod absently without looking up. He didn't really want to know; he was just being polite.

The night was no different from any of the previous ones. By the time she joined him in bed, he was fast asleep. She sat staring at him for a long time. She had decided finally to tell him about Indra visiting the ashram, but now she wondered if she ever would.

It made her feel excited and reckless, recalling every moment of the encounter till the instant she had walked past him, her head bowed, as if wanting to hide not just from him but also from the world and, most of all, from herself ...

She was still unnerved when she reached the ashram, stumbling into her home for sanctuary, only to be met by her husband.

She tried again in the morning to tell him about Indra.

'There was an unexpected visitor to the ashram ...' she began, her voice hesitant and low.

'Yes?' Gautam said impatiently, looking up with a frown. 'This list needs to be updated. Why has Jabaali left this unfinished?' he barked, irritated. He jumped to his feet. 'I shall ask him right away.'

He strode out purposefully, a scowl on his face. Her words remained unspoken. She swallowed convulsively. She had lost yet another opportunity.

Gautam was to leave again by the end of the week, and whilst he was busy in the classrooms, Ahalya found herself feeling more restless than usual. She calmed herself with the thought that with him and the children not there, she might get more time to concentrate on her studies. She had discussed it with Rishi Vashisht the last time she was at Kampilya. One look at his face had told her that she had disappointed him too.

'I am surprised you are still at it,' he had remarked quietly and gone through her work. 'Keep at it and don't give up,' he had cautioned her.

She wouldn't. But she needed a constant guide, and with Gautam not mentoring her now, she was like a boat without a sail in the churning sea. He was everyone's guru but hers, she thought with a twisted smile. He was her husband, but no longer her guru, no longer her guide, no longer her friend, no longer her lover; she trembled, scared of the storm churning within her.

That night, as she placed dinner before him, she was surprised by the long, probing look Gautam gave her.

'Ahalya, why did you not tell me that you met Indra?' he asked quietly.

He saw her stiffen and go white, her hand shaking as she held the spoon to serve him rice. She looked at him, her eyes opening wide, and it startled him to see the utter fear in them.

'Ahalya, don't be so scared,' he said. 'I know you met him, and I want to know why, but that doesn't mean you have to be so frightened ... Did he scare you?'

Yes, but oh-so differently this time, she thought.

'No, I–I suppose not,' Ahalya said huskily, and made an effort to control herself. How much did he know, she asked herself, her mind cold with panic. Did he know about her response? Was this only the opening gambit? 'You startled me, Gautam. I didn't think anyone knew about that.'

He nodded, unsmiling.

'Jabaali saw both of you talking near the river last evening,' Gautam said. 'I presume you met him when you went for your evening stroll?'

She nodded. How much had Jabaali seen? Had anyone seen them the last time too?

'Why was Indra here?' he asked.

Ahalya almost went limp with relief. Gautam didn't know! The relief was so great she wanted to cry.

'To ap–apologise.' She stumbled over the words.

Gautam raised a brow. 'Now? After so long? Didn't you meet him at Divodas's wedding? He could have apologised then.'

'He behaved like a boor even there,' she said.

His brows shot up. 'You didn't mention that either.'

'I should have,' she said, and her mind darted about trying to think of a reason he would believe. 'But it didn't matter ... He doesn't matter,' she finished weakly.

'For God's sake!' Gautam exclaimed. 'Why didn't you tell me? I would have broken his neck!'

'That is why!' she cried. 'I didn't want to anger you. I...'

'You should have told me,' Gautam said, his face hard. 'The little rat! I know he is a weak loser, but I never realised he had sunk as low as that. Ahalya, don't hide things like that from me again. I could have fixed that coward in a moment.'

'But it was my fault too ...' she said, her face bowed, watching herself wring her fingers and clenching them to stop her mounting terror. 'I was too ashamed of myself!'

'What do you mean?' he said, astonished. 'But, my dear, you needn't be ashamed—he does. What have *you* done wrong?'

Her face reddened.

'I ... I am guilty of ...' *Having responded to him so treacherously.* '... picking a quarrel with him at the wedding,' she said awkwardly. 'I was furious that he had disrupted your yagna when you were trying to bring rain and provide water to Godavari. Oh, it was so silly of me to pick a fight at a public occasion ...'

She was rambling, she knew.

'So then why did he come *now* and apologise?' Gautam asked, interrupting her thoughts.

'Because his wife told him to,' she provided promptly.

Gautam looked incredulous.

'He ... he ... also wanted to apologise for his conduct at our wedding,' Ahalya explained hurriedly.

Oh, what was wrong with her, why had she reacted to Indra the way she did, she thought despairingly. She had reacted like a desperate, lonely woman. A hot wave of shame flooded her. She had acted like a jaded, sexually-deprived woman, excited by this attention from a man who so clearly wanted her after all these years. *For all these years.* She had been shaken by his ardour. She had never felt more flattered and excited, secretly pleased that she was not the dreary drudge that she believed she was and had reduced herself to.

But if Gautam ever found out ... She shuddered with fear. She knew he would never forgive her. He was a trusting person, but an unforgiving man as well. She was not going to deceive herself that his present sympathetic attitude would last. Also, he seemed to despise Indra more than he loved her.

His next words confirmed her doubts. 'I don't trust him, Ahalya,' he said tersely. 'And you needn't be so scared—you have done nothing wrong. In fact, I shouldn't be demanding your explanation at all. It's up to you if it was worth recounting and discussing. You don't have to tell me anything. You needn't have told me of this meeting if you thought it not worth mentioning.'

He paused, stroking his jaw, his eyes brooding. It was a habit of his when he was troubled.

'All these years, I have never discussed or mentioned Indra not because he made me angry, as you seem to think, but because I didn't want to make you feel awkward. Ever,' he said quietly. 'He was clearly an embarrassment for you. So what? Most of us have done something at one time or other that embarrasses us later in life. But *you*, Ahalya, did nothing wrong. Indra makes *you* feel guilty and fearful for what *he* did—that's why I despise him! You were unlucky with him and he's unlucky not to have you,' he said, his tone soft, and Ahalya felt her heart breaking. 'That's what I worry about. It's him, not you, I don't trust.'

She shook her head. Her lips moved into a stiff smile.

'No, no, don't worry about me. I can look after myself.'

She got up and went into the inner room. His worried eyes followed her and he sighed, frowning down at the floor. He sat still, his face thoughtful, his mind busy. He had a vague feeling that Ahalya had not told him the whole truth.

'Now I wonder what you've been up to, Ahalya?' he said, half aloud. He got up and started pacing while Ahalya waited for him in the next room.

Now was the time for love and trust, she thought desperately; everything had been straightened out. She felt the fear slowly ebb away, but her heart still beat hard and her mind raced as she thought of Indra holding her close, his face tortured and passionate, his eyes begging, his beautiful lips close enough to taste ...

Oh, I want to live! she cried silently, feeling her body melt with desire. *But, O Lord, can I not control myself? Something's happening to me!* She tried to shut off the wild image. *Oh, how I despise myself! I shouldn't attempt to justify myself! It's not Gautam but myself that I am deceiving. And not only now; I have been deceiving myself for a long time. Gautam is a good, honest man, but he is not mine any longer. I don't know what he does, what his work is, but I know he is inaccessible to me now. And then there's Indra—loving me to madness for so long now. He loves me, he wants me, I knew it all along, but now I realise it ... I am being tormented by my treacherous desire, my treacherous curiosity. I want something better!* She wept into her pillow, her head buried deep as if to stifle all amorous thoughts.

I want Indra, she admitted to herself at last. For the first time, Ahalya had recognised Indra as a man. His image came to mind instantly: handsome, young, erotic—male beauty in all its virile splendour. Never had he fascinated her as he had now. She wondered what it would be like to be made love to by him—by a man who was so besotted with her after all this time. It was a very gratifying, almost exhilarating, feeling; it felt good to be admired, she thought, awash with a surging, warm wave of confidence and passion. To be again filled with a sense of self-assurance arising from *his* appreciation of *her* desirability, to be wanted, to be needed ... To have him look at her with those hungry eyes, to have him in this bed with her. Her body grew hot and yielding at the thought.

'I beseech you,' she whispered to herself, tormented. 'I love and want this feeling as much as I want a pure, honest life. I don't know what I am doing!' It had been a moment of madness—now she must forget it.

Angry with herself, she got out of bed and walked to the window. She looked down at the river where she had met Indra last evening. In the silver moonlight, the waters did not seem warm and welcoming anymore. She went back to bed, feeling the sensual warmth of her body evaporating.

Where was Gautam? *Come here*, she cried silently, *I want you to love me* ... She moved impatiently, closing her legs tightly together, shutting her eyes in pain. Was it to be another lonely, cold night?

23

The Surrender

Gautam was back, Indra fumed. He had hoped that the wretched man would stay away longer. But here he was, just when he had been making some headway with Ahalya.

The thought of Ahalya filled Indra with happiness. There was still a chance. He had thought he had nothing to lose when he met her again, that having no fear of losing her would make him invulnerable at last—but seeing her again made him understand that he had just lost something more, as surely as if he had married her and seen her fade away before his eyes.

She had been taken from him once, but now she was close, so delectably close ... Feverishly, he pushed the palms of his hands into his eyes and tried to bring up a picture of himself as he had held her hard against him. Her lips, upturned towards his face, her large eyes melancholic one moment and anxious and wild the other. The intoxicating fragrance of her body, her silky hair, her fair skin—it had all permeated his senses ...

She had struggled, her soft body twisting against his, looking helpless and so arrestingly beautiful, exciting him, inflaming him more. The colour in her cheeks feverishly warm, like the colour of her delectable mouth. He was a frenzied, demented bee, driven mad. Would Ahalya, this beautiful flower, not allow him to taste her?

She still drove him insane with desire, she always would. Till he had her, till she surrendered to him ...

Ahalya, he moaned, what was he to *do*? Indra had surrendered a part of himself to this dream every day of the last many years. It began like it always did—and continued, with varying shades of intensity, rising to a crescendo but hanging precariously on a tantalising note, never reaching the dénouement. She was the untilled land in Gautam's ashram, and he, Indra, the plough. Ahalya and he were meant to be together. She was not, as he had been made to believe, beyond his reach. She was close, oh-so close, and he meant to have her.

From his hidden spot, he observed Gautam walk out of the hut in the dark hours to take his bath. He had been noting Gautam's routine too: every morning he left his hut at dawn. He walked to the river for his bath, ablutions, prayers, and then returned home after two full hours. *But not today*, Indra thought to himself with a smile. He had managed to convince Chandra, the Moon God, to take the form of a cock to wake Gautam up much before dawn, hoping he would get some additional time with Ahalya.

Indra listened as Gautam's footfalls faded away. It would be another two hours till he returned home. The hut was empty. Ahalya would be alone, sleeping, her soft, white body curled up and warm, her hair spilling over her pillow, the face serene and eyes shut. The image precipitated in him a sort of ecstasy, and it was in that trance that he walked across the courtyard and stepped inside the hut. He was filled with a sense of intense anticipation, a sense that, for once, he was magnificently attuned to life and love and lust. Everything about him was parched, and he was racked with a raging thirst he might never know again. Trembling, he looked down on the sleeping form of Ahalya. She was as he had imagined her ...

Ahalya felt the bed move. Was Gautam back so quickly from his morning bath, she thought drowsily, her heavy eyes refusing to open. But then why would he return to bed, to her? She frowned in her sleep, perplexed. She felt him settling himself quietly next to her, and then she felt his hands on her waist, gently drawing her close. He buried his face in the warm crook of her neck. She felt the length of his body, hard against hers. One hand moved over her smooth shoulder, down her bare back, sliding from her waist up to cup the softness of her breast ... She froze. Her eyes flew open. She twisted around to face the man.

It was Gautam. His craggy face was close, his eyes inflamed with passion. He looked as taken aback as he stared into her dark eyes.

'You are not Gautam!' she muttered, pushing against the hard, beating chest.

She felt him tremble next to her.

'I am your husband, Ahalya,' he mumbled, his voice thick, his eyes drinking her in: her parted lips, the creamy length of her neck, her ebony tresses tumbling over her bare shoulders on to her exposed pale breasts, the soft, uneven breathing making them rise in erotic unison. He could have wept at the wonder of her beauty.

He lowered his head desperately, his lips seeking to touch their voluptuousness.

She pushed away harder, causing him to throw his head back, forcing him to half sit up.

'You are not!' she cried, her eyes wide open now. She pulled herself half-upright, tugging at her sari to cover her nakedness.

She stared at the man in her bed.

A breeze blew through the moonlit room. His hands tightened spasmodically, hungering to touch her. He stayed perfectly quiet, his nerves in wild clamour, afraid that if he moved he would find her gone. He was filled with a sudden dread.

'You are Indra!' she whispered, sure and shocked. He heard her draw in her breath and shape her mouth for a scream.

Indra moved quickly. His tall frame pinned her under him, one large hand covering her mouth.

The terror on her lovely face was ugly to see. She pressed her body against the bed, straining away from him, like an animal trying to get back into its burrow; her fingernails clawed at his bare shoulders in a futile, panic-stricken quest for escape.

'Yes, it's me,' he said hoarsely. 'Don't be scared, please ... please. I won't hurt you, I could never hurt you.'

His tone was pleading, slowly sucking the fear out of her writhing body. She stopped struggling.

Her mouth trembled against his clamped hands, hesitated, then closed. She stayed where she was and stared at him; questions, not fear, lurked in her eyes.

He felt his heart lurch, but she kept still. He felt her body relaxing against his. They lay together like that for a long moment, looking at each other.

'You know who I am, don't you?' he whispered, his breath fanning her face.

Her throat tightened, but she managed to nod. She waited, her eyes searching his face. They were not Gautam's eyes: they were twin pools of despair and desire as they swept over her face.

'Forgive me, but I had to,' he muttered brokenly, gently removing his hand from her mouth and cupping her pale face. 'I couldn't bear it anymore. I need you, Ahalya!'

She felt her throat go dry. She nodded weakly, feeling the pleasurable heaviness of his body weighing down upon hers. Passion had replaced fear.

'I can't stay away from you ... !' He buried his face in the crook of her neck, breathing in the scent of her bare, damp skin, gathering her gently in his arms.

She began to breathe quickly.

'Still scared?' he questioned huskily, raising his head from the fragrant spill of her long tresses.

He gently raised her chin, forcing her to gaze up at him.

'Look at me,' he whispered urgently. 'Look what you have done to me.'

Ahalya gazed at him with new eyes. Indra was in the guise of Gautam, and she wouldn't have known the difference. Had his dark desire made him stoop to such duplicity? But right now, in the pale shadow of the moonlight, Indra looked like a man desperate, begging for love. He wasn't Indra. He was the Gautam she had hoped for and wanted and loved. He looked like Gautam when Gautam had first made love to her: eager, earnest and hopeful.

Her heart stirred. She could feel her blood coursing through her veins as though dams that had been holding it back had been opened, unlocked by Indra's touch. Her body tingled deliciously. She lay still, wishing he would touch her again. She now wanted him with an ache that tore through her, overwhelming and drowning any further thought. She wanted him to peel off her clothes and take her with this sudden gentleness he had revealed and which she hadn't believed possible in him.

'Don't,' she whispered, touching his face tentatively with quivering fingers, setting his blood on fire.

He stiffened. 'Don't what?' he murmured.

'Don't be Indra, be Gautam,' she whispered back.

He flinched. She wanted to make him love her as Gautam, not Indra, knowing he was not her husband. What fantasy was she playing out, he thought wildly.

But he didn't care.

There was a pause. Then she smiled, and there was an almost imperceptible arch of her back, straining against him, melding her closer to him as she looked straight into his eyes. A lump rose in his throat, and he waited breathlessly for his lips to touch her soft ones ... that touch he had waited eons for. The touch of their lips aroused in him a more voracious renewal of that hunger, demanding more, ravenous, greedy and gluttonous. He felt his heart would explode. She communicated her excitement to him, lavishly, deeply, with small, tentative kisses that were not just a promise but a fulfilment. Each enflamed him, each touch scorching him with a pleasurable fire, melting her against him ... Kisses that were bounteous, craving a fiery want by holding back nothing at all.

'You are beautiful, oh-so beautiful!' he said thickly.

The desire in his voice excited her. She couldn't remember when Gautam had last spoken like that to her; a long time ago, she thought dully in a heightened haze as she watched him, looking at the breadth of his shoulders, his slender hands and his masculinity. Ahalya again felt the warm, tormenting urge swamp her. The brush of his lips across hers sparked a longing deep within. It did not unfurl gradually: it erupted violently. When he kissed her mouth fully, she moaned urgently, revelling in the feel of his arms round her, his breath quick against her neck as she leaned fervidly into him, feeling the solidity of his body burning against her softness.

What were these overpowering physical sensations? She touched his throat with her lips, his skin so warm. She breathed deeply his smell, so familiar to her now but so very forbidden until this moment, when she didn't deny herself, drinking it in, committing it to memory for life ... It was Gautam she was making love to, it was Gautam whose lips burned every inch of her face, trailing down the white slender expanse of her neck to the wildly beating pulse at the base of her throat, down to the voluptuousness of her breasts. She moaned again.

Indra stiffened. She had mumbled the name Gautam. He paused, rage tearing into him. He tightened his grip on her wrists. She strained harder against him. Hot blood drummed in his ears and he feared his wrath would douse his desire, but the licking flames of fury fuelled it more. For a brief, wild moment he recalled how he had uttered Ahalya's name over and over again as he had made love to Sachi ... He shut his eyes, pain and pleasure slicing through him as he again felt Ahalya's moistened lips against his prickling skin.

'Love me,' she whispered. 'Love me more.'

Indra trembled, but he was willingly surrendering, the moments rushing into a whirl of drowning passion.

'Ahalya, I have wanted you for so long ...' groaned Indra, turning her so she could see over his shoulder as he held her. 'Look at us.'

Ahalya felt a sudden prickle of apprehension crawl up her spine. She was looking into the flashing eyes of Gautam.

24

The Parting

She stiffened, her face ivory pale, forcing her numbed hands to push Indra away.

Her mouth opened in a soundless, horrified scream.

'Gautam!' she whispered, but no sound came from her frozen lips.

Indra caught her frantic outbreath.

He whirled around.

Gautam!

Why was he back so soon, he thought in fearful frenzy. Gautam's glare seared him to the bone, blazing hot and furious. Indra had never felt so vulnerable before; he was paralysed with terror, completely exposed to the wrath of this man. He realised he was naked and threw a desperate glance at the discarded garments at the long end of the bed. He tried to sidle away but he was pinned by the look in Gautam's unblinking icy eyes.

'I knew you were a coward, but you are worse than the worst.' Gautam's voice broke the stillness of the room. 'Seducing her in my guise ... You could not have lowered yourself more, you dastard.'

With a shock, Indra realised he was still in Gautam's guise. In quick reflex, he returned to his original form, wondering wildly how he was going to escape Gautam's wrath. Terror grabbed at his throat: Gautam was going to curse him! All thoughts of Ahalya fled from his petrified mind as he thought desperately for some way to save himself. He waited with bated breath and a thudding heart for the words of condemnation that he knew were coming.

Gautam looked as if he had gone out of his mind. There was a wild, crazy glint in his eyes. His mouth was working, the muscles in his neck were standing out like knotted ropes, and he began hissing through his clenched teeth.

'You are proud of your looks, using them to charm women and seduce them,' started Gautam, his voice now dipped low and controlled, his cold eyes flicking contemptuously over Indra's inert, naked form beside his trembling wife. Ahalya had a dazed look on her face: Indra trying to flee in self-preservation had brought her quicker to her senses than the subsiding desire. He had no eyes for her, no care; he was busy scrambling to get away from the wrath of her husband. He had never been in love with her, she thought dully. It had been just raw, naked lust. And that she once refused him had made the chase more exciting. She had hurt his vanity deeper than his heart. What a blind fool she had been!

Gautam came at him with two quick strides. Indra was handicapped by his shock and nakedness. He thought Gautam would slam his clenched fist against the side of his head, but it was his terrible words that did the damage.

'May this very body, the beauty and strength of which is the reason for your pride and transgressions, be covered with what you seek—a thousand vulvas. The female parts you so openly lust for! And may you lose what is needed to unite with it!' he pronounced, staring at Indra's exposed form. 'May the world know of your indecent thoughts and actions. Henceforth, carry your shame with you, Indra!'

Indra recoiled like he had been hit by a bolt of thunder. The words had barely been uttered when Indra felt awash with a strange gush of heat, penetrating from his loins. His flesh crawled and before his unbelieving eyes, his fair skin tore open into orifices, the livid apertures fast spreading down his legs and riding up his chest, to his neck.

'*No!*' he screamed in terror. But only silence greeted him as each angry female organ glinted back at him in a collective, accusing glare. His knees buckled, and dimly he felt his throat constricting. There was nothing he could do about it. Indra felt shock, then a white flash of light scorched his eyes.

Indra blindly scrambled to his feet. 'What have you done?' he shouted, but the cry came out of his dry throat in a whimper. He was crying, feeling the hot rush of tears of terror and mortification coursing down his face.

The note in his voice made Ahalya turn away. She shut her eyes at the bruised, swelling pores filling the once handsome face.

'Leave my sight—and my house!' growled Gautam, his voice flat and final.

For Indra, groggy with pain and shame, his voice was like the sound of the sea pounding on the beach. Then he became aware of a dull ache throbbing throughout his body. The ache reminded him of the fist of the curse flashing towards him, slamming him into torpidity. He shook his head disconsolately, throwing a last glance at the white-faced Ahalya. The fear and repulsion in her eyes made him cover his face with his hands. His body racked with sobs: this was not the first time he had taken a blow, but he could not recall taking a harsher one. Gautam had destroyed him.

He looked around, then levered himself unsteadily to his feet, snatching his silk robe from the floor to cover his castrated genitals. He suppressed another sob. How could he ever show himself to the world? He, the king of gods, in this pitiable wretchedness. Where could he go? Who would take him? Sachi? No, he couldn't go to her either. Not now, not like this ...

He spun around, gaped at Gautam, flinched, then stepped back where he had no room to step back. He cannoned off out of the hut, his shoulders heaving in dry sobs.

His cries rung through the silent room even when he was long gone. It was the sound of her silent cries, too, Ahalya knew with sickening certainty. What had she done?

She continued to stare at Gautam, her eyes glazed yet wild, her expression dazed. He was staring at her like one might stare at a lizard that had dropped into one's path.

She flushed and looked away, trembling. Now it was her turn. With sweat running down her pale face, she waited for Gautam's curse.

She felt the heat of the smouldering coal eyes on her, as they began to probe her face again. She stiffened, bracing herself for the lash of fury. She started to tremble, more fearful that he had noticed her reaction. His sharp eyes never missed anything and were trained to notice a thing like that.

The silence stretched and crackled between them. *Say the words and let it be done with*, she thought.

'Why have you always been so scared of me?' she heard Gautam say sorrowfully.

Ahalya sat motionless, her shaking hands between her knees, her eyes a little wide, listening.

'I could never curse you, Ahalya, I have loved you too much ...' His voice shook.

Her eyes widened in shock as he gazed down at her. She could see herself in their twin reflections. She saw that she was looking tense, but in his deep eyes, there was more grief than anger.

'It is my fault. You were Ahalya, the perfect, most precious gift given to me by Lord Brahma himself, and I could not cherish you ...' His voice broke.

'No,' she managed to whisper. 'I loved you, but I betrayed you.' She swallowed convulsively. 'Oh, I knew what I was doing, but I was too carried away by—'

'Your vanity or your desire, Ahalya, or both?' he accused bitterly. 'Did you perceive his guise and not his motives?' Gautam stepped forward, the blood rising to his face. She winced, pressing against the bedpost.

'Yes, I knew he was not you,' she affirmed, her voice strangulated.

'I cursed him, Ahalya, to a miserable life—but you, you, Ahalya, had enough powers in you to stop and curse him! You are not just my wife, you are a powerful yogi yourself. But desire overcame the spirit. The desire of the flesh took over the spirit of the mind and soul.'

She looked up earnestly, her hands spread out. 'With you, not with him!' she stammered. 'But you just did not want ... !'

His face flushed a deep red, and he clenched his jaws. 'Don't, don't explain!' His voice was not a bark but strangely controlled. 'I saw what I had to ...' He broke off, turning away from her. She could hear his long, shuddering breath.

'Gautam ...' she said shakily. 'You said you would forgive me, if I ever was wrong.'

He whirled around, his eyes blazing. 'Don't try me, Ahalya, don't allow my anger to consume me and you!'

He struggled for control, clenching his big hands into fists, straightening his shoulders.

His blazing eyes met hers.

'Yes, I once said that,' he said slowly. 'I had said that no matter what, I shall love you. That I shall look back and I'll forgive you if you hurt me. That's what I said,' he said contemptuously and paused. 'But then it's not about love, is it?'

Panic showed in her eyes.

'You think I have destroyed Indra with the curse and that I shall now curse you, too, and destroy you as well.' He drew in a deep breath. 'But don't you see, Ahalya? *You* have destroyed *me*. *You* have destroyed *us*!'

She nodded desperately before looking down at her clasped hands, cringing against the accusatory words.

He stood for a long time, staring down at her; her head was bent low as if afraid to meet his eyes, his wrath, his grief.

'You broke that love, that trust, Ahalya. Will my forgiveness ever restore it all?'

'It was a moment of vulnerability ... I was weak ...' she mumbled, staring beseechingly at him through her unshed tears.

He regarded her, his eyes dull.

'And I was hard,' he said flatly. 'Such is the irony of life.' He sighed. 'Your knowledge leaves your side when you need it most. If love is complicated, faith is oddly simple. You have to treat it with an honesty—which is often hard. You think you have erred, you think you have betrayed me—but did I love you enough, did I give you enough, Ahalya?' he asked, shaking his head. 'I assumed once I had you, you were mine forever, never realising there would come a time when you would lose interest, that I would lose you ...' His voice had a slight catch. 'I knew you were the right woman for me. But was I the right man for you?'

He waved a hand to silence her protest.

'I thought you would be the pivot of my life: that I would find everything important revolving around you. We shared not just marriage but our children, our work, our ashram.'

'Did we?' she said then, raising her eyes sadly to him. 'How much of you is the "we", Gautam? Perhaps I would not have needed an Indra in our "we",' she said bitterly.

Gautam flushed.

She continued. 'In such a blissful partnership, why then did I stray? Blaming our unhappy marriage is easier than dealing with our own weaknesses, our unresolved problems, our longings, our ennui ... shaping not just our individual destiny but asserting existence of ourselves, our marriage ...'

'Yes, we did not resolve our differences,' he agreed, his voice raw. 'You made your choice, Ahalya. And unless I have a full understanding of why you made this choice and the circumstances that led you to it, I cannot—and I shall not—judge you.'

'But I shall be shamed for this,' she cried, her eyes opened wide in sudden repressed fury. 'I had my reasons to do what I did—but will you—will anyone—understand? My reason may not be good, my decision may not be good, but to shame me for it is cruel and unfair! I am not an infallible being, I am not a god, I am a woman!' she said furiously. 'Is it that when a woman is not "good", she does not receive sympathy? Do I have to be perfect to deserve that sympathy? I was not.'

'Nor was I,' he reminded her, his face rigid. 'No one has to be perfect to be deserving of justice. I have no right to judge you. I couldn't make you happy, I couldn't keep you happy,' he said. 'If it was your desire, perhaps even your vanity, then it was my arrogance, my negligence, that failed both of us.'

'You realise all this now?' she said painfully, her voice low. 'Not when I pined and pleaded for your attention? Did I have to do this to gain it, losing myself, my respect, my everything?' Her lips curled in a bitter sneer.

Gautam turned his eyes away, flinching from the contempt in hers.

'We all do what we think is expected of us,' she said slowly. 'You were always the guru, and I was the wife of a guru, never *your* wife, Gautam. I don't think I was ever yours.'

A spasm of pain contorted his face. 'Even if you had different ideas from me, I respected them—as they should be. I saw your ideas, but I failed to gauge your emotions in my self-absorption. I assumed I had arrived at a position where I believed I was right, even when I knew that you might not agree. I had to do one of two things: either spend a lot of time persuading you to see it my way or else stamp over you. The first way would have told you that I respect your opinion, even if you are wrong; the second way would have conveyed that I was still in command. I did not give you the time and respect to persuade you, and I headed the way I had to, and I stamped over you!'

'Gautam ...'

The sound of her voice, again scared and unsteady, hit him in the heart.

'No, let me speak, Ahalya, as this is the last time we shall ever talk.'

Ahalya felt raw dread pierce her frightened heart. 'What are you going to do?' she asked fearfully, but she could feel anger stirring in her. 'Punish me, Gautam, like you do your students when they err? The punishment you think would give me my redemption?'

He did not miss the disdain dripping from her voice.

'Punish you? For what? No, I cannot, I won't. Is it so hard and so easy, Ahalya? Retribution cannot always be redemption,' he said, his eyes anguished. 'Everything comes with a cost; everything has a price—our love, our marriage, our relationship. I didn't know your worth and you didn't value me or us. Is that not penalty itself? You can often lose in an inexact proportion of what you gain. It is this breach that separates useless fulfilment from hope ...' He shrugged resignedly. 'That becomes our reckoning, the avenging of our misdeeds.'

'Don't be so cryptic, Gautam,' she cried hotly, standing up and pacing the room. 'Say plainly what you want. Don't we go deeper than that, as you once claimed? Oh, Gautam, you talked about Rishi Veda and Rishi Agastya once—you understood what their wives were going through. Can you not understand *me*—for once?!' she cried, her face pale, her eyes bright with anger. 'You cursed Indra, now you are going to punish me too?!' she mocked.

That brought him up short. He hesitated, then lifted his hands helplessly.

'Punishment—you throw that word as a taunt. Would that make you feel better?' he said gruffly. 'Is that a way out?'

'No, it will help me know myself!' Her eyes were bright with angry tears, but her mouth and chin were firm.

His brow cleared. 'Then why do you need *me*? Ahalya, you are your own teacher.'

Ahalya raised her head. 'It might make *you* feel better, more righteous, more vindicated. Punishment is a harsh word and a harsher option—for the offender, not the upholder. For it is easier to serve punishment than justice, is it not?' Her tone was now openly sardonic.

He shook a quivering finger at her. 'You accuse *me*, when you are the culprit,' he hissed under his breath. 'Do you hear yourself?!'

She laughed in his face. 'Yes, I do, but have *you* ever heard me?' she said, her voice even. 'Then *you* have no right to punish me!' She paused, collecting her breath. 'And punish me for what? That I felt desire—a desire you, as my husband, could not perceive or satiate?' she said brutally.

Gautam seemed suddenly to lose control of himself. He leaned forward, his eyes snapping fire, and his great face turning mauve with fury. Words failed him and he paused, gathering his flailing dignity. A look of despair sprang in his eyes, and he spoke carefully. 'Then it is me who should get the punishment, Ahalya, not you.'

Her head shot up as she stared at him in disbelief, her fury fading. A stab of fear sliced through her. What was Gautam saying?

Gautam continued tonelessly, 'Man believes he is free to do what he wants. He can explore lands and knowledge and passion all so easily. Not so a woman. She is not allowed to be free. Rishi Veda allowed it. Rishi Agastya realised it. I did neither. Like other men, I treated you not as a wife but as most men treat most women: I thwarted you, made you inert and compliant, restricted you to home-keeping and legal subordination. *Me*,' he said contemptuously. 'Me, who made laws for women so they could uphold their rights ... I couldn't cherish my wife!'

He exhaled a long breath. 'I made your will like the angavastra you are wearing, quivering at the slightest breeze that blows. But there will always be desire that compels, as against convention that constrains.'

'Gautam, I don't understand ...' She shook her head, trying to shake off what he was implying. She forced herself to stay calm. 'You are going to blame yourself, castigate yourself,' she muttered, swallowing painfully. 'Not me. Is that to be my punishment? To see you punish yourself? Is that my curse?'

'We are cursed, Ahalya,' he said. 'We have punished each other too long—in our ignorance, in our arrogance, in our passion ...'

He stood looking at her for a long moment, and then turned away abruptly. It took her an instant to realise what he was saying. She stood stunned.

'You are leaving me, aren't you?' she said fiercely. 'That is what you are saying; you are escaping from our truth!'

He looked over his shoulder and gave her a ghost of a smile. 'Yes, I am,' he said quietly. 'I need my redemption too ...'

'But that is what you have been doing, always!' she cried. A tear ran down her cheek and she flicked it away impatiently. 'Turning away from the obvious. Why don't you say that I strayed because our marriage failed to deliver the love and passion it promised?! You are punishing me, you are judging me—I am the promiscuous wife, you the wronged husband. Say it!' she demanded, her face tight. 'That cheating is cheating, and there is no justification to it! It is cruel, it is selfish, it is dishonest, it is abusive!' she cried. 'It is my fault. But then, did you see my disempowered position as your wife, my resentment and repressed anger, my struggle to avoid conflict, the claustrophobia I felt? It was me, not you, Gautam, don't you see? Oh, Gautam, you don't need to leave for me to run away from our unpleasant reality. This ashram needs you, I need you—don't you understand? I wanted *you*, not Indra, never Indra!' she mumbled, her voice breaking. 'I wanted a man, my man to make love to me ... in that search, I got lost!'

Gautam stood still, like she had struck him.

'Yes, I know,' he said after a strained pause. 'The redemption you seek, Ahalya, is for the curse of ignorance, not for your mistake,' he said gently. 'I hold you to no moral trial—I have no right as I have erred too. But the lesson we need to learn is however severe or deadly one's oversight, one may hope to be free from its consequences through penitence, not punishment. Penitence is self-realisation, and regret is the first step to repentance. Instead of condemning others for one's mistakes ...'

'Then why are you blaming yourself for my weakness?' she demanded.

'You did what you did because of me. I realise it now,' he replied. 'I am as guilty as you are, and we need to look within our hearts and minds and make our own amends, cleansing ourselves in the process and finally achieving tranquillity. The best of us have a need for eternal vigilance; we cannot escape our faults, our decisions, our choices. That is the moral of our error, Ahalya. There comes a time when one chooses oneself over duty and responsibility. One needs to respect oneself and walk away from a situation that is harming and harmful, to walk away from those who take love and loyalty for granted.'

She nodded. 'Yes, I did,' she said, her voice breaking.

'No, Ahalya, we both did,' he replied.

She shook her head. 'I made you suffer the ignominy and agony of the betrayed ...'

'I betrayed your trust too,' he said hollowly. 'Infidelity is not a violation of trust, it is the splintering of the magnificent objective of romantic love. I broke yours. I broke your heart. It is a shock, a realisation that makes us question our past, our future and even our very identity. Strange as it may seem, infidelity has a lot to teach us about marriage,' he said with a twist of his lips. 'And us: about what we want, what we expect, what we feel entitled to. In this one moment, I realised what I hadn't all this time: my inadequacies as well. Give it time, you too shall soon know. It shall unknowingly reveal to us our personal bias and social conditioning about love, lust and commitment.'

'Gautam, I know contained within the marriage vows are vastly contradictory ideals!' she cried. 'Where love remains unconditional, promising intimacy with one person forever. But is it for ever? There was never a gradual melding of two individuals into a "we"—it was you and there was me. Both alone in our marriage.'

She exhaled slowly. 'It is not my desires that are different today, Gautam, but the reality that I ... I felt entitled, even obligated, to pursue it, to succumb to it. My desires were my need, my right to my sanity, my satiation, my self-actualisation, possibly even my freedom, my last defiant show of individuality.'

She threw him an agonised look, struggling with grief and guilt.

His eyes remain shuttered hearing her speak, the emotions raw and naked in her anguished tones. 'The conscious choice I made to free myself from it is proof not of my unfaithfulness; it is evidence of my physical need. Turning back on it so long was proof of the seriousness of *our* commitment or rather to conform and confirm to the uniqueness of you, of you as my spouse, my only one.' She bit her lips to stop them from trembling. 'But does our desire for others evaporate by the assurance of this singular promise of marriage? Is our marriage so perfect?'

She glanced desperately at Gautam.

'But I changed, Gautam. I am not the Ahalya you married. I wonder if you realised that. You are leaving me to punish me, to punish yourself. Why? What I did had nothing to do with you, Gautam. I now realise that I sought another not to turn away from you but to turn away from the person I had become. I wasn't seeking a lover so much as another version of myself ...'

'It's not a new partner you were seeking but your new self,' interposed Gautam, his eyes sad but a glimpse of pride in the twin pools of despair. 'You are your own equal, you don't need anyone but your perpetual thirst for "otherness", Ahalya,' he said gently. 'Go find it, seek it.'

He stepped closer to her. 'Forgiveness is bound by terms too. We need to forgive each other first, because if even forgiveness is violated over and over again, it is time to leave. You forgave me for too long, and in my ignorance and insentience, I assumed it to be your love and duty.'

'I chose myself,' she choked.

'For once,' he reminded her softly. 'And that is why it is time to leave ...'

She stifled a gasp, her throat dry.

There was an interminable pause as he looked at her sadly, without anger or accusation. She could feel her heart beating wildly, the silence and his look breaking her. 'I shan't make the same mistake,' he said. 'But I see chastity is in the mind, not in the body. It is your mind that wavered, your emotions you could not control. You said you wanted to be a rishika, and you *were* one, Ahalya. But you got distracted and drawn to the notions of love and marriage, and then the responsibilities of family and children, getting caught in loneliness and desire, not that peace and illumination you had always hoped for. The greatest of rishis and philosophers have lived their lives searching for this truth. About oneself. It is about you, yourself, Ahalya. Just *you*.

'May you remain invisible to the human eye but visible in your mind's eye, surviving on air and lying in ashes till the time you receive your blessing, your enlightenment, Ahalya,' he said softly. 'In that quest you shall receive your salvation—the deliverance you searched for so long all these years.'

Those were his last words. Gautam stood for a little while, listened to the stillness swirling around them, and then, when all sound had died away, he left her.

She watched as he strode away from the hut, his steps long and purposeful as he walked away from her. Forever.

She could not shed any more tears; they had dried on her immobile face. She seemed frozen, like a sculpture, life draining away, her face pale and rigid.

25

The Meditation

The clouds broke abruptly and a rush of cold rain hit her face. A vague memory stirred her: she had first met Gautam in the monsoon. The recollection loosened a cluster of benumbed sensations: longings, regrets, imaginings, the throbbing brood of the only spring her heart had ever known. It was strange that she could miss him in spite of the wave of negation flooding her. She seemed suddenly to see her action as he would see it, and it chilled her blood with humiliation. Was she to live with guilt and shame forever, or would she someday see the ray of light Gautam had promised her? All her pain at his coldness was swept away in this overwhelming rush of recollection.

She was motionless, senseless to the outer world. She was a pariah: quickly repositioned from devoted wife to adulteress. Gautam had left her, retreating to the mountains for his enlightenment, hoping she would find her own one here. Was it his blessing or his curse?

The world saw it as a curse, and the fact that he had left the ashram seemed to confirm the rumour that he had left her for good. Her children never returned home to her either. Each had taken up shelter in different ashrams started by their father: they wanted no contact with their mother.

Ahalya thought she was beyond pain, but her children's dismissal of her had destroyed her more than the world's denunciation. What was more hurtful than seeing the shame writ large on her daughter's face? Anjani had left her, as had her sons, judging her guilty as accused. No words, no explanations. Just that one shrivelling glance of contempt. Of condemnation.

It is just one single moment of weakness, that momentary lapse of judgement—that is all it takes for us to make us lose our all in our struggle between good and bad, right and wrong, allowing the wrong to win. It was her absurd dreams of passion, romance and impossible love. In sheltering those broken dreams and passions, she had tried to seek solace for her own expectations. That momentary weakness, that small slip that led to her big fall.

But does that one lapse of judgement define a person? Yes, it did, and worse. It condemned her to eternity. She would always be known as the infidel wife of Gautam. Was that her identity, circumscribed by that one mistake?

She chose wrongly; her choice was an error. No justification or guilt could erase that and make it right. It was too late for rectification ...

She had made herself invisible to the condemning eyes of society. For years now, she had withstood the blatant speculation, the insinuations, the prurience and sympathy of all she knew and those whom she did not. She was known as the woman who had cheated and deceived her good husband.

And she had no choice but to bear the humiliation and the pity with as much fortitude as she could muster.

She found herself frozen into stone, not in defence against the insinuations and barbs, but in the hopeful quest that she would seek her sense of peace. It was her symbolic death and the world seem to revel in it. That same world that once revered her as Rishi Gautam's wife, the mother of the ashram. Did it warm the cockles of this heartless society to see a woman subjugated and subjected to a trial of chastity and fidelity? Gautam had claimed he did not hold her guilty, but the world did by the fact that he left her. It was his action that condemned her, as much as her infidelity. He was not condemned for his redemption, she was.

But had she been falling, from a long, long time? Ahalya recalled her childhood days. Even then, her wish for education and learning had been thwarted. She should have never fallen in love with love, or got wedded to the concept of marriage. She should have pursued her quest for learning and what had truly been her dream. Had she realised that, then she would not have had to limp on the crutches of love and lust and longing and wishful romance. Her yearning for education had remained as unrequited as her physical desires. Be it in the palace or the hut, she had spent her life with imposed conformity and eternal expectations.

Ahalya remembered when she'd had Anjani after three sons. When she had held her sons in her arms, she had not been filled with a sense of her past powerlessness as a woman. But with Anjani, she had prayed that her daughter would never have to suffer that same feeling of helplessness. That same powerlessness that enveloped her now ...

Ahalya shivered.

What a long way she had travelled since the first day she had met Gautam. Even then, her feet and heart had been set on the path she was now following. That of remorse? Of regret? Or redemption? Gautam had said it was to be her enlightenment—what she had sought all her life.

She had conceptualised her husband with her own dream of eternal adoration, hoping for a new life—and that had been her first mistake. Gautam had not been what she had hoped him to be. In her desire for more, she had fallen into this act of transgression. She had tried to articulate her desires and discontent to him ... Had he addressed them appropriately, would she have surrendered to this weakness of flesh? She knew she would not have. Yet there was no argument for her infidelity, the voice of the world taunted her. It was also her conscience speaking, as she found herself caught in this realm of distinct moral codes and conduct.

'And are you not disappointed in me?' she had cried.

'I would be a liar if I said no,' he had said. 'Let me leave before my anger overwhelms the hurt; let me leave you to yourself for you to seek what you search for ...'

What was she searching for? She had lost all, her everything. Well, that part of her life was over: she did not know why her thoughts still clung to those memories. She was not to think of them. But the longing to see him and her children remained— she had to bring herself to not hunger for it anymore.

Ahalya sat still, unconscious of her surroundings. She was still treading the buoyant ether that emanates from the high moments of life, of love, of living. But gradually it shrank away from her and she felt the dull, hard ground beneath her. The sense of weariness returned with accumulated force. The warmth of living had passed out of her veins into a bloodless death.

It was like being turned into a rock.

She could not breathe, not move, not touch, not feel ... Was this what Gautam had turned her into, for the journey he hoped she would make eventually? That journey from a beautiful woman to the unfeeling rock she was now, stripped of pride, love, lust and longing, encrusted in a shell of indifference and detachment as she watched the world go by. The wheels of her life were still whirring slowly in her state of oblivion, her comatose mind experiencing the complete whole, the full turn of the wheel of experience and events. If life was meant to be an accretion of extreme forces and feelings working together, was her insatiable desire just a bridge to cross from ignorance to knowledge? Connecting the good with the bad, the just with the unfair, beauty with ugliness, faith with deceit, hope with disappointment, trust with betrayal, the sheltered, reverent life of the ashram with the exposed life of disgrace and humiliation. From the palace to the hut, from a princess to a rishika, she thought she had travelled across boundaries, but she had now crossed that one line she thought she would never pass. Her righteousness was a lie, her transgression her new truth.

Ahalya soon realised she had been exploited by these two men: Gautam in his righteous neglect and Indra in his obsessive lust.

Ahalya smiled, recalling how Indra had failed to protect her in his desperate scramble to flee from the hut and the curse, which she had heard had been duly nullified after the other gods had begged Gautam. The thousand vulvas on his body had been replaced by a thousand eyes. While Indra was still a god, she was standing stagnant in time ...

Her curse of immobility was more self-inflicted, as Gautam had hoped it to be. She would rather keep silent, stay invisible, away from the harsh hypocrisy, and remain a silent victim of societal convention. Would anyone hear her anguished wail, her cry for justice? Would she be deemed the infidel for eternity? Her transgression came because of a man, her retribution too from a man. Did the world expect her redemption to also come from a man? No, she told herself fiercely, she would not wake into such a world. She would decide when to wake up, when to live again, when to breathe.

Nothing but this silence around her, not calming at first, but racking her tired mind like the loudest crash of a wave. She had not imagined that such a multiplication of wakefulness was possible: her whole past was re-enacting itself in a range of consciousness. The terrible silence was like being inside an empty shell. Her heart, her mind, her home, her love were all empty. Would this silence still the legion of insurgent thoughts? But, slowly, in the mysterious separation from all outward signs of life, she felt herself more confronted with her reality. The noise of the outside world had ceased, the barbs were less piercing. The sense of exhaustion was sweet, cutting the shrill taunts of a mocking world, the weariness had suddenly dropped from her ...

Ahalya did not stir once. She was not alone. She was with herself.

Slowly, she thought of the world fading around her and a lull began to enfold her. She did not struggle; there was an indistinct sense of drowsy peace, one which, suddenly and surely, dispelled the last dark flash of pain and loneliness. Guilt and remorse were torn asunder. She started up again, cold and trembling with relief, the recovered warmth flowing through her once more, and she yielded to the soporific lull, sank into it, and closed her eyes ... It seemed as though the most complicated and difficult part of death was only just beginning.

EPILOGUE

The Meeting

Ahalya peered out from her window. The woman was still at the gate, hesitating. Ahalya decided for her.

She opened the door and called out, 'Come in, sister. Are you lost?'

The young woman gave a small laugh. 'No, I am searching for my sons. They are twins. About ten years old,' she said.

'Oh, they are here.' Ahalya smiled. 'I found them in the garden, trying to judge the age of that banyan tree!

'They have had their lunch and they are sleeping inside,' she told the young mother. 'It's very hot outside, and I promised them I would drop them to Rishi Valmiki's ashram later. You are staying there, aren't you? That's what they told me.'

Ahalya noticed the reluctant look on the woman's face.

'I'm sorry, I'm talking too much,' she said with a reassuring smile. 'I didn't mean to be intrusive. But this is a forest, small but wild, and this ashram is even smaller. And visitors rare.'

'Yes, we stay at Rishi Valmiki's ashram,' the young stranger finally said with a soft smile. 'I am Sita. The mother of Luv and Kush. And you are?' she ventured shyly.

'I am Ahalya.'

The expression on the other woman's face changed swiftly; she showed her surprise.

I am still infamous, thought Ahalya dryly.

'You have heard of me clearly,' she said with a smile meant to ease Sita's obvious discomfiture.

'Yes. My husband used to praise you,' Sita said and then seemed to regret her words.

'Do I know your husband?' Ahalya said with a frown.

'Yes ... You met years back.'

Ahalya's frown deepened. 'I have been in meditation for years. If I did meet him, it must have been eons ago!'

'Ram, the king of Ayodhya,' said Sita, her tone low.

Ram! Ram. Ahalya had a quick vision of a tall, slim, dark boy.

'Yes,' she said finally, 'I remember. He was a prince then. A mere lad. He was with Rishi Vishwamitra and his younger brother ...'

'Lakshman,' murmured Sita.

Ahalya gave her a quick look. 'I recall they were on their way to Mithila then ...' Her voice trailed away. 'You are *Sita*, the daughter of King Janak!' she exclaimed in sudden realisation.

Sita's shy smile widened into a sparkling one, joyful that she was being greeted as her father's daughter.

Ahalya crossed her arms. 'Yes, I remember these two princes of Ayodhya. It was Ram, clearly the older, who touched my feet, followed by Lakshman. They came and life touched me once more ... I was alive again ...'

Her eyes misted over as her mind travelled back to that day. Then she blinked and looked at the young woman in front of her.

'If you are Sita from Mithila, then you must know Rishi Shatanand too,' murmured Ahalya, her tone hesitant.

'But yes, of course, he's our royal priest!' said Sita. 'My first teacher! He—' She halted abruptly. 'He is your son, isn't he?' she asked, her eyes widening.

'Yes,' said Ahalya shortly.

'He worshipped you!' said Sita.

Ahalya gave her a strange look.

'When Ram first came to Mithila and narrated how he had met you at the ashram, I remember how Rishi Shatanand broke down. I had never seen a man weep ... He insisted they were happy tears, happy that you were alive again, that you had been ...' Sita faltered, looking anxiously at Ahalya.

'Liberated from the curse?' interrupted Ahalya dryly.

Sita flushed.

'Yes. Shatanand eventually did come to meet me,' continued Ahalya, her tone calm. 'So did the others. My daughter, I heard, got married to Uttank. He is a renowned rishi himself, like Gau—' She stopped abruptly, a small sigh escaping her lips. 'Everyone is busy in their own world now. I have mine here. And I am happy as well, as never before.'

She looked it, observed Sita, much to her surprise. This woman with her gentle smile and strangely distant eyes seemed to be brimming with hope and optimistic wisdom. She was as lovely as she had been variously described, but her loveliness gave an immediate impression of granite-hard strength, not softness. She had heard so much about Ahalya and Rishi Gautam from her father, Rishi Shatanand, and, of course, Ram.

Her heart contracted painfully, and Ahalya was swift to notice the twinge of sorrow on her face.

'I am happy that the children visited me,' commented Ahalya, her tone wry. 'I guess one would be more happy with fewer expectations: from others and, more importantly, from oneself.' She shook her head. She leaned back and stared into the burning embers of the dying kitchen fire, her fingers laced around her knee. 'It is futile identifying yourself always as a daughter, a wife, a mother; both husband and children can disown you—and then what?'

Immersed in her words. Ahalya failed to observe Sita stiffen, her face going pale.

'A woman has so many roles, but each has a perimeter. You have to step out and away and yet move forward,' she continued. 'But the world won't allow you that: it defines you as someone who has been born a daughter, to live as a wife and die as a mother. Who sees the woman behind that daughter, that wife, that mother? Women are not told that they also belong to a bigger world—of freedom, of knowledge ... of passion, of ambition ...'

'Is that why you took that form for your meditation? Is that your purpose in life now?'

'Yes, and it was meant to be my curse too,' Ahalya responded wryly. 'But I made my curse my blessing.'

Sita gave her an apologetic look. 'I didn't mean to pry,' she said.

'No, you are not; we are just chatting, are we not?' said Ahalya, reassuring her with a smile. 'It is a tiny world we live in, though. Imagine meeting you here in this forest!'

Sita flushed again.

'Is it my turn to apologise?' asked Ahalya, noticing the rising colour on Sita's fair, delicate face.

'No, I am not ashamed that I am here,' said Sita stoutly.

'You need not be,' said Ahalya quietly. '*You* did nothing wrong.'

'I did not,' she agreed grimly. 'But often we pay for other's transgressions.'

Ahalya raised her brows.

'Ram did nothing wrong either,' continued Sita intensely. 'He did what he had to as a king.'

'I am not implying anything,' said Ahalya, her voice gentle. 'It is so easy to judge. Who should know better than me!'

'I hate it when I am seen as a victim. I am not one!' said Sita, her eyes defiant. 'Nor is Ram a culprit. It's so difficult for the world to know what we have been through,' she whispered, her eyes darkening.

'Should it matter? It's that same world in which you gave your agnipariksha to prove your blamelessness; it's that same world which cast despicable aspersions against you,' Ahalya reminded her gently. 'Then why bother about what this world has to say? It shouldn't affect you. Does it still matter what they believe?'

Sita tightened her jaw, the muscles on either side standing out suddenly.

'Yes, what they say matters to us—I am a queen and Ram is a king. We are not just a wife and a husband,' said Sita. 'That world is not just society, it is the citizens, the subjects of the kingdom.'

'But they are people,' reasoned Ahalya. 'People who drove the husband and the wife apart, who forced the king to banish his queen, a blameless woman ...'

'Because they did not accept me as the ideal queen,' said Sita, her eyes bright with a disguised emotion. 'And as a queen

I had to agree with their decision. Just as Ram did. He is the seeker of truth, the king who has devoted his life to his people, the king for whom the opinion of his subjects matters ...'

'But do the people deserve him?' asked Ahalya dryly. 'If they desire an ideal king and an ideal queen, are they as people and society ideal themselves?'

'As kings and queens, we are expected to be,' Sita said. 'It was a moral dilemma for both of us; I saw Ram struggle with it.' She paused, a sigh escaping her lips. 'A king cannot afford to be selfish and think of himself and his personal happiness. His subjects come before and above the self. That's the ideal both of us grew up with. We were not taught to think of ourselves first. We understood each other and love each other because of our shared beliefs,' she said with defiant pride.

'It's not just about love, is it, Sita? It is about justice and many things other than just love,' interrupted Ahalya quietly.

Sita's pale face told her nothing, but her dark eyes were hard, her lips pursed.

'You fail to recall that it was not Ram but *I* who demanded the agnipariksha.' Sita's tone had gone glacial. 'I was not proving my innocence to him or the world: I was challenging them instead. And I won, did I not?' she asked, throwing Ahalya a sardonic look.

Ahalya gave her a measured glance. 'Just like Ram won the war,' she murmured. 'Ram and Ravan went to war, they say, for you, but did *you* want it?'

'Who wants war but men, for their pride and greed?' retorted Sita scornfully. 'But yes, I wanted a fair fight. I wanted my justice!' she said fiercely. 'I was as aware of his pride as I was aware of mine! I could have returned with Hanuman when he visited Lanka surreptitiously, but that would have been an easy way out. Ram had to fight, he had to fight for *me*!' she continued violently. 'He had to challenge Ravan, defeat him, dishonour him, kill him if need be. *That* is war, Ahalya!'

'Don't I know what war is? I am the sister of the most powerful and mighty warrior, Divodas,' Ahalya said, chuckling softly. 'He created a huge empire, and his son Sudas has followed in his father's footsteps. My nephew has won the Great War of the Ten Kings, defeating a confederacy of ten kings—an alliance of all the powerful Puru tribes—and firmly establishing the ascendancy of his Bharata clan.'

Ahalya smiled, but it was a sad smile. 'Wars make men into victors and even the vanquished are winners in their heroic deaths. But the women: they are always the victims.'

Sita's eyes narrowed. 'You faced a similar battle like I did, Ahalya. Men fighting for a woman's honour, deciding, judging and putting the woman on trial!' Her lips curled in contempt.

Ahalya sat still, but Sita noticed the clenched fists in her lap. She said, her tone gentler, 'Like Ram, I think Rishi Gautam too made his war his mission.'

Ahalya had a thoughtful look on her face. 'I agree,' she said after a long pause. 'But was it solely to save us or was it to save one's inflated sense of honour as a man, as a husband, as a rishi or as a king? Ram banished you, Gautam cursed me.'

Sita shook her head. 'Yes, for honour and pride, but whose?' she said dully. 'Men talk of wars, but the fact is that these wars never end, do they, for us?' She shrugged, lifting her shoulders tiredly. 'Wars have been fought for land and greed and pride and egos, but most of all, fought over the bodies of women, in the name of the "honour" of their women—be it wife, daughter or sister. In the name of protecting the chastity of women, men have stamped their proprietorial rights over them, and there is no end to the violence perpetrated by them. It is a continuum ... the scale just varies,' she said with a sigh. 'Be it the battlefield or home, a woman has to be punished, put in her place, disciplined, for real or imagined sexual slights by men who are strangers as well as men inside their own homes.'

Ahalya gave a wry smile.

'You are talking of me again?'

'I am talking about all of us! It could be that washerman who accused me, or Ram or Gautam or Indra ...'

'Indra got away easy,' scoffed Ahalya. 'Gautam was forced to dilute his curse when pressured by the gods. He didn't think I was fit even for a second thought, forget a second chance!' She gave a short laugh, devoid of bitterness but full of ironic mirth. 'That's what I meant, Sita. I don't need anyone's sanction or blessing. I had to seek my own salvation.' She paused, exhaling sharply. 'Societal expectations are hypocritical, dear. They enjoy a woman being subjugated, subjecting her to a moral trial. And then lament her "fall" from the lofty pinnacle of female virtue, her projected chastity and fidelity. It was your chastity that was questioned and my fidelity. But what makes yours worse is that you were innocent, Sita. I was not.'

'And you were made to suffer greatly,' said Sita, a touch of anger in her voice. 'You were pardoned by the unforgiving world only when you were redeemed. By Ram.'

'Pardoned,' Ahalya murmured softly, but Sita detected scorn. 'Punished. Redeemed. Such severe words for what I did—and my crime was that I succumbed to desire, to feel a little alive again.' She stared at the dying flames, licking the coals weakly. 'I searched all these years for myself—and I only found Ahalya, the woman I was supposed to be born as: unblemished, without any faults. I had no hala in me, no sin, no crime, no guilt. What I had done was to respond to the call of life within me ...'

'That was how Ram saw you too,' Sita said quietly.

'Yes, he did. I was at last seen by a person who recognised me for what I was—that rare person sensitive enough to know my plight, a person who did not pass judgement, a person honest, fair and rational.' She grimaced. 'Sita, is not suffering, penance; self-denial, reparation? I redeemed myself long ago; I needed no one else. Did I, as the cheating wife, punished into an inert lifelessness, need to seek her salvation through someone else?' Ahalya raised her chin. 'I did not. I had to seek my own salvation.' She paused, inhaling deeply. 'I promised myself that I would wake up from my meditation and show myself to the world only in the presence of a just, enlightened soul. Ram was ...'

'Ram is,' defended Sita quickly.

'Yes,' said Ahalya with a smile. 'And so was Rishi Vishwamitra. And in their presence, I ended my meditation to come back to this world to give what I had gained—and lost. But did I need my redemption to come through these men? No. *No!*' she repeated more strongly. 'It was *my* decision. You may call it a mistake, but it was *my* mistake and I was ready to suffer the consequences and obtain my redemption myself. No one else. Just like my happiness or unhappiness need not depend on any man—or anyone else. Both come from within: the joy and the sadness.'

'Yes, you seem happy ... content,' commented Sita after a pause.

Ahalya laughed. 'Do I look it? Yes, my dear, I have no anger against anyone, nothing to be resentful about. I am beyond all that anger and bitterness and rancour. I *am* happy.'

'Then why did you not return to Rishi Gautam when he came to take you back?'

Ahalya threw Sita a thoughtful look.

'Because we were no longer the same people; those two people who had met, fallen in love, married—and made mistakes,' Ahalya said with a smile. 'We had changed. Irrevocably.'

'But he came for you because he loved you.'

'And I love him, Sita, but love cannot be enough. There is respect and then there is trust. It was not the same; it could never be the same. I wasn't what I was. Nor was he anymore.'

'Was it because *you* did not forgive *him*?'

Ahalya gave her gentle smile.

'Possibly. There was resentment from my side initially—a certain bitterness,' she admitted, sighing. 'But I have sought my peace,' she added thoughtfully. 'I had to save myself first. We had gone through our trials and inquests and our judgements. I was beyond that now. I couldn't hold it any longer.'

'Why?'

'Because all this—the tests and the enquiries—means distrust. Trust comes above love; once broken it shatters into a thousand pieces of doubts, guilt and suspicion. Distrust is more fatal than being condemned as guilty or cleared as innocent. It allows neither. There is never closure. And I couldn't live in that world anymore.'

There was a sudden stillness, elongated and awkward, broken by Ahalya's short laugh. She regarded Sita steadily, her chin up, a small smile on her lips. 'Gautam and I were probably not meant for each other, though the world believed we were given to each other. He, Gautam—the light so bright and scorching—and me, Ahalya, the fallow, untilled land ...'

'... who needed the rain, which Indra supplied ...' Sita finished.

Ahalya gave a start. 'Is that how it was? And did I bloom after that? I did! Perhaps that was our tragedy: we never knew what we were for.' She paused briefly, her smile widening. 'You know what my redemption was, Sita? It was my recovery, my reclamation ...' Ahalya stared down at her clasped hands, then looked up, meeting Sita's gaze, her black eyes distant. 'It was my self-discovery. It was my rebellion against myself. And it was the most difficult journey. It started off full of pain, guilt, loss, self-condemnation and confusion about my past, my misdeed and the aftermath of Gautam's departure. And then there was this stubborn confidence in the notion of virtue and love and family and faith. Women have to be "punished", put in their places, disciplined ... In my case it was for a real sexual transgression, and in yours it was an imagined one, Sita.'

After a protracted pause, Sita looked at her, her clear eyes enquiring, almost sympathetic.

'Were you deceived into infidelity by Indra?' she asked bluntly.

She was taken aback by Ahalya's loud laugh. It rang of defiance.

'You know, this is one of the most enduring questions of all time!' she remarked, her laugh subsiding, her face unsmiling.

'It has intrigued all. Even my daughter asked me the same thing, condemning me with that very question, hoping to find my innocence in it!' There was a sudden catch in her voice. Ahalya swallowed and continued. 'But that's another convenient way of looking at it—is it an attempt to extenuate my offence?' she continued grimly. 'No, I wasn't duped. I knew what I was doing.'

There was a flat, final tone in Ahalya's voice. Ahalya saw one of Sita's eyebrows lift in disconcerted surprise.

'And I don't regret it, either. Regret is not remorse. I felt sorrow, not shame, for what I did. It was *my* experience, *my* emotion. More than the act itself, it was that erotic feeling of being sensual, of being animated ... It was life ...' She cut off abruptly, noticing the expression on Sita's pale face. She gave a slight shrug. 'That small pleasure gave me a lifetime of pain, and I regret the consequences that were bound to happen, not for myself but for the others. My children got swept up in the turmoil. But it will always remind me of what I already knew and how I lived then. Condemnation cannot capture desire; this passion is unjustly maligned. Desire, like other emotions, can change, and change means evolving,' she said. 'I think all of us are aware of our desires—the range and depth of them. We're aware of our right over our bodies and our pleasures, but yes, it is easier for some of us to deny this to ourselves based on supposed virtuousness.'

Sita was motionless, her hands resting on her lap, her eyes a little wide, listening. Then she said, 'It's an all-encompassing dilemma. In the forest here, I find myself doing what you are doing, Ahalya. Seeking my answers. The forest is a more truthful place; there is something brutal in its honesty.'

Ahalya leaned back against the wall. 'That is why I remain in the forest, away from Man's rules and falseness. And in this quest and questioning, I found myself confronted with truth and fidelity—it holds as precious to us as we are affected by it. I had to know and understand the value of *my* existence in this world. For that, I had to be alone, and made this curse a blessing. I didn't need anyone, neither to love or protect nor to save or salvage me. I was the seeker of my own salvation. I liberated myself from it, from me, from Gautam, from the others. For the first time I felt the meaning of freedom: it was an accomplishment, it was accountability to oneself. I was in control of my body, my mind, my heart, my desires, my dreams, my life. I had lived in the forest without understanding its meaning: it was never a punishment or an escape, it was my very fulfilment,' she said and laughed quietly. 'It was in the forest that I found my mistake, my infidelity, my recovery, my rumination—all were meant to liberate me from others, to be myself, to secure me for myself. I fought, I struggled, I obeyed, I compromised, I rebelled, I surrendered, but above all, and at last, I think, I found myself. I found the truth that is *me*. I lived the life given to me as a woman with all honesty, true to my instincts and faithful to my impulses, eager and yearning, but always true to *myself*. Always.'

Ahalya heard Gautam's velvet voice in the cool evening breeze. *'The greatest of rishis and philosophers have lived their lives searching for this truth. About oneself in this life. It is about you, yourself, Ahalya. Just* you.'

Ahalya smiled. His words came clearly to her as she sat with Sita on the veranda, feeling the hot sun on her face, soaking in the sense of self-fulfilment she had never had before. She was ... Ahalya.